IN THE MAT

*Nikola Tesla*

A ROMANCE OF THE MIND

ANTHONY FLACCO

DIVERSIONBOOKS

*Also by Anthony Flacco*

Impossible Odds
The Road Out Of Hell
Literary FAILS
Publish Your Nonfiction Book
Tiny Dancer
The Last Nightingale
The Hidden Man
A Checklist For Murder

Diversion Books
A Division of Diversion Publishing Corp.
443 Park Avenue South, Suite 1004
New York, New York 10016
www.DiversionBooks.com

For more information, email info@diversionbooks.com

First Diversion Books edition January 2013.

Print ISBN: 978-1-62681-160-7
eBook ISBN: 978-1-938120-91-6

Toward the end of his days, the brilliant inventor Nikola Tesla tried on several occasions to describe the muse whose inspirations filled his mind. His stories were dismissed as lunacy, despite the fact that this was the man who lighted the world with a package of forty U.S. patents representing the complete technology behind the western world's electrical power grid. Those patents were only a small portion of the hundreds of international patents awarded to him over the span of his productive decades.

In one of his last interviews, Tesla revealed details about his muse and his Universal Power System to author John J. O'Neill, then editor of *Collier's Magazine*. O'Neill refused to print Tesla's comments, claiming the choice was made with respect for his reputation. However, years later, O'Neill publicly expressed his personal regret over that decision. With time and thought, he was left with the unanswered question, *Tesla was right about everything else — what if his story was true?*

# *Chapter One*

## 1895
## *Menlo Park, New Jersey*

Thomas Alva Edison stood in the deserted laboratory and gazed into a cloudless night, straining to see some distant sign of his rival's burning building. He quickly polished his glasses and slapped them on his nose, squinting toward the distant conurbation of Manhattan Island. He had not wasted a moment; as soon as the young messenger boy rushed in with news of the fire, Edison tossed the lad a copper to send him on his way and immediately turned to the window to scan for any sign of a distant glow.

The snapping cold air was crystalline and brought the pre-dawn horizon closer, but the great New York City sprawled some twenty-five miles away as the crow would fly, and there was no sign of fire. There was nothing out here to dim the glory of the stars and the silver-blue constellations, so clear and sharp they seemed to beam directly down onto this place and onto him.

He reassured himself that the lack of a glow in the sky could simply mean the destruction was over. A fast burn might be the expected thing for a five-story wooden building. Why not?

Why not indeed. Edison choked back the urge to gloat. He was painfully aware that such indulgences belong to people of lesser discipline. Venal people. Still *if his worst rival had truly been devastated by fire*, then 1895 promised to be most interesting. And the year was still young. He had finally lived to witness the season of the purge.

He smiled when the day's ironic date struck him: March 13 was only two days from the famed Ides of March on the old

Roman Calendar. That was when the Romans rid themselves of that tyrant, Julius Caesar. Edison felt a whiff of pride over knowing that fact in spite of his grade school education.

He pressed his gaze toward the horizon again and strained to see any faint reddish colors, reminding himself that even if the fire still burned, it was hardly possible for the flames to be visible at this distance. Waste of time. Still…

He belched for the second time since hearing of the blaze. Absorbing this news was like digesting a spicy meal. He fought to keep the hot sensation packed under his ample belly, though as a gentleman, he made no display of it. At the age of forty-eight, Edison believed in a successful man's need to maintain his dignity.

He accepted the tenet that it is never good for the soul to gloat over the suffering of others. Not even that of a certain ungrateful former employee who has eclipsed your accomplishments and set about to shatter your plans for a power system covering all of America—an employee who actually showed the gall and the sheer *temerity* to tell some popular magazine interviewer in words that burned themselves into Edison's memory the first time he read them: Thomas Edison "never discovered any basic science behind the universe's elemental forces," and he "merely constructs devices which rely upon the raw creativity of others."

The man had actually called Thomas Alva Edison, *builder of the first practical light bulb*, a mere tinkerer in the field of generated energy.

A tinkerer.

Edison's stomach lurched. The pain stabbed through his midsection the same way that it did back when he was a young boy chasing the plow horse too soon after dinner. In those long gone days, his mother's cure for a stomachache was a mixture of buttermilk and cornbread, but tonight the deep burn ate at him with a power no home remedy could quell.

It came from the gloating. He knew that. One particularly nasty little sin struggled to take control of his behavior. This gloating sought to make Edison sneer, chuckle, maybe laugh outright, perhaps even dance with glee and shout like a rambunctious schoolboy. The gloating assured him that any reasonable person would understand and condone an expression of joy from him.

But no. He had already resolved that no one would ever be able to say Thomas Edison was swept away by this news like some giddy miser who has cornered another man's gold. No need for that. Edison's reputation was established; his place in history was secure.

He turned in reaction to the thought and ran his gaze around the main laboratory: a long row of neat lab tables, each one a tableau of an ongoing experiment. Assistants toiled every working day, pounding out solutions to the challenges endlessly presented by Edison's designs.

"The Devil really *is* in the details," he liked to tell the boys in the lab. He also took it on faith that the Devil could be hammered right back out of the damned details if enough trained assistants were put to the task—each one a relentless perfectionist. Each one hungry to be noticed by the Boss.

The Boss, that would be him: Mother Edison's oversized, hard-of-hearing, semi-educated farm boy. For the humble lad who still lived inside the famous man, this silent workshop was a reassuring sight. All the more so on this night. Edison's electrical research laboratory was now the finest in all of America—no longer merely the biggest or the most expensive. From this night on, he could trust his army of inventions to march forth unopposed, hungry soldiers sacking the world's cities on his behalf. They would send back ever more fortune to him, ever more fame. And benefit humanity.

Alone inside that silvery moment, Edison silently affirmed that no matter how tempted he might be, he would never be so crude as to pay a visit to the blackened remains at the first crack of daylight. He would not stroll by and casually look out of the corner of his eye to see if *that man* would be on his knees, filthy from sifting the ashes.

And even if he did decide to go and the two men's paths should happen to cross, Edison would never stoop to snubbing the arrogant bastard the way Edison got it from him back at the

Chicago World's Fair. Why, the fool actually walked straight past him and a group of reporters with his head up in the clouds! Too preoccupied to merely tip his hat like any ordinary gentleman of the trade. Too "pure" for all of them.

Right there in front of the nosy journalists.

"Arrogant bastard" was the right term for him, sure enough. And so Edison repeated his position again, just to fix it in his mind—*to engage in mockery now would be unseemly, beneath my station* (even if no one could blame a man for being human, for suffering certain jealousies). The first Mrs. Edison liked to say the measure of your refinement isn't whether or not you feel temptation, it's in how you handle the urge. He figured she usually got such things right.

He took a deep breath and belched like a sailor. *That's it, then,* he thought. *Time well spent.* It was good to work the news down through his innards, chew it into cud, consider the many implications.

At last, when he was ready, he squared up his shoulders, took a deep breath, and issued himself a standing order: *In the face of extreme temptation, the thing that matters most is to just hold everything inside. Use a battering ram if you have to, but stuff it fast and stuff it hard.*

He knew the order was good, understood it with his own combination of horse sense and quick thinking. He vowed to live up to it.

On the heels of that decision came a larger realization—it carried a message from the tiny part of him that would always be a barefoot farm boy, running like the wind to catch a freight train and praying on his knees with a full heart. It chilled the bone marrow of the man he had become. He could not risk a single witness to any rejoicing, not here in the privacy of his darkened lab, not even in the silence of his heart of hearts. Otherwise trouble would descend upon him. It would surely find him whether his sin of gloating was witnessed here in this world or from the next.

*You must do this,* he assured himself, *hold it all inside.* This remained true even though the early gossip brought by the newsboy hinted neither the building nor the contents were insured against fire. That was such a spectacular turn of events it begged the question, did Holy Angels sing while everything burned?

Toss in the ancient Roman season for doing away with a tyrant, and a perfect picture came into view. Why deny it? Wouldn't any blathering fool understand that such sweet irony could never be a mere coincidence?

That part was a touch of the Divine. It made everything Perfect.

# Chapter Two

## 1874
### Twenty-one years earlier
### Smiljan, Lika, Austria-Hungary

Reverend Milutin Tesla held out the teapot toward the town doctor, offering another refill. The scowling physician made no move to accept. "Please Doctor," Reverend Tesla urged in his softest tones, "wait until the storm eases up a little before you leave."

"No," the doctor growled. "This rain is too cold for midsummer. There will be others taking sick. Even those not known for delicate health." He did not need to add, *like your son.*

"Then let me apologize once more for his behavior," the Reverend continued. "Surely the fever caused his outburst tonight."

"Perhaps," the doctor sniffed. He rose to don his coat and offered them no relief from guilt over the indignities he suffered inside their home.

Reverend Tesla pressed harder, tagging close behind his guest. "Doctor, at least–what can you tell us about his health? What should be done to pull him through this crisis?"

The doctor smiled. "What can I tell you that your *son* does not know better than I do?"

"Doctor!" Reverend Tesla cried in alarm. "Surely you forgive the lad for his outcry—"

"Throwing leeches in my face? After I come five miles in driving rain to help him?" The doctor was at the exit, turning the latch, opening the door; now it was safe to let his full outrage show.

"I am not of your faith, Reverend, and yet I minister to you and all of your flock just as I would to any others."

"And we appreciate—"

"But you may have risen in your church ranks so fast that your family has forgotten simple manners many people hold dear."

"Doctor, my family is always on the best possible behavior!"

"Really, Reverend? Even if we forget about tonight, can that excuse Nikola's behavior this afternoon at the cemetery?"

"He was that young lady's tutor for nearly a year. He was exceptionally fond of her, and—"

"She was the daughter of the town's most powerful family; he had no place in her life except teaching! By showing up uninvited at her funeral he created a humiliation that *you* will work long and hard to live down! And even so… I came here tonight to help him fight back a fever that no doubt comes from standing in the rain at the cemetery all afternoon!"

With only a glance toward the upstairs bedroom to make his point, the doctor raised his rain hood and prepared to step out the door. "Your son has attracted the wrong kind of attention since you took over this parish, Reverend. No one questions his intellect; it's the nature of his thinking that people find troubling."

Djouka, the Reverend's wife, had remained aloof from the two men up until this point. But with this talk about her son, she spun to them and brought her dark gaze to rest on the Doctor. If he had been paying attention he might have taken warning.

"Please Doctor," Reverend Tesla persisted, "let's not end this with anger."

"Reverend, if the rumors that I hear on my rounds were to take on any real weight, people might begin to seriously wonder why the parish pastor doesn't discipline his boy to be more normal." He glanced at Djouka. "And keep his wife from reading dreams and telling fortunes." Reverend Tesla knew that he had to hold back any further objections. This angry visitor spent his days circulating among the homes of the populace; the power of gossip rested in his hands.

It was Djouka who advanced on the doctor. She held her eyes fixed on him while she reached out and yanked his hand away from the door latch. His mouth opened uselessly while she pulled the door back wide in front of him.

"Get out." She nearly whispered it.

Milutin gasped and shouted, "Djouka!"

She ignored him and continued to the doctor, "Get out right now." She smiled and added, "Or you don't know what I might do, what spell I might cast." She riveted her gaze to the doctor's eyes. Before the stunned physician could object, she pressed her hand against his chest, pushing him out the doorway and into the rain. She banged the door closed and locked it hard behind him, then glared at Milutin as if daring him to scold her.

The Reverend remained silent, shaking his head. The background din of the driving rain was too strong for the couple to hear the doctor's buggy while it slogged away. But after the next peal of thunder rolled past, they both heard their son softly laughing upstairs. The long laugh ended in a rasping cough.

Each avoided looking at the other. It was not the first time he had been embarrassed by her pagan spirituality. But she was a headstrong woman and he was a married man of God. He could not raise his hand to her and she tended to laugh at any other form of threat. The pastor finally sighed, walked over to the fireplace, and dropped into his favorite chair.

"It was only the fever," he muttered. "The fever made him behave that way."

Djouka didn't want to fight either. She made sure Milu never heard her whispered reply while she moved toward the stairs. "It was *not* from the fever."

She stopped at the first step and stared upward toward her son's room. The last words did not leave her lips.

*There is something else.*

Eighteen-year-old Nikola Tesla lay alone in the darkness of his bedroom and trembled on sheets damp with perspiration. His reedy body was a mass of cramping muscles. Nevertheless he held himself perfectly still while he attempted to slip out from under his pain by creating a great challenge of distraction for his imagination. The effort was the only defense he could conjure against his tormented condition.

His central question for the last few hours had been how to handle the challenge. He was convinced that he must not allow local doctors and their cut-and-bleed pseudoscience to come near him, but the fever's symptoms were baffling. His hearing had somehow been sharpened by the illness so that even though the storm pounded away outside, he could still hear his father's tall clock downstairs, tolling the midnight hour.

Midnight. Nikola let out another weak laugh when he realized midnight was probably the right time to start his experiment. He knew by using the last of his strength to rip the leeches off his arm and throw them into the face of the village's only doctor, he had crushed all hope of conventional medical help for the pneumonia gnawing at his chest.

It seemed plain enough that if he was going to force his illness to be useful, he needed the fever at full strength. It was time to see how much visualization power his fevered hallucinations might deliver. He lay back on the bed and prepared to completely give himself over, drinking up the symptoms like a willing victim. Time slithered by while the ringing in his head and the ache in his chest assaulted him in waves.

Nikola began to sense that his rage and frustration were somehow giving him a form of strength. Inside of that strength, an inspiration formed. It felt as if he had waited all of his life for it to appear. The challenge was to use his visualization powers to raise up the complete and detailed image of a human being.

Years ago, with his very first secret urge to turn his visualization power onto a nearby woman, a frightening gush of sexual pleasure flashed through him with such force that it shocked him away from ever tampering with such adventures. Not while he lived in the Reverend's house.

But now, in his pain, he resolved to raise up the solid image of one specific human being. The continual overflow from his gushing imagination was about to be harnessed. Its task would be to bring him as close as possible to the experience of what it would be like to have a last visit with Karina—a chance to reveal his feelings to her before saying goodbye.

He turned a deaf ear to the persistent voice in the back of his head, jabbering about forbidden things and Satan's territory. Nikola's real concern was that he was going to have to create this thing without a living model. He intended to raise the image of someone already dead. If that didn't use up his mental energy sufficiently to ease the internal fire of his grief over Karina's passing, nothing would.

He reasoned that as long as his father never found out what he was doing, then the internal voice would just have to remain in its mental corner and talk to itself. He laughed at the thought, which set off another series of racking coughs.

This time he didn't care.

"What is he doing up there?" Milutin bolted up from his chair at the fireplace and started for the stairs. "For the love of God, he sounds like a madman!"

As if to punctuate the Reverend's words, rasping laughter came again from Nikola's room, followed by another round of deep coughing.

"Wait," Djouka stepped in front of her husband, laying one hand on his arm. He stopped in surprise. On the rare occasions when she spoke out with such force, he knew it was pointless to object.

Djouka turned toward the upstairs bedroom. "He needs to spend this time alone."

Milutin exhaled. He shrugged and turned back to the fireplace but didn't move toward it. His big chair now seemed uninviting. Instead he began to slowly pace before the fire, asking himself why a sincere man of God should have so much trouble understanding any of God's children—especially his own son.

He got no answer, but he kept on pacing. The throw rug under his slippers was deeply worn, and the frayed pattern matched his steps.

Nikola knew that the beautiful Karina had only been marginally aware of him. She was two years younger—two classes behind him at the local school. They were only acquainted through his tutoring sessions at her home over the past year, after her parents hired him on the school's recommendation. The study process frustrated her—something about not seeing letters correctly on the page—but she proved to be a quick and able student. To Nikola she was not only the most fascinating girl in the province, she was also the most graceful and charming and feminine creature he had ever seen. Despite her frustrations with the written word, all he could see when he looked at her was a young woman blessed with the best of graceful human traits.

He even loved to watch other people's reactions to her. She carried a radiant sense of ease about herself and remained graceful and outgoing in any situation where he got the opportunity to observe her. Other girls at school clearly envied her, which she seemed to easily ignore. Clever young men became loud and brash in her presence, and perfectly mannered boys transformed into oafs simply because she walked into the room. He might have done the same thing during their lessons if not for the comforting constraints of his professional role.

He had always kept himself tight and proper in her presence in spite of his fascination. There was really no choice, given the difference in the social positions of their families.

None of that mattered to anyone but him. For all of his pains, Karina barely seemed to notice anything about him. If she had ever held special feelings for him, she kept them to herself. He hadn't been able to do more than follow her with his eyes in the agonizing knowledge that she was most likely indifferent to whatever feelings he harbored for her.

He never even knew that she was ill until early that same morning. Lying upstairs in his room and already sick with a heavy chest cold, he overheard a neighbor downstairs tell his mother the girl of his dreams had died and was to be buried that morning. The woman spoke in a matter of fact tone, having no idea that her words had stopped time for him. She confided that the burial was being rushed in spite of the heavy autumn rain due to fears of contagion.

When he heard that, Nikola felt his movements compelled

by a force beyond his control. He had barely taken time to dress before charging past both women and out into the relentless downpour. He rushed to the cemetery and lingered outside the fence during the abbreviated service. Afterward, he remained behind until all of the invitees left and only approached the grave site after everyone was gone. He remained for hours, feeling the need to honor her with a vigil. The long wait undid him.

Tonight, laid flat with fever, Nikola raged at the obscene circumstances. He raged at himself for not seizing some opportunity to get to know Karina when he had the chance. Finally he turned his fury toward his own illness and at the fever for being strong enough to put him in this bed while still failing to distract him away from the depth of his shock.

A wave of familiar pain seemed to pinch every nerve in his body; he knew this meant the pneumonia was settling in. But his anger powered his muscles and made him strong enough to sit upright while he gathered every ounce of his energy.

He realized what he was about to do would be more difficult than anything he had ever attempted. Such a thing might be considered a sacrilege. Perhaps it was. He could already hear his inner version of his father's voice screaming warnings of eternal doom.

A blinding flash of lightning distracted him for an instant, then he began focusing his eyes at a spot in mid-air, just beyond the foot of the bed. In seconds, the air began to shimmer as if heat waves were rising through it. He kept his gaze focused there while the "heat waves" grew thicker. Before long, his entire body pitched into the strongest act of visualization he had ever attempted.

He vowed to raise Karina's image into the air in front of him tonight or expend his life in the attempt, simple as that. The strength of his will locked out any other possibility. For the first time, his power of visualization was going to be good for something more than parlor tricks and some impressive school work. Tonight he would raise her image so clearly she would appear to be solid flesh. She would be a sculpture no one else could see, and her image would be his to cherish. He had no better way to honor her or bring her close to him.

His gaze went straight to the center of what appeared to be a mass of congealing light. The mass hovered in the air accompanied only by the sounds of the driving rain and Nikola's labored breathing. His body trembled under the force of the effort.

All sense of time fell away.

The storm outside subsided, but there was no peace in the darkened bedroom. To Nikola it simply felt as if the storm had moved into him. Sweat rolled down his forehead without cooling his fever. He felt the hot droplets and the salt stinging his eyes, but his concentration was locked onto his task. Nothing mattered anymore but this new portrait of Karina. Brushstroke by mental brushstroke her image took shape in the air before him, sharp in every detail.

Djouka Tesla stood alone at the foot of the stairway and listened to the sounds of her husband pulling the carriage from the barn and hitching up the snorting horses in preparation to hurry away with their sleepy-eyed daughters. The couple had agreed it was best to get the girls out of there after they woke up complaining about their brother's shouting. Milu was glad enough to grab them and go. By then the good Pastor had taken all he could stand.

For her part, Djouka had no doubt that the forces at work in their house were better left alone. Her son could deal with them as well as anyone else might. This was the first time she had seen his *power* truly tested, but so far her clandestine support of Nikola's *power* was one of the great secret projects of her life. Beyond this point, she could only hope he had inherited enough of her infamous abilities to win his current struggle. For now, he would have to ride his chosen roadways alone up in that room, just as her Milu and their three daughters were riding the rain-soaked roads out there in the gloom.

She moved to the fireplace and sat in her husband's big chair, keeping the door of Nikola's room within sight. If the town fathers could hear Nikola's unchecked ranting, they would surely be convinced that the Pastor's house played host to some kind of devil's holiday. Still, Djouka Tesla simply smiled and began to slowly rock in the big chair, comforting herself with the thought that most of the graces a mother radiates onto her family take place without their knowledge.

Nikola was panting with exertion by the time he found himself staring, astonished, at the image just past the foot of his bed. It looked just like Karina—exactly as he remembered her. Impossibly, her image actually showed fine points of detail that he did not consciously recall. And yet there she was.

Rather, there *it* was.

"It doesn't simply look like her," he breathed, "she looks… *it* looks alive." He smiled at his own words, referring to a hallucination as a living thing. If the Doctor reappeared and observed that, Nikola would take a short trip to the nearest mental prison.

But it was still true, and there it was. She (it) not only looked just like Karina, but somehow Nikola felt self-conscious in the presence of this illusion, as if there actually was another conscious entity in the room.

Trembling, he inched closer, and her eyes (its eyes) flashed with a presence unlike any of the other simple images he had ever raised before. In the first moment, he tried to pretend that he was analyzing his work. A moment later, he threw away pretense and drank in the lure of her beauty.

"It," he reminded himself out loud this time. "*Its* beauty."

She or it, he gave himself over to drinking up every detail of this life-sized image that seemed so real. But instead of finding solace, somehow his frustration only increased—the impact tightened his chest until it felt as if it would cave in his ribs.

He picked up a wooden match from a small matchbox next to the oil lamp on his nightstand. A globe of red-yellow light enveloped his bed and the floor around it, leaving the walls in shadow. But the detail that nearly stopped Nikola's heart was that the lamplight played across the image's face, as if the real Karina stood before him.

His fingers trembled while he reached out to touch her (it). Even though he knew there was nothing to touch, the act itself made him feel as if he was chasing an orgasm through an erotic dream, racing against awakening.

Temptation had him firmly in its clutch, as he did not doubt his father would frantically remind him, so he forgot he was sick and rose on the bed. He forgot he was in bed and clambered to his feet while he stretched his arms, his hands, his fingers closer to the image of her. He moved with equal amounts of anticipation and dread.

He hadn't yet been able to take the full vision of her, and didn't notice himself getting used to thinking of it as a "her." The face was as much of her that he had dared to really study—as if the rules of modesty somehow applied to illusions projected from a fevered brain.

Now he was close enough to the image that the end of the bed no longer blocked her lower half from view. He could see she was dressed just as he last saw her. He stepped onto the floor and stood, staring. A rush of excitement tingled through him while he allowed his eyes to travel down the pale skin of her neck…down to her breasts, her belly, her hips, her thighs…all the way to her feet.

Her feet. They were tucked into light slippers, and to all appearances, she was standing on the solid wood floor.

He had no explanation. None of his past visualizations were this complete, and they always faded away if he stared at them too hard. This image appeared solid.

It baffled him to feel so timid in the presence of a beautiful illusion. When he raised his eyes to meet the gaze from this illusion, a hot rush blasted through him.

"My God!" he whispered without meaning to. "It's as if you're really there."

The image's lips seem to curl just a bit at the corners, sharing the delightful joke in this scandalous secret of their aloneness together in a darkened bedroom. He knew that he needed more of whatever this experience was, but he had to wonder if this girl's image was an actual creation of his own doing, something of his natural ability. Was this an illusion born in illness? Was all of this the simple product of a fever?

If so, once he recovered from his illness, he would find himself without the ability to do it over, wouldn't he? And in that way, Karina would be torn from him again. This phenomenon he had created in the air before him might be something he would never be able to repeat.

*Talk to her.*

"Say your name," he whispered, no longer caring if the fever had made him insane. He didn't even care if anyone should come in and see him. "I promise I will hear it, even if you just move your lips. I *will* hear it."

The image of Karina appeared to look at him quizzically, as if asking him why he should want to hear her name. Nikola had never visualized an image that was accompanied by sounds, and he had no reason to hope that anything like that would happen now. Still he still kept his gaze fixed on her lips and waited.

And then in a clear and perfectly natural voice, the image looked directly into his eyes and said, "Karina."

Nikola gasped from the bottom of his lungs and grabbed his nightshirt, twisting it in both fists while he stumbled backward and struck his calves on the bed board. He fell backward onto the mattress amid a squeal of bed springs. For several seconds, the room remained silent.

He kept his gaze turned away from the image while he tried to slow his breathing and wondered what to do if the thing spoke to him again. He stalled for time by taking stock of his condition—strangely enough, he felt all right. Any awareness of being ill or of being in any pain had completely left him. It was as if his pneumonia and fever dissipated under the sheer power of his amazement.

*Oh yes. This one did it all right.*

So it seemed this visualization talent of his was a power of both the eyes and the ears. He took a deep breath, then slowly turned back toward the image.

It was still there. He quickly reminded himself that it was all right for the image to be there. It was good for it to be there.

"Say my name," he whispered out loud.

*For God's sake,* he told himself, *the damned thing is an illusion. You don't have to be nice to it, just control it. Make it do something.*

"Your name is Nikola," the image replied in a voice that sounded exactly like Karina's voice. Again the image appeared to smile, as if this was all some amusing game Nikola would surely explain in a moment.

This time he kept calm. After all, the hallucination hadn't done anything more than respond to his own suggestions. The voice sounded exactly as he recalled—clear, sweet, feminine, and slightly low in timbre. But at that moment the image gave him a wan smile and added: "And you're under the impression that you created me."

Nikola had no awareness of bellowing in shock while he involuntarily leaped sideways. He was also unaware of bouncing off the wall and ricocheting over to the other side of the room. He landed on his back and rolled halfway across the floor, knocking over dozens of his homemade models in the process. Each one represented days of work, yet he paid no attention to the destruction—not even when his prized little chariot, built to run on bug power, flew into splinters. Or when he felt himself flatten the fragile turbine water wheel made out of twigs. A score of his most prized possessions became instant trash under his flailing body, and he felt no concern for them at all.

By the time he was able to collect himself and scramble back to his feet, Nikola happened to be facing away from the image. He rubbed a bump that was quickly rising on his head and vaguely noticed that whoever was doing all the yelling had finally shut up. So he inhaled deeply and counted to three, then gritted his teeth and turned to face her.

She was gone.

He spun in a circle, stopped, spun in the other direction, stopped, then staggered to the door. When he reached the door, he realized he had no desire to leave, so he turned back toward the foot of the bed again as if she might reappear. But the room remained dark and quiet. Heaps of freshly manufactured trash reflected points of pale silver from the moonlight streaming through the open window.

The realization faded upward into existence like a lantern flame being cranked higher: *The window is open. During a rainstorm?*

The window had been tightly closed against the storm, and there had been no time to open it after the rain stopped. He shuffled toward it on stiff legs. When he grew close, he heard a voice—Karina's voice. He stopped in his tracks. It was faint, but there it was.

"Nikky!"

He spun around once more. Nothing.

But a moment later the voice came again, stronger, though still far away. "Out heeerrre!"

He reached the window, looked out, and there—perhaps a hundred meters away—the image of Karina hovered in the air. She was as high as his second story window, floating at his eye level.

"Come out, Nikola," she called again. When he didn't move, speak, or even blink, the image laughed. He could barely hear it at this distance, but he knew the sound of that particular laugh. Karina used to laugh often.

"What are you?" he demanded, his voice a dry rasp. She only answered by laughing again, then turned as if she were about to float away.

"What are you?" he bellowed after her.

Farther away now, she turned and called back to him. He had to strain to catch her words.

"You really want to see, Nikola?"

"Yes," he barely breathed the answer. His voice so weak that no one could have heard him from more than an arm's length away. She heard him anyway.

"All right," she called from out in the distance but sounding if her lips were pressed to his ear. In the next instant, the image rushed toward him. It struck with the force of a heavy sandbag and crumpled him to the floor.

Several moments passed while he lay stunned, able to do

little more than breathe. Disorienting sounds filled his mind, mechanical sounds unlike any he had ever heard. The depth of their power vibrated his bones.

He tried to rise and got as far as his hands and knees, but then the floor began to feel like it was mounted on a swing. When he raised his head and opened his eyes, the image of Karina hovered right in front of him.

"Are you…" he whispered in awe. "Are you Karina?"

She smiled and raised a finger to her lips, then pointed to her eyes. Before he could question the gesture, a flash of light exploded from her eyes and blinded him for several seconds. He remained helpless on his hands and knees while a metallic thunderstorm pounded between his ears.

After a few seconds he realized that even though his eyesight was still useless, he could "see" the sources of those mechanical sounds in his mind's eye. His inner vision was filled with images of strange metallic devices. Some were small and others were massive in size, but each one was perfectly clear in detail.

The strange creations glowed, revolving like images in a kaleidoscope, pulsating with energy. When he forced his eyes open to test his eyesight, he gasped again; the devices were still there. They were in the physical world of his bedroom—the hard world.

This state of illusion was beyond anything he had ever experienced or intended. Somehow the act of calling up a three-dimensional memory of a real person appeared to have set off reactions that ended with these objects leaping from his imagination and into the air in front of him. They were things he had never heard of. He suspected they might not even exist.

"But they are real, Nikola." She spoke as if he had asked her a question.

His brain felt like it was boiling. He rose onto his knees and grabbed his head with both hands in an attempt to stop the violent activity. But new visions spewed into his mind. It no longer made any difference if his eyes were open; Karina had started a flow of energy that he could not stop. He could not slow it down.

He stared up at her and felt her gaze meet his eyes, while the images whirled in the air before him. He heard himself alternately laughing and crying, and he could not stop the flow of emotions any more than he could turn off the geyser of images.

Even if it was all his own creation, he could not will himself to stop seeing this beautiful, magical hallucination of Karina. He was grateful to his fever for bringing her back to him for these few moments at least. She stood before him, as real as anything else in his world.

The deepest part of the mystery was her appearance of self-awareness. She stood before him and stared straight into his eyes, something Karina had seldom done in life.

On the other side of the bedroom door, Djouka Tesla lingered with her hand on the latch.

"Impossible!" she heard her son cry, his voice trembling with amazement. "Free will! It has a will of its own! It…she… she…"

Djouka had always hoped that her *power* would someday arise inside Nikola, but it tested her deepest faith and all of her inner strength to pull herself away from the door and return downstairs. She returned to the big chair by the fireplace to quietly await her husband's return. If her son didn't calm down by the time everyone arrived, she would insist that Milu and the girls go out with her for an early morning walk. Her daughters had good hearts and intelligent minds, but they did not have the *power*; there was no way for them to understand what was happening here.

They were all so frightened by Nikola's outbursts that they would do as they were told for a while before they started getting cantankerous. Milutin would be glad to avoid all this and leave the house again with his wife and the girls, if she gave him the excuse. In this way, Djouka pulled an invisible blanket over her struggling son.

Nikola lay pinned on his back by the firestorm of energy inside him. It felt like lightning bolts were ricocheting around in his skull. He could only cry softly, staring in amazement while the countless images whirled and danced before his eyes.

When Karina moved to the side of the bed and smiled down at him, he gathered just enough self-control to whisper to her.

"For God's sake, what is happening to me?" he breathed. "I'm not insane, I know you're just…you are something I imagined."

The warmth immediately drained from her face. "I am?" she snapped. "Well, why tell me that since I'm not here? After all, you're only talking to yourself!"

She moved closer to the open window and spoke without looking back at him. "Nikola, you're as alone right now as you have always been."

"Karina!"

She stopped moving at the sound of her name, but she didn't turn around to him.

"Please," he breathed. "I have to know. Is it really you? Are you Karina?"

He hardly dared to breathe while he watched her for a reaction. Finally, the stiffness in her shoulders seemed to ease. When she turned around her expression had softened, but her words teased him.

"How could I be Karina? She died."

"Yes, but you—she—what *are* you?"

She smiled. Again, her eyes flashed with brilliant light. This time the blast of energy hit Nikola so hard that it tore a scream of shock out of him. The blast wave snatched him up and carried him away.

Nikola clearly felt Karina somehow riding that giant wave right along with him. He knew it was impossible; even so, he sensed her closeness in the midst of the chaos all around him. The touch of her fingers brushed over his cheek and the soft warmth of her breath played upon his neck. It made no sense and he did not care. He relinquished all of his fear and relaxed into the powerful wave while it swept them far away.

Djouka finally felt her resolve shatter when she heard Nikola's scream. The sound brought her running to her son's room. When she yanked open the door, the sight in front of her left her frozen in the doorway.

Nikola lay on his bed, face up, with his feet wide apart and arms thrown back over his head. His entire body seemed as rigid as an ice sculpture. The eyes were wide open, staring upward.

She ran to him and knelt beside him, touching his face to gauge his fever, but found to her astonishment that it was gone. The pallor was nearly off of his skin now, even though his breathing remained fast and shallow. His lips moved slightly, mouthing silent words.

Only the expression frozen on Nikola's face kept panic away from his mother. He showed no pain, no fear. If Djouka had to put a name to it, she would say what she saw was fascination. She focused her gaze and sank back inside of herself as far down into the root of her *power* as she could go. Soon she peered out from that familiar old place and saw Nikola with clearer eyes. She could not quite focus on what he was seeing, but it was plain to her that he was surrounded by a strong aura of energy.

Not all of it was coming from him.

It struck Djouka then that she was witnessing an epiphany in her son's life. There was no point in calling the doctor back again. She could only hope that she was doing enough by keeping her Nikola safe from prying eyes and away the misunderstandings of others while he lay in such a vulnerable state.

The church authorities, had they been looking on at that moment, would have been horrified to see that instead of calling upon religious intervention for her son, Reverend Tesla's wife simply kissed Nikola's forehead, covered him with a single sheet, then closed the window and walked out of the room.

## Chapter Three

### Spring, 1876
### The Polytechnic Institute
### Gratz, Austria

Once Nikola's fever subsided, the visitation did not return. There was nothing of her for over two years. In moments of guilty reflection, he remembered his father's many sermons about how Satan tempted new disciples in strange and imaginative ways. As long as he thought about such things during daylight hours, he usually concluded there was no such danger to him.

Once he accepted that he could not recreate the experience in an ordinary state of mind, he only managed to endure going back to the routines of daily life by spending as much time as possible inside of his head. He consumed countless hours with the extraordinary new visualization ability left behind by the fever dream, or whatever it was.

That version of the story sustained his strained coping devices until the spring of his twentieth year, when he lost all control over his inner life once and for all. The event, when it finally happened, snatched him up in a single instant.

It overtook him while he stood in the rear section of the Institute's largest lecture hall, amid row upon row of ferociously competitive science students. Thirty pairs of eyes focused on him, along with the famously bored sneer of condescension from Herr Doktor Poeschl, the class's esteemed professor.

Herr Doktor was tutonically schooled and excruciatingly opinionated. Only a fool challenged his teachings the way Nikola had just done. Now the entire class awaited his explanation.

"Mr. Tesla, we're waiting!" Herr Doktor's voice rang upward

over the sloped seating of the packed hall.

The rest of the class would have already lost patience by now and stopped craning their necks to see him, but they had witnessed this before. The air in the room tightened while the tall student with the jet black hair and snow-pale skin appeared to stare into space. They knew that Nikola Tesla always managed to avoid imminent disaster with some arcane line of reasoning. He still had a moment or two of their faith left.

But Herr Doktor called out again, his voice full of good cheer, "If you *please*, Mr. Tesla! We await your defense with bated breath! You must be so good as to justify your theory that even though alternating current is uncontrollable, and—"

Here, the professor grinned and confided to the class in a stage whisper: *"Despite the proven fact that it is the same force as a lightning bolt…"*

His voice returned to its normal boom, "…it might nevertheless drive this small machine with 'more efficiency' than our standard direct current?"

The professor was a canny public speaker; he flashed a smile that somehow included every person in the lecture hall except Nikola. He added, "the *infinitely safer* direct current?"

That did it. The spell was broken. A wave of appreciative chuckles rippled through the hall while Nikola's overshadowed peers felt free to let their jealousy emerge. Clearly, this time he was going to lose.

After all, the renowned Herr Doctor Poeschl had just been interrupted in the midst of his famed annual demonstration of his French-made "Gramme machine." When he proudly pointed out that the Gramme machine was so well designed that it could serve either as a power generator or a motor to drive machinery, Nikola raised his hand to question whether the entire machine and its DC power were not "examples of poor science."

Herr Doktor frequently ignored questions while in the midst of his favorite lectures. However this was more than a question; it was a clear challenge to the lecture itself.

At first Herr Doktor had appeared absorbed in removing a bit of dust from the sleeve of his lecture gown. Finally he had cleared his throat and forced a wan smile. Then to the amazement of the class, he not only acknowledged the impertinent interruption, he actually set aside time to address the issue.

The students knew the old scholar would exact his revenge. Nikola found himself reeling under the professor's withering attitude. A horseshoe of staring eyes peered back at him from the lecture hall's rows of seats, sending prickly waves of snide energy through his clothing.

He struggled to clear his thoughts and focus his *vision* onto the impossible alternating current generator that hovered in mid-air directly in front of him. The shock came when he mentally dissolved the machine's housing and attempted to focus on the essential components; he discovered that although his intuition felt rock solid, his image of the machine was foggy in key areas.

And the classroom clock was ticking. Herr Doktor, after all, had stopped his lecture for Nikola's impertinent outburst. Nikola felt panic rise. It was suddenly apparent; completely new forms of circuitry were required to convert the alternating current to a useable form, and at this agonizing moment he could offer no proof that such circuits could be made to work.

It was useless to offer intuition; he needed to justify the disrespect of his interruption. He grasped for anything that might deliver him from the burning stares of his peers and the jolly derision of Herr Doktor Poeschl.

Nothing came to him except for a single fact, a real Grim Reaper of truth. It leaned on its lethal scythe and exuded itself at him:

*It's not going to happen for you this time.*

Herr Doktor's voice perforated Nikola's reverie with the Devil's perfect timing and snatched him back to the hard world. "Thank you then, for today's entertainment, Mr. Tesla! This class is concluded."

The students immediately began to stir, preparing to leave. The professor raised his voice over the din. "Facts, ladies and gentlemen, not speculation! Alternating current cannot be turned into a one-way power source for the same reason that a *direct* force, like gravity, cannot be converted into a *rotary* force."

Herr Doktor turned on the Gramme machine for emphasis. It hummed to life. "This is why we refer to the two forces as *fundamentally different*, you see."

The students collectively chuckled and began to file out, but a loud gasp from Nikola stopped them. They turned back to see his eyes lit up and his face covered with a broad smile of relief.

"Professor, the *straight* pull of the earth's gravity acts as a *rotating* force upon the moon's mass!"

"Mr. Tesla, class has been dis—"

"The moon rotates around the planet," Nikola cast a nervous glance around the room, "although gravity is constantly pulling the moon straight down. Toward us."

The classroom became very quiet.

It remained quiet.

Except for Herr Doktor Poeschl, no one moved. Even he, at first, did nothing more than drop his gaze back to the sleeve of his formal lecture jacket. He picked away another bit of invisible lint, then forced the wan smile back onto his face. When he lifted his gaze up to meet the eyes of his happily inspired student, Herr Doktor's professionalism nearly allowed him to conceal his wounded pride.

"Well, certainly. That is… if you…" He rubbed his eyes. "Right you are. Right enough. Class dismissed. Mr. Tesla, if you might remain for a moment?"

The rest knew enough to make a hasty retreat.

Ten minutes later, Nikola and Herr Doktor sat only a few seats away from one another in the otherwise empty lecture hall. In spite of the close distance, Nikola strained to hear the older man's voice. He was well aware of the import of the occasion— why, to not only be granted his point of argument by Herr Doktor in front of the entire class, but to be publicly invited to remain for a private conference! When did such things ever happen? He made a note to find a good poker game while his luck was running hot.

"…and while I can certainly appreciate your analogy of planetary forces, of course the *feasibility* of alternating current remains elusive."

Nikola was determined to display the best of manners in this situation, despite the raw envy in the professor's eyes. It was clear that the older man was trying to show him some sort of special attention, even an attempt at kindness.

"Sadly, you will soon graduate with a degree that indicates a level of education which, in truth, you have long since surpassed." The older man leaned closer. He shifted into a tone of respect Nikola could not remember ever hearing him use.

"Genius is a word best applied in retrospect, Mr. Tesla. I can't tell whether history will mention you on that short list of names, but it's clear to me that you are one of the most gifted students I have ever seen. Perhaps the most gifted of them all."

"Sir, I certainly do not think of myself—"

"Spare me!" the professor snapped, then returned to his gentler tone. "A gift can often be the result of nothing more than luck. Do you believe in luck?"

"Well, the question of luck is undermined by the existence of free will, so that if—"

"Rhetorical question, Mr. Tesla. Requiring no response. Do you understand that?"

Nikola started to open his mouth, paused, and closed it.

"Perhaps there is hope," Herr Doktor responded, then shifted in his chair. "Mr. Tesla, it is the *proper use* of one's gift which provides the true challenge. Do you have a plan for yours?"

What Nikola had was the strong intuition that this was some sort of a test, but with no idea what the Professor's agenda could be, his only hope was to be honest. He took a deep breath. "Actually, aside from learning everything that I can about physics, I spend a lot of time battling my father's strong intention for me to follow him into the clergy."

"The *clergy*?" shouted Herr Doktor. He stared at Nikola for a moment, then exhaled sharply and shook his head. "Spend your life wearing a hair shirt."

Nikola started to express concern, but stopped himself before any sound came out.

Finally, Herr Doktor cleared his throat and began again.

"Let me approach the issue this way. Many years ago I had a student—in some ways, your talents remind me of his. And like you, he seemed to have the ability to take a few of these tiny pieces of knowledge that we offer here and then leap ahead with them. Advance them to places where lesser lights like myself do not shine."

Nikola started to object to Herr Doktor's excessive humility. The older man silenced him with a wave of his hand. "No, not even me. And the other students? The other professors? Were they able to follow him on his intellectual journeys?" He flashed a derisive sneer. "Forget about them! All of them."

"Sir, I appreciate your mention of me in the same category with this outstanding—"

"He hanged himself at the age of twenty-four."

Herr Doktor let that one hang in the air for a moment while he paused to light a match and put the flame to his briar pipe. He took a puff or two before he continued.

"It was less than three years after he graduated from these august halls, as we ourselves call them. His family claims he left no final note—not that I believe them. He was too brilliant to be silent. The only silence for him was in death. I received a farewell letter from him, however, in the mail. And this, mind you, after he had already been dead for several days. You do not believe dead men write notes, do you?"

"Of cour—" Nikola clamped his mouth shut.

"He must have mailed it immediately before," Herr Doktor stopped and cleared his throat. He continued in a tighter voice. "I was his strongest supporter, you see, and so I like to think I was among the last people with whom he chose to communicate." Herr Doktor gazed into Nikola's eyes and let the pain show itself, just for an instant. It nearly knocked Nikola backward.

The older man resumed with his voice constricted nearly to a whisper. "I was fool enough to allow my own petty jealousy to keep me from giving my prize student a fair warning. In fact, I spent two years of labor in constructing fantasy castles inside his mind! Then I and the rest of this 'august institution' ordered him to go forth and slay the great scientific problems of our time. But I did nothing, you see, to provide him with *protection*!"

"From what?" Nikola blurted it out before he could stop himself. He tensed for a rebuke, but this time the professor did not seem to mind the question. Nikola tried to recall any other time when Herr Doktor Poeschl did not mind a question.

"These great abilities also have the capacity to create *the very demons* that haunt you. There is no need to turn to the afterworld to encounter demons, Mr. Tesla; they will appear in this earthly life, anywhere you allow yourself to be weak!" '

The professor fumbled to relight his pipe, thought better of it, and set the pipe aside. He looked straight into Nikola's eyes. "You seem to possess unlimited memory skills. Naturally, the more you develop and refine these skills, the more they will impress people. They will impress people almost as much as they will make them feel *stupid by comparison*!"

"Sir, I have been raised to show respect to—"

"My experience is that people do not like to feel that they are stupid. Worst of all, as you may have already discovered, it is the *truly* stupid people who are the most opposed to being reminded of their condition."

The professor paused and looked away while he searched for the words. "If you are not very, very careful, then the stupid ones, Mr. Tesla, they will become your demons."

He again leveled has gaze straight back at Nikola. "So, when the inevitable time comes that the *ignorami* are using their stupidity as a weapon against you, you will not attempt to beat them by dealing on their terms, correct?"

"I'm not sure what you—"

"*No*! You will not! You will remove the white gloves! You will use your superior ability against *them*!" At this point he paused again. He stared off at some distant place.

Nikola waited a few moments, then decided it must be time to go. With a little bow, he started to rise.

Herr Doktor's voice stopped him before his legs were fully straightened. He quickly sat back down.

"I believe that's how they got to him. Loneliness opens the doorway to despair, and despair is the worst demon of all! Many people will react to you with fear. The more they are afraid, the more envious and dangerous they become."

A dry smile played across his face. "But the smart ones are the worst. Listen to me, don't scare the smart ones! Understand? You have to come up on them slowly! You do not simply introduce yourself at a party and then proceed to destroy their logic, as if it is some sort of exercise in conversation."

"Herr Doktor, it is never my intention to—"

"I've seen you do it. Or things just like that. Close enough. Stop interrupting. People don't like to be interrupted! That's not part of the topic; that's me telling you. The topic, the topic is isolation. Now you listen to me—a wonderful mind, a mind which I had the pleasure to know and to teach, somehow reached a point where oblivion was preferable to existence.

"Why? Why would he do that? I think you *know* why! And better you should tell me, because I wonder what it is like to remember everything you read, to, to imagine complex things without writing them down—without even referring to drawings! To instantly grasp sophisticated concepts that the world's great minds spend years or decades—"

The professor's voice broke. "I wonder how you volunteer to put an end to such a gift. Where do you get the right? You have *no* right, that's all! What you do is avoid becoming weak enough to allow stupid people to make your life so frustrating that you give in to despair. *This* is how despair becomes a demon and destroys you!"

Herr Doktor turned away with a heavy exhale. He took several deep breaths but otherwise remained silent, staring off through the wall.

After a moment, when nothing else came from the older man, Nikola decided to test the situation. He took a deep breath and straightened his back as if he were about to stand. There was no reaction from Herr Doktor. Nikola put both hands on his knees and inhaled. The professor only stared into space. Nikola stood up, waited, picked up his books, waited again, then leaned forward and quietly uttered, "Thank you."

Herr Doktor still made no reaction. Nikola guessed that the

correct response was to respect the man's private thoughts and quietly leave. He turned and started up the steps, pausing for just a moment. There was nothing from the professor.

Nikola sneaked a glance back toward Herr Doktor Poeschl once he reached the exit. The older man was busily dusting off the Gramme machine, making a real chore of it, working away as if no one else was there.

# Chapter Four

## 1879
### On The Night Train
### Outside Budapest

The steam locomotive thundered away on the night run from Budapest all the way out to the northeast provinces. The moon was already down for the night, so at two in the morning, the long freight train rumbled and squealed across the countryside nearly unseen. The meager starlight produced only dim flashes of light along the glass and steel of the swaying cars.

Inside the single Pullman car, gas lamps were dimmed down to the glow of a single candle. Every one of the dozen other passengers was asleep except Nikola. He sat wide awake in the darkened car knowing he was unlikely to get any rest on the twelve-hour ride to his parents' home.

The telegram that sat folded into the breast pocket of his overcoat only contained a single stark line in his mother's words, urgently summoning him.

His head was still spinning. He took out the message and grappled with it again. The actual words were kind, but he saw their intent: Your father is dying. It had taken him only half an hour to pack his bags and be on his way. Now the clackity racket of steel wheels over wrought iron tracks combined with the rhythmic sway of the coach to lull the other passengers into sleep and leave Nikola staring into the darkness.

He struggled to overcome motion sickness partially caused by the moving train. Most was a reaction to the images in his mind's eye that appeared to float in all directions.

He was certain that in order to get himself back into

balance he needed to overcome the visual chaos, but had no idea how to go about it. When he tried closing his eyes as tightly as he could to block out the images with blindness, the floating devices simply took on a glow of their own and danced in the air before him.

In desperation, he clenched his eyelids until the physical effort gradually moved across the muscles of his face, his neck, his torso. Finally every muscle in his body was clenched. He felt like he was made of stone, with no idea of why he sensed that he could staunch the flow of images if only he could bear down on them with enough strength.

His awareness melted out from under physical reality while he concentrated on the task. At last, when the noise and motion of the train began to fade beneath his exertion, any sense of passing time dissolved away.

The breakthrough moment happened when he squeezed all the muscles of his body so hard that the floating images began to fade. He kept up the pressure and gradually they disappeared. But they only stayed gone for a few seconds before they returned.

Even though he could not explain why it worked, he had just proven that this full-body "squinting" somehow suppressed the gushing products of his vision. It was only a temporary effect, but it was some measure of control.

He jerked forward with excitement and tried it again, this time with his eyes wide open, and once more it worked. If he clenched all of his muscles, the effort itself "squinted" his mind's eye. His physical eyesight remained the same, but the distracting images quickly faded from mental view. His breathing came fast and shallow while he dared to wonder, *had he truly just stumbled across a way to stabilize his visions?*

Nikola burned through the next several hours practicing his control over the flow of images. He worked in stages. First he would relax, letting them pour through his mind, then he closed off the flow by bearing down with his new full-body muscle squeeze.

Once he began to get the hang of it, he increased the challenge by standing up, then slowly pacing the aisle while he practiced tensing and walking at the same time. To make it work, he had to stiffen his joints and channel all of his energy into the effort, which left him moving along like a man with wooden legs. At least the unwieldy learning process was enough to distract him from his dread of going home, and it never occurred to him to wonder about his effect on the other passengers.

It was hours later that he landed back in the hard world when the conductor called out his stop. But when the voice snapped Nikola back to full awareness, it broke the protective spell of his reverie. The purpose of his mission returned with all of its weight.

He managed to squelch his dread for another few minutes while he went about disembarking and collecting his bags. It was some comfort to know that at least now with this new full-body squinting technique, he would avoid burdening his family with his reactions to the spontaneous images—especially since he could not explain them and had no idea why the things were there in the first place.

The frailness crept up on Djouka again while she waited for her Nikola to arrive. It caught her unaware while she busied herself with all the routine chores of preparing Nikola's room and tending to her dying husband. The frailness gnawed at her like a sneaky parasite that works its way deep inside before the host realizes it is there.

She retreated to Milu's big rocking chair next to the red-orange glow of the fireplace and huddled under two extra blankets. The warmth defrosted some of the frailty back out of her, but her bones still felt hollow and thin. Most of what used to be Djouka's bodily self was now simply otherness to her; it dangled from her skeleton like slow-dripping mud. It served no purpose but to anchor her in time and place, to pull her down into the awful frailty.

On most days, she still felt strong enough to beat back the coldness in spite of her years. She could still fire up her blood using special breathing techniques she learned as a young girl.

She could even employ a form of self-hypnosis that she picked up somewhere in her study of ancient arts, and with it she was able to drive away most ordinary aches and pains.

None of that was working for her today. The sense of frailty gnawed at her joints like a hungry jackal. It rose from her spirit itself, because her spirit felt the pulse of this household and it told her the light and warmth of her husband Milu was nearly gone.

More than ever before, Djouka felt thankful for the special knowledge accumulated over the course of her life. It helped her remain steady within herself now. And so she was not entirely alone. Today she clearly felt that her trait of insatiable curiosity, bequeathed to her by generations of her family's best women, had given her the tools she had needed now to endure the terrible loss of her life mate.

Generations of distilled folklore had long ago mixed with her personal store of myths passed down through her family's women, plus an accumulation of white witchcraft learned from her own studies of the world and its universally desperate inhabitants.

Throughout her life, Djouka had found great comfort in seeing beneath the world's surface, watching the flow of life energy passing back and forth between people, connecting them and driving them apart. In such things, she found a source of comfort that had eluded her in her husband's religion ever since the Lord so capriciously stole her precious boy Dane from her.

The grim side of her unique ability was that it delivered knowledge to her whether she desired it or not. On this cold afternoon, in addition to whatever protection Djouka's abilities gave her, there was a feeling of hollowness inside her chest. It told her that Milu was so close to dying that he only held on with the hope of seeing his son one last time.

She reaffirmed for herself the idea that her husband was eager to see their son and make peace, surely to make peace between them at last. She pulled the two blankets tight around her shoulders and quietly made her way to the bedroom to check on Milu. The door was half open and the room itself was dim, with a thick daylight curtain covering the window. She stepped inside and lit a small candle at the bedside to see if the flame's light would reveal any changes in his coloring.

Djouka relaxed her eyes and focused her gaze a few inches above Milutin's sleeping form. Shimmering heat waves appeared to rise from his body, forming a small energy cloud around him. The cloud looked weak and thin. Milutin Tesla was worn out from a life spent as the walking embodiment of his faith. She could feel that Milu's spirit cried out for rest, but that he was determined to fight for life until his son came. The girls had already been there to hold their father and say their private goodbyes with him. Djouka sent them back to their homes and their young families with useful white lies about perhaps visiting Papa again tomorrow.

She did not doubt that Nikola's presence was crucial to her Milu, allowing him to let go. Within the family, Reverend Tesla's lifelong disappointment in his only remaining son was no secret—Nikola had long since taken to withdrawing into a sullen shell every time he and his father occupied the same room. Since Djouka had eventually found that the ability to smooth the road between them was beyond her reach, she could only yearn for both men to greet each other with an open heart on this day.

So she busied herself with small things. After she checked on Milu, the next thing to do was to get a pot of tea ready to offer her son. Perhaps Milu might take a few sips also, if he gathered his strength. After that, the next thing was to add wood to the fire.

Just when the tea water reached a steamy rolling boil, there was a knock at the front door. It came in a funny little rhythm that Nikola always used, and Djouka's heart cheered at the sound. She hurried to the door feeling sure that the synchronized timing of the boiling tea and her son's arrival was more than coincidence. Perhaps it was a sign that there could be harmony for all of them in Milu's final hour.

When she swung the door back, the cold afternoon's light revealed her son standing there—so tall—holding a dilapidated suitcase. He hardly seemed to see her at first. He stood on the porch slightly hunched over, staring at a blank spot on the ground. It appeared that he was tensing every muscle in his body.

She dismissed his behavior as simple nervousness and stepped forward to embrace her son. She felt some of the tension in his body melt away as soon slid her arms around him and pulled him into the house.

After a few hurried greetings, the pair moved toward the bedroom door. Nikola walked with his arm draped over her shoulder while she nervously prattled, "I can't tell if he's going to get through the night or not. This time, for some reason, I can't see a thing." She stopped Nikola outside the door and smiled up at him. "But I do have a feeling, as a mother, that he is hungry to put matters to rest between you. You will let him, yes?"

Nikola took her hand and nodded in agreement. Djouka exhaled a deep sigh of relief, then gestured to the door and gave him a smile. "You should go in alone." She patted his arm and walked back out to the main room to wait near the warmth of the hearth.

Nikola took a deep breath and clenched his entire body to lock off the flow of images once again. Then he reached for the door handle.

Reverend Tesla lay in bed with his face sallow and sunken while Nikola sat next to him and held onto his hand. The old pastor struggled hard to speak. His weak voice faltered between labored breaths.

"I was too hard on you, Nikola. After your older brother died—"

"Dane."

"After your older brother died, I tried to push you to fill his shoes. But what could you do? You were a little boy, you tried to please, but it was hopeless."

"Not hopeless, father! I can still—"

"You had nothing of his talent! And yet even after I saw that you lacked his spiritual potential, I pushed you to at least equal his intellectual powers. I did not take your problems seriously enough—one problem in particular, in fact."

"Well, Dane was so young. I mean, how can anyone know what he would have actually accomplished, if he—"

"I want you to know that your mother gave me every paper you sent home from school over the years. I read all of them."

Nikola flushed with pleasure. "You did?"

"Of course. I have a responsibility to be informed of the doings of all of my children. You are my son." He paused for a moment and appeared to be gathering up all of his energy. Finally he took a deep breath and went on.

"Nikola, your writings—they all seem to concern pieces of the same puzzle. Do you have some larger idea in mind?"

Nikola was happily taken aback. "Yes! I do! Papa, I want you to take comfort in knowing that even though I didn't go into the clergy, I am devoting my life to being a priest of sorts. A monk of science. And everything else in my life will be second to that mission." He inhaled deeply and spoke with all of his energy, willing his father to grasp every word.

"Papa, I am convinced that this force of electricity can be harnessed on a *grand* scale! There are fundamental discoveries yet to be made, but—"

Nikola dropped his voice to an excited whisper and gleefully confided, "This force can provide power for *far* more than mere local telephone lines. It can drive messages around the entire planet. From anyone, to anyone!"

The Reverend was listening carefully despite his illness. He held up his hand to interrupt. "Then you are describing communication back and forth freely? Between all of the world's people?"

Nikola beamed at that. "Yes! Only in theory right now, admittedly, but I am convinced that all of the obstacles can be overcome!"

"Yes," Reverend Tesla muttered. "I gathered as much." The old man turned away from Nikola before he continued. "But I had hoped you would tell me something else."

Nikola's face clouded. "...What else?"

The Reverend closed his eyes. His soft voice took on a tone

of gentleness exaggerated to psychotic proportion.

"Nikola. Experience shows us that people are weak in the presence of Evil. Yet you envision— No! You do not simply 'envision,' you propose to *build* this horrible thing!" The Reverend paused to take in a deep breath. When he went on, his last bit of mortal energy began to well up.

"You would construct a civilization where every single, struggling, child of God is constantly exposed to everyone else's *conniving stench?*"

For the first moment Nikola could only gape. In the next moment he felt the spike hit his heart. He recoiled from the bed, felt the storm flare up again inside of him, and the flood of images rushed through his brain. He blinked as if flies were buzzing at his face.

The Reverend's stare bore into his son from under hooded lids, while Nikola slammed his eyelids closed and stiffened his body, clenching the muscles and staring at a blank wall. It took several seconds before he finally exhaled.

Reverend Tesla's failing eyesight had missed nothing. When he began to speak, his voice sounded loving. His tone was gentle, but his eyes narrowed. A trace of a bitter smile curled the corners of his mouth.

"You show the demon in you when you slip like that."

Nikola gasped and leaped to his feet. "What demon? Why do you say that to me?"

The Reverend continued, sweet-voiced, "I know, Nikola. And I know you can't stop it. Your mother confided in me years ago." He managed to give his son a knowing grin. "She told me everything she heard the night you had that high fever when you were eighteen."

"Papa," Nikola whispered, but he could not make himself look his father in the face. "I thought you sent for me because you want the two of us to make peace."

"Peace!" Reverend Tesla's voice was instantly cold and sharp. "You listen to me—this plan of yours is not merely insane, it is Evil! And I *do not doubt* that it was inspired by this demon that haunts you. This piece of filth!"

"There is no demon in my life!" Nikola barked in shock and outrage.

Reverend Tesla continued as if Nikola had not spoken. "*If* you have any free will left, take a good look at yourself! Realize that this so-called 'plan' of yours formed at the same time that your demon appeared to you. And that it was at the same time that it began to haunt you with your *visions*." Reverend Tesla spat the final word.

"Papa!" Nikola pleaded. "That was— That was years ago! And I *know* she was an illusion! She has never appeared to me since that night! Not once!"

"*She*"? His father's eyes bored into him like iron spikes. "You can try to hide it from me… from the whole world… but a demon will always break through. Nikola, I want you to do this one thing right and *seek salvation from this Evil.*"

At that point the exhausted man's breath seemed to catch in his lungs. His expression flashed with a startled look. He fell back on the bed and began to visibly fade. With no more warning than that, Reverend Tesla's eyes went blank. A moment later the death gasp rattled in his throat.

Nikola slapped his hand over his mouth to keep from crying out. He spun to the door to make sure that his mother had not heard her husband's final words.

In the three days between Reverend Tesla's demise and his burial in the shadow of the church steeple, Djouka asked Nikola several times to recount their last moments together. He realized she was torn by not being present at his bedside, even though she was grateful Nikola arrived in time for their final reunion.

Each time Nikola retold the deathbed scene to her, he repeated every line of it for her just as she insisted. It warmed his heart to see the gratified smile that came over her while she listened to the story of forgiveness and reconciliation. It was plain the beautiful last moments between Milu and Nikola gave her tremendous comfort. She drank up the words of love and wisdom, which her Milu had bestowed upon Nikola at the end of his life, and she especially loved to hear of her husband's final blessing upon his wife and all of their children. Nikola was happy to repeat the story as much as she wanted.

When the burial service was over and the family slowly walked away from the cemetery, she moved close to Nikola's side and took his arm. She lowered her voice to a private level while she walked along next to him. "You know he would want you to finish your degree."

"I will Mama, but it's settled," he tenderly replied. "I'm going to find work as soon as I graduate and send money back to help you."

Djouka turned to face him, but she kept walking. "You plan to do this because your mother is a widow now? I have your father's pension, you know."

"And that's enough in good times. But if I earn a good enough salary, I can bring you to join me. Or at least if you become sick, I can see to it that you get the best care."

Djouka stopped walking and gently laid her hand on his cheek. "This is still my home. You think I would leave here?" She gave him a seductive smile. "I think that my Nikola looks like a young man who has had his heart broken. Are you planning to move somewhere far away so you can run from a woman?"

"No!" he snapped. Her startled expression caused him to quickly repeat it in a more restrained voice. "No."

"Good," Djouka replied, patting his hand and mimicking his tone. "Good."

She resumed walking. "A broken heart doesn't care if you run from it or not. Either way you take it with you."

# Chapter Five

## 1881
## Two Years Later
## Budapest

The Budapest Telephone Company was a brand new offshoot of the Budapest Telegraph Exchange. When Nikola showed up for work after prematurely ending his studies at the University of Prague, the telephone "company" turned out to still be more of an idea than an actual creation. At least it had a source of government funding, so he found himself hired and employed as a draftsman, helping to design the remaining equipment necessary to get the fledgling telephone exchange up and running. The need for quick production in finalizing the new system created a dream job for someone with unusually high levels of personal energy. From the worker-efficiency standpoint, Nikola Tesla was a model employee, which is why his troubles began there.

He indulged in his work frenzy without considering the impact on the other workers, despite his awareness of the hostility he had generated in people who felt intimidated by his abilities. The other workers, mostly male, shared an enthusiasm for this new telephone invention like everybody else. These men, however, were not monks of science; they had wives, children, and circles of friends to occupy their time. They were used to putting in their ten or twelve hours, possibly fourteen, but then going home to other interests and concerns.

It was with real consternation that they witnessed this new man, Nikola Tesla, always being there, always working. No matter how early any of them arrived, no matter how late anyone went home, Tesla was there and busily occupied. The man seemed to live without sleep.

Eventually a few of the boys noticed that whenever Tesla got all excited about some new little improvement in the current project, he would turn his back to the room and sort of stoop over and clench all of his muscles. When he opened his eyes and stood back up again, he moved carefully, like he had something balanced on his head.

But the thing was—he would then sit down and draw out a diagram of whatever he was trying to improve, and the workers would build it. It would work. It always worked. He never did any preparatory sketches, even though he designed certain parts in tolerances of a thousandth of an inch. He frequently stepped up to one of the industrial sized tools and helped to cut and grind the crucial parts himself.

Nikola completely forgot Herr Professor's warning about making smart people feel stupid and forgot the profane world of office politics. Instead he lost himself in the joys of discovery.

Since the other workers could not come near his levels of productivity and innovation, they began to question his flashy feats altogether. Maybe there was something fishy going on with him, some form of trickery.

They also found that when they tried to probe him for more information about his little tricks, the usual techniques that worked in dealing with other men of the trade somehow did not apply to him. Plying him with drinks and throwing in some flattery ought to have worked. Instead he only sipped at his drink while he gave them doses of incomprehensible science, always delivered with precise diction and a quite formal level of behavior.

He was willing enough to sit with them and freely speculate about the ways that things work and the ways they can be made to work better, but he never stayed around. He radiated a sense of duty so strong that he seemed to have no time for ordinary pleasures like a few steins of beer with the boys or a group fishing trip. He agreed to attend their poker games, but his consistent winning made him unwelcome.

His ironclad work ethic and ability to endure long hours

were regarded with unabashed awe. His peers wanted to stop his outrageous work pace, all right, but not until they found out how he did it.

Within eight months, Nikola was running the new Central Telephone Office. In the ninth month, his health collapsed from overwork. His co-workers got the relief they longed for while he stayed at home and struggled to recover.

Nikola lay in bed in his tiny Budapest apartment with his senses so distorted that it felt like he was bobbing around on rough water. The symptoms that finally put him on his back had started out like a case of the flu. At first he had assumed a few days of bed rest were all he needed. Instead his condition deteriorated.

On the afternoon of his second day at home, he felt himself developing a fever. By evening it was higher than any he had ever experienced—except for that one unexplainable night back in his parents' home.

Later while a sliver of moon rose into view outside the bedroom windows, it occurred to him that this fever appeared to be growing strong enough for him to force another visitation. *Wouldn't it be something to find out if such a thing could be possible twice?*

Why not?

Why not indeed? He threw back the blankets, jumped out of bed and ran to the window to let the cold breeze into the room, then flopped back onto the sheets stark naked. He invited the fever to eat him alive.

It didn't seem as if it would take much; those small efforts left him gasping for breath. The sound coming from his lungs reminded him of several people wheezing in unison. He let out a small laugh at that thought, which was enough to send him into a coughing fit that lasted nearly a minute. It left him raised up on his elbows gasping for air while his head throbbed with hammer blows.

The sensory distortion grew. He felt the ticking of a grandfather clock reverberate in his skull, then realized that it was only his pocket watch next to the bed. The dim light of the room's gas lamp seared his eyes. He was in agony. It was perfect.

The next coughing fit starved him for air. He became so light-headed, silver flakes sparkled in front of his eyes. Soon they were thick enough to block his view.

The sense of floating developed into an overpowering feeling of vertigo. It created a rush of pleasure that was almost sexual, tingling his senses and making him hungry to drink up more of it.

All awareness of the little room left him. He couldn't tell if he had passed out or not. *If this is death, I'll go.* He thought the words, or maybe he spoke them out loud, or perhaps screamed them at the top of his lungs.

"NIKOLA!" Karina's voice.

His eyes snapped open and everything was pitch black. He was floating in warm water or warm air. All of the pain was gone. The fever had disappeared and his fear along with it. The sense of loneliness was replaced by stunned amazement.

Karina stood there in front of him. There was no light but he could see her perfectly, as if she gave off light of her own. This light didn't hurt his eyes.

"It worked..." he barely whispered. It felt like he whispered; he was not sure his lips even moved. And yet and yet and yet— Karina was right there before him for the first time in years. Her image was so faint he could see through her into the empty blackness beyond, but there she was.

He noticed she appeared to be about his same age. She, it, the image, Karina, looked nothing at all like a country school girl. Today she was dressed in a fashionable outfit. Nikola remembered seeing one like it recently on a young woman in an elegant restaurant. It was a practical sort of attire, the combination of a simple skirt and long-sleeved blouse that allowed unfettered physical movement.

Karina playfully reached out to run her hand across his cheek. Her touch was nothing more than a wisp of moist, cool air. She spoke, but her voice was barely audible. "—just a dream. Don't be afraid. Don't close me off..."

Fear shot through him.

Something felt wrong, completely wrong, about a dream woman informing him that she did not exist. He had already dreamed of Karina often enough, sometimes clearly and sometimes amid a jumble of chaos, but her dream image never seemed to be anything more than a ghostly presence.

Now his instinctive response was to use his muscle-clenching trick to bear down on the dream image and make it disappear. He focused all of his strength onto squeezing her out of his mind. He felt the process starting and he saw her faint image grow weaker.

Except that just as Karina's image was about to completely disappear, she reached out both of her arms and placed her fingers on Nikola's temples. A bolt of energy flooded his skull.

His mind filled with visions of elaborate, unexplainable machines. The force of the incoming imagery was so great that powerful physical sensations began to wash through him, as if created by the overflow of energy. Again he was a leaf, spinning on water. Again his vision clouded and filled with silver flakes, blinding him—but this time each silver flake was a tiny functioning device. Each had its own unique sound and radiated a sense of its purpose, which he instantly understood. With so much information gushing into him he could grasp none of it. The machines kept coming and the speed of the flow increased.

Panic hit him with a sensation of drowning. In terror he mentally bore down on the geyser of images with all of his might, trying to force them of his mind. Slowly, slowly, it began to work. He could feel something happening. Something was definitely changing…

He opened his eyes.

He was awake in his bed. It was still the middle of the night. Karina, the image, the dream, was gone. The distorted sensations caused by his fever were also gone. So were his symptoms. So was his fever, just like the first time.

The countless tiny machines, however, continued to float around in front of him. Nikola was too amazed to question any of it. Fascination overwhelmed him until he was aware of nothing else.

At that point, the only thing that prevented him from fainting in astonishment was his burning determination to not let go of whatever was happening to him. He seized it as fistfuls of treasure in the hands of an awakening dreamer. He would have to make sense of it later. Now, more than anything else, he was compelled to embrace this and somehow make it his own.

Along with this new attack from Satan, or this new symptom of his mental defect, or this magical new gift whose purpose he did not understand — there came an entirely new ability. Now, when he mentally dismantled a machine, there were no gaps in the image. Everything was laid out in front of him. The cruel twist was that elaborate scientific principles, which he was only beginning to understand, caused the apparent objects to be composed of a web of riddles. There in front of him were answers to scientific mysteries, some employing levels of knowledge he did not have. Yet the results were there in front of him. Their mystery hit him with a bull's-eye blow and lodged in the part of his mind where he spent most of his time.

His heart raced while he recalled the Reverend's death-whisper about visitations from demons. On the other hand, he could also feel the cool mist of Karina's touch along his cheek. Whether he was remembering an entity of substance, a delusion, or even a demonic trick, the mere memory of her was enough to send pleasure radiating through him. The delight nourished him; it energized him and would not allow him to turn his back.

# Chapter Six

## One Year Later
## At The New Telephone Office
## Budapest

Four disgruntled engineers with the Budapest Telephone Office huddled together in a quiet corner, livening up their day with a little intraoffice conspiracy against that buffoon, Nikola Tesla. They made no effort to be discreet.

"That's it then," said the one who liked to get things going. "We've got a clerk who was at the City Manager's meeting last night, and they are *not* going to replace Tesla."

"Idiots! He was gone for *two weeks*! Nobody's ever stayed out sick that long!"

"Remember that machinist who took four days off and lost his job?"

"Yeah," agreed the first one. "It was close for Tesla this time though. In the end, they started talking about how, you know, since he came back he's working as hard as ever."

"And that he also invented the 'repeaters' to boost the sound."

"Hey! Whose side are you on? Anybody could have done that! It's basic science!"

"Parts of it. But the rest… I don't know."

"What, you think he should keep his job? Keep making the rest of us look bad?"

"See here! I didn't say that."

"Listen! The clerk says that they all went around and around about it, and they eventually decided he is 'too valuable' to fire. *But* this is the thing—they came close to going the other way! Why? Not because he stayed out two weeks, but because they're getting too many complaints about his *behavior!*"

"I've seen it! People are getting spooky around him."

"He's worse since he came back."

"Everybody notices now."

"Oh, you'll notice too, when he suddenly clenches up all his muscles, head to toe."

The men chuckled at the image.

"Or if you miss that, you will absolutely notice after he straightens back up and starts moving around like he's got a bottle balanced on his head!"

The men laughed heartily at that. They were pushing the boundary of acceptable behavior, right there on the job site, and it gave them a brave feeling. The brave feeling made them laugh even harder. It prolonged the moment and allowed them to enjoy the novelty of beer hall camaraderie in the middle of a work day.

"If we could just get something else on him. If his behavior really got out of hand at some point."

"Or if he did something to embarrass the company."

"If that's all it takes, we should just watch him close. Sooner or later he'll do something strange enough to get him pushed out the door."

"What, now you're saying we have to take turns keeping an eye on him?"

They all laughed at that. The laughter drove away the guilty feelings over conspiring against another man, leaving them free to settle down to consider the idea of actually doing it.

One checked his watch. "We have a lunch whistle in half an hour. Where does he usually go?"

"Ever since he got back, he's been going off on 'health walks' with some old friend of his."

"Anital Szigety. I met him. A real muscle fanatic. He likes to brag that he's going to get Tesla in top physical condition after his illness."

"Then maybe we should kill Szigety."

They burst into laughter at that one, then became quiet…

A moment later they realized what they were all thinking and exploded into laughter again.

"All right, maybe we could start by just following them."

"Right! Once they're away from here, Tesla is sure to feel freer. You know, free to, free to…"

"To *what*?"

"I don't know! Who knows? Anything we can use to add to the reasons to get rid of him."

"It doesn't have to be a big thing. He's on thin ice."

"I'll follow him!" volunteered the one who really wanted the others to like him.

"When?"

"What do you mean 'when?' Today! As soon as he leaves with that Anital fellow."

"Anital Szigety. It might help to know his name in case you need to talk to them."

"What for? To ask if he minds being followed?" The one who really wanted to be liked turned to the others for an approving laugh, but they just looked back at him, waiting. He quietly continued, "I'll, uh, just follow them, that's all."

"Not too close!"

"But follow!" added the one who liked to keep things going. "See how he behaves when it's just him and his healthy friend."

"Be sure to let *him* start whatever happens, so that he'll be the one who's actually—"

"Responsible! Right!"

"You just write down what he does!"

"But only if it's something… you know."

"What?"

"Something good."

"How do I know if it's good?"

"All right, anything then."

"Anything at all?"

"Anything good."

By that point the four workers were grinning in the squinty-eyed satisfaction of outlaws with inside knowledge. They sealed their agreement using nothing more than a few silent nods.

Moments later the unofficial lounge area was empty.

\* \* \*

The two young men who strode through the tree line of the large urban park were both swinging heavy wooden clubs the size of bowling pins. Nikola pumped his long legs in rhythm to the fast-paced strides of the ridiculously fit Anital Szigety, but no matter how hard he pushed himself, he remained several feet behind him. In spite of the exertion, he insisted on gasping his way through a conversation because his brain was alive with heat and light. Talking helped him bleed off pressure.

"In fact, you can compare the effort of learning to control it to the process of learning to play a musical instrument." Nikola laughed. "At first it seems impossible, but with practice—"

"Breathing. Deep breathing. I don't see how you can be taking your deepest breaths when you talk so much."

"Take the repeaters, for instance—I invented them, it's true, but Anital, I *copied* the design from a working model that was already in my head!" He laughed again and added a little skip to his step.

Anital ignored that and continued, "It is impossible for me to earn the money you are paying me unless you start breathing harder than that. Swing the weights higher! Don't you ever want to get your lungs back from all that pneumonia?"

Nikola laughed louder. "Yes! Of course you are right! And I want my strength back, to be sure. I'm going to need it. There's so much to do! Of course I can't tell anyone at work. You wouldn't believe how hard it is to keep it all pushed into the background, so people don't take offense at—"

"Wait a minute! Did you actually hire me just so you could tell me this story?"

Nikola considered that for a moment. "I don't think so, but then again it was killing me not to tell *somebody*!" He laughed with glee, then dropped his clubs on the grass and stretched his arms wide, pulling in deep breaths.

"Good!" Anital injected. "Because I don't know enough about any of this stuff to be able to tell if you are making sense or not. Mostly what I hear is that you are either too eccentric or too inspired or whatever you call it to be able to give me your best efforts. Is that it? Because it seems as if you want me to drive the remnants of the fever out of your lungs, but how am I supposed to do that while you chatter like a gossipy old woman?"

"Chatter?" Nikola leaped into the air with delight. "That's perfect! Chatter! You understand? Because the images come in a stream of chatter and they're just as hard to stop as gossip!" He ended with a happy laugh.

"Yes, good. Why are we stopped here?" Anital groused. "I suppose you want to take a nap now?"

"You have not heard the extraordinary part, Anital! Even when I have no idea what sort of device I am dealing with, they can be dismantled to any degree! You hear me?"

Nikola whispered the next part, the good part: "I don't have to devise the machines before seeing how they work; I pick apart what is already there and allow it to teach me!"

"Nikola, if we were still back in physics class I'm sure you could turn this into one of those bizarre presentations that you always managed to pull off against all odds, but—"

"There are such things, aren't there, Anital?" Nikola interrupted, suddenly serious. "You've heard of such things, at least? Visions one can learn from? I mean, there is not necessarily anything demonic about them. Wouldn't you say?"

Anital dropped his clubs with a deep sigh. "All right! I admit it. You have defeated me. If you want to avoid exercise so badly that you come up with *merde* like this..."

He raised his hands high and cried out, "This scrawny man has beaten me!" Turning back to Nikola, he added, "Lucky for you I can tolerate abnormal people. It's a gift. But you need to calm down, my friend. Slow down your brain and speed up your body."

He looked around the area and focused on a sandwich cart on the other side of the clearing, parked in the shade under a large tree. "Maybe we should at least have something to eat. You watch our clubs; I'll see if he's selling anything that won't kill you on the spot."

"I could bring the clubs wi—"

"That's fine! The clubs are fine where they are. You stay with them." Anital was already halfway between Nikola and the sandwich cart.

In the opposite direction, a solitary male idly scuffed at the ground, stooping to pick up attractive leaves. The solitary male so desired for the other telephone company workers to admire him that he was putting extra care into his spy duties. However, when he followed Anital toward the sandwich cart and realized that Nikola was not going along, he stopped, suddenly trapped between them. He was in the middle of the clearing, uncomfortably close to his subject, so he began drifting back to his observation spot among the trees. But he saw that the maneuver was going to require him to turn his back for a few moments in order to avoid walking backward and drawing suspicion. He checked for possible problems, glancing around under hooded eyelids; nobody else was in the vicinity, except for the subject Nikola Tesla on the opposite edge of the clearing. The subject appeared to be doing some sort of stretching and deep breathing exercises.

It was a good time for the spy to make his risky move. He turned away and casually began relocating himself, drifting like a man with nothing on his mind, studying the grass all the way back to his protected observation spot. No rush.

If he had been watching Nikola at that instant, he would have seen his subject abruptly stop and stare in disbelief at an empty space in the air next to the nearest tree.

"I must be wrong..." It was a young woman's voice.

Nikola turned in the direction of the sound. He gasped and his eyes flew open wide. He barely dared to breathe. He was planted there, rooted in the ground by the solid image of Karina standing next to the tree line. Hands on hips, she regarded him with a wry smile.

She stared straight at him, dressed in filmy white and appearing more mature. The adult facial features had settled into themselves. She seemed complete. And she was even more beautiful than he remembered her.

"Because it sounds to me," Karina continued, "as if you are

giving up. You're not really going to do that, are you?"

Fascination paralyzed him while warnings of demonic possession rang in the back of his mind. This time he had no fever to excuse such a sight. But before his fears could convince him to run, the first whiff of the familiar delight radiating from her began to blow across his nerve endings. The far sensation pulled hard at him and made him hungry for more, but at that moment Karina casually stepped behind the closest tree and disappeared from sight.

Her absence broke the spell just enough to allow Nikola to spin away from her, but he was unable to run. His legs could do nothing more than stand, electrified. He could still speak, and he struggled to keep his voice down to a bare whisper. That was all the control he could muster. He had none left over to stop the words from spilling out. "She is not real. *It! It* is not real!" He took several deep breaths, keeping his eyes closed while he struggled to clear his thoughts.

So he only heard her voice. "You force my hand, Nikola?" Her tone was gentle, teasing.

He had to open his eyes at that. When he did, he found himself face to face with the image of Karina as a middle-aged woman. Her brow was lined by the years, and her hair was shot with gray. She was attired in a fashionable "day in the park" dress that would fit next to any contemporary lady who might stroll by.

His knees trembled. He fought to keep his balance. "You are not real," he said through clenched teeth.

"You argue with illusions?"

"…This is a haunting then. You died! I have no fever to explain you!"

"Karina died."

"Whatever you are! You are not real."

In reply, Karina simply looked into his eyes with a mischievous smile. She took a long, deep breath and then lightly brushed her hand across his cheek.

Nikola's vision exploded into a flood of oncoming lights. He fell to his knees, crying out. A few moments later, the blinding lights began to resolve into individual sources that were everywhere and in all directions. At first the lights appeared to be glowing halos of energy. After a few seconds his vision cleared enough that he realized the "halos" only radiated from living things.

The grass was a carpet of glowing energy. A small shrub exuded a crackling aura of energy. The nearest tree was a towering blaze of radiant energy, humming with power.

Nikola remained on his knees and buried his face in his hands to cut off the overwhelming imagery. The sheer volume of information flooding into his mind felt as if it would tear him to pieces. While he fought to steady his thoughts, more than all the other questions flooding through him, there was one thing he needed to know most.

"Where have you been? My god, so many years. Where were you? Why have you not come to me?"

"Why would you not let me near you?" Her voice was close, as if she whispered in his ear.

"Nonsense!" he hissed. "Why did you turn away from me?"

Her reply was soft, but her tone was rock hard. "Your fear closed me off. Your fear kept me from you. Is *this* what you fear? *Look!*"

He opened his eyes but Karina was nowhere to be seen. His field of vision was filled by a giant, blazing mass of energy that surrounded the nearest tree. The huge mass duplicated itself, as if Nikola suddenly had double vision. A moment later the duplicate energy mass moved upward, leaving the original behind. The duplicate stopped and hovered overhead, then began revolving at such a high speed that the motion generated a deep whine.

Before Nikola could react, the spinning mass of energy stopped cold. There was a moment of dead silence, then—just as abruptly—the huge halo reversed direction and immediately resumed spinning in the other direction at full power.

Once Nikola was struck by the meaning of what he was seeing, he lost all sense of inhibition. Proof! Notions of social propriety or the dignity of his professional position suddenly meant nothing. Proof! He had no sense of arching his back and hurling an exultant scream into an open sky, "Proof!" Nor was he aware of throwing his arms open and bellowing, "Prooooof! Prooooof!"

It was proof that Karina came from somewhere outside of his imagination because the scientific value of what he was seeing was far greater than anything he could conceive on his own. However she might be described, her visitations brought him more than mere delusion—and the proof of *that* was spinning in the air over his head.

He was staring up at the link between matter and energy. The connecting link. A *provable* way of joining the visible world with the invisible powers driving it. The missing piece to his failed insights on alternating current had just fallen into place with a metallic clang.

This supposed "problem" of alternating current—that it continually shifted from positive to negative charge—was actually its greatest strength, because when the charges between two magnets are rapidly shifted back and forth, the magnetic field between them will spin around to keep up with the shifting charge. This spinning magnetic field will invisibly grab onto any solid object that contains the element iron. If that object is the end of a metal axle, then that axle will be turned by the rotating magnetic field around it, and it can be used to power every kind of machine and operate at any speed the metal can withstand.

*A magnetic field can whirl thousands of times a second without friction—just like that giant mass of energy is doing, whirling away up there in the sky.*

The power of the revelation took control of him until he became a lanky meat puppet dancing on strings of pure joy.

Nikola could not tell if he screamed the words or if some inner voice screamed inside him. *A magnetic field invisibly engages the physical world in the same sense that the mind moves the body!*

On his knees there in the grass, for the first time, the ever-present ache from the burning coals in his belly finally vanished. He leaned back and howled with laughter over the wasted years spent fearing that his inspirations were only some useless form of torment.

He had no awareness at all of a man watching him from the edge of the clearing, slack-jawed with amazement. He was barely even aware of Anital Szigety when he ran to Nikola's side, spilling two perfectly good mutton sandwiches over the grass in his efforts to pull Nikola to his feet. And neither of the pair caught a glimpse of the telephone company spy hurrying back to the office, moving like a man with big news.

# Chapter Seven

### The Next Day
### The Telephone Company Office
### Budapest

The voices came at him with speedy urgency. "Mr. Tesla, you do not seem to realize that the City Manager's office is trying to bestow an honor upon you."

"We thought you would be thrilled."

"You should be, you know."

"Anyone else would be."

"Surely you can see that."

"My god, *I* would be," the telephone company spy interjected. He now spoke with the confidence of a man who knows that his words are heeded. All five representatives of the City Manager's office nodded in vigorous agreement.

"Gentlemen," Nikola kept his voice quiet, careful to weigh his words. "I am certainly, ah, flattered by this, but I—"

"'*But*'? Before you say 'but', mister, you should know that the City Manager is personally sticking his neck out for you!"

"Like a long tree branch."

"Just hanging out there waiting for your response."

"Out there where any damned bird on the planet can land and shit all over his head. Perhaps that means nothing to you?"

"But you see, gentlemen, my mother lives alone now, and Paris is so far away. I don't think she will want to move."

"Mm. Yes, correct, actually."

"She's quite firm about it, you can be sure."

"Excuse me?"

"We contacted her yesterday."

"You spoke to my—?"

"We sent a man on the train to explain how you are to be honored."

"She is delighted for you!"

"And yes, as you predicted, she refuses to move."

"Even at company expense!"

"But she *strongly* desires you to take the opportunity! She is sending you a letter to that effect. Our man would have brought it with him, but he had to come right back."

"And of course she needed time to write it."

"Gentlemen, why would you contact my mother without speaking to me first? She is not—"

"Come now, Mr. Tesla! You are far too intelligent to play dumb with us. Are you holding out for more money?"

Nikola snapped his eyes closed and turned away, then stooped over slightly, clenching all his muscles. A moment later he took a deep breath, stood up straight, and turned to them, moving as carefully as if he had a bottle balanced on his head. The representatives threw grim looks to one another.

"Gentlemen, I am not 'holding out' for anything. I am simply overwhelmed by the company's determination to, ah…"

"*Honor you.* After all, for you to be able to move from our humble little local telephone office here, to the Continental Edison Company in Paris? Well!"

"On Saint-Germain-des-Prés, yet!"

"Not only that, you will be a 'consultant'! Not just some bureaucrat!"

"That's almost like not having to work!"

The representatives all laughed in appreciation of not having to work.

"Better! It's almost like *not having a job*!"

A bigger round of laughter greeted the suggestion of not having a job.

"Gentlemen, please—I do not seek to avoid work. Quite the opposite."

"Then work yourself to *death*, mister!" The largest one was tired of the game. "You need to grasp the simple fact that the

City Manager has pulled *strings*, very high-up *strings*, to get you this opportunity! In Paris!"

"But why?"

"Because the Edison company there needs to figure out how to repair all of their failing generators, and the rumor is that you are a smart guy."

"But for you to have done all this in secret…"

"The point is that if you turn up your long nose at this opportunity, if you slap the City Manager in the face and humiliate him in front of—"

"I have no desire to offend him! And certainly not to humiliate—"

"Good! You might as well have the rest of this week off to get your affairs in order here. You can take the train to Paris over the weekend. You start on Monday."

"This Monday?"

The yes-men began to all talk at once.

"Here's your letter of introduction."

"Read it if you like."

"You'll see how it praises you."

"Cheer up! This letter is like having a magic wand."

"It's going to open up doors for you!"

"*Open, Ses-sa-meeee!*" cried the formerly neglected telephone company spy, enjoying his new status. All five representatives rewarded him by howling with laughter.

Nikola stumbled out of the Manager's office and into the centuries-old metropolis of Budapest. He needed to burn off the confusion and anxiety overwhelming him. At least his feet were on familiar turf. He had taken many late night walks along the embankments of the Danube River when sleep eluded him. Long on daydreams and short on rest, at one time or another his boot heel had touched nearly every cobblestone within many blocks of his apartment. He could maneuver all of those streets and most of their alleys in complete darkness and never take a wrong turn.

The ability came in handy that afternoon. He was so baffled by the honor of being transferred to Paris that his confusion kicked the spontaneous mental images into overtime. While he walked along, his vision filled with secondary lines and angles. They rose from physical objects and continuously joined themselves into odd shapes and configurations. Each completed object gave off a definite sense of function. The images soon crowded Nikola's field of vision like frenzied children grabbing at bits of his attention. His awareness of the hard world dimmed to a background glow.

It was late when he finally noticed his immediate surroundings; he was stumbling west on Victor Hugo Avenue, less than a block from the east bank of the river. He had been walking for long enough that the afternoon sun was low in front of him, nearly at the horizon. The shock of awakening into such an unusual situation sent a jolt of fear though him. He wondered if the hours he had spent virtually sleepwalking that afternoon could be excused as a condition of absent-mindedness, or had he come to inhabit places outside the boundaries of sanity? There was no answer, only the single admonition: you have to go to Paris. They need you in Paris.

His inner demons sneered. *They need you to go somewhere far away, so you will not embarrass the City Manager for allowing a madman to run the city's telephone exchange.*

"Maybe it's because of the repeaters I invented for the city's phone system. More sound for less energy. Perhaps the Edison company hopes I can do a similar trick for them."

*They are only doing what they have been told to do by political cronies.*

"Not true! There are people who value my abilities!"

*There are people who are afraid of you. They don't know if you will do something dangerous.*

"I have *never* given anyone cause to believe such—"

*You have shamed yourself in front of your colleagues with your bizarre behavior!*

"No!" Nikola shouted as he passed a fruit vendor, who dropped the shiny apple he was holding out.

*Your demon gives off an evil stink. You can't smell it, but others can.*

"Nobody has ever said—"

*Why should they take the chance of being honest about it?*

"No more of this!" Nikola grabbed the sides of his head, but he kept moving. He didn't even slow down.

*So why shouldn't they just get rid of you? Quietly.*

That one stopped him in his tracks. He immediately glanced around, relieved that no one appeared to have noticed him. He could practically smell his father's dying breath. He had to do something to clear his thoughts.

It occurred to him that he was standing next to the low stone wall along the river's embankment. Only a few other people were around, and at the moment, none were looking in his direction. He stripped down to his bare feet, trousers, and shirt, then set his clothing in a neat pile on the wall, kicked off the stone surface, and dove into the chilly water. The bracing shock of cold felt wonderful, as if it could clean him inside and flush away his guilty fears. He swam hard.

Eventually the effort and the cool water cleared his mind. A renewed sense of things allowed him to see that it no longer mattered if his detractors were right about him. As of that day, his fledgling professional life in Budapest was effectively over.

He swam back to shore with all his strength, using the exertion to drain more energy away from his spinning thoughts. It was effective enough to help him remain focused after he climbed back on shore, and even while he slipped his dry clothes back over his wet body.

He took bearings; the apartment was less than a kilometer away, and it was time to get off of the streets. He started out at a fast walk so that it only took a few moments for his blood to heat back up. Soon the geyser began to spew. Line segments floated up off of the sidewalk, the curb, the edges of buildings. Nikola employed his diminishing mental clarity to set a repeating command in the back of his mind, ordering his legs to continue moving toward home. Out of habit, he also set a mental timer to measure the trip. He focused on it for a second to set its image so clearly in his memory that the timer would continue to work even after he turned his attention away.

By the time he had gone another block, Nikola was picking up spontaneous images from the surface of every object that came into view. It forced him to choose his footsteps and to carefully separate the components of his inner world from the hard world around him. He moved down the sidewalk as if walking through a dream.

This time, at least, the dream was not a nightmare. Rising sensations of delight began to tease him, sensations he had come to associate with the presence of Karina *or whatever she is*.

It took all the willpower he could muster to keep from dissolving into the experience. Out on the streets, there was no choice but to hold back his awareness and control his behavior long enough to keep himself out of trouble.

When he finally opened the door to his apartment, the geyser of images overwhelmed him, but not before his mental timer confirmed that he covered the distance from the river back to the apartment in four minutes and fourteen seconds.

# Chapter Eight

The building's large sign proclaimed the home of the Continental Edison Society, and Nikola arrived beneath it dressed in humble finery. He eagerly strode up to the door of the building and found his way inside through a maze of hallways until he reached the Manager's office. A prominent sign next to the door read, "Maurice Baudelaire, Manager-of-the-Works." Nikola leaned into the doorway and gently knocked.

Moments later he found himself standing across from Manager Baudelaire, a righteously fat man in his mid-fifties who sat wedged behind a bed-sized desk. Manager Baudelaire squinted and held Nikola's reference letter at arm's length, already radiating resentment and disgust. He wore his long side-hair swirled over a bald pate. The tonsorial self-delusion crowned a hundred and seventy-five kilograms of jellied anger. *Three hundred and eighty-five pounds,* Nikola automatically reminded himself.

While Nikola waited, the room's dead silence was broken only by the nearby sound of dripping water.

Drip… drip… drip…

Meanwhile he stood with posture so stiff he was nearly at formal attention. Finally Manager Baudelaire muttered under his breath, speaking in French, "The older I get, the smaller everybody writes." He squinted harder at the letter. "They are making a very bad joke." He glanced up and fixed his eyes on Nikola. "A dangerous joke."

Nikola had no idea how to respond, so he said nothing.

Finally Manager Baudelaire tossed the letter down and regarded him with a bored smile. "Well! How does a genius from Budapest expect to communicate here in Paris? Impress me."

Nikola replied in perfect French, "I have found French to harbor a highly logical structure. I'm happy to converse for a while if you'd care to test me. Of course, I must do more work on my accent."

Manager Baudelaire looked equally impressed and embittered. He glanced at the letter again and pretended to reread a line or two. "Now the vague referral in your little letter here seems to indicate some extraordinary talent on your part."

Baudelaire studied Nikola a moment, then snorted. "So *this* is the sort of utter shit that people are willing to say, just to get rid of you?"

He laughed out loud at Nikola's expression. "Oh, yes! I know about such things, believe me. Conspiracies? People do it all the time, just to get someone out of the way. You should never try to fool me on such a matter.

"Well. You're nice and young. Keep the syphilis out of your scrotum and you can have a good life." He gave a dismissive wave with his left hand and set about scratching his pen across the surface of a printed form, pretending to fill in boxes.

Nikola went on, unfazed, "You see, I have what one might call an enduring obsession with inventive science." He added in a confidential tone, "That is what I have decided to call it, at least," and smiled.

Manager Baudelaire raised his gaze to Nikola as if he didn't expect it to be worth the effort of lifting his head. He let out a long sigh and rubbed the palms of his beefy hands over his face. When he spoke, he switched to German, saying, "Some of our seasonal workers are from Deutschland. How would you communicate with them?"

Nikola immediately replied in perfect High German, "My father was a pastor; he wanted me to be able to communicate with as many people as possible."

The Manager dropped his head slightly, took a breath, and then raised his face up once more. "Ach! A preacher's boy!

Brought up to follow after papa also, ya?"

Nikola's face darkened. "For a while. At first." Then he broke into a delighted grin. "Do you know—well no, of course you don't, but let me tell you—he actually gave me a one-day share of his salary, every time I learned a new language!" He paused, struck by the memory, "Think of that…"

Manager Baudelaire switched to badly accented Italian. "And how many times did he have to pay your one-day cut of his salary?"

Nikola's Italian reply was fluent. "Eight, but I'm only truly fluent in six. He eventually grew tired of the game."

Manager Baudelaire slapped the desktop hard and leaned forward to growl, "if your brain is that good, why would you even *want* a job like this? The Edison dynamos are huge. They are filthy. They are completely unpredictable! You'll spend your life tangled up in their guts, just trying to keep them working!"

He stopped when he realized that he was addressing Nikola's profile and that Nikola's attention was distracted. Baudelaire decided to wait…

After a moment Nikola turned back and asked in an affable tone, "Is that water, dripping? Somewhere out on the factory floor, I think?"

Manager Baudelaire stared at Nikola for several seconds, trying to make himself believe this intruder's impertinence. When he recovered his voice he replied, "Yes. Water. Yes." He made a vague gesture in the general direction of the sound. "After a while, you don't even hear it."

"However, would it be, dare I say, a poor combination? Electrical current and leaking water?"

Manager Baudelaire leaped up from his desk, knocking his chair backward, ready for hand-to-hand combat. "You sneer at me? You dare to *sneer* while you are here asking for a *job*? You come in here and ignore me while I speak and worry yourself about something so trivial as a little dripping water?"

Nikola stared for a moment, uncomprehending, then his face broke into a beaming grin. "Ahh! *No!* No indeed. I have not come to ask for a job!"

"…No?"

"No, no! Simply a misunderstanding, nothing more! I am here to report for work."

"You— You are here to report for work."

"Oh yes! It's all in the letter. Right there."

"Oh I see. Thank you, yes, you are right. It's all in the letter, and you don't have to ask for a job because you are already here to report for work."

The Manager released a sardonic chuckle. "Why, you don't even have to ask as a *simple* gesture of courtesy to *me*! Eh?"

"How would that be a gesture of—"

"*Perhaps* you are one of those people who assume a common man cannot also be brilliant? Far beyond his job function! A man who may have also fallen victim to any number of *plots*, eh? Plots by others to hold you down! Envious dimwits! Resentful plebeians! Every low-brow lickspittle who can finger the dial on a monkey wrench! When in *fact*, Monsieur Genius, my position also requires several languages, as you heard!" His eyes narrowed. "Perhaps you will soon want *Manager Baudelaire's* job. Eh?"

Nikola's eyes glazed over. He slowly turned away from the Manager and squinted hard, then relaxed and took a deep breath. He opened his eyes again, stood up straight, then smiled and turned back again. He answered in reassuring tones, "I don't believe your job is why I'm here. However, I am given to understand that there is a malfunctioning dynamo I can see? Somewhere nearby?" He added, "It's all in the reference letter."

Manager Baudelaire stared at him, radiating disgust. "What did you just do? When you turned away just then?"

Nikola stood gazing into Baudelaire's eyes for a moment before he pleasantly replied, "Nothing."

"…Nothing? Just now, that was nothing?"

"Correct."

"Nothing. What you just did."

"Yes.

"You are actually going to stand there and try to call that 'nothing'?"

"Nothing at all."

Manager Baudelaire let go of a deep sigh and rubbed his eye sockets with his fists. He twisted the knuckles back and forth, back and forth, back and forth.

Nikola politely cleared his throat. "The, ah, malfunctioning dynamo?"

Baudelaire dropped his hands to the desk. Now his eyes were wide open, as if he had just remembered something. A sour yellow grin spread across his face. "Now that you mention it, I am reminded that we *do* have one. Of course you are correct. How silly of me."

He leaned toward Nikola and brought his face close enough to whisper, "In fact, Monsieur Genius, it is waiting for you *right down the street!*" A low-pitched giggle bubbled out of him. He squelched it before he stood, then gestured for Nikola to follow him out the door.

The cavernous warehouse served as a Continental Edison repair shop, and it was large enough to service dynamos the size of a railway locomotive. Stacked along the walls were ruined experimental devices ranging from breadbox-sized contraptions to major machines larger than the workers who toiled on them. The machines competed for space among piles of electrical scrap and boxes of spare parts.

The center of the warehouse was dominated by a huge iron and copper dynamo. The burned-out machine was a scorched disaster, as if it had been repeatedly struck by lightning. Manager Baudelaire and a dozen rough-looking shop workers clustered on the front side of the machine while they waited for Nikola to finish his initial inspection in the back.

Manager Baudelaire maintained a tense, expectant silence and a tiny smirk of anticipation; he already knew that this impossible remnant of ruined metal had no future beyond the nearest scrap pile. But he also knew that the combined size and complexity of the thing was guaranteed to intimidate anyone at first, even the most self-confident upstart.

The silence finally ended when he heard Nikola break into a giggle from the other side. The giggle stopped immediately, but the sound echoed around the warehouse's hard surfaces.

None of the workers moved. The Manager stole a glance at his men, but quickly looked away. He had no way to tell what any of them were thinking so he remained in place, arms folded.

Nikola giggled again. The Manager began to shift his weight back and forth, but still he kept quiet. A moment later Nikola moved around to the front of the dynamo and came back into everyone's view.

The workers watched him climb all over the machine, studying each section. His moving lips produced no sound, but his intense stare methodically took in everything about the ruined system.

He finished his inspection, brushing his hands with a white kerchief, then took a deep breath and let out a long, slow exhale. Finally he took a couple of steps back, still keeping his eyes fixed on the dynamo. He paused, contemplating the huge machine.

And giggled a third time.

This one was so forceful that mucus flew out his nose when he tried to stifle it, and he wound up making a sound that was a cross between a cough and a sneeze. He clapped his hand over his mouth and threw a guilty glance toward the Manager, but the large man was so aghast that the expression on his face completely overcame Nikola, who exploded into laughter. He was only able to stop by faking a coughing fit.

There was another moment of silence.

Still none of the workers moved.

The Manager only stared.

Nikola quickly recovered himself, turned to the workers with an apologetic shrug and spoke to them in French, "Gentlemen, I *am* sorry. Please forgive me. It's just that—"

He stepped closer to the dynamo. "Look over here, for example." His voice took on a tone someone might use to describe the work of an adorable child. "All of the wiring in here is of a gauge *too light* for the current! You see? And oh! Oh! Over here! Look, look, look! Capacitors of this size? Who decided that? Why, the entire contraption works out of phase with itself!" He turned passionately toward the workers. "Do you see? You see, don't you? Gentlemen—this machine is one hundred percent reliable, provided that it was *specifically engineered to break down!*" Nikola finished with a happy laugh.

He stopped a moment later when he noticed there was no other sound in the warehouse, no other movement. All of the burly men were staring at him as if he had just relieved himself on their floor.

He inhaled sharply and continued, "Of course that is not the case. No! Not the case at all. No. For us, this is merely an opportunity to, ah…" He swallowed hard and went on. "I could demonstrate, if perhaps someone would be kind enough to loan me their toolbox?"

The workers glared. No one moved.

Nikola carefully stepped up to the biggest factory worker. The man outsized all of the others, but his placid expression and dull eyes caused Nikola to guess that he was the safest choice. As soon Nikola he got close enough to the man, he gently reached down toward a large toolbox sitting at the worker's feet, keeping his eyes on the man's face while he gingerly picked up the box and then took several steps backward toward the burned-out dynamo. He made sure to be well out of reach before he turned his back and faced the huge machine again.

He stopped himself, held up his hand and gestured for a moment's patience from the men, then turned away and hunched over slightly, clenching all of his muscles. A few seconds later he straightened up again and turned back to them, moving with deliberate care. He staunchly avoided any further expression of humor while he made his demonstration adjustments.

Manager Baudelaire and all of the workers kept their eyes riveted on Nikola. Not one of them had moved or reacted to Nikola's eccentric behavior in any way. After spending their lives in provinces where ethnic and political struggles were a persistent fact of life, the men had each mastered the craft of masking his thoughts. Even if Nikola had studied their faces, none of the men would have had any trouble in preventing him from reading them.

However, all trace of Manager Baudelaire's little smirk was gone.

# Chapter Nine

Autumn
Paris

Late at night in the following autumn, Nikola sat in his darkened apartment on the Boulevard St. Michel and stretched his senses to the utmost, trying to reach through the walls and somehow determine if a storm was approaching.

The air inside was so moist and heavy that his nightshirt was damp throughout, and his hair hung in his face. He ignored the discomfort and continued his endeavor with the concentration of a musician working on a difficult piece.

There were no other indications of rain but for the damp air. The potential for thunder was poor; at that time of year there was rarely enough energy in the storm clouds to generate lightning—thick sleet was just as likely to fall. Nevertheless he kept his windows closed and curtains drawn, trying to force the rest of his perceptions to sharpen until they could detect a faraway storm's electrical energy. He wondered if it might come via a faint tingling sensation, like a cat feeling a breeze across its whiskers.

By the time he arrived back at his apartment that evening, his usual eruptions of imagery had been suppressed for several hours. The longer he held them back, the more pressure they built up. He arrived through the door feeling like he was holding back the world's biggest sneeze.

His skin prickled with a growing sense of anticipation. In the back of his mind lurked the hope that it meant he would be getting a much overdue visit from Karina. Such a thing didn't seem like too much to ask, but so far the place she occupied in his heart had remained empty and silent all through his stay in Paris. With his frustration building, he sometimes fumed that she left him bare of her company without explanation.

A floorboard creaked behind him. Nikola spun in the direction of the sound, eager for the sight of her.

Nothing.

With that, the pressure exploded and the mental sneeze blasted through his brain. A geyser of imagery spewed into him with overwhelming force. By this time, Nikola's prime exercise of the evening was completely lost to him and he had no idea whether an electrical storm was approaching or not.

Early winter was on the scene by the time Manager Baudelaire found himself standing in front of the same dynamo that twenty-eight-year-old Nikola Tesla had faced on his first day in Paris. This was the machine no one could fix. What was there to fix? It was a ruined hulk. Nobody could have fixed it with anything short of witchcraft or pacts with the Devil. Manager Baudelaire needed no further proof of trickery afoot.

He left Nikola to suffer politely in the background while he performed a grim and protracted inspection. Maurice Baudelaire was not so easily impressed with such shallow affectations as the big machine's restored metal surfaces. The Manager-of-the-Works hardly considered himself some tulip-brained schoolgirl with moist panties for this upstart from Budapest. Would he piss himself at the sight of the giant ruined dynamo running under full power with a low, steady hum? Oh no. He did not marvel upon noting that all the working components had either been retooled or replaced, or that after two solid weeks of continuous operation, it was still running smoothly.

Baudelaire knew for a fact it had been running without interruption because he had a team of three employees watching the place around the clock. That left the inspection itself as a footnote, a formality. Manager Baudelaire had already walked into the room that day already knowing nothing remained for the Continental Edison Company to do but move the refurbished generator into one of the city's newer power stations. He also knew there was nothing forcing him to reveal this to Nikola before he had the chance to toy with him about it.

Some measure of payback was compulsory. Baudelaire nearly ground his teeth smooth while he read from the field report, knowing a copy would be sent to The Man over in the land of the Puritan assholes—the young upstart had also fixed several other big generators during his few months of tenure. So far, not one had failed. This was unusual, since they routinely burned out under full load.

*So*, Baudelaire mused, *this Tesla fellow thinks that his one little repair assignment is to be the extent of his initiation here?* He sensed an opportunity to issue a far more interesting and humorous challenge. All that remained for him to do was inform Tesla that he was being sent on a temporary assignment to Strasbourg. There, Continental Edison had just constructed a power generating system for the new railway system being built by Kaiser Wilhelm I, only to have the gargantuan thing short out and blow a hole through one of the depot walls. The Kaiser had informed Continental Edison that he refused to pay for the job until the system was put into good working order. He sent the message through his administrative staff in Strasbourg (*or "Strasburg," Baudelaire reminded himself, as the Royal Anus prefers it to be spelled*). Why, the spelling issue alone was merely one more sign that of the two, Baudelaire was the unappreciated superior being.

"Royalty." Baudelaire grumbled under it his breath. He harbored a whiff of nostalgia for the days when France had a stroke of the guillotine for every imperial head.

*So,* he concluded, *why not let the upstart try his genius out on the situation? Oh yes. Let us see how far Mr. Nikola Tesla's fabled brain takes him in dealing with the vagaries of a Royal court!*

Manager Baudelaire decided that Tesla would be on the train for Strasbourg by the end of the day. He took a deep breath; that was it then.

He extended his arm upward and snapped his fingers for the upstart to join him, having already concluded that the best way to deal with an intellect as sharp as this one is to hit hard and fast. Don't give him an instant to think.

A moment later Nikolas stood at Baudelaire's side wearing an eager expression.

"Nikola," Manager Baudelaire began.

"Yes, Monsieur Baudelaire?"

"*Manager* Baudelaire."

"Yes, ah, Manager Baudelaire?"

"This repair work of yours."

"Yes?"

"I don't think it presented much of a challenge to you."

"Excuse me?"

"I am not a tool user myself. Clearly, I overestimated the difficulty of the task."

"...Sir, this machine has not only been repaired, but I have also corrected half a dozen blatant design flaws. Any one of them would have prevented it from ever working for more than a few hours without burning up."

"Funny, it looks just about the same to me."

"Sir, if I may take you through the job, point by point—"

"No need for that. It runs. Good work. Thank you."

"Every one of the dynamos had to be rebuilt, as you know, not just repaired! And now all of them are working without a problem!"

"Yes, yes. No one is belittling your, ah, repair work, Nikola, but after all, repairs are really just a matter of having access to good tools and plenty of cheap labor, eh?"

"No. No sir. If I may say so. Not at all. The very architecture of each individual system had to be addressed!"

Manager Baudelaire grinned. "'Addressed'? Well, that is just fine, Nikola. Now I am 'addressing' you! If you want to earn a hefty bonus, you are going to have to show Continental Edison that you can be a genuine problem-solver for the company! Can you do that?"

"A bonus?"

"Only if you can solve our current dilemma, my friend. Relax. I am positive it will be nothing for a talent such as you.

Did I say 'nothing'? No, no, I trust that for you, it will be *less* than nothing!"

Nikola's face clouded. "Can anything be less than nothing?"

Baudelaire laughed out loud. "He asks if anything can be less than nothing!" He slapped Nikola on the back. "Well, *it can today!*" He threw one arm over Nikola's shoulders like an understanding mentor.

"Get on this afternoon's train up to Strasbourg. Report to the administrative offices for the Kaiser first thing tomorrow morning. Himself is in Berlin, but they say he's going to visit again soon, so I'll wire them to expect you. Before he returns from Berlin, you have to 'address the architecture' of the dynamo we designed to light the railway station there. It appears that the godforsaken thing does nothing except spark its own gaps and blow out the Kaiser's railway station walls."

Nikola gasped with delight. "You will—you will allow me to represent this company to the Emperor of the Prussian Empire?"

"Allow? Oh. Yes. But here's the challenge: you have to keep the old man on our side. If he returns before you are finished, you must somehow prevent him from getting impatient while you complete the repairs. Have you ever had anything to do with royalty? They have no use for patience, Nikola. None at all. Nevertheless, you *must* keep him content so that you have time to do the job right, in order to be certain it doesn't fail this time. So! Your challenge will not be as a mere tool user, my friend. This time your true challenge is political! Your success or failure at this project may well determine whether or not the Kaiser helps us gain further acceptance on an international scale! *That* is why it is worth a 5,000 franc bonus for a job well done." He paused, then decided to add, "—on top of your regular salary, of course."

Nikola was so overwhelmed with excitement that he had to squint his eyes and clench his muscles just to keep the images in his mind's eye from spewing all over and rendering him hopelessly confused.

Manager Baudelaire could barely believe his eyes when he saw Tesla turn away from him. A rush of panic hit him. After all of the promises, was this fool still too smart to be tempted into accepting an impossible assignment? Would he actually *turn down the job*? Baudelaire had no intention of allowing that to happen.

"Nikola," he smiled. "Let me finish. We are *also* going to raise your salary by ten percent while you do the job. Use the extra money to travel about the city and soak up history. Medieval city, you know. All the way back to the seventh century. Try the *fois gras*; they're famous for it."

But the upstart's eyes were not even focused on him; they darted back and forth, barely even glancing at Baudelaire in the process! *Christ on a hobbling beggar's crutch, the man doesn't even show interest in a raise! How can that be? Is it the amount? Is it not enough?*

"And of course," Baudelaire continued, "in addition to your *raise*, we will pay your living expenses—reasonable living expenses—while you are in Strasbourg."

"Mm? Oh. I see. Is there just the one dynamo and distribution system? Perhaps all they need to do is to employ non-conductive baffles at the contact points between the commutator and the armature. Then there would be no need for me at all."

Manager Baudelaire stared for a moment. Tesla had just offered to tell them how to fix the problem themselves, in spite of the alternate prospect of a bonus and a raise. That was how *unimpressed* he was by Baudelaire's offer! It took another moment for the manager to find his voice.

"Well, Monsieur Tesla, why spoil the suspense? The job might be impossible for anyone else, but there can be no doubt that it will be *easy* for you!"

Baudelaire nearly screamed in frustration; this idiot was still showing no interest! None! All right for that, then; it was time to deploy heavy artillery.

"Oh yes, you will have full access to the repair shop, of course. You know, the experimental lab."

"An electrical laboratory?"

This time Baudelaire saw Tesla's eyes almost come into focus. So, somebody was awake over there after all, eh? The Manager marveled; this upstart was turning out to be a negotiator of far more skill than he had predicted. All right then, it was time to pour it on full and be certain this recurring Tesla problem was taken care of, once and for all.

"Of course! Use the lab! After all, you have to have *somewhere* to try out your new parts for the system. To make sure they work. Correct?"

"Actually, I do all of that in my head before I build a single piece of anything."

Baudelaire suddenly looked like the neck of his shirt was two sizes too small. He stared at Nikola for several long seconds. The only movement that came from him was the slight heaving of his chest, and the only sound was the wheeze of air through his ample nostrils.

"Oh. You are saying, then…" Baudelaire's voice broke, "… you are unimpressed with my offer?"

"Unimpressed?"

"Because you didn't let me finish. You really should allow a person to complete a thought, Nikola! When they speak! Let them finish! You know, what they are… trying…" He sighed. "*Anyway*, you may even use the lab for your own fiddling around. As long as you go in after hours. On your own time."

*Aha!* The upstart's eyes lit up like fanned coals! Manager Baudelaire felt a rush of excitement—*now* he had him! Even though this Tesla's negotiating style had proven more subtle than expected, Baudelaire had hooked the fool by simply being canny enough to throw in some free lab time, a nice raise, and a fat bonus.

Years of practice at shuffling employees out of his office had polished his skill at the task, so it only took a few seconds to get Monsieur Upstart Tesla moving out the door and happily on his way to professional annihilation. The routine was *pro forma*. Once Tesla was gone, Baudelaire could barely even remember the actual *bon voyages* or even that odd formal bow that Tesla seemed to prefer to an honest handshake.

That was it, then. By the time Monsieur Tesla finished scandalizing the Royal staffers with his eccentric behavior, the inevitable failure of this doomed mission would already have him in its grasp. Baudelaire knew the Prussian situation was already hopeless. There would be nothing more for the "genius" to do but to accept the blame for Continental Edison's engineering calamity and keep Manager Baudelaire's reputation clear. It was nearly a *fait accompli*, reason enough for extra champagne with dinner.

Still, in the aftermath of his amusing little scheme, Baudelaire found himself lacking any sense of fulfillment. Once again there had been precious little challenge from the opposition. *Shit on a stick! Where is the difficulty needed for an enjoyable victory?* Baudelaire wondered, *is my search for a worthy rival doomed to disappointment such as this?* In that ongoing conversation of blades which was the contest of wills between himself and Nikola Tesla, Manager Maurice Baudelaire was the clear winner, yet somehow his level of satisfaction amounted to nothing. Nothing at all.

Less than nothing, he realized.

# Chapter Ten

## The Next Six Months
### Strasbourg, France, near the German Border

Many of the Parisian workers in Strasbourg who initially installed the aging Kaiser's unsuccessful generator either spoke only French or refused to admit that they understood another language. This behavior was thus coded into the actual workmanship of the installation itself and, along with certain design flaws, explained the blown out wreckage sitting where a railway power dynamo was supposed to be.

Nikola's fluency neutralized the language problem before it became an issue. His additional fluency in German also opened other doors in dealing with the many local workers and supervisors from Germanic regions.

The job itself presented little physical difficulty. From his first glance he recognized that the dual problems of conductivity and resistance were obvious; someone had literally designed the flaws into the system. He spent the rest of the year organizing the rebuilding tasks and suffering through the arduous paperwork involved. Following the earlier failure, every step of the process had to be formally approved by the Kaiser's administrative staff.

Once the long months of the actual work process finally began, Nikola eventually came to consider the slow pace a gift. His personal access to the electrical laboratory combined with his spare time, which allowed him to build his first working model of the alternating current motor. It was a relief to craft it in metal at last; the motor and its whirling magnetic power source had existed nowhere but in his imagination since the inspiration first struck him back in Budapest.

By the time summer was ripe, the railway lighting project approached readiness for its demonstration, and the aged Kaiser came for a brief visit. He also brought his fifty-two-year-old son, the Crown Prince Frederick William III, to handle all the details and make the final approval.

When the big moment for revealing the finished work arrived, the old man did no more than throw a bored glance at the generating system. After that, he spent the rest of the afternoon in a long conversation with Nikola about the nature of electrical energy. By evening, the Kaiser was on his way back to Berlin, leaving the Crown Prince to tidy it all up.

Weeks later in Nikola's hotel room, Strausburg's Mayor Bauzin had joined the Crown Prince in observing Nikola's tabletop electrical energy generator in action. The three men clustered around a small wooden table under the hazy yellow light of the gas flame sconces high on the wall to watch the hand-tooled machine run smoothly, even at thousands of revolutions per minute. It was powered entirely by the "impossible" alternating current. Both of the high ranking visitors realized that even in this age of emerging gadgets, they were looking at the first such device ever to exist.

"Amazing," said the Crown Prince. But he was not referring to the generator. "Not *one* offer of sponsorship?"

"No, Your Majesty," replied Mayor Bauzin in a tone of muted sorrow.

"And you gathered these men together from the list of names my secretary supplied?"

"Oh yes, Your Majesty. Just as you directed, but…"

Frederick William waited for a hopeful moment. When it became apparent that Mayor Bauzin was not going to finish his sentence, the Crown Prince sighed in a tone of monumental boredom.

"Monsieur Mayor, I dislike it *intensely* when people stop in the middle of a sentence, simply because they have something delicate to say, and thus choose to *test my sensibilities* by seeing whether or not I will ask them to continue with what they have almost—but not quite—actually said."

"Yes, sire," Mayor Bauzin replied, crushed and not sure why. "...So?"

"Ah! Yes! Well, sire, they, ah, each one of the investors, that is, ah, they kept asking when *you* were going to arrive."

"Idiot! You were to inform them that I was called away!"

"Oh I did, sire. Most assuredly. They simply didn't..."

"Monsieur Mayor, you just did it again!"

"Forgive me! I meant to say that they, ah... I am afraid they did not believe the story, Your Majesty."

"Didn't *believe* it?"

"They feared that your absence indicated that your father has not fully embraced this new kind of power system."

"Yes! Correct! He hasn't! My father is an old man in poor health! What does he care about new inventions?"

"Yes... but then... he *is* the Kaiser." Mayor Bauzin quickly added, "Just as you will be one day, Sire! But since he is in Berlin and has left the handling of Herr Tesla's work up to you, your presence was really what they... seemed to desire."

"'Seemed to desire.'"

"Strongly. Strongly desire. It was what they strongly desired, Your Majesty, some direct assurance of cooperation with the Kaiser's government. That is, in order to feel confident enough to invest in Herr Tesla's electricity device."

"Polyphase alternating current generator," Nikola spoke for the first time. His gaze was fixed on the working model with a dreamy cast to his face. "And it is more powerful than a dynamo twenty times larger."

He turned to the Mayor. "Mayor Bauzin, I am grateful for your efforts on my behalf, but I fear that the failure tonight was mine. I was simply unable to make them see. It is a mistake I do not intend to make again. Because this—" he gestured to the motor and finished in a near whisper "—and the entire branch of technology it represents, is going to change the world. That's correct, gentlemen, the entire world."

The Mayor and the Crown Prince looked at the strange little

device humming away on the tabletop. *Change the world?* Their eyes met in a skeptical glance. For a moment, for one tiny moment, the two men were united by doubt. The Crown Prince and the Town Mayor were momentary brothers in the presence of this eccentric's world view.

The camaraderie was brief. The Crown Prince had many such moments of fleeting *simpatico* with eager underlings on a regular basis; he had long since learned to shrug them off before people got the chance to use the false sense of intimacy to cozy up to him and start asking for things.

The Crown Prince grabbed Mayor Bauzin by the elbow and firmly escorted him toward the door. "Well, Monsieur Mayor, good of you to accompany me here this evening so that I could personally get the story on the financiers' reaction to Herr Tesla's interesting device."

The Mayor tried to resist by dragging his feet, but he was no match for His Majesty. "But Sire," he protested, "we came in the same carriage!"

The Crown Prince automatically slipped into the practiced tone he reserved for small children and the feeble-minded. "No problem at all, Herr Mayor, just tell the driver to *return for me* after he *drops you off.*"

Mayor Bauzin planted his feet at the door and made one last attempt to remain a part of the evening. "But Sire, that will leave you with so much time on your hands until—"

"Tut-tut! My curiosity is centered on the technical nature of Herr Tesla's work. Heady stuff. Not for you."

"Sire—"

"I insist! Goodnight! Goodnight!" The Crown Prince firmly waved the man into the hallway. Nikola gave a quick bow in Bauzin's direction just as Frederick William III personally closed the door and Mayor Bauzin vanished from sight, still gasping with exasperation.

The Crown Prince immediately spun to Nikola. "Good Job! I was afraid you were going to say something."

"Certainly not, Sire."

"My staff follows me like hounds. There was no other way

to get here without causing questions."

"I'm not sure I understand, Sire."

"My father, Herr Tesla! He admires your scientific skill but fears you practice witchcraft with your healing apparatus. He has forbidden me to take more treatments. 'Good Of The Empire' and all of that."

"Sire, I explained to him that I cannot prove the healing powers of magnetic energy without more experimentation, and that you insisted on volunteering because of your recurring throat problems."

"Yes, and the fact that I assured him I feel benefit from it no doubt convinced him something is unnatural here."

"Disease is natural. Do we not fight it?"

"You preach to the converted, Herr Tesla." He clapped his hands together in anticipation. "Now! With the Mayor gone and pretense behind us, I would like for this last session to be twice as long in length."

Nikola blanched. "Session? Your Majesty, the Emperor has forbidden us—"

"One! He does not understand. Two! He is not here." The Crown Prince pulled up a chair next to the table and sat down by the electrical generator. "Three…Please get out your electrical coil device, Herr Tesla. I am not here to waste time."

Nikola felt himself squeezed between the two opposing forces of disputing rulers. But in his moment of hesitation, he realized that Frederick William must be suffering from unusually strong pain today; a slight grimace played across the older man's face every time he moved, though he was trying to conceal it. Since the Crown Prince was a combat soldier, Nikola knew it would take an extraordinary level of pain to force him to seek out radical treatments that his own family and many of his subjects would consider witchcraft.

His need was real, and Nikola had the means to help. The choice seemed to make itself. He set about getting the spiral coil of copper tubing and preparing it for use on the Crown Prince. As soon as everything was set, he laid the coil over Frederick William's shoulders like an elaborate necklace, then turned on the power. The dynamo produced a low hum, and the coils quickly grew warm from the electrical resistance.

The Crown Prince smiled in satisfaction. "Mm, that's better, now." He closed his eyes and smiled. "You know, Herr Tesla, I really believe that these treatments of yours will prolong my life; doctors could do nothing for me. Some days I can barely swallow food—not even soup! But after one of these treatments, I feel better for days."

"I am very glad to hear it, Sire. Once I have the opportunity to experiment more thoroughly in this realm, I am sure there will be many medical uses for magnetic fields and controlled bursts of electrical energy."

"Ha-ha! Invisible forces! The rabble will hang you, Herr Tesla! They will burn you at the stake. Higher. Turn it up higher. There… Now, I hope you can assure me that you plan on going to America at your first opportunity."

"America? I've not thought about—"

"One! They are not as superstitious in the New World! Two! There is more money floating around there! Three! Here, if the Kaiser of the Prussian Empire decides that you really *are* a witch, you can still be tossed in prison and forgotten, even in this day and age! Remember, my father is the man who took a loose coalition of Prussian states and pulled them together for the first time into the true German Empire. This is where his concerns lie. All of Europe should expect to see big things from the Germanic race! Just not you. Conclusion: get yourself to America. Do it quickly."

Nikola sighed. "I suppose you are right. I went to Paris for her, and nothing has happened."

"What, 'her' again? That muse you talk about? Nonsense. But do not say 'nothing' has happened here! Your work in Paris is what sent you here, and *here* is where you built your machine for the first time! Here, we both learned that your theories about magnetic healing have promise! As for me, I do not doubt that this device has given me a new chance. This throat, it was going to kill me. I could feel that."

He lovingly patted the copper coil. "Why don't you just

accept that this 'muse' of yours, whatever she may be, actually sent you on a most productive adventure?"

Nikola stepped away and softly replied, "Perhaps I should. Especially if she is merely a reflection of my own dreams."

"Or your insanity," the Crown Prince cheerfully interjected. "Because I am convinced that you are of superior quality in your mental powers, Herr Tesla, and everybody knows that genius is always accompanied by an equal dose of insanity. It's a Universal Law of some sort."

"Sire... you consider me insane?"

"Tut-tut! Sane, insane, genius, witch, just relax and proudly play with your own excrement or whatever it is that you do in private! Ha-ha! Don't look so shocked; you're talking to an old soldier! You did not forget that, did you? Soldiers know all about playing with their own excrement, my friend—every time a cannonball lands too close! Ha-ha! Frankly I never enjoyed soldiering as much as I pretended to. But it was the only avenue out of my father's castle if I wanted to avoid being constricted into the life of a royal moron. Now listen to me, I have information you can use: twelve years ago I commanded the Prussian army in the siege of Paris, and after my experiences with that city I am not surprised by the uncouth treatment that you received there!

He curled his lips into the expression of a man who has bitten into a lemon. "The French? Pah! And French art? I sum up all of French art in two words, my friend—*frilly nonsense*! Do you paint? No? Good. I don't care what kind of image the Parisian town dignitaries try to create; after a decent fellow washes down one of their fattening meals with a bottle of the local wine and then tops it off with a trip to the nearest whorehouse, he has *completely* exhausted the list of worthwhile pastimes to be found in Paris! I'm sure you agree."

"Well, I—"

"I have polled every single one of my advisors and *not one* can explain to me how the French people justify their attitude. You cannot either, I'll wager a new saddle! Ha-ha!"

He squinted in concentration while he adjusted the coils

tighter around his neck, then smiled at the sensation of warmth flooding his upper body. An additional thought occurred to him. "The Parisians are the worst, as one might expect, but all the French have it. Even their dogs. Those poodles. Somehow their national attitude seems to originate in their noses."

Abruptly, the Crown Prince laughed at himself and clarified the concept, "Excuse me! I must apologize. Ha! What an ignorant thing for me to say! You must think me a fool."

"Certainly not, Sire!"

"Because of course I mean the *people's* noses, not the poor dogs! You would be the man to determine what mechanism is at work there, but make no mistake, the French point of view has something to do with the nose. You can hear it in the basic sounds of their language. Well, never mind. As no doubt you already know, Francophiles are peddlers of illusion!"

He leaned closer to Nikola and spoke in confidential tones, "Which is precisely what my aged father fears *you* to be, dear fellow. A peddler of illusion! Not that he isn't pleased with the new railroad lights and all, but that little talk you had with him about 'invisible magnetic fields'? About shaping these unseeable things 'as one shapes a piece of clay'? Herr Tesla, the man is finishing his seventh decade, do you understand?"

"Of course, Sire."

"Now, *I* see the difference between you and some godforsaken Francophile! Oh yes. I can feel the difference working on me through this magical coil of yours. This e-lec-tri-ci-ty of yours makes me feel warm right in my throat, right where that awful coldness always starts. I swear I feel it working already."

He flashed a grateful smile at Nikola, then turned away and relaxed his gaze onto some faraway point while he soaked in the sensations of relief that the odd little machine created in his troubled throat. Frederick William III, Crown Prince of Prussia and heir to the Kaiser's throne, leaned his head over to the side and dropped into that fast sleep of a retired soldier who has learned from the tedious rituals of state how to put the best use to his time.

\* \* \*

Many hours later in Nikola's hotel room, the ticking clock was the only sound while he lay sleeping. It happened between ticks—the image of Karina walked through the outside wall and strolled into the room. Her presence snapped him out of his sound sleep. With no further warning, she stepped to Nikola's bed and sat on the edge of the mattress as if this was something she did every night. The mattress seemed to sink under her weight, *odd for an illusion*, he thought. In a single motion, he contracted his body into a sitting position with his back to the wall.

All he could do was stare. She appeared to be about his same age, nothing like her former schoolgirl image. Her hair hung loose around her shoulders. She was dressed in a silver-white garment with the consistency of mist—a finger's width of thick steam that somehow clung to her skin.

He found a little bit of his voice. "I know this is only a dream. You are a dream."

The image of Karina smiled. "You are strange, then, to take time to speak to a dream. I'm pleased that you waste the effort on me. That is, I would be pleased, if dreams had the ability to feel. I don't think they do. Do you?"

Nikola considered the question while he looked for hidden angles to the query. Finally he shook his head and replied, "No. But I..." He sighed.

In the next instant he realized that if she was not real, then here was someone he could safely tell about his tentative plans. What risk could there be in confiding to someone who doesn't exist? He forced himself up into a normal sitting position, feet on the floor, and began.

"If I am ever to get started translating the visions in my mind into objects that people can see and touch and use, then Prince William thinks I must to travel to the New World. To America."

Nikola stared into her eyes for a long moment before he broke his silence and urgently whispered, "If I am to go so far away, can you still..."

Karina looked at him with a coy smile. "You mean, can I

still find you when you are so far away, *if* I am real? I don't know. Will you be taking your thoughts?"

Before he could respond, she reached out her hand and pulled him out of his body. It happened so quickly that he had no chance to react or even to cry out. The sensations were like the sudden silence and pressure that follows a plunge into deep water.

He glanced down and realized that he could see through himself, just as if he were looking through colored glass. He stood next to his body, supine on the bed.

In the next instant he saw the entire physical world transform to a completely ethereal state. Even the most solid objects were like translucent versions of themselves. He might have stopped to marvel, but at that instant Karina's fingers brushed his face. The sensation made him realize they both appeared solid now, while everything else around them had the aspects of a ghostly mirage.

He felt their bodies entwine, marveling at how real the sensations felt. When he tried to wonder how any of this could actually be happening, he couldn't even get the thought to form.

# Chapter Eleven

*Months later*
*Continental Edison*
*Paris, France*

Manager-of-the-Works Maurice Baudelaire appeared to be in a better mood than usual on this particular morning. This was true even though his office was as dank as ever and he still encumbered his long suffering chair. He gazed in silence across the top of the oversized desk, listening with a vague smile to a familiar pulse of distant noise.

Drip… drip… drip…

The sound of leaking water was music to him today. *How perfect!* he thought. How excellent to employ it as the background for this occasion! After all, the upstart, Nikola Tesla, had made pointed mention of the water upon his very first visit, the fool. This morning, the dripping would serve to mock Monsieur Tesla while Baudelaire boxed him into a trap of frustration and uselessness.

He was well aware that the young Tesla had only been back in Paris for a few days, barely enough time to get himself reestablished, but the knowledge did nothing to engender mercy. And so at that moment he had the upstart himself standing on the receiving side of the oversized desk, waiting to be told why he had been summoned. Up to this point, he noticed that Tesla had displayed a complete lack of concern over what the meeting was all about. That would change momentarily.

He leaned back in his bedeviled chair amid the squeal of metal joints, then pushed himself away from the desk with the elation of a circling buzzard watching its dinner die. "I am feeling like to speak English today. This is not a problem?"

"English is fine," Nikola happily replied. "Once you get your Latin, some German perhaps, the descendant languages practically map themselves out."

The Manager stared, radiating disgust, but Nikola was captured by his own rhapsody and blindly sailed ahead. "Whenever I have to wait for a train, I like to compare two vocabularies by building mental diagrams. Just to see how many levels I can hold." He grinned at a happy memory.

"Last fall I had to miss six trains in a row—trying to finish, you see! Alphabetical lists of shared words between Middle English and High German. Finally, I just laughed out loud and everything came crashing down! Ha-ha! Crumbled words, ankle deep!"

Manager Baudelaire scowled, shaking his head. Resentment darkened his eyes and graveled his voice.

"Yes. Now to business. Monsieur Edison's *personal* secretary writes me a letter. He says the man himself wants to know how you managed to repair the Kaiser's entire dynamo system *and* light up his railroad station. How you do this without one failure…" He looked Nikola up and down. "Or a single mishap."

"It's no secret. I construct a mental model of what the thing should look like. Huge, weightless machines! I tow them along like so many balloons!" He laughed at the thought. "I do not tow them, of course; I simply call them up whenever they are needed, so that I take all of the necessary models right along with me to every job site."

The Manager gave a tiny laugh of disbelief. He addressed the ceiling in a whisper. "I can think of nothing cruel enough." He turned to Nikola and spoke with a voice that started softly but steadily built in volume.

"I make it simple so you understand. If you want the bonus of 5,000 francs Edison Continental promised you for your fine work… your brilliant work… your stunning work… your *miraculous* work…" The Manager gave a smile so fetid that Nikola nearly smelled it. "You will go to America and get the money from the great Mr. Edison himself."

"Oh. All right."

It took a moment for Manager Baudelaire to register that.

"Oh all right?" He turned away and repeated it under his breath, deciphering, "oh all right." He shook his head and turned back to Nikola. "Good! Now say 'oh all right' to this: your ship sails *tomorrow*! Eh? You can build more word lists while you wait for train… take you… seaport!" Stress was collapsing his linguistic skills, so Baudelaire simply pulled a ticket out of his desk, tossed it down in front of Nikola and waited for a reaction.

Nikola remained placid. He offered no indication that the ticket presented the slightest concern.

Baudelaire made a final effort to do some damage. "Oh! And if you get lost inside your little daydreams and do not be there for ship going? Finished! No refunds! … *Nothing*!"

Nikola reached down, picked up the ticket, and turned it over in his hand. "I'll be there," he smiled.

By that point Manager Baudelaire looked as if his bitterness could effectively petrify him, convert him into a man-shaped chunk of solidified rage, a frozen statue helpless to avoid eventual humiliation under a layer of guano.

Nikola leaned forward and lowered his voice to a playful whisper. "Actually, I've been curious about America all my life." He extended his hand to the Manager with a giddy smile.

Manager Baudelaire regarded Nikola's hand with distaste. Then he glared up at the ceiling and snorted a bitter laugh at the universe.

"Monsieur Baudelaire," Nikola began, "it is not—"

"Manager! Manager Baudelaire! Manager-of-the-Works!"

"…Yes indeed. And it is my desire that we part on good terms. Personally I do not make it a habit to shake hands at all; the Japanese bow seems to make more sense as an issue of public health. However the custom here is to part by shaking hands, so I do this to show respect."

Nikola kept his hand out. Baudelaire closed his eyes, inhaled deeply, then reached out and shook Nikola's hand without looking at it.

Nikola tried to be subtle about compulsively wiping his

hand on his shirt when he turned to leave. After a few steps, he pivoted back. "Oh, and please believe me, I am sorry about my reaction when I first saw the Edison dynamo. In front of your men. It was just so adorable there! With its coiling all out of phase with the current!" A fond laugh escaped from him, like a father telling a story about his wonderful toddler. "Forcing an overly strong current into wires that are too thin to carry the right load in the *first place*! Capacitors the size of beer kegs!"

Nikola turned and walked out, still chuckling at the picture of the adorably ignorant design and so lost in the memory that he forgot to extend any further goodbye.

Silence filled the office. The petrified Manager could do nothing but sit and begin the long process of accumulating a thick guano crust. After a while, a familiar sound began to tickle at the edge of his awareness.

Drip… drip… drip…

Very slowly, Manager Baudelaire turned his head in the direction of the dripping water.

# Chapter Twelve

### Eleven Days Later
### New York

The trans-Atlantic steamship *Saturnia* reached New York City in June of 1884. It took less than an hour to have the ship's compartments emptied of immigrant passengers and packed into the yammering chaos of the Castle Garden Immigration Office. The rituals and practices there baffled most of the arrivals, who experienced complex bureaucratic torture administered through a series of winding lines. The lines were each capped by uniformed workers who stung them with personal questions, but to the relief of many of the frightened immigrants, the government officials stabbed no one, arrested few, and never opened fire.

Among those huddled masses one particularly tall and ragged hobo wore a torn greatcoat that was once a fine garment. His hat was a black felt derby which, in its pristine condition, would have been fit for anything short of a formal occasion. In spite of the hobo's deteriorated condition, he managed to be one of the first to get through the processing center. He did it by showing a facility for language that greased him through the arcane official procedures.

The hobo emerged early from Castle Garden immigration receiving center in the Battery Park area of lower Manhattan and walked away into the gathering twilight. His age was obscured by whiskers and dust, but he was only a month short of his twenty-eighth birthday. He carried no luggage away except one small valise, and it held little more than a few drawings and some written notes that would strike most readers as gibberish.

He moved through a daze of exhaustion, although in spite of his fatigue, he could not help but marvel at his first sight of an American city. The constant noise struck him first: all the noises of a city back at home, but with the intensity somehow increased. Motion was everywhere in spite of the hour, and most businesses appeared to still be open. Horses and carriages moved in every direction, leaving the dusty aroma of powdered horse manure churned into the breeze. Every single person on the street had the look of somebody who has just realized they are terribly late for something urgent. The sight struck him as impossibly strange, almost real but not quite.

The hobo stumbled on through rising darkness. City workers began to light the pale yellow street lamps, using long torches as wicks to ignite the gas flames.

He continued walking north, knowing nothing more than that the rest of the city lay in that direction. While he headed into the crowded area of storefront businesses, his stomach growled with hunger. His thin frame was emaciated by a ten-day sea voyage with practically no food. He reached into his pocket and fingered the four cents of American money that represented his total net worth. Even in his depleted condition, the hobo knew that four cents might get him a bite or two to eat but would do nothing to secure a place to get clean and rest.

He passed through one patch of lantern light after another with his feet scraping along the sidewalk. Aimlessly, he allowed the light pools to pull him one by one into the guts of the city.

The hobo began to think that if he could just find a quiet little park or even a cemetery, he could at least lie down and sleep. He consoled himself with the thought that anything was better than another night on that ship. Any quiet spot that held still was good.

On the long trip across the Atlantic, he had only been able to determine for certain that his wallet was indeed with him when he boarded the train to the seaport. He needed his papers to get aboard. His pocket had to have been picked during the train trip. If he had not slipped his ticket into a separate pocket, he never would have gotten on the boat. Once aboard the ship and safely underway, he discovered his wallet gone and found himself with no more than some loose change, one suitcase, and his small valise.

The suitcase lasted until the crew mutinied during the trip and the resulting riot separated him from it, never to be seen again. He was grateful that at least he kept his precious letter of introduction snug in the inner pocket of his vest. He felt sure that he could overcome any other obstacle as long as he had that letter to open doors for him.

Hunger was making it hard to think. He paused to lean against a lamppost. Did he have a destination? He couldn't recall. The stomach pangs gnarled inside him. He looked around for anything to distract himself.

Another few doors up the street, he noticed a small machine-repair shop in the gathering darkness. The shop's lanterns were burning away inside while the front window revealed a pudgy and unattractive man, impeccably dressed, bending over a long work table to toil on a small electrical device.

It was the device that caught the hobo's eye; the sight of it made him smile for the first time since stepping into America. It was a Gramme machine, a combined generator and motor driven by a battery, just like the one that Professor Poeschl once demonstrated back in school.

At that moment, the shop owner's hand slipped and scraped against the outside of the machine. He swore a loud oath, threw his screwdriver down, and paced around the floor holding his hand like a man who has spent far too much time on this chore already.

Nikola forgot his hunger. The fog in his brain burned clear and a sudden sense of purpose focused him. Even his sense of balance became sharper. He stepped through the door of the repair shop and happily informed the owner that he knew what this machine was, and that he could surely fix it. The mere idea of such a challenge filled Nikola with a flush of strength that he had not felt in days.

Half an hour later, he flipped the switch on the newly repaired Gramme machine, and it immediately hummed to life.

The repair shop owner clapped his hands in delight. "Look! Look at that! Wonderful!"

"Thank you," Nikola smiled. "It was a pleasure to be able to make something come out right, even this small victory."

"I was ready to give up!" the owner enthused. "That would have been tragic! Believe me! Tragic!"

"Tragic?" Nikola asked, confused by the use of the word. "Sir, these machines are not so expensive and should not be difficult to replace."

"Replace?" bellowed the owner. "Replace? Ha! My friend, you don't know what you're saying!" He pulled out his wallet and opened it. "And in case you think my gratitude is limited to a few words of thanks—" He removed a twenty dollar bill and handed it over.

Nikola's eyes widened. "Sir… that is a twenty dollar bill!"

"Okay, if you know what it is, take it then. Believe me, my friend, you earned it! Ha! Oh, you earned it, all right!"

Disbelief paralyzed him. "But sir, the entire machine can be purchased for less than that."

The owner leaned forward and tucked the bill into Nikola's shirt pocket. "That's what *you* think, brother. Replaced? Not a chance!" He whispered confidentially, "I bought this machine for my mistress. She uses it as amusing toy for her parties. Loves the attention it gets."

"Could you not simply buy her a new one?"

"Oh, no-no-no! That's just it! *This* one is hers. See the initials engraved on the side? If I buy her another one, she'll immediately know it's not the same!"

"I don't understand."

"You want me to spell it for you?"

"Spell understand?"

"*She thinks I can fix anything!* Get it? She says it's one of the things she loves about me. Men who can do things, you know? Now my wife, she knows good and well I can't fix half the junk that people haul into this place. Ruined garbage! Broken pieces attached to broken pieces!" He patted the repaired machine. "If this thing belonged to my wife I wouldn't bother."

The owner grinned at Nikola and winked. "Believe me, mister—you earned that money! From the looks of it, you could use it."

"You are certainly right about that. I am so tired, it will be a relief to pay for a good bed and something to eat."

"Perhaps a bath?" the owner sniffed.

"First of all."

"Good enough then! Well, time for me to close up. I have a young lady to impress, thanks to you."

Nikola's light-headedness was making it hard for him to comprehend what had just happened. He allowed the shop owner to usher him back into the evening, then stood on a nearby corner for several minutes, fingering the twenty dollar bill and trying to pull his wits together. After such a difficult trip and undignified arrival into this bustling city, he had just earned a sum that was close to an average month's pay back at home. He had heard about things like this but never expected to see proof of it in his first hours ashore. A person could do anything here.

It felt like a message from the heavens confirming that he did the right thing in coming to America, and that somehow, he would find the means to thrive. A cool white rush of energy coursed through him. The sensation expanded. For a few moments, it was enough to lighten his anxiety and ease his racing thoughts. Its presence seemed to assure him that he would not remain a stranger in this place.

He took a breath, hunched his shoulders, and clenched every muscle in his body; the chaos in his head receded like the screeching of passing crows. After another moment he steadied himself and took a quick check of those few things he still knew to be real. He felt for the letter of introduction in his pocket and fingered the twenty dollar bill. Those two paper touchstones were about to launch his new life.

He set out to find the nearest hotel. His steps were lighter, as if rest had already reached him. Surely, those two small pieces of paper were all he needed to fulfill his mother's vision for him and to prove his father wrong about the "Evil" in his mind.

Most important, this new land was where he was determined to have the whirling magnetic field introduced to the world of industrial science and accepted by its leaders. If he was ever going to attempt something truly monumental with the strange abilities that alternately blessed and haunted him, now was the time, and this rough-hewn country was going to be the place.

On the following morning, the hour of nine found Nikola fresh from a good night's sleep, immaculately groomed, and attired in a cheap new off-the-rack suit that was only passable on him because of his ramrod posture and elongated frame.

He called upon the Edison Company's famous South Fifth Street laboratory building in lower Manhattan, hoping for nothing more than to make an appointment to see the famous inventor. But the strangeness of his new life in this place continued to confront him. To his astonishment, the letter of introduction proved so effective that he quickly found himself ushered into the building and seated on a low chair in the middle of the office of Thomas Alva Edison himself. Nikola could only shake his head about the way things happened in this new country.

Edison stood surrounded by several extremely agreeable staff members. Everyone kept a keen watch on the Boss while the famous man quietly studied Nikola's letter of recommendation.

"All right then, Mr. Tesla," Edison finally intoned while still reading, "Charles Batchelor is an admired colleague in the Paris office, so I suppose I should respect his good words about you." He glanced up to his four staff members. "Listen to this part, fellas: 'Mr. Edison, I only know two great men. You are one, and I believe that Nikola Tesla is the other.'"

Edison turned to the highly agreeable staff members and made a comically exaggerated look of being overwhelmed, then turned back and addressed Nikola directly. "I am also inclined to be impressed by your accomplishments in Paris; they prove you have talent—I can always use men of talent. But as to this 'bonus' owed to you by those French fellas, well… my companies overseas are locally owned."

He tossed a glance at his men. They sneered in anticipation.

"Locally owned?" Nikola repeated the word with a blank face.

Edison turned and muttered, "His English is good." But he kept his eyes on Nikola, like a man talking out loud at a play.

The yes-men chortled, overlapping each other's replies. "That it is." said the first one. "Almost American," said the second. "He talks like a professor," remarked the third.

The fourth had done his homework: "I took a look at his resume; he speaks eight languages. He's college educated. Basic physics, electrical theory—" He caught the flash of a warning glance from Edison and barely paused before he added, "Foreign schools."

Edison smiled at Nikola with the same mixture of kindness and pity that a grandmother might show a backward offspring. "Local operations pay their own way," he patiently explained. "You see? The Edison Company owes you that money, all right. But *only back in France*! I'm afraid you have been victimized by that notorious French humor." Edison and the yes-men watched intently for Nikola's reaction.

The best Nikola had for them was a small laugh. "It is unfortunate that they cannot know how well their joke worked. My wallet was stolen on the trip here. I arrived with four cents in my pocket."

There was a brief pause... then Edison and his men exploded into laughter. Nikola was too confused by this to do anything but wait for something else to happen.

"See that, fellas?" Edison finally crowed. "He might be a college man, but he'll be coming up the hard way here, just like the rest of us!"

He turned back to Nikola. "I'll hire you. The Paris office tells me you're full of ideas for improving my generators. Well, they're failing all over the city. You figure out how to stop that, and I'll turn your five thousand francs into fifty thousand dollars. You hear me? Fifty thousand dollars! And meanwhile, you'll make my basic wage." He couldn't hold back any longer. "And *I know you'll take it*!"

Edison and his men burst into laughter again, harder than ever. Finally, Edison gestured for one of them to take Nikola away, saying, "You go along with this fella here, he'll get you all signed up."

Nikola cooperated and started to go, but as he reached the door Edison called out to him. "And Mr. Tesla?" He grinned good-naturedly. "In commerce, in industry—*everybody* steals. Only an educated idiot opens up a negotiation by revealing that he doesn't have a leg to stand on."

Nikola waited for another moment, as if unsure that Edison had finished his point. Finally he looked down at his legs, then back to Edison. He smiled. "Mr. Edison, my legs are fine."

Groans and laughter erupted from all the other men. But after a moment, Nikola held up his hand for silence in a manner so self-assured that they all obeyed him before they had time to question why they should.

"However, I must point out that this was not a negotiation. Surely you are much too wise not to hire me, and I am too great an admirer to walk away. And as for the money, the Paris office may have it as a parting gift from me—I have reason to believe everything will work out." He gave a short, polite bow, turned around and left.

Edison stared after him for a long moment. He forgot that anyone else was in the room. Even though he could see plain as day that he had just met someone truly unique, someone whose mind he ought to cultivate, he could also see that this Tesla fellow was an overeducated foreigner. Another heavy flash of anger went through him. That was enough nonsense. It was time to turn his attention to something productive.

Edison dismissed his yes-men with a wave of his hand, then made a determined effort to resume his study of light bulb filaments. There would be a proper occasion for dealing with this new foreigner in good time.

Show him how things are done.

# Chapter Thirteen

## Later That Night
### New York

Late afternoon was already giving way to evening by the time Nikola completed the Edison Company's hiring and orientation process. He was rewarded with a short-term hotel voucher and a small advance on his humble salary.

It was more than enough to send him ecstatically on his way. After his first twenty-four hours in this new land, arriving too broke to pay for a meal, he already had a foothold with a job and a bed and even some pocket money. Excitement gripped him so hard that he was barely more than a block away from the company's Manhattan location before he had to stop and tightly clench all of his muscles, just to avoid being overwhelmed by elation-generated imagery.

He hesitated there on the sidewalk. Every part of his undernourished body still ached with fatigue. He wondered if he should return to his hotel and soak up one more good night of rest. After all, he was to report the next morning at seven. While he thought it over, he slowly turned in a full circle, counting off the compass points and taking in the sights all around him. By the time he came back around to face north, his hesitation was gone. His state of wonder had become a power source that moved him in the opposite direction of his hotel and stretched his long-legged stride. Soon his muscles warmed up and his wind came deep and even. It felt wonderful to push himself after nearly two weeks with very little exercise. The hard world began to grind by under his feet.

Most of the buildings he passed were around five stories

high, as with European cities. Even though they were constructed
of the same types of brick and granite as their prototypes in
Europe, each of these buildings looked like it had been built
within the last few years. He found the subtle difference between
the original European buildings and their stylistic American
copies as distracting as an odd smell. These new buildings were
made of bricks formed well within his lifetime. Their granite
slabs had been cut and shaped within the same years. Overall,
the appearance of universal newness gave him the odd notion
that he was walking around on the set of an elaborate opera.

Nikola took a misstep off a curb to avoid a rushing buggy;
the resulting flash of pain shot through his ankle and traveled all
the way up his body. When it passed through his head, it struck
off a glowing moment of extra light. This shared architectural
style between the European cities of his past and this New York
City were at once the same and different, like two harmonic
waves of electrical energy. In the complimentary world of
architectural style, the walls and windows of Europe's original
constructions rode down the lines of time on different waves
than their American progeny, no matter how identical they
might be in form. There was a permanent phase-shift between
their energies.

It occurred to him that the reason he noticed the contrast
might be that he was also stranded in a phase-shift between his
past and his present. An involuntary shiver rattled his shoulders.
He clenched his muscles and kept on walking until the gathering
darkness thickened enough to blur the details of the hard
world at last.

The rhythm of his stride worked a hypnotic effect. He was
able to risk switching the task over to his automaton, so he split
off the tiniest possible slice of his awareness and put it in charge
of operating his body, walking it in a consistent direction and
avoiding obstacles.

He employed a long-distance stare that was useful in
preventing people from trying to engage him in conversation.
It deflected them as well as the cow-catcher on a train's engine.
It was much too soon after his arrival to begin taking the

social risks of trying to determine what the slower ones were talking about, then managing to concentrate on their plodding thoughts, and then coming up with responses that avoided making them feel stupid.

He imagined a tiny version of himself residing inside his skull and looking out from the eyes as if through large picture windows. This miniature version of himself sat comfortably on a tiny rocking chair and let his thoughts fly free of the hard world. The kilometers rolled by, or as his splinter of awareness reminded itself, *twenty blocks to a mile, northbound in Manhattan, or one point six zero nine kilometers.* He automatically kept count of his steps in groups of three, keeping a running total that felt as important to him as anything else in his mind, even if he had no explanation for it.

Soon night was fully settled in with a new moon overhead. The view out the picture windows of his eyes dimmed to a world of shadows. With the exception of a few passing carriage lamps and some occasional dim window light, the only illumination came from gas street lamps. At every corner, double sets of glowing glass spheres hung from cast-iron poles standing nearly five meters high—*fifteen feet, here.* Each pair of lamps cast down gentle splashes of amber that didn't actually light the way so much as offer glowing patches to use as reference points. He navigated the darkness by connecting them and randomly moved deeper into the city.

When he eventually checked in with himself long enough to notice a street sign, he was near the great Central Park at the intersection of Fifth Avenue and 59th Street, both wide boulevards. It was an area of fabulous private residences and churches with towering steeples. The well-cobbled streets could allow as many as six horse-drawn buggies to pass side by side. There was little of the congestion that marked transportation in Paris or Prague, although there was traffic even at that late hour. He unintentionally calculated the flow rate to average out at five and one-third carriages for each city block. The wide streets easily swallowed the rolling buggies. They created the impression that these grand avenues were constructed for mightier vehicles of far greater size.

Central Park rolled out far to the north. For years, he had read of it in books, studied it on maps. Now he felt a rush of excitement at the thought of taking long walks there during heavy rain storms. It would be a magical place to continue his long habit of easing stress with physical activity. Several different pathways into the park were visible from his corner. He felt a rush of thankfulness for the park's semi-wilderness, graciously left intact by the original city planners.

The exertion had cleared his head enough for him to realize it was getting late. Even if he didn't bother to eat dinner, he still needed to a few hours of rest before morning. He was already fairly certain that most of the problems with these American Edison generators were matters of tuning and balance, and he could usually do such work sleepwalking, but he wanted to arrive looking refreshed and ready for any challenge.

He turned south and began the return trip downtown, then tightened the focus on his concentration until his awareness of the hard world began to slip away again. He relaxed back into the automaton state and settled into the little chair behind his eyes for the long walk to his hotel.

Free again, he narrowed his concentration down to a point so fine that he became like an engraver working a design into steel. The design itself was Nikola's resolve to fulfill this opportunity to its utmost, do everything that Mr. Edison asked of him, and then look for ways to go beyond that. He burned the design into his will. Nikola would allow the legendary man no doubts about his potential. With an ally such as Thomas Edison, what wonders might be achieved within Nikola's lifetime? No doubt Mr. Edison had the power to utterly transform the life of a worthy assistant, to raise him to the realm of acknowledged scientific discoverers. Together they could ease humanity's burden of hardscrabble struggle and pointlessly heavy labor.

The heat of the moment intensified until Nikola's usual concerns over his father's interpretation of his gifts faded away. If he could accomplish such things using the *vision* that had somehow come into his life, there would never be better proof his inspiration was genuine.

Feelings of pure elation began to fill him like helium gas. There was no end to the great changes a mentor like Edison could render in Nikola's life. All Nikola needed was the chance to show him what he could do for the great Thomas Alva Edison.

He was back in his hotel before ten o'clock that evening, already eager for daylight. He knew there would be no sleep for him yet; he still had all of the day's suppressed imagery to release. Soon the things would explode through him on their own.

It was a rare luxury to relax into the present moment and appreciate his sense of gratitude over the personal circumstances. It was clear that every moment of his past and all of his extensive education had combined to propel him to this place.

At last his life was transforming from a single note to a fully voiced chord. Sleep could wait. Now more than ever, he could not bear the thought of missing anything.

# Chapter Fourteen

## The Following Day
## Menlo Park, New Jersey

Thomas Edison began his day early at the Menlo Park compound by making sure his foremen were off to a running start and that it was safe to leave them to their own devices for the rest of their shift. Then he called up a couple of his company wagons to carry his most trusted project managers to the ferry across to New York. He and the boys used the travel time to conduct a series of huddled meetings to make an efficient trip of three hours between the Menlo Park compound and his Manhattan lab.

There was plenty to occupy them. He huddled with one project manager after another, riding herd over accomplished scientists and technicians. It took solid brass cow balls for Edison to step up to every last one of them and go belly to belly over the best way get things done. He could always spot the gleam in their eyes, that flash of condescension while they gazed up at their farm-sized taskmaster. He could practically read their thoughts. They were so certain their brains were superior to his, and didn't their massive educations prove it? Edison's authority over them reflected nothing more than his money and political clout, did it not?

And so it was magic, no-tricks-and-no-foolin' pure magic to witness the uncertain flicker in their superior gaze at the precise moment that their self-opinions once again ran into the hard fact that Thomas Alva Edison was already a man of world renown back when they were still stuck in their fancy schools. Every one of his fancy-schooled workers swung their lunch buckets to and from the office every day, hacking away for a salary like everyone else except the fortunate few who controlled them all: people such as Mother Edison's oversized, hard-of-hearing, semi-educated farm boy. It would be inconceivable to him not to love a country where such things could happen.

He arrived back at his South Fifth Street lab in the mid-afternoon. The first thing that caught his attention was the sight of that overbold new fellow. The fresh one. Nikola Tesla it was, already up to his elbows in dismantled parts on the lab's main power dynamo.

Edison was surprised by his own reaction to the sight. Everything was just as he had ordered the night before, so why was he so tight in the shoulders? It made sense for the new fellow to start his repairs; the plan was to make sure Edison's lab could keep churning out work while the other generators around the city were gradually taken out of service and repaired.

Still that rationale brought Edison no relief; his stomach tightened at the sight of the Tesla fellow. Half the company workers were grouped around him while he delivered an impromptu lecture on "harmonic balance among the energy waves." Edison's stomach tightened harder; pain solidified in his middle while he stood for a quiet moment and strained to hear. It angered him to see a group of employees standing around on shop time, even though he realized they couldn't do much else while the main power source was shut down. They sure as hell didn't have to stare at the new man like he was delivering the Sermon on the Mount.

But he also realized this was his own doing; Tesla was merely following instructions. Edison had unwittingly set the man up to spend his first day on the job being observed by everybody else at the lab, playing the role of conquering hero.

So he had called that one wrong, that's all there was to it. He wondered if he was slowing down. His innards tightened when he first met the Tesla fellow, but he allowed his other distractions to deflect his attention. He had neglected "the wisdom of the body," as the first Mrs. Edison used to say. She usually got such things right.

How did he become so lax? Why, he was still three years

away from his fortieth birthday—much too young to rest on his laurels. If he needed any reminder of that, all he had to do was look at this Tesla fellow, nearly ten years his junior with a vastly superior education. Equal to any of Edison's top men, maybe better.

In other words, precisely the type of man who could stand to gain by trying to steal Edison's thunder and beat "the Wizard of Menlo Park" at his game. Well, such things might all be in the nature of life, but he was not about to tolerate any of that nonsense, not for many years yet. There was too much left to do, first an entire country and then an entire world to be spread with Edison's electric light and power system.

"Oh Mr. Edison! I am so glad you are here! I was just telling these ladies and gentlemen about harmonic energy balancing—"

Edison was already on the move up the stairs. "Fine. Continue on, then. We all have lots to do." He disappeared in the stairwell without making eye contact, leaving his foremen to themselves while he strode to his office and closed the door behind him.

He had a ship to run and a world to conquer. Not a single one of these fancy-pants private school boys would be given the chance to take anything away from Thomas Edison while he moved his operations toward that goal. How did the fools think he got where he was?

Nikola felt a harsh rush of fear shoot through him when he watched Mr. Edison leave the room. What just happened? He was doing exactly as ordered, yes? The repairs were going just fine. The other employees appeared to be interested in what he had to say. Nevertheless, the Boss just left the main floor as if something there had irritated him, without even looking over to check Nikola's work.

He wondered if that could be a good thing. Was it that the Boss trusted Nikola already? If not—if Edison was rejecting him for some reason—*how on earth* did Nikola manage to anger the Boss on his very first day?

He was suddenly aware of the other employees' stares. They showed no reaction to Edison one way or the other and appeared to be waiting for him to continue his lecture. Another startled chill shot through him; was their silence during his little speech only a form of social grace? Were they actually aching for him to shut up?

It struck him that this was just the way he felt at that awful moment back in Herr Doktor's class when he finally realized how much hostility he had engendered with the other students by making them feel stupid. Was he doing that now? Was that why Edison stormed on through the room and barely acknowledged him?

The other employees were still politely waiting. He was unsure how long had it been. Two or three seconds, perhaps? He closed his eyes and squeezed all of his muscles for a moment, then stood up straight, took a deep breath, and turned back toward the others.

"Well then. As you see, there is still much left for me to do here." He thought for a second, then added, "As I am sure is the case with you." He put a period to the sentence with a tiny bow, then turned back to the large dynamo and busied himself.

The others, polite strangers, seemed to have no trouble accepting his dismissal; they drifted on their separate ways. Only two of the youngest lab assistants showed any reaction. A subtle pair of mutually fond young men tittered back and forth over Nikola's intensity while they made their way outside to savor this rare chance for a smoke in the middle of a work day while the main generator was shut down.

Panic gripped him. How had he allowed his social graces to fail him so soon? All the way around, it was completely unacceptable to fail Mr. Edison; the shame would be impossible to bear. He had to do everything so well that they could not replace him.

Habit rose to protect him. The simple but laborious task of restoring the hulking Edison dynamos required only a few more slivers of awareness than he needed for ordinary walking and talking, so he kept moving through the world and working on the tasks before him, one giant electrical dynamo at a time. Meanwhile the rest of him condensed into the miniature version of himself. He got comfy in the tiny rocking chair behind the picture window eyes while his imagination raced free of the hard world. Time began to slip past him.

In this way, Nikola was able to pass unchallenged through his initial task. Subsequent encounters with Edison were seldom and brief, always with Nikola rising from his tiny rocking chair and pouring himself back down into his body in order to ensure sufficient awareness to remain socially proper with the Boss.

Weeks went by. The best Nikola could say in terms of evaluating his own performance was that as far as he could tell, he avoided offending the Boss. That was a feat, since he had already witnessed that the Boss could get angry with anyone over anything.

Beyond that, the Boss himself remained a mystery while Nikola's automaton moved about the city, repairing and replacing the Edison dynamos wherever they were installed. He once again added refinements to their functions and increased the variety of their controls, as he did in Paris. It took anywhere from several hours to several days to get each one working, but the pace of his progress was relentless. He only slept for three or four hours each night and stayed fit by swimming in the East River every morning.

In the meantime, throughout the days and nights, he soared through a realm of questions regarding energy and matter. Was there any real difference between the two, beyond simple density? Insights begged for answers; if energy and matter are fundamentally the same, shouldn't the transmission of energy be possible without wires? Is it not obvious that the path to that goal must somehow utilize the specific mutual traits between energy and matter? Further questions rose from every answer.

The challenges to his mind were not quite enough to keep him from being haunted by the desire to see Karina again. But unlike the thought problems he could grind away on at any hour, she remained a mystery in her absence. There was nothing he could do to reach her.

* * *

Edison worked away on a new light bulb connection until he shocked his finger with a loud zap. He yelped and popped the fingertip into his mouth, failing to notice when Yes-Man #1, Hawkins or Haughton or Harper, appeared in the open doorway.

"Excuse me, sir... Sir?"

Edison glanced up. "What is it?"

"Oh. Tesla, sir. He just installed the last of the new dynamos. Twenty-four new designs in all. He completely eliminated the use of long-core field magnets and replaced them with shorter magnets that have proven much more efficient."

"Mm-hmm, fine. That Tesla has turned out to be a damn good man."

"Well, yes."

"*And?*"

"Oh. For the last two dynamos he invented automatic controls. Just for fun, he says. These controls won't allow the wires to overload. And they work! That is, I saw them."

"Mm." Edison was busy. Anyone could see that he was so very busy. It was vital that he get this new filament tied off right at that instant. "That's good. Talented fella."

"Oh. But it *was* the last of them, sir." His voice nearly faltered when he added, "He... ah... asked about his bonus?"

*Hawkins* was the man's name. Hawkins. Edison finally looked up and stared his favorite yes-man squarely in the face. "I heard you, Hawkins. Dare say, I hear as good as you do."

"Yes! I just wondered what—"

"Send him around." Edison was already back at work. "Probably best to do it tomorrow. Tell him to come see me in the morning."

Hawkins nodded, started to leave, then spun back around with a certain angry force, as if he just might give the Boss a piece of his mind. That snagged the Boss's attention for a moment or two, long enough to see if this young fellow was going to actually muster the fortitude to speak up for himself.

It was after a very little bit of time and perhaps even a moment's thought that Hawkins made his choice. Yes-Man #1 turned to the door and quietly walked out.

# *Chapter Fifteen*

## *Weeks Later*
### *New York*

*It must be the news*, Nikola thought, feeling himself drain back into his body. Surely it was the sheer power of the news pulling him out of the automaton mode for the first time in many days. He returned to the hard world as soon as they told him. This was the first time he felt the need to be fully present for many weeks. It was, after all, a momentous achievement to be summoned for a private meeting at the Boss's office.

He was well aware that no one had expected him to be able to complete the massive repair tasks, even though they only required a fraction of his attention. This personal meeting with Mr. Edison was the goal he had kept at the front of his mind throughout all the long months of numb routine, and at last he was being accepted as a proven colleague. He could hardly wait for the appointed hour to visit with Edison at his office.

It was nearly midnight while he walked through the Battery Park area at a fast stride. The slaps of cold shoe leather on colder ground sent stinging sensations through his feet and legs. He felt the fatigue that racked him, but the heady prospect of a personal meeting with Mr. Edison filled him with such anticipation that sleep was out of the question. He needed to move and burn off nervous energy.

He had not only met the Boss's requirements, he had done much more than necessary to earn the fabulous bonus. *Fifty thousand dollars!* Such an amount assured him that even if he could not convince his mother to move to the New World, he could permanently secure a safe living situation and guarantee proper care for her inside her own home. And so despite the late hour and the frozen ground of early spring, the sheer magic of this new nation seemed to radiate up from the earth and fill him with vital force. He felt better than he had since leaving Paris.

A cold wind blew in over the black water and made him wince and shiver. The sea breezes were so alive with energy and the air so fresh and invigorating, it was hard to imagine the choking clouds of daytime traffic.

Every few blocks, he passed another one of the local power generators that served small groups of homes or businesses. Many of the generators were subjects of his repair and redesign work over the past months. The direct current generators were so weak in power, with such poor transmission efficiency, they could never be more than a mile apart or the energy on their wires wouldn't be enough to light a bulb. Even then, the customers farthest from their local power station had noticeably dimmer light than the lucky users closer to it.

Now without the protection of the distancing exercises that Nikola had employed over the last six months, he felt the full impact of the ugly and unnecessary D.C. dynamos. He heard each one humming away while he walked past, and the sound might as well have been music played on badly tuned instruments.

It struck him that his newfound credibility with the Boss had brought him the perfect opportunity to broach the subject of switching to alternating current, getting away from this direct current mess once and for all. This was going to be his first chance to show Mr. Edison that direct current is for things that run on batteries, whereas alternating current will drive the most powerful machine at any level of force from distances of hundreds of miles.

How to do it? How to maintain proper respect and humility while convincing the Boss to convert his entire power generating system to the "impossible" alternating current? He knew that citing the mathematical formulae would do nothing; Edison made it a loud and frequent point to value common sense over education. How was Nikola to communicate with a powerful man who placed such high value on something as hard to define as "common sense," and liked the meat of his life served plain? For the Boss, the term "common sense" seemed to boil down to whatever he thought was right on any given topic.

The mid-morning appointment time at Edison's office stretched into early afternoon while Nikola sat stranded in the lobby. Edison's secretary repeatedly came by and apologized for the delay, but the Boss remained huddled in his office, calling in one engineer after another in an interlaced series of meetings.

At lunch time, Edison blew by Nikola without glancing at him while he tossed off a quick comment about having a very busy day and that he would see him when he returned. Since Edison didn't indicate how long that might be, Nikola didn't feel safe in leaving the building to get lunch for himself. Instead, he wandered around the factory until he found an engineer who wasn't working at his easel and convinced the man to loan it to him, along with a drafting pen and a large sheet of paper.

He decided that as long as he was stranded in the lobby indefinitely, he might as well use the spare time to work up a detailed schematic drawing that would illustrate the potential power of his alternating current technology. He worked quickly, copying the lines and shapes straight from the empty space in front of him where the illustration was clearly visible, hovering in midair.

Hours passed. The afternoon dwindled. Evening arrived. The last worker shuffled out the door, yawning, while Nikola continued to sketch away at the large schematic and occasionally checked an empty space next to him for reference. By that point in the day, the design had advanced to a state of sheer elegance, with balanced forms that represented whirling magnetic fields joined by winding lines of circuitry. The whole schematic was laced with tiny paragraphs of annotation crammed next to each component.

Nikola managed to feel relieved that he had been made to wait there for so long; perhaps it was even a blessing in disguise. The opportunity to create a detailed schematic might prove to be just the thing to disarm Mr. Edison's objections to alternating current and show that the technical problems around its use had truly been solved.

There on the easel was proof that he had surmounted all of the obstacles blocking the use of this gigantic power source. More importantly, it was evidence that he had indeed fulfilled his family obligation; not only had Nikola discovered his source of greatness, he was pursuing it with due determination. That $50,000 bonus was practically in his pocket.

Edison stepped out of his office and closed the door behind himself, putting on his coat as he walked away. He stopped, squinted at Nikola for a moment, then nodded and started toward him. When he walked down onto the main floor of the lab and saw Nikola's elaborate sketch, a puzzled look came over him. Nikola was too absorbed to be aware of Edison's approach.

Edison cleared his throat. "Still here, Eh? Good for you, Mr. Tesla. You are the only man I ever met who sleeps less than I do."

Nikola continued sketching while he replied, "Actually, I've totaled your nap time throughout the day to an average of—"

"Care to tell me what you're working on? My wife will be waiting with supper."

"Yes! Thank you! I was hoping we could discuss this very thing! You see, this is an induction motor for alternating current. Sir, I have built three of them. They work! If you rotate a magnetic field fast enough—"

"Alternating current? You're talking about putting the power of *lightning* inside of a thin copper wire? How is the public supposed to cope with such outrageous levels of power? *Eh?* No, no. Direct current, Mr. Tesla! America must run on direct current! There is no other safe means of electrical power for the masses. That includes industry, if you're wondering. Industry is run by people, and people can't be jeopardized by handling such a force! Otherwise, they will shock themselves to death, one right after the other."

Nikola fixed Edison with a blank stare. He exhaled so deeply that the effort felt like it shrank him by two inches, but he steadied himself by clinging to the thought that he could always visit the alternating current debate with the Boss some other time. At the moment, the far more important matter was his bonus money—and the changes to his life that it had the power to bring.

"Ah. Well, then," Nikola began, "I was merely passing time, waiting for you. You see, I have not been able to send much money to my mother, but if I may collect my bonus now, I can—"

"Your what?"

Nikola stared for a quiet moment. When he replied, he spoke in a slow, deliberate tone. "The fifty thousand dollars."

"…Oh. That." Edison picked up a light bulb filament off of a lab table and busily fiddled with it. "Your mother is back in Croatia somewhere?"

"Yes. But with the bonus, I hope to bring her here or at least take better care of her at home. She is very ill. Of course she won't admit it in her letters to me, but with that money I can see that she gets the best care."

"I looked for your home town on the map, the other day. Wasn't there."

"Lika is only a small province, and unless your map—"

"Is it a primitive place?"

"…Primitive?"

"Do you want money to use in support of un-Christian things?"

"Do I what? Sir, what are you saying to me?"

"I'm saying that I am a *Christian man*, Mr. Tesla! And so I want you to tell me God's Truth this very instant: Has anyone in your family ever eaten human flesh?"

Nikola could only gape, speechless. After another long moment, Edison broke into a wide grin.

"That was a *joke*, Mr. Tesla! A joke! You see? That's the problem with you foreigners! You do not appreciate the American sense of humor!"

"Mr. Edison, I need to send my mother—"

"Do you have a contract to show me? Do you have any proof? In America, sir, our courts deal in *proof*."

"I have earned this bonus."

"And I just told you, Mr. Tesla—you obviously don't appreciate the American sense of humor. Your 'bonus,' you see, was just a little joke." He smiled with a kindly expression. "But you can rest easy. No need to get riled over such a thing. Take it from me, there's plenty of money to be made in this country by a hard working young man. You'll get your chance."

Nikola's expression moved from shock to rage. He felt his breath become ragged and uneven. On quivering legs, he stepped up close to Edison's face and spoke so quietly that his voice was nearly a whisper. "So you share a sense of humor with your French counterparts…"

"Eh? Speak up!"

Nikola raised his voice a notch. "Mr. Edison, we are men gifted with the future. Dishonor is beneath us. And if you fail to understand that simple idea, then your reputation will be the only real inventing you ever do."

"Now you listen to me, mister! That is the kind of talk that will get a man fired!"

"Fired!?" A sharp laugh burst out of Nikola before he could stop it. "You think I would come back to work here? I brought you a gift, tonight! Drew it out right in front of you! But what for? What could *you* do with it?"

Nikola moved in closer to Edison until he was nearly pressed against the big man's torso. "Your reputation is a sham. Your greatness is stolen from others." He turned his back and walked out the door.

The moment was so unexpected that Edison could only stand wide-eyed with indignation while he disappeared.

*Incredible!* Edison could hardly believe his luck. The gullible fool was actually gone! And it cost him not one *nickel* in bonus money! He drew a deep breath and walked over to the easel, then took a close look at Tesla's schematic of the supposed "alternating current motor." He ran his gaze over the diagrams for a few seconds, then his eyes lost focus.

*Arrogant bastard!*

He snatched the schematic off the easel, crushed it into a ball, and tossed it into the nearest trash bucket. Right spot for the thing—the night cleanup crew could deposit it out back in the building's large incinerator. And since the crew was already arriving, he was free to walk straight out the door and head for his Manhattan overnight apartment without even pausing to lock up.

The short walk helped to get him started on calming down. He knew that as soon as he arrived at the apartment, he would use the private telephone that he had installed right inside of the kitchen to place a call and inform Mrs. Edison of his plans, then hang up the device and dip into his valued supply of Mother Edison's bromo recipe. Even when his stomach troubles were at their worst, the bromo always straightened him out quick enough. She usually got such things right.

The early creep of sunrise was already on before Nikola could feel anything more than a tormented mix of rage and humiliation. After walking throughout the rest of the night stuck in his automaton mode, he found himself standing outside the New York Stock Exchange Building while he returned to the here and now.

When he glanced around at the surrounding downtown buildings, stone block constructions three to five stories tall with facades of either fine red brick or silvery New England granite, the one eyesore on the overall image was mounted on every rooftop. Crossed wooden beams supported dozens of wires running in every direction: guide wires, telephone wires, telegraph wires and electrical power lines, all mounted and strung according to the needs of the moment. There was obviously no real source of oversight or control. The vaunted financial royalty depicted by Wall Street's first-rate architecture wore a twisted crown of hot wire.

To Nikola's eyes it was plain that some of the lines had negligible insulation where they contacted the poles, inviting short circuits and major fires. Even in this district, the crown jewel of America's foremost city, every rooftop was tangled with the reckless trappings of an emerging society's inability to understand how the electro-magnetic force must be handled.

It gave some weight to Edison's desire to keep high-frequency power away from the general public.

But the situation before him was a complete mystery. He could see one aspect of his calling right there in front of his eyes: educating the general public on the safe handling of electricity. Even the low voltages of the direct current were enough to start fires on wooden roofs. It was apparent, then, that part of his mission was to organize these chaotic technologies into an effective and sanely delivered power supply.

It was an achievable dream, wildly ambitious in a time and place where wild ambition ruled. In this new society, burgeoning with massive land holdings and abundant natural resources, it was assuredly an achievable dream, except that he had just quit the employ of Thomas Alva Edison, who at age thirty-eight, only nine years older than Nikola, was already world famous as an inventor and a major presence in the American business environment. Nikola Tesla, the unknown immigrant who worked for the Wizard of Menlo Park, had just openly sneered at the great man's scientific value, derided his honesty, and chided him for lacking personal honor.

*What have you done to yourself?* It was not really his father's voice screaming inside him, no matter how much it seemed to be; he knew that. The knowledge did nothing to stop the words from slashing at him.

*What have you done to our family name?* His father was dead; the snarled accusations were nothing more than stray bits of his own thoughts, but he still felt the old belly fire beginning to heat up inside of him.

*What have you done to your future?*

Leave me alone!

*If you want to be "alone" why don't you get rid of the demon inside of you?*

There is no demon in my life!

*Oh? Is she merely a "daydream" then? A daydream who conveys information to you that you have no way of knowing on your own?*

Nikola began to jog, traveling at a brisk pace, but he could not leave the torment behind.

*Since the visions she brings to you are clearly real, leading to inventions you can demonstrate, you know she is real. Whatever she is, you must admit that, yes?*

Yes. I think she is. She must be.

*Then the inventions she reveals to you are nothing more than bait. They are her way of getting in and taking control of you. See how determined your demon is?*

Stop it! She does not control me! Stop it!

*You stop it, Nikola… You stop it.*

He blindly ran on, hungry for relief through physical exertion. He kept going until he came to the East River. Within a few minutes he had slipped between a couple of warehouse buildings to reach the riverbank. He pulled off all of his clothing except for his thin black trousers, then he waded in and swam halfway across the wide expanse of water before turning around and coming back.

On the shore, an older man hollered at him not to swim in that area, but Nikola pretended not to hear and kept going. He pulled hard against the current, using his long arms to reach as far as possible into each stroke and pushing himself to the brink of exhaustion. It was as if the body's fatigue could burn away his inner torment. It almost worked; when he finally staggered back onto shore he was so tired that his sense of anxiety eased a bit.

Whatever crime he committed by swimming in that spot was apparently not serious enough for the man to wait around; Nikola was left undisturbed once he got back. He dressed still soaking wet, letting the fabric towel up the water.

Then he turned from the river and jogged away at a pace he could keep up all the way back to his hotel. An added plus was that his speed prevented passers-by from hurling questions or taunts at the tall, thin young man trotting past them in wet street clothes.

Twenty minutes later, he padded into the hotel lobby. His clothes were still damp from the swim/run but at least they were no longer dripping; nobody paid any particular attention to him when he slipped through and quietly climbed the stairs. As soon as he stepped inside his room, he closed the door and then turned around to lean his forehead against it. A sigh of relief escaped him over the knowledge that he was finally safe at home again, alone.

"At least you admit I'm real."

The sound of her voice stabbed into the back of his neck. He gasped and spun around—there she was, and she appeared to be made of solid flesh.

In that first moment, before anything else happened and before he could manage a sound, Nikola recalled that he had been saving up a *long* list of questions for her about where she had been and why she ignored him, along with demands for proof that he could trust her. His full intention was to refuse to deal with Karina at all until she satisfied his need to know more about her.

He forgot about all of that.

"I know you are no demon," he whispered. "But I have to fear that you may be… some malady of my mind."

"Ah! So I am madness that inspires," she teased. "Or am I only a creation of madness itself?" She reached out to him, almost-but-not-quite touching him, and gently guided him toward a worn sofa near the window.

"I am not sure of anything," he replied, "except that I don't want you to go."

She guided him into position on the sofa until he was lying on his back and facing the window. "All of your visions," she whispered to him in a lover's private whisper, "the spinning magnetic fields, and their power to control the flow of energy— all these things spring from only *one note* on the energy scale, Nikola. A single note. There is an entire range of energies above and below that note."

"Surely such a thing is more than anyone's mind could grasp or even withstand."

She smiled, closed her eyes for a moment, and then right in front of Nikola's dumbfounded stare, Karina began to quickly age. Within seconds she completely converted her image into a wizened old version of herself. He could still recognize her, but this version appeared to be a hundred years old. The sight itself was enough of a shock; he felt no desire to hear the rasping remains of young Karina's musical, playful voice. A bolt of shame immediately nailed him for feeling that way, but he was still thankful that she did not attempt to say anything to him. Instead she merely looked into his eyes, smiled, and extended her thin hand to him.

He surprised himself by recoiling in panic, so that he only felt the briefest brush of her fingertips across his arm before he was out of reach. The touch was so slight that it was already over when he felt it.

It was still enough. He gasped in shock when his senses traveled up out of his body on the sound of rushing air and he saw himself change to a translucent state, as she did. It made no difference to him that this could not be happening; in the next moment he clearly felt all the sensations of sailing out the open window and rising up into the night. Powerful vertigo whirled inside of him.

A bolt of lightning fanned the black sky, and an avalanche of thunder splintered out of the silver-blue flash. The sounds changed in rapid-fire with every twist of the bolt. He did not mean to scream at the top of his lungs when a second giant lightning flash pulsed with the impact, but something not of his own will tore the sound out of him while every crook and twist of the lightning bolt threw off an array of pitched sounds and prism-like sprays of color. The colors quickly overwhelmed his visual field.

In the next instant, everything disappeared into blackness. His inert body jolted with two or three full-body spasms, then he lay still for a long moment. His eyes snapped open and he struggled to regain his inner balance. As soon as he could manage it, he leaped to his feet and staggered to the window. He immediately threw back the shutters, gasping, and then leaned outside just as another lightning flash split the sky.

This time the impact was so hard that his eyeballs felt like they could explode from the visions. With that single flash he immediately grasped what she meant by "the single note of energy" giving way to the many notes, the endless tones above and below it. He was so filled with delight that he stretched his arms out into the darkness as if he could pull the whole sky into his embrace while he bellowed with joy.

# Chapter Sixteen

### The Following Evening
### New Amsterdam Hotel
### New York

The darkening sky was heavy outside the posh dining room of the New Amsterdam Hotel. Thunder continued to roll through the air with another full downpour only a breeze away. Inside, cast-iron potbelly heaters baked the air dry for the comfort of a full complement of customers, mostly small groups of stylish diners. They moved through their evening from within the formidable constraints of Victorian manners and the physical restrictions of evening attire. Certain dispensation was enjoyed by men who used tobacco: fat cigars, ivory pipes, rolled cigarettes for the dandies. The bright colors of the gilded decor were muted to half-tones by a pall of blue smoke. Females were left to delicately sniff for strands of breathable atmosphere, using whatever strength remained to them with their midsections compressed in whale-bone slats and cotton strapping.

Nikola sat alone near the rear of the dining room, although he had instructed the confused waiter to set his table for two. The chair across from him was slightly pushed back; he gazed with a self-conscious smile toward the space over the empty chair. He pretended to cough, covering his mouth with both hands, then murmured, "It's a pleasure to have a dinner companion for a change."

From behind Nikola's eyes, the sight of Karina seated across from him was a plain as day.

"Mr. Tesla!" a confident-sounding woman's voice sliced through the room's thick haze, coming somewhere from the direction of the entrance. He was momentarily startled when he turned to see a gussied-up dowager of a certain age moving directly toward him.

"Mr. Tesla, I'm so glad to see you here! I'm Corinne Watters." She paused for a response, got none, then added, "My late husband was one of the city's leading architects."

Nikola stood and kissed her hand in the courtly style he had learned in Strasbourg. She gasped in pleasant surprise and flashed him a blushing smile while he greeted her saying, "I am pleased to meet you, Mrs. Watters. What may I do for you?"

Watters leaned in close and spoke in confidential tones. "Actually, it's the other way around, Mr. Tesla. Do you, ah, have a moment?"

"Certainly," Nikola replied, already puzzled by her behavior.

"Good!" She pulled out Karina's chair and plopped into it before a horrified Nikola could object.

He blanched and quickly sat in his own chair, trying to discretely glance around the table.

Watters continued, "I am blessed with many friends, Mr. Tesla, and let me simply say that I have been told of your recent treatment by that Mr. Edison."

"What, already?"

"Oh, quite confidential, I assure you. Nevertheless, you are a young man with a reputation of being on his way up. People describe you as being a bit strange but brilliant." She gave him a warm smile and looked him up and down.

To Nikola, the movement of her head caused the patterns in her hair to dance like grass in a windstorm. The reflections from her pearl necklace writhed in opalescent flashes of color that tasted sticky sweet on his tongue and made him feel dizzy.

She smiled into his eyes. "You don't seem particularly strange to me."

"...Thank you." It was the best he could do. Nothing in his past had equipped him with sufficient social graces to steer through a conversation with a woman of apparent American royalty. Tension grabbed him; every word he spoke only increased his risk of making some sort of verbal gaffe—perhaps even causing her to think he regarded her as stupid. Now more than ever, he was desperate not to repeat the tidal wave of ill will that he managed to generate among the other telephone workers back in Budapest or among his fellow students in school. The sight of an entire group of human beings converting into demonic versions of themselves and staring straight at him was nothing he cared to repeat.

So far, it appeared that he was still on Mrs. Watters good side; she leaned closer and added, "Not everyone in America is under the spell of Thomas Edison, dear boy." Then she raised her voice and spoke for the benefit of the rest of the room. "I'll hold a party for you, Mr. Tesla! We'll call it your Independence Party! Ha-Ha!"

She looked at him and somehow managed to whisper while barely moving her lips, "I also have three daughters of marriageable age. Well, four really. Lovely girls."

"Ahhh." He turned away ever so slightly, clenched every muscle in his body hardly more than a twitch, then took a quick breath and turned back to her. "Mrs. Watters, I would be delighted to visit your home. I should tell you, however, that shortly after attaining the age of majority, I realized it was necessary for me to remain unmarried."

She stared, trying to grasp what he was telling her. "… Surely you like women?"

He laughed out loud. "Yes! Yes indeed! That is not the issue at all."

"Fine. It's settled then! At any rate, you will also have a chance to meet several other young men whose fortunes are also emerging. Just as yours surely will."

"I can see that you possess a most generous heart, Mrs. Watters. But I have so little time to spare for a social life." Nikola's eyes popped open for an instant focused at a point behind Mrs. Watters. He quickly tore his gaze away and made himself stare down at the table, fighting a smile of relief.

"Mr. Tesla," Corinne Watters continued, "would you *kindly* tell me how you can have 'no time' as you say, when we both know you are now unemployed?"

"Oh! 'Unemployed,' meaning no job!" He laughed again. He lowered his voice and cheerfully confided to her. "That only leaves more to be done!"

At that, Watters indignantly rose from her seat. "Really sir—ambition or not—I must know how a vital young man gets along without those things a good woman can add to his days." She flashed a coquettish smile and lowered her voice. "And to his nights?"

Nikola made a gesture of surrender. "Madam, I suppose I must confess at this point... there is already someone in my life." He paused, then added, "One might say it is she who inspires me."

"Well," Mrs. Watters sniffed, "if that is the case, you ought to show her off once in a while. My goodness, at least be seen with her! I hardly appreciate making a fool of myself."

"Please, madam, you have done nothing of the kind! And I would be very happy to be seen with her. But she is—" he exhaled in exasperation. "She is completely baffling! She tells me I am the one who draws us together, but it seems to me that she only appears whenever *she* sees fit!"

"Ha! There's an idea! I like the sound of her." With that, Corinne Watters turned and walked away, calling back over her shoulder loudly enough for everyone to hear, "Friday night, eight o'clock, Mr. Tesla! At my home! Ask anyone for directions!" And then she was gone.

Nikola sat unmoving trying to decipher what just happened. Answers did not come. At least the sense of nausea caused by the reflections on her pearls was subsiding. But within moments, any of the diners who happened to be watching him would have been puzzled to see his eyes slowly track over to a spot near the empty chair and then follow the motion of an invisible someone sitting down in it.

He nearly snickered out loud and barely managed to stifle it. But the humor he managed to restrain only continued to expand inside him. At first he was determined to uphold his decorum and did well enough until he dared to glance across the table again—a surprised laugh barked out of him. He made a show of clearing his throat and covered his mouth with a fresh napkin.

He looked up and realized half the people in the place were staring at him. He turned toward the empty chair across the table while his eyes tracked the motion of an invisible someone standing up from the chair.

He also stood and bent forward to sign the bill, then straightened up, took a deep breath, and started toward the exit. He felt himself moving against the suspicious stares of the other diners until it became like walking into a head wind. He only achieved the distance by keeping his gaze locked on the doorway and his posture stiff with dignity. When he finally reached the exit, he paused long enough to crook his right arm as if to receive a female companion's hand. Then, still in full view of the other patrons, he escorted his invisible partner out into the stormy night. His badly suppressed giggle was not entirely concealed by the sounds of the rain.

When Friday evening arrived, Corinne Watters clutched the arm of her guest of honor and steered him through a strolling series of lengthy introductions. Hers was the soft-handed relentlessness of a genteel woman on a serious mission. The purpose of her evening was to send an invisible dagger through the heart of Thomas Edison for pretending to be oblivious to her attempts to seduce him. Hardly famous herself, Corinne Watters nonetheless possessed the social and financial means to exert an entire series of jabs at her audacious rejecter. Did he honestly expect her to accept his high-and-mighty "married man" excuse? Where in the world was a man who would turn down feminine favors if he found the lady attractive? Clearly, Mr. Edison did not merely fail to find her attractive; his actions also implied that he was, at his core, a better human being for obvious ethical reasons.

One must not tolerate such things. Coldest of all, none of his explanations disguised the sad and blunt fact that Edison's lack of interest in her was due to their age difference.

Due to their age difference.

Due to her age.

Due to her.

Her pain was real and the anger burned deep. Corinne Watters planned to grant helpful social boosts to this Tesla fellow and also function as the personal mentor to any other angry competitor burned by the oh-so-gallant Thomas Alva Edison.

And so on this happy evening, she carefully introduced Mr. Nikola Tesla to the dozen young single women and men who composed her evening's selection of desirable peers. In truth, the clear opportunity for romantic connection between one of these eligible men and one of her four eligible daughters was at the top of her list of priorities. Running a close second was the fact that it would be most telling to closely observe Mr. Tesla's reactions to the guests, including the men; Corinne Watters was nobody's naive school girl.

Her eyes remained sharp for any trace of warmth between her main guest and the others, the flash, perhaps, of sudden heat. She chortled to herself. It was lovely to be in control of another social event right there on her home turf, where everyone was under the cultural obligation to allow their hostess to say almost anything. Her unseen palette of human relationships forged connections, established bonds, and changed lives in ways few of the attendees understood.

Oh, but she did. This evening's party filled the entire ground floor of her fabulously well-appointed three-story Victorian home. Watters moved among her hovering guests with the smooth and casual sweep of a shark in well stocked waters. She was aware that her guest of honor was feeling awkward and overwhelmed— his reluctance to be shown around the room was plain in the stiff shuffle of his gait and in his ramrod posture — but she decided that whatever Mr. Tesla's apprehensions, they would have to be a matter left to him. The alchemy of personalities she intended to mix was a complex endeavor, requiring her full attention. For Watters this protracted round of personal introductions *was* the party; the rest was nothing more than a *de rigueur* amalgam of light conversational filler, an abundance of sweet-cream pastry, and a calculated soaking with New York champagne. At ten dings on the grandfather clock it would be time for everyone to go—keep them smiling but head them toward the door. She and her staff had the procedure down pat.

Nikola curled up inside his skull while he allowed Mrs. Watters to steer his automaton through the house. Introductions flowed by while he left it to his partial consciousness and his automated body to sift through the obligatory social graces. The young guests all appeared pleasant enough, but they were socially mobile people with an aura of personal ambition that reminded Nikola of the Kaiser's entourage. He did not doubt some of them would become movers and shakers of tomorrow, but he was not yet confident enough to comfortably attempt American social graces and express polite conversation with American females. Besides, the energy coming from most of the young men had a prickly, competitive feel that he thought must consume tremendous amounts of stamina to sustain. Their gazes were hot with attitude; from their general responses Nikola surmised that the goal of their comments was not to simply employ the required remarks of social convention but to always deliver them dripping with musically sarcastic tones and local references that everyone except for Nikola seemed to understand.

Their laughter felt overly boisterous to him. Most of their conversation appeared to involve displays of wit in belittling other guests, generally but not always concentrated on those who happened to be out of hearing range. With his peripheral hearing he was aware that any guest's status or lack of it was reflected in the degree of negativity in the remarks made about them, combined with the volume of disdainful laughter that followed.

He heard someone refer to the process as "teasing," which seemed to refer to verbal remarks intended to symbolically pull the carpet out from under the feet of the victim, causing them to appear foolish and, in the process, tumbling their status within the group. The clannish jockeying again reminded him of the Kaiser's royal entourage, those frightened sunbirds.

With either group, one's complete absence of social status was revealed when they joined the unlucky few who were openly ridiculed, not behind their backs and out of hearing, but in their own presence.

Even from the safety of his tiny rocking chair perch, the party atmosphere felt ominous enough that his skin was clammy and his legs were stiff with tension. A loud crash startled him from behind, and he turned to see that one of the butlers had dropped a tray of champagne glasses. Mrs. Watters released her grip on him and asked him to "wait right there," then hurried over to supervise the cleanup.

He was on his own for the first time since walking in the front door. He tightened up as hard as he could and left only the smallest part of his awareness to navigate the hard world. The rest of him focused on considering the shared traits between electromagnetic attraction and gravity.

The point of fascination lay in the question of whether gravity is in fact created by mass, such as the planet earth, or whether it exists as a vibratory state throughout the universe, with harmonic points of frequency creating pockets of attraction, accumulating the cosmic debris and packing it into masses which are then credited with generating the force themselves—

At that point a young woman broke into his reverie with a polite but insistent tone of voice, "—and so you see, Mr. Tesla, I was hoping that a man of your skill could explain to me why the sky is blue? When you split up light from the sky with a crystal prism, it breaks into all the colors of the rainbow."

*What was that? An actual question?* He pulled some energy away from the gravity issue and focused on the questioner. She was one of the Watters girls, the eldest, he thought, the one who would not look him in the eye when they were introduced. But her name... *what* was her name? When they first met he noticed in passing that she was the only one of her sisters who was not voluptuously plump; her tall and thin frame was dressed in dark colors and her gaze seemed to stare through the floor. A few minutes before, her mother had brushed over the introduction as if it were a foregone conclusion that it was a waste of time to attempt to interest a man in Watters' skinniest daughter.

But what was her name? Too much of his attention had been diverted when they were introduced. He failed to capture it. Now here was this very interesting question from someone who did not appear shy at all while she planted her feet in front of him and gave him no choice but to pay attention. A good portion of his awareness was back in the hard world by the time he began a reply.

"Well! Yes! Why is the sky blue? It is a fascinating question, is it not? It opens up so many other implications about the nature of light energy and of energy itself."

"Perhaps. But why blue? Why not green or yellow?"

Nikola was fully aware of the hard world now, and he could feel the prickly hot gazes of a number of other young men who were attentively eavesdropping. He supposed that a lot of people must have wondered about the blue sky at one time or another, but he wanted to avoid delivering some kind of lecture and causing resentment from the crowd or creating some offended reaction. It seemed best to pretend to be unaware of anyone else and concentrate only upon her, so he answered in a quiet voice.

"The question opens up the entire issue of light refraction," Nikola smiled, "because it can truthfully be said that the sky is not blue! Rather it is, as you mentioned, all of the colors of the rainbow. Light from the sun is scattered by the photochemical properties in the atmosphere—dust, what have you—but the wavelength we call blue light is the most efficient wavelength for bouncing off those particles and into our sense of vision. Thus blue is the dominant color of the sky, but only as far as the human eye is concerned. Other creatures may see a different color."

Everyone else in the room now seemed to be watching for her reaction. Nikola felt a pleasant sensation when he abruptly realized she was not looking at him with the same confused expression he encountered so often in social situations. She nodded thoughtfully, mulling his answer.

Her eyes were clear and her gaze was straight and strong while she replied, "You are saying, then, that the impurities and distortions of the atmosphere filter out the other colors so that they are still there but we don't see them?"

Nikola laughed out loud. "Yes! Yes indeed! Simple as that!"

She smiled in satisfaction. He was already wondering how to continue the conversation when Mrs. Watters returned looking both surprised and pleased to see Nikola with her black sheep daughter.

"So, Mr. Tesla! I see that you have my daughter enthralled. However did you manage to say something she will listen to?"

Now he was expected to converse with both women at once! Time stopped. Panic shot through him.

But he still could not recall the daughter's name, someone to whom he had just been introduced and who then took the time to initiate a conversation on a most interesting topic. Worse, he had answered her so casually that it certainly would imply that he indeed remembered her name.

Could he simply call her Miss Watters? That was a point of American etiquette he had not grasped. Would it be an insult if he did, since she and all the daughters were introduced by their first names?

Perhaps he should have spoken up right away—candor was usually appreciated in this country. Instead, he tried to bluff his way through, and he had obviously been much too familiar with her. But now if he admitted to that, wouldn't it only make him look deceitful? Surely that was offensive to anybody, was it not?

Nikola stood inside of the frozen moment convinced that it was happening again; he was going to cause hard feelings no matter what he attempted to do. At least, he thought, the grim assessment of his situation simplified things—gentle honesty seemed to be the only option.

"Mrs. Watters, I am afraid that I must confess—"

"Mr. Tesla!" The speaker was one of the young men who had been drawing closer. "You're response to Miss Watters' charming question indicates that you see some relationship between light and electricity—in the sense of frequencies, I mean."

*Miss Watters!* Nikola exulted. If this fellow could use the term without seeming too formal then so could he! Relief flowed through him. "Yes, as you say, Miss Watters opened an issue—"

"Because if you understand such things, which I myself do not—I'm a businessman, that's all—then you ought to be able to convince every city in America to install electric street lamps so that the lights are actually bright enough to do some good, eh?" He gave a quick mock bow and grinned. "James D. Carmen, in case you need a reminder.

Nikola noticed that Mr. Carmen was speaking to him but that his attention was directed at young Miss Watters; it seemed as if Nikola had somehow amplified Miss Watters' social value by addressing her in such a cordial fashion. Nikola felt glad to see the effect on behalf of a young woman clearly out of step with the expectations of her world.

"That is kind of you, sir," Nikola replied. He ignored Mr. Carmen's rudeness in focusing so intensely on Miss Watters while pretending to converse with him.

Miss Watters tossed an irritated look at Mr. Carmen and said, "I wasn't thinking of street lamps, Mr. Carmen. Aren't the ones we have sufficient?"

"Sure," Carmen laughed. "Unless we can do better!"

"Mr. Carmen, I am in the process of receiving patents on an alternating current electrical generator which would be capable of lighting the streets of an entire town using a highly refined form of arc lamp. Even if one insists on using direct current for a power source, such a system would be powerful enough to re-create daylight, outdoors, at night."

Gasps rose from the crowd. The polite ones indicated that the idea was fascinating, while the more blunt ones scoffed at the grandiose aspiration.

Nikola noticed that Mr. Carmen, however, squinted slightly at him, studying him the way Nikola used to study bugs under a magnifying glass. Before Carmen had a chance to pursue the question, one of his hovering companions jumped in.

"Joseph Hoadley, Mr. Tesla!" called out a pampered-looking fellow dressed in a new and very expensive-looking suit. He drew close, reeking of champagne, grabbed Nikola's hand, and pumped it up and down before Nikola could draw away. "And don't you believe a word that Carmen here, says," He smiled and winked as if he had just told a great joke. His gaze lingered on young Miss Watters.

She looked flustered by the boyish attentions, but her mother was beaming. Nikola had no idea if a response was expected. It didn't matter; Joseph Hoadley went on, asking him, "Where'd you say you were from, again?"

Everyone within earshot had paused to wait for Nikola's answer, meaning that he would have to stop talking about the prismatic factor of light proliferation and change the topic to the status or lack of status in one's physical address, which perfectly encapsulated his reasons for avoiding parties whenever possible.

The distraction factor made him feel like he was in a cloud of stinging bees. With nothing else to do, he decided to try a direct response and to keep it simple. "My birthplace is a small town in the province of Lika, along the Austro-Hungarian border."

Miss Watters forged on, trying to ignore the host of distractions. "Word has it that you speak several languages, Mr. Tesla," Nikola turned toward her but didn't get the chance to reply.

"*Austro*-Hungarian? Hey!" Joseph Hoadley called out like a man who has just had a revelation, "isn't everything upside down there?"

Nikola noted with dismay that the fellow actually seemed to expect an answer. "Sir, why would everything be upside down?"

Hoadley beamed with glee and shouted, "Why would everything be upside down? That's funny—I heard you were a genius! But you should know your 'Austro' place is on the bottom side of the planet, *right?*"

Several onlookers burst into laughter, which immediately drew the attention of everyone else. It was followed by a short pause during which they all watched the guest of honor turn slightly to one side and clench all of his muscles. He straightened up, took a short breath, and turned back to Hoadley. "I believe you are thinking of Australia."

"Oh," Hoadley replied. Then he grinned and shouted

so loudly that everyone in the room could hear, "What's the *difference?*"

All the young men and several of the young women burst into laughter.

Corinne Watters was eager to see how well the young Mr. Tesla responded to such a fool. She knew the insufferable Mr. Hoadley to be one of New York's codfish aristocracy: new money, rich enough to live like royals, and smarmy enough to belong in a bawdy house. The situation was rendered much more interesting because, impossibly, it was Watters' wafer-thin bookworm of a daughter, so different from her other three plump and charming girls, who had grabbed their guest of honor's attention and sparked the rest of the room's competitive urge. Now the customary wallflower stood there beside the evening's guest of honor, smack at the center of the evening. Unexpected, yes, wonderful nonetheless.

Nikola blinked heavily several times, then turned slightly away and took another deep breath. Too much of his awareness was present, and he began to feel that he was suffocating. He glanced up and smiled apologetically to Mrs. Watters' wallflower daughter, who came so alive in his awareness when she flashed him a glimpse of her lovely mind.

Back inside of himself, Nikola lost all control of the automaton, and the automaton opted for survival. Corinne Watters and all of her guests watched in silent consternation while Nikola gave her a slight bow, nodded to the beautiful wallflower, then turned toward the exit and calmly walked out of the house. The empty expression on his face told them nothing.

Less than two weeks after Nikola walked out of Corinne Watters' party and spent the rest of the night berating himself for failing to comprehend American social wiles, he found himself once again in her presence. He and the grand social doyenne stood together outside a converted industrial garage in Rahway, New Jersey, while he stared in amazement at a long wooden sign mounted over the doorway.

# THE TESLA DYNAMO COMPANY

Nikola had arrived with no idea what to expect, and could not believe his eyes. He heard her she was speaking to him at that moment, but the events had left him so disoriented it was difficult to comprehend her.

"—and if I learned *anything* from watching my late husband amass his fortune, it is that you always compensate someone who does you a good turn." She exploded in a girlish laugh and grabbed his arm. "Remember to act surprised when they bring you here in the morning!"

She pulled him close and spoke in hushed tones. "They will most likely offer you something like two thousand dollars earmarked for laboratory equipment. But I happen to know that they have room in their budget for five!"

"Five?"

"Five thousand dollars for necessary equipment, Mr. Tesla. And the salary may not be much, but it will keep you going while you build their lighting system. It's true that they're refusing to employ your, ah, 'experimental' form of power, but otherwise you have the job. You will be delighted to rise to this occasion, will you not?"

Only now did he fully grasp that he was standing in front of the reason for the personal note sent by Corinne Watters. It arrived at his hotel that morning and urged him to cross the river into New Jersey and to meet her at this address to "discuss investments."

"Listen to me, Mr. Tesla," Watters hissed, punching through Nikola's thoughts. "I realize you may have some point of pride about accepting their offer because they want to use Edison's power generators, but you will still design the system and the lights. So if your pride is going to make me sorry to have done this, well, I can hardly wait until tomorrow to find out in front of the others, can I?"

"Ah." It was the best reply he had.

"I prefer not to be the object of ridicule, Mr. Tesla, whether or not such a thing seems like a bother to you."

"Ridicule? Why no madam, I hold no such—"

"Perhaps you can afford to be eccentric. Truth be told, I rather think that most people expect it. Do you agree? Whiff of madness and all that? My reputation, however, relies upon having my public displays of good works accepted by the beneficiary, you understand. Not rejected as somehow unsuitable."

"Yes… Yes! I see now. You wanted to tell me in advance about what these men want to do."

"Damn what they 'want' Mr. Tesla! They are doing precisely what was suggested to them, and they are doing so without giving it much of a thought. The ability to do that comes from *social credibility*, Mr. Tesla. Coin of the realm. You and I are here today to protect mine while I boost yours."

"Well, I… Good."

"The attention you graciously showed my eldest daughter threw so much glory onto her that several men began to show real interest. She is already engaged to a clever fellow who mostly leaves her alone and treats her like royalty when he does not."

"You mean…" the daughter's name was still gone.

"Yes," Watters agreed. "And if a woman in my position should fail to secure proper husbands for her own daughters, that would not reflect well upon her *social credibility*, would it?"

"No?"

"Of course not. In one evening, with a single conversation and one garishly dramatic exit, you did for my eldest girl what years of forced elocution lessons could not."

"Mrs. Watters, I merely explained—"

"You showed her to be *worthy of attention*, Mr. Tesla. Others *saw* you do that! They saw a man whose mind frightens them turn his attention onto a young women they had not even noticed. They saw that you did not frighten her at all. They saw that you took her seriously. They watched you give her your full attention. For a clever girl like her, that was all she needed."

"Well, she certainly did not require—"

"The other girls are pleasantly plump and soft in the face and not nearly so bright." Mrs. Watters gave a happy titter. "Give me half a year and all three will be plucked like winter berries!"

Nikola could think of no adequate response. In six months winter would have passed. All he knew for certain was that the meager amount he had saved during his time with Edison's company was nearly exhausted and that this woman clearly had some motive of her own for helping him, whether he understood it or not. Watters seemed to consider the value of this marriage to be much higher because of her daughter's perceived lack of social viability.

Beyond that point, the number of variables behind Watters behavior toward Nikola grew to such huge proportions that her reasoning struck him as hopelessly complex. He had no idea what else to do but keep his hands folded and solemnly nod every few seconds while she continued her baffling explanations. Winter berries, yes.

# Chapter Seventeen

## One Year Later
## New York

Edison's assistant, Harlan Walsh, looked worried while he hurried up to the Manhattan branch of the Edison Company. When he reached the Boss's office door and peeked inside, the renowned inventor sat alone at his desk. His posture was fixed in an alert position but his eyes were closed and he was sound asleep. Walsh gave a light knock on the doorframe. Edison's eyes snapped open. He grabbed a stopwatch and switched on a light bulb in a single motion.

He looked up to see Yes-Man #2, Wallace or Walden.

"Um, Sir? Sorry for interrupting your—"

"Timing bulb-life."

"Yes." He took a breath. "Oh. Our man in the patent office says that over in Rahway—"

"Where?" Edison kept his focus on his study of the filament.

"Oh. Rahway. Small town on the Jersey side. Not far."

"Yes, yes?" The busy inventor clearly had no time to look up from his work.

"Sir, the, ah, financial backers of Mr. Tesla's lab announced a public demonstration of that city's new outdoor lighting system." He paused to swallow. "For tomorrow night."

Edison's back stiffened, but he kept his eyes on the filament. "Parading for the press is best left to circus clowns."

"Yes. Oh. He was contractually obligated to use direct current, which he did. But he has been using it to power new types of lamps, sir. Arc lamps."

"Arc lamps are inefficient. Why do people think I work so

hard to find the best damn filaments? Arc lamps don't work."

"They never did before…"

"The amount of power they consume? Just to give off that feeble little spark? Ridiculous."

"It always was…"

"Mark my words, this is some foolish public relations stunt. A hoax."

"Um, hoax is probably not the word."

"Eh?"

"Our man confirms that Tesla has just been granted seven new patents."

Edison finally turned and glared straight at him. "Will you *please* speak up?"

"He-just-announced-to-the-press-that-his-next-power-system-will-be-run-on-alternating-current!"

There was an ominous pause.

"No." Edison spoke in a soft, reassuring voice. "That is not possible. You understand that it is not possible, don't you? It isn't even good science. Dangerous, irresponsible—"

"Certainly! Yes sir! One would think…" His voice dropped to a weaker tone. "But our man says all the components for Mr. Tesla's new arc lamp system worked on the first try."

He reached this dangerous place in the conversation with so much momentum left over that he unwisely continued, "Sir, they say that he gave each of his engineers perfect drawings. Detailed schematics drawn straight from his mind! No sketches."

Edison glared disapproval, but Wallace or Wells was a freight train with a stuck throttle. "He claims that before long, a single Tesla powerhouse will light an entire city—using alternating current."

This time the Boss's stare sent a beam of heat straight through him. Yes-Man #2 hit the wall like a spent bullet, emptying the air from his lungs. He offered a weak smile and disappeared.

Edison stood abandoned to a tornado of emotions. He sank into the news, dropping down and down into its repercussions. He resumed his head-up posture in the chair and went back to holding himself so still that he could have been asleep again, except for the long ordeal he made out of crushing an experimental light bulb filament between his fingertips.

Nikola was practically a silhouette while he stood in the brisk night air behind the raised and decorated lectern on Main Street in Rahway, New Jersey. His public grand opening was designed with a low-key beginning and this was its bottom moment. A single oil lamp sat atop the lectern and threw off a pale yellow-orange wash. It was one step better than moonlight.

"Dear ladies and gentlemen, thank you for coming out on this chilly evening. I offer my promise to you that none will be disappointed!"

He maintained rigid composure and delivered his memorized speech to the gathered crowd, but the audience members themselves were mostly dark shapes to him. He counted one citizen for each intermittent puff of steam.

There were two sets of wooden grandstands, five rows high, lining both sides of Main Street for the event. Many of the little town's people turned out, so the grandstands were mostly full. In the center of the street, next to Nikola's fancy lectern, a sawhorse stage held six of the town's top elected dignitaries, along with their six wives and two mothers-in-law.

"…everyone on our team joins me in thanking you for the opportunity to—"

While he forged on with his necessary bit of memorized political speech, he could not fail to notice that his own steaming breath matched that of the others, tempting him to consider the ramifications of regarding the crowd itself as a single, aggregate being—an assembly of conscious steam engines. The raised the question: if they were somehow linked together, how high might the crowd's total energy output go?

Spontaneous estimates beckoned to him like streetwalkers, challenging him with energy estimates for the output of each of the adult bodies present. Was a crowd, then, a living engine? He realized that the answer was yes, of course—but that they do not travel well unless you have a good transmission.

He nearly laughed out loud at that and had to cough to cover up losing his place. He immediately went on, focusing even harder on the speech.

Several of the dignitaries nervously eyed the bleacher crowd. If the public's expectations were not met, things were likely to turn ugly for the dignitaries, their wives, and the two mothers-in-law, all of them perched in the midst of the event and right there within easy grabbing reach.

The mayor had wisely declared the event a "dress-up occasion" and made it an opportunity for the ladies to wear their nicest outfits. Experience had taught the mayor that nothing was more effective at preventing the married men and bachelors with sweethearts from jumping into any kind of brawl than the prospect of damaging the ladies' best clothing and facing the consequences.

Still the mayor could not help his apprehension. A combination of chilled night air and early spring darkness was working on the crowd at a bone deep level. The usual drunks were already radiating grumbly boredom; soon the semi-drunks would start getting antsy.

Now several of the folks on the dignitary platform began noticing that since the non-drinkers among the crowd were likely to do the sensible thing and hightail out of there if the situation went bad, that would leave the dignitaries alone among a drunk and disappointed populace.

The long anticipated demonstration and the much ballyhooed slogan, "daylight, outdoors— at night!" had raised a vaguely defiant attitude from a skeptical public. Now that the demonstration was about to begin, there was no room for the slightest margin of error on the inventor's part.

The dignitaries, their wives, and the two attending mothers-in-law all had reason to suddenly wonder who this Nikola Tesla *was*, and precisely what was so special about him that he got the job of creating and building this supposed "daylight" system? Most of all, why on earth was he permitted to refrain from giving any sort of demonstration before this night?

By that point it was far too late for the answers to make any difference. They could only cringe and wait, tentatively shifting their eyeballs in search of the right person to blame. The inventor spoke to the crowd in tailored formal attire. He seemed a cool and confident presence, a tall, almost gaunt young man not yet thirty. His manner of speaking was unusually formal, but full of enthusiasm.

"—and the full year which your town council gave to us to create the project is actually the reason it succeeded. Since current science had no answers, this entire system had to be invented from the ground up!"

He stepped to a valve on a thin pipe that led to the gas lamps and closed the shuttlecock. The amber glow of the gas street lights faded. In the darkness, Nikola continued at full voice — "After tonight there will no longer be any need to argue about the proper source of lighting for the future. Tonight I simply *demonstrate* it for you!"

Nikola reached for a large iron switch and forcefully pushed it closed. In the next instant, all of Main Street was filled with dazzling white light from rows of electrical discharge arc lamps mounted over the old gaslights.

A collective gasp rose from the crowd, equal parts shock and wonder. It was followed by several seconds of silence…

The town dignitaries stared. They glanced back and forth to each other, at everything all around them, trying to make their eyes believe it.

The sight of the crowd's astonished reaction filled Nikola with such delight that he felt like half the artificial light was coming from him when Main Street erupted in cheers. No matter how much time he had already spent with this system in his imagination, nothing could compete with the thrill of seeing it out here in the hard world and watch people suddenly *understand.*

Relief flooded the faces of the town dignitaries, their wives, and both of the mothers-in-law. They each added their applause to the din. The mayor cued the waiting saloon band, who launched into a fair guess at what an Irish jig would sound like played by musicians who know how.

By that point the crowd was so intoxicated on pure

amazement that nobody cared if the music was good or not. Once the bawdy ones started dancing in the streets it was not long before the proper social animals joined in alongside them. A giddy cloud enveloped everyone as surely as if they had all levitated into the air.

Daylight outdoors, at night—the first minutes of the never-before-seen bright magic stabbed at their eyes and made them squint while it filled them with elation and charged them with the idea that anything at all was truly possible in this emerging country.

Every resident was fully aware: nowhere else on the planet was the lantern-lit night made so bright as it was right there in their little home town. An instant metamorphosis of public perception took place in Rahway. It was happening already — the crowd began to move in unison, behaving more like a single being than a group, trying to get closer to this Mr. Nikola Tesla. The same personality traits that branded him eccentric suddenly imparted a compelling mystique. The people swarmed him in an unspoken hope of soaking up some of the unbelievable good fortune emanating from him.

From a nearby side street covered in shadows, three men watched the reverie of the dazzled crowd. The largest man, the one in the middle, took a few steps forward. Pale moonlight brushed his features—Thomas Edison stood with his gaze locked onto Nikola Tesla. He held it there while the saloon band played a happy waltz, and delighted couples whirled amid the only artificial daylight anyone there had ever seen outdoors.

Edison was still cringing at the sight of Tesla's fawning dignitaries when he saw a young couple step up to the inventor. The husband gestured for Tesla to honor his wife with a dance. It appeared to Edison that Tesla was attempting to graciously decline, but the crowd egged him on. Finally he relented with a smile, bowed to her, then waltzed her away. His movements were stiff but poised enough for the Kaiser's court. It also appeared that every other female present locked her gaze onto the young inventor. The dancing wife was clearly thrilled to be sharing the moment with the man of the hour.

Edison knew well enough what it was like to be on the receiving end of such nonsense. *More irritating than anything else really.* He stared from beneath hooded eyes until he wordlessly turned around and walked away into the alley's darkness. His two companions hurried after him.

# Chapter Eighteen

## Immediately Following
## Rahway, New Jersey

At no time during the year-long labor in Rahway did it occur to Nikola to ask himself if he was prepared for public scrutiny—until one brief moment after his dream came true. He felt a shift in the public gaze; eyes bored into him from every direction, stinging his skin like thin sunbeams.

His skill set was entirely insufficient to the task. That crash course in proper social behavior assimilated in the company of the Crown Prince was difficult enough to navigate in Europe, but at least over there a person's public responses were much more predictable. Here in America, Nikola was entirely off balance when it came to maneuvering through a street party among minor politicians and a giddy public.

He reflexively pulled every bit of himself up into the tiny rocking chair behind his eyes, leaving just enough consciousness behind to run the automaton and get him out of the party environment as quickly as possible. While his body steered its way through the social maze, the rest of him sat curled up before the splendid, wide-picture view and sank into the fascinating notion of considering a human crowd as an organic steam engine, then estimating ratios of caloric intake versus energy burn regarding a potential output expressed in foot-pounds of lifting pressure.

While he moved through the crowd, bowing and smiling and doing his best not to shake hands, the faces in all directions were looking straight at him, mostly smiling. There were others. From them he sensed a familiar and angry jealousy—an American variation on the same unabashed envy he often saw in

Europe. Nikola had no idea what else to do but stride through the crowd, hoping to pacify a few of them with a moment of conversation in hopes it would prevent them from being inclined to turn vicious on him.

However, Nikola was just as unused to moving through a public place at night in full "daylight" as any of them. The bright overhead lighting exaggerated people's facial expressions, and the hunger on their faces made it impossible to tell if he was placating them or not. The only thing he knew for certain was that he intended to get back to the safety of his quiet laboratory as soon as he could manage it.

He was barely able to dodge a young woman who stepped free of her escort to stare an open invitation at Nikola. He kept moving without returning her gaze, but that put him straight in the path of three young men from his work crew, locals hired to do heavy labor.

He had already spent much of the past several weeks ignoring the dire predictions for this lighting system that each one of these fellows had made in Nikola's presence. They always seemed to be speaking just loud enough to guarantee he heard it. The game appeared to be for them to make increasingly bold and disrespectful remarks about the job in Nikola's presence. Now under the bright lights of fresh proof, they clearly sensed how foolish they looked.

The taste of their energy was sour enough that Nikola decided to avoid eye contact. There wasn't time to form a plan. So when an elderly woman next to him reached toward her companion to accept a glass of champagne, Nikola seized her hand in mid-air and pressed it to his lips. He followed with a deep bow. She flushed with such pleased surprise that she was not aware of him gently spinning her in a half circle while he pressed his lips to her knuckles, which allowed him to avoid the three crewmen by departing in the opposite direction.

This new direction set him on a course that now made the town Mayor an inevitable encounter; the man's head floated unswervingly through the crowd, moving toward Nikola like a high-riding river log. Nikola sensed that the politician would not be too difficult to handle at the moment; all traces of the hostility and suspicion that the man had embodied for the last year were gone from his wax-fruit imitation of a smile.

In the next moment the Mayor had Nikola by the hand in excitement, giggling like a teenage boy on his first trip to a brothel. He pumped Nikola's arm and shouted congratulations over the music, the laughter, the crowd—something about how this was a great night for Rahway and oh yes, Nikola should see him soon about investments that could offer a real opportunity to an up-and-coming something or other. Nikola smiled and replied in German, which was garbled by the music well enough to leave the Mayor thinking that he didn't hear it right.

Inspiration struck him; he could avoid the admirers for those who did not exist. Every time someone stepped in close enough and attempted conversation, he pretended to recognize someone else just over that other person's shoulder. He was nearly at the edge of the crowd and almost within the safety of darkness when his peripheral vision picked up the sight of a matronly woman headed toward him. He might not have noticed her but for the shy beauty of a daughter she escorted in his direction.

The young woman's party outfit revealed enough skin to identify the mother as a husband hunter. The daughter on display was a voluptuous delight, wide through the hip, perfectly built for churning out healthy babies, one after another after another after another.

Panic stabbed at him while the woman and her young charge closed in. The enraptured crowd closed off all the ready escape routes. He had no idea how to talk to a mother about her daughter in that daughter's presence, especially while the young woman was being pushed toward him. Surely he would offend one or both of them no matter what he tried to say. Would she start shouting at him right there in front of the others? She could damage the evening's positive tone and somehow limit future opportunities if he offended her.

Inspiration only saved him at the last possible moment. At the instant before mama could latch onto his sleeve and set a sale in motion, he began slapping his hands at his pockets as if he had just realized his wallet was missing and he was hurrying to retrace his steps. The illusion of urgency gave him the excuse to bolt past them and make his escape without causing personal offense. It appeared to work.

He kept moving until he made it out of the light, then continued with long strides toward his temporary Rahway lab. At such a late hour, the deserted work space offered the luxury of a safe place for solitude. There he would be safe to do what he really wanted, really needed—wait for Karina to come to him, as she surely must do now.

After all, he had made the system possible only by perfecting arc lamps to a far higher efficiency than ever before, and in spite of the ridiculous mandate placed by fearful town authorities to use the weaker direct current. Nevertheless his first inventive and engineering project in America was complete, less than two years after his arrival. Satisfaction soaked so deeply into him at that moment that the old stomach fire of self-doubt had no power over him at all.

He was aware of little else, practically nothing else besides his strong hunger to be with Karina. The need was so intense that it surrounded him like a magnetic field. It radiated from him in every direction while he walked on through the darkness. It passed as easily through the earth as through the sky.

# Chapter Nineteen

### The Next Night
### New York

He sat unmoving on a simple wooden chair under the open skylight, bathed in a fog of moonlight and dust. Nothing so far, but she was coming. He knew she was coming. And because it was only a matter of time, he did not stop the vigil. He remained in the same spot long after the shaft of moonlight moved completely off of him and traveled several feet across the floor. He got up once to relieve himself in the back house facility, but quickly returned because she would be there at any second.

He was still waiting by the time the patch of moonlight had traveled high up the wall. By then, with his body slumped over and nearly asleep, he saw no reason to leave. Surely Karina would not spurn him after such a night like this. He lowered himself off the hard chair and sat on the floor to continue waiting. If she was real, she would arrive.


Somewhere inside of himself, Nikola was aware that he was asleep and dreaming. He knew of no reason why he should not sleep or dream. He had a vague sensation of pressing his entire body sideways, as if trying to push himself through a wall. The wall's cool surface flattened the side of his face, the left shoulder, hip, knee, and ankle.

In his dream, he felt vibrations buzzing through the wall, felt them on the side of his face, his left shoulder, hip, knee, and ankle. Next he seemed to hear stomping noises. They sounded like heavy boot steps. Those sounds were accompanied by voices, adult male voices approaching him and growing louder.

One voice seemed particularly loud, while others spoke out in subservient tones. Sharp knocking sent waves of vibration through the wall. Their impact rapped at the side of his head. Within a single dream-moment, the sound became that of a pummeling fist striking a large door. In the next dream-moment, the pounding vibrations were capped by a splintery crash. Even within the dream, Nikola had no trouble identifying the noise as that of a door being kicked open.

That was when he woke up. And in the moment of waking, the cool wall rotated sideways and became the laboratory floor. Nikola opened his eyes and squinted hard. A bright morning glare filled the room. He knew in the first instant that everything was wrong. As if to confirm, the sounds of stomping boots now seemed to be approaching. He heard that voice again, the big one: harsh, commanding.

"Anybody else worried about us not having a key, say so right now! The new owners are taking over the whole place *plus* everything in it, so we can do whatever we—"

The speaker stopped cold the instant he entered in the room and saw Nikola in the middle of the floor. The man was big, and did not seem intimidated or even particularly surprised by the sight of Nikola rising from the floor and staring at them in shock.

"What— what are you doing here?" Nikola stammered.

"Not so fast!" the big man hollered. "What are *you* doing here, might be the real question. This is private property, right here!"

"It certainly is! This laboratory is owned by my company and you gentlemen are trespassing! I must insist that all of you immediately—"

"Wait! You're *Tesla*? The inventor! You're the inventor?"

Nikola felt a small sigh of relief. "I am. I was, ah, working all night and apparently fell asleep on the floor."

"Ohh!" the big man beamed as if the mystery was solved, the situation explained, the mistake cleared up at last. "That's why nobody got the message to you, even though you would *think* somebody would have thought to look here."

He turned to the other men and called out, "All right you guys, get started on the small stuff until we make enough room to get the big things out."

"Stop!" The word seemed to leap out of Nikola's mouth on its own.

"Look Mister, ah, Tesla. Mister Tesla, I don't usually have to go to work until the bank has already had other people come and explain the situation, move everybody out, you know, clear the work space."

"What are you— *please*, what are you talking about?"

"I mean you can talk to a lawyer. I would. But that's not my concern here, you understand. They pay me to hire a crew and collect up all the—"

"Enough! It does not matter what you say—*this is my lab*. Get out of here at once! All of you! I am willing to have the door fixed myself, but if you do not leave you will pay the costs of repair—"

"Hey! Hey! Hey! You can't threaten me—not any of us! All I know is your company was sold to the bank by the financiers about thirty minutes after the lights went on last night. To pay off all the debt. We got to clear out everything in here so the bank can rent out the space."

"These machines are mine."

"Bank says your company owns them."

"Well, yes, but—"

"So it's not your company, Mister Tesla. Your creditors owned the title. They sold it. All legal."

"These devices are of no use to anyone except—"

"Well yeah that's what they figure, but there's good scrap value and the bank is claiming their right to sell it off."

"Scrap value? *Scrap value?*" Nikola grabbed an iron measuring bar in sheer panic and began swinging it at the men like a long sword. "Get out! Get out of here! No one is going to steal—"

The big man gave out a shrill whistle; the entire crew responded at once. In an instant he was tackled high and low, pulled to the floor, buried under the pile. The men held him down so tightly he barely was able to breathe.

When the big man spoke, he sounded like a man trying to remain calm and collected. "Mr. Tesla. What can I say to you? The 'promoters' of your work not only sold the building and all its contents to the bank, they also closed the company account. And unless you have got personal funds to cover the bank's price, your situation is impossible."

He gestured to the men. They helped Nikola back to his feet, but remained close on either side of him.

Nikola straightened up, still panting. "Impossible is the word, sir. Much of the proceeds of this company are deeded to me, as payment for my work."

"Way I understand it, your share was only in profits."

"Yes, but after last night you understand that profit will absolutely—"

"It's sold, Mr. Tesla. Maybe your promoters just wanted to play it safe. Who knows? The bank owns all this now. You can still have your shares of stock or whatever it is. You can keep the company name if you want it. But all this stuff, well now, if you want to keep it you'll come up with the bank's price for the building plus all the contents. And that amount is, uh..." He pulled a slip of paper from his pocket and checked it. "Three thousand, one hundred, forty-one dollars and fifty-nine cents."

Nikola gave a peculiar laugh. The big man looked up at him with a surprised expression, so he explained, "That amount is the first six digits of the numerical value of *pi*." "Have to be a pretty big pie."

Nikola brightened for one quick moment, "No, no, circumferences! You know: three, point one, four, one, five nine, etcetera, or in this case, three thousand, one hundred, forty-one..."

The smile left his face. "I wonder how they could arrive at any figure without knowing what these machines actually do?"

"Who knows? Maybe somebody on the board of directors. One of their friends. Who knows?"

"Well sir, they are no doubt already aware that I have no funding of my own! My salary has barely been enough to live on."

"Oh hey, that's no surprise. Lots of people can't get work at all, Mr. Tesla. I tell ya, a guy sees everything in a job like mine, so listen to me—times are not good. Just be thankful you don't owe the bank any extra—"

"They owe *me*! And as for not notifying me about this, that makes no sense at all! My partners are well aware that if they want to contact me they should look here to pay me for the value of my—"

"To pay you? Mr. Tesla, do you *hear* yourself? Contact you to *pay* you?" The big man exhaled in frustration. He shook his head and turned to the men. "Better take him outside so we can get started."

Nikola's eyes widened as the men grabbed him again to hustle him out the door.

"Gently!" the big man cautioned the others. They used softer motions but continued pulling Nikola toward the exit. "I know it's a hard way to start your day, Mr. Tesla. This is absolutely not personal. For me, anyway."

Nikola planted his feet at the door, stopping the men long enough to steady himself and ask, "Is it personal, then—for someone else?"

The big man simply stared at him with an even gaze that revealed nothing.

"Tell me!"

The big man turned away without a word.

*"Tell me!"*

The other men wrestled Nikola out of the building before he had the chance to hurl another question. They tossed him out through the doorway with enough force to make it clear that he could not re-enter. Then just to be certain that the message got through, one of the men stopped on the way back inside and reached up over the doorway to the painted sign, "TESLA ELECTRIC LIGHT COMPANY." He tore it off of the wall and tossed it onto the ground.

"I built everything in this place!" Nikola rasped at him. "All of it is mine."

The man stepped back inside and pushed the broken door closed.

Nikola's knuckles were already stinging from knocking on his landlord's door by the time a grubby man opened up, bare-chested under denim overalls and holding a roasted turkey leg in one hand. He wiped his greasy mouth with the back of the other, then poked his grim face at Nikola with a look of experienced boredom.

"Sir," Nikola began, "please! I spent the entire day searching for my partners. They are not making themselves easy to find, but I am sure that I can——"

"Your rent is due yesterday."

"I know this. But *as I told you this morning*, my entire monthly salary was also due at the time that they sold the company! Now, I have almost twenty dollars in cash, which I could give to you as proof that——"

"I changed the lock already." The landlord picked a sliver of turkey from between his front teeth. He spit the turkey so that it struck the front porch a polite three feet away.

"Sir!" Nikola whispered with fierce urgency. "All of my clothing, my books, even my personal effects, they are all——"

"Yes!" the landlord yelled. He continued like a man trying to make himself understood by a deaf simpleton. "The law says I keep *every single thing* right here, until you pay what I'm due. What, don't they do that wherever you come from? Don't people pay their bills, there?"

The landlord sneered with the self-satisfaction of a man who has justly prevailed over one of the scum who make life needlessly unpleasant. "This isn't your Old Country, eh, you European piece of shit?" He chuckled and leaned halitosis-close. "Go find some money." He stepped back inside and flipped the door closed.

For a moment Nikola could only stand in baffled silence. Finally, he turned and shuffled away into the failing daylight. The hours since that morning had passed in a frenzy of activity while he ran around town trying to resolve this catastrophe. Now the condition of disbelief that protected him in the first few hours had faded, and the emotional shock set in. He saw with cruel clarity that in the wake of his first triumph in America, even after proving the value of his new lighting system, he had nevertheless been reduced to abject poverty by base trickery.

Every time he attempted to focus himself and reason his way through the situation—the likely effects or any possible course of action—he was reminded that his intellectual ability was useless with this problem. It was as if he became a simpleton in the face of questions about business procedure and financial planning. Surely there was an answer, most likely a simple cause-effect product. But every time he tried to plod his brain through the mind-numbingly dull analysis, the feeling of confinement was so intense and suffocating that it took all of his physical discipline to refrain from panic.

So far the responses from everyone he spoke to about his crisis indicated that he must have brought it all on himself. The throbbing ache under his stomach that his father used to be able to create with such ease was back in full force.

Night descended while he pushed deeper into the city, block after block. Every fear of failure that had ever crossed his mind reappeared to torment him. He passed the entire night in motion until he was so hungry that he felt like a hollow balloon. But still too disturbed to hold down solid food, he kept walking along the paved streets toward the northern end of Manhattan, then zigzagged through the neighborhoods in a generally northern direction. Hours later, when he finally reached the top edge of the island, he turned around without pausing and headed south again, back toward the downtown financial district, a distance he estimated at about twenty-one kilometers or thirteen miles.

He felt as if he had spent the entire night walking at top speed by the time sunrise rolled around. Still dressed for his Rahway demonstration, he found himself in the middle of Central Park. For no reason at all, he was hiking ankle deep in the autumn leaves between thick stands of American Elm and Spanish Oak.

Once inside the urban grove, he could barely tell that he was in a city at all; everything around him looked like a piece of land in the middle of the country. A few early morning equestrians were out for dawn rides, posting at the trot and clipping along in steady rhythms. His light-headed condition combined with the surroundings to make it seem as if he had left the city altogether. Before the sun got any higher he found himself walking into a secluded, grassy clearing within the grove.

It was there that he stopped cold in his tracks, and amazement filled his face. Because in the shimmering morning air not twenty meters ahead of him, Karina stood waiting. Her face lit up when their eyes met. She lifted her arms to him.

He cried out and rushed across the clearing to sweep her into his arms. He pulled her close to him and watched the background whirl while he spun her around in glee. Karina's expression was ecstatic as she placed her hands on both sides of his face and seemed to drink him in with her eyes. Then she leaned back to ride his twirling bear-hug while he held her as close as he could and brushed his lips across the smooth skin of her neck.

In the space between one moment and the next, Karina turned into Nikola's dead father. Nikola gasped and recoiled just as Reverend Tesla's face transformed into a horror of putrid flesh. His rotting hands pulled Nikola's face toward his. Nikola screamed in shock and horror, bellowing his outrage and rejection of everything that was happening to him.

In the next instant he bolted upright in bed, gasping, and found himself in a large dormitory flophouse.

"Shaddup!" an annoyed voice called out in the darkness. Still gasping, Nikola gazed all around his cot, plastered in a cold sweat. Windows allowed in enough faint moonlight to reveal a long, bare room filled with rows of cots. Each cot held a slumbering load, with boots and bags stashed underneath. When he finally realized where he was, the dismay that overwhelmed him was heavy enough to anchor a body to the ocean floor.

# Chapter Twenty

### Days Later
### New York

Nikola emerged from the flophouse carrying nothing and still wearing his ruined suit. His legs felt heavy, and his steps were daunted by the shock of rising to yet another day filled with the one kind of difficulty he never prepared himself to face. He had been conserving his small wad of pocket cash as tightly as possible over the past three days, but even the cheapest food and lodging took their toll on his dwindling funds. In another day or two he would run out of money altogether. He was already out of time.

The first twenty-four hours after his eviction were wasted in the struggle to find his investors. His efforts got him no further explanation for why a year's worth of his work was taken from him as easily as a breeze changes direction.

The day after that was filled by his search for decent employment before abject poverty confronted him. He started with places that should logically be able to utilize his extensive education, then broadened the search to any place that might only need some small part of his abilities. By the end of the second day he was knocking on the doors of any place that was somehow related to his wide range of skills. Still there suddenly seemed to be a thousand applicants for every available position.

This third day was his deadline day. The night before, he promised himself when he lay down to sleep that he would begin the day by seeking any kind of work at all, no matter what the job might be. He fingered a few coins in his pocket, wondering if he could allow himself fifty cents for a sturdy breakfast. That would leave him with three paper dollars.

When he passed a large newsstand, the day's headlines caught his eye, warning of the "Depression of 1886." He smiled at that notion; until three days earlier, Nikola had no idea that an economic "depression" was going on in America, or that such a thing was even possible in a land where opportunity oozed from the ground.

Cool air blew in from the Atlantic ocean with the unfortunate effect of bringing him fully alert; he would have been more comfortable in a daze. For the past two days, the urgency of his situation had helped him avoid the issue of Karina's continued absence, but now the question nagged at him. He hated to ponder whether his father was right or even partially right about Karina, but the old fears that she might be a symptom of his madness tormented him again. They mixed with his guilt over doubting her.

His day had barely begun when he passed an alley where a tattered mother hovered over her three small children. The mother's eyes met his and she extended her palm to him. The ache behind her expression resonated so powerfully with his own that without giving it any thought, he handed her all three of his paper dollars and kept only the coins for himself. The faces of the three children flashed with excitement when they realized they would all eat that morning.

The mother's eyes radiated such gratitude that Nikola spun from her and hastened away. He heard words of thanks but made no reply. If he tried to speak, he could feel that his words would only snag in his throat.

By the late afternoon Nikola had lost count of his job inquiries. He had not come close to securing a job and a deep sense of panic was setting. Late in the afternoon he approached a construction company office with a line of job applicants trailing out the door, mostly strong-looking men. The sign over the door read, "Men Needed. Heavy Back Work. $2.00 per day."

Nikola glanced down at his slim frame—the luxury of preference was long gone. He straightened his shoulders and stepped into line. It made no difference what the work was. It paid two dollars a day.

Since an applicant for "strong back work" had no need of powerful intellect, he wisely decided to withdraw himself up into the little rocking chair behind his eyes and give the automaton just enough consciousness to go through the application process. Meanwhile he avoided the terrible temptations to drown in self-recriminations. Present circumstances were his own doing, no doubt, but in ways that he could not fathom.

There was no real interview. His height at over six feet, two-inches was enough to earn him a chance at his two dollars per day in spite of his slim frame. He emerged from the office just as darkness was falling, with instructions to return at five o'clock the next morning to pick up his company-issue tools and the day's work order.

A job that paid for each day's work at the end of the day was perfect for a man starting over with nothing. It was safe to spend his last coins on a flophouse bed, even though there would be nothing left for food. After that all he had to do was work tomorrow's twelve-hour shift without eating, then collect his two dollars. That would be just enough to cover the expenses of returning the next day and doing it again. Still, he was surprised at how reassuring that little sliver of security felt.

On his way back to the Bowery flophouse region on the Lower East Side, he came across a long line of men streaming all the way down the block. The line ended at the steps of a large Catholic church. When he asked one of the waiting men about it, he learned that the church hosted a soup and bread service especially for unemployed workers.

He could see the line was a study in desperation, mostly males but a few women as well. Many appeared to have taken such a beating already that they could do little more at this point than wait for the final blow.

*These are my colleagues. And after so many years of education.* He felt his own dry laugh followed by a shiver of fear. Then he walked to the back of the line and took a place. For the first time, he was grateful to have no family at all in this country. It would have been unbearable for any of them to see him in this condition.

# Chapter Twenty-One

## Winter – Summer, 1886
## New York

The dead of winter hit New York City a few weeks later. The temperatures only added misery to the lives of outdoor laborers.

Icy blasts swirled powdered snow over a crew of rough-looking ditch diggers forcing a trench into the frozen earth. It measured six feet deep and three feet wide, running along the side of the street. Nikola worked with the men, dressed in thick work clothes and swinging a pick. He had to struggle to keep up with the burly laborers, but he was able to hold his own. The crowds of unemployed workers grew in the streets with every passing day, constant reminders to hang onto any paying job by all possible means. After weeks of steady work and those daily payments of two dollars per shift, nobody needed to persuade Nikola that even the meanest labor was better than the shame of being useless. On that pittance of a salary, he was slowly improving his circumstances. The crowded streets reminded him every day: the torture of contradictions that he felt eating away at him was hardly unique. It was known throughout society during those hard times, leaving him with a curious mix of shame over his daily labor and gratitude for the opportunity to earn a survivable wage.

Icy weeks dragged by. His muscles screamed and his spirits flagged, but the trench grew longer in the hardened ground. When that job eventually petered out, there was another. There was another after that one, as well—all positions he was able to secure only because they involved labor so heavy most men simply could not sustain the effort.

By the time that the spring thaw began to soften the earth, Nikola spent most of each day up in his tiny rocking chair looking out the picture window eyes. Even with his concentration pleasantly occupied, he was unable to forget his most pressing problem. It outweighed passing issues of labor and money, because no matter how badly he wanted to deny his father's interpretation of Karina's presence in his life, he had to admit that disaster had been a frequent occurrence since he first encountered her.

The memory of his father's voice rang through him. It implored him to reject any further presence of the demon in his life. Nikola had no desire to listen to the warnings, but neither was Karina there to convince him otherwise.

Where was she? Would she ever offer any sort of assurance that he was not consorting with some dark force? He was afraid to actively reach out to her, to attempt calling out with his mind and begging her to come to him. When he thought about daring to do such a thing, he could not avoid also being a preacher's son and wondering what sort of dreadful consequences might result.

Summer rolled around. Nikola still worked as a day-job laborer in the deep seasonal heat. Now his crew was breaking up the inside of a condemned post office building. The day was so hot that he and all the other men reacted automatically when they heard the lunch whistle blow; they dropped their tools and reached for their lunch boxes. On his way outside to sit in the open air, he stopped at the large drinking bucket and dipped a ladle of water for himself just as foreman Fritz Lowenstein pulled up a wooden crate and sat near him.

Lowenstein was a few years older and sounded as if he grew up in that city or somewhere nearby. He tone of voice was generally one of pleasant irony.

"Mr. Tesla, I notice you spend a good deal of time lost in thought. A real thinking man. A smarter man than me would fire you for the crime of thinking on the job. Dangerous practice. But maybe you can get away with just telling me what's so good about whatever you are thinking, that you have to do it while I'm paying you to work. Ha? Make it good, though.

"...What I'm thinking?"

"You find the question odd?"

"No, Mr. Lowenstein, that is, I'm not accustomed to—"

"Call me Fritz. Still, make the story good!"

"Yes... I was, well, thinking of the magnetic field. About its physical effect upon the element of iron. You see, there are endless implications to a non-physical force which produces controlled movement of physical matter."

Lowenstein regarded him for a moment, then turned and shouted to everyone in general, "Hey you guys, one of my laborers right here likes to consider the 'implications' of magnetism moving solid iron! Anybody wanna top that?"

"—because the specific point of interaction between those two realms is a *mirror image* of the connection between our invisible life force and our physical bodies."

"Excuse me?"

"A magnet moves iron but is invisible. Is this not the same way the energy of life animates a physical body?"

"Ahh! Also you're a philosopher?"

Nikola smiled and shook his head. "As you see, I am a laborer."

"No shame in that; times are hard." Lowenstein grinned. "All right, now tell me: what are you really?"

"I was, rather I still am, but I'm not employed at it now, or perhaps it's more accurate to say that I am not being paid to do it at this time... What was I saying?

"What.

"What?"

"What. You are what."

"Oh yes. An inventor."

"Inventor... Hey! *That* Tesla? Those new street lamps! No! Nikola, right? Nikola Tesla!"

"Why, yes... You know my work?"

"Know? Yes! I know!

"But how?"

"*How* do I know? I *read*, perhaps?" Lowenstein yelled to the world in general, "Mr. Nikola Tesla is in here today helping my crew pull down an old post office!"

He turned back to Nikola with a wide grin and addressed him in confidential tones. "So Mr. Genius, what other sorts of things do you like to think about while you're busy failing to help me meet my quotas?"

"Well, sir, with a few—"

"Fritz."

"Mr. Fritz, with a few months of research time, I could produce far more than bright street lights."

"Such as?"

"For one example, it is possible to create the wireless transmission of electrical power to any point on the planet. Not information, but electrical power itself, and enough to drive any kind of system, large or small."

"What, rays of electricity shooting through the air?"

"No, no, no!" Nikola paused, stared into space, laughed out loud, then sobered himself and turned back to Lowenstein, "Not like that at all."

Everything paused for a long moment while Lowenstein regarded Nikola with freshened interest and a level gaze. This time he spoke in a whisper. "And how much money would such a clever boy-chick need? To start up, I don't know, perhaps a small laboratory. Hm?"

"With tools and equip… Why do you ask?"

"Mr. Tesla, a man spends his life in this city, he learns the way things work. I mean that this depression has got plenty of people—investors, I'm talking about—believe me, plenty of people very anxious to grow money. I happen to know of just such a group who is seeking someone who has something to offer that is valuable and unique. Something *nobody else* can offer. And what you just said, Mr. Tesla, what you described just now, if you convince them you can really do it, *that* they will pay for!"

"There is much more that can be done, Mr. Lowen— Mr. Fritz. Without any further research, I already know how to generate electrical power for the entire state of New York—"

He dropped his voice to an whisper that matched Lowenstein's, "—for less than it presently costs the Edison Company to light all of the homes in a single town!"

Lowenstein studied him with a poker face. Empty seconds passed. Then his eyes took a definite sparkle. He broke into a wide smile and called out to one of the nearby workers. "Hey Jacob, take over for me today and keep these guys hopping!" He threw one arm over Nikola's shoulder. "Right now there are some people who want to meet Mr. Nikola Tesla, here, whether they know it yet or not!"

He grabbed Nikola's coat sleeve and pulled him out to the street. There he obligingly hailed a taxi for them while Nikola bent slightly and clenched his muscles in an effort to prevent himself from being overwhelmed by the way opportunity danced in and out of his life.

Two weeks later, after a long round of meetings with an increasingly large group of well-suited cigar smokers, he could only stand and stare in amazement at his new laboratory. Small and bare, but clean, the lab's walls were lined with empty shelves and glass-topped cabinets waiting for tools and equipment. It was a place of science delivered to him by what appeared to be, for all intents and purposes, sheer magic.

Lowenstein and several of the backers proudly flanked Nikola while Lowenstein explained, "It's small. It's small. But we can get you supplies and all the tools you need, and—"

"No matter! Gentlemen, no matter. I can work here! This will be acceptable. I can, I can work here." Nikola looked around, eyes glowing. Under his breath he added, "Ohhh, yes."

He dared to consider that this might not be magic at all. It might instead be an example of how his way of thinking and of describing his thoughts created this opportunity by causing complete strangers to place confidence in him. The thought reverberated through him: *This is the way it's supposed to happen.*

Lowenstein grinned. "Hope you don't mind working down here on South Fifth Street, 'cause in the morning you'll see that we are actually *within sight* of Edison's lab. I swear it was an accident." He gave a dry smile and added, "But I don't know, it's fitting, somehow, eh?"

Nikola walked over to the window and looked out. His eyes strained to penetrate the darkness until they focused on the main building of the Edison Company Headquarters. He could just make out the lettering on their large sign.

"I wonder how fitting he will think it is."

# Chapter Twenty-Two

## December
## Menlo Park, New Jersey

In the late evening of Christmas Eve, 1887, Thomas Edison paced his Menlo Park office like a hungry bear, ranting in fury at his number one Yes-Man, *what's-his-name, sounds like Holbert or Kolbert*. "Why can't anybody tell me what's going on there? The man has the audacity to put a new lab directly down the street from my Manhattan location, and after seven months I still can't find out what he's working on?"

"It's a closed lab, sir."

"I am *damn sick* and *tired* of everybody around me mumbling all the time!"

Yes-Man #1 forged on. "So we sent two private investigators to pose as job seekers, but he interviews everybody himself, so we—"

"I do the same thing. It's a good idea!"

"Yes, but he realized what they were up to, sir. He said to tell you. . . that he means no disrespect, but the Tesla system will light the world." Yes-Man #1 quickly leaned closer and spoke with reassuring confidence. "We're all sure such a thing won't really happen, sir."

"I already know what he *wants* to do! Did the Great Dreamer explain *how* he plans to actually carry out such a massive undertaking? An entire field of science and enterprise, constructed from the ground up?"

"He only mentioned something about, um—" He paused and sighed, knowing what was coming— "having a 'destiny.'"

"A what."

"*Destiny*, Mr. Edison."

"A destiny," He scoffed. "*Oh*, I see." Edison turned his back on what's-his-name until the hapless fellow got the hint and left the room. For a long time after that he stood in silence, glowering out the window.

Nikola huddled in the tiny rocking chair while he focused most of his energy out the picture-window eyes and onto the object of his concentrated *vision*. He sat high on a tall accountant's stool before a tilted drafting table while he applied finishing touches to his current rendering: a single white six-inch by five-inch page filled with the cutaway view of a large battery. He left just enough consciousness to his automaton so that his hands could accurately reproduce the detailed scale-model drawing hovering in his mind.

He raised the automaton's eyes and shifted its gaze back out into the room, where his *vision* of the large battery hovered in the air no more than an arm's length away from him. The battery was split in half to show a clean cutaway view, but a moment later the image rotated and moved closer to him, providing a clear view of the detail while he matched it to the schematic. Nikola watched his pen hand make a small correction on the drawing, then he lifted the drawing from the table and turned slightly to the side, handing it to a female assistant in a clean white lab coat. She accepted it with a nervous smile and backed away from Nikola for a few steps before turning toward the laboratory floor.

He glanced around in a quick check up on the lab work. Several male assistants were hard at work at constructing a giant "Tesla coil." It was only half completed so far, but already filled much of the lab—a wooden fence, ten feet high, had been formed into a circle twenty feet in diameter. A carefully weighed inch-thick copper strand of insulated wire was wound around the wooden circle in several ascending rows, then tied off until it could be finished.

The iron core was already braced into place. In the middle of the wooden circle, a tall metal pole rose to a height of twelve feet over the floor. The tip had been painstakingly affixed with a shiny copper globe that provided the coil's discharge surface.

Next to the Tesla coil, another assistant worked on a nearly-finished hard world copy of the large battery that Nikola had drawn from his imagination. Tesla's female assistant handed another fresh detail drawing to the worker, then sneaked a glance back toward him—he was already absorbed in the act of drawing another schematic, while yet another assistant waited nearby.

She continued watching while Nikola looked up every few seconds and stared intently into empty space, then returned to his drawing. The process went on until the young woman saw Nikola's spine abruptly straighten while a startled look flashed over him. She saw him sneak a quick glance around as if he had just sensed someone's presence close by. But just as abruptly, he stopped himself with a shake of his head. He took a deep breath and went back to his drawing, checking the empty space in front of him for reference, while the young male lab assistant working next to him politely waited for the next drawing and pretended to be interested in something else.

The year of 1888 had not yet brought full recovery to the American economy's deep slump, nevertheless an extraordinary Victorian-style office building in New York City was being occupied by the financial offices of J. Pierpont Morgan, where he comfortably rode out society's lean years astride a mountain of polished stone, beveled glass, and a tradition of family banking he did not intend to disappoint.

The crowning corner office declared itself via richly polished woods carved into intricate scrolls, fine leather furnishings, and heavily gilded decor. It was the Lair Of The Alpha Male for nineteenth century America, an appropriate place for a man of these times to contemplate his domain while he relished his power.

Morgan was in his graying fifties, stocky of build, and while he had no trouble relaxing in this place, his visitor, Thomas Edison, nervously paced the floor. Morgan reclined in a huge desk chair while Edison sputtered in barely-controlled frustration.

"The man is mentally incapable!"

"I do not agree," Morgan amiably replied.

"I *meant* incapable of capitalizing on his own work!" Edison corrected himself. "How could a man like that be any real help to you?"

Morgan smiled. He shrugged in a practiced gesture calculated to indicate nothing. "My people in the U.S. Patent Office tell me that he was granted a total of forty new patents, just before Christmas. Forty. That's a large number, isn't it? For patents? I tell you, Thomas, it sounds like a lot of inventing to me, in a very short period of time, on the work he's done *just* since he opened that new laboratory. Down the street from yours."

"It isn't forty. It's not that many."

"Well yes, he only *asked* for seven. I'm aware of that. But my little birdies also tell me that when the boys at the Patent Office saw what ground-breaking concepts Tesla was outlining, they made him break it up into forty individual patents—and then they granted every one of them."

Morgan sat forward in his chair and lowered his voice to a specific tone meant to indicate that good fortune would not follow if his listener failed to cooperate. However he also smiled, for his own amusement, just to confuse Mr. Lightbulb with mixed signals.

"They tell me he could be grinding out an entirely new field, Thomas. They are calling it 'Undiscovered Science.'"

"He's not right in the head! He could never organize anything so vast. His blasted 'genius' is half speculation! His so-called 'undiscovered science' is *unproven* science, that's what it is! Where's the *proof*?"

Morgan smiled again. He puffed lightly on his excellent cigar, like a man who had all the time in the world and most of the money. "Doesn't a patent require proof, Thomas?"

Edison glowered but before he could reply, a butler pushed a wheeled food cart to the door. Morgan glanced over and waved him in. Edison watched in confusion while the butler pushed the cart over behind the desk. It carried a sumptuous layout and was only set for one. Morgan's face lit up at the site of the meal.

He rubbed his hands in anticipation.

"Mm-hmm. Now here we go! Oh, look at this! This is why you get out of bed in the morning!"

He grinned up at Edison and then gazed around at the food items while he rubbed his belly.

"And look at this—these little things, they're toasted, I think! Morsels! One of the greatest things about being rich is eating too much. I tell you that as a *solid fact*, my friend! When you feel yourself slowly covering up in a thick blanket of too much good food, why, you know you're doing something right in this world. You must be! Or you wouldn't be able to put on that much weight in the first place!" He laughed at himself, then glanced over to the butler and spoke in a practiced monotone, "Wait over there. You can take this back when I'm through."

Morgan dove into the platters with obvious relish, a gourmand at his leisure. He seemed to forget Edison was even in the room.

"...Mr. Morgan. If we could *please*—"

"Thomas!" Morgan interrupted with a slight wave of his fork. "Worry is not good for a man. It ruins his digestion."

"I'm not eating. You are."

"Rest easy! Rest easy." Morgan leaned a bit closer to Edison without actually looking up and paused in forking the food long enough to say, "Just don't speak another word about an increase in your funding..." (Scoop, lift, chew, swallow. Scoop, lift, chew, swallow.) "...and my support will remain with you."

Edison's throat clenched with outrage. "Mr. Morgan, it is *vital* to my work that—"

"Our work."

"Yes of course. Our work."

"For now."

"For...?"

"Now. You know; 'for the time being.' All that." (Lift, chew, swallow. Sip, chew, sip, chew, swallow.)

"Mr. Morgan!" Edison nearly shrieked in frustration. He stopped himself and lowered his voice. "Mr. Morgan. My company is poised to become the nation's leading source of electric power."

But Morgan was again consumed with the fascinating task of plundering his private feast. His mouth was full to bulging, which seemed to require that he take another long sip of wine. Thus occupied, he gestured with his free hand for Edison to run along.

Edison nearly choked on his need to scream while he fought to keep his voice even. "All right! All right, then. The increase…"

"Yes, yes, the increase?" prompted Morgan while he slathered butter on a roll.

"…is not necessary."

Morgan nodded without bothering to look up from his meal. He lifted his fork and twirled it in a "run along now" gesture and then returned it to the task at hand, leaving Edison nothing else to do but turn and stride out of the room, mindful of not making too much noise.

As soon as Edison was gone, Morgan tossed down his fork with a grin, picked up his cigar and relit it, saying, "Mmm. I love that one…" He waved in the butler. "All right, take this back down to the kitchen and freshen everything back up. It should all be steaming hot for my next appointment — I need to persuade George Westinghouse to run a little errand."

The Butler gave a slight bow and turned to wheel the cart toward the door.

"Three minutes after Westinghouse enters," Morgan added, "bring it in again. Three minutes sharp."

"Yes sir."

"Wait," Morgan called out. He make a quick mental calculation…

"Make it two."

The butler nodded, whisking the cart from the room, and the fragile peace and quiet returned. Morgan basked in such rare times as this; leaning deeper into his unapologetically comfortable chair, he took another deep pull on his cigar.

J. Pierpont Morgan was acutely aware that a man in his position had no choice but to love his life if he was right in the head. And Morgan loved his life, all right. Not just the myth of it as it existed in public perception, but also the truth of it as it really was: sour with indigestion, stiff with arthritis, paunch across his beltline, bald skin stretched across his graying skull.

He loved the life he had built for himself because it allowed him to drain the blood of satisfaction out of every single day. The process fueled itself in that the more power he got over others, the more it seemed foolish to waste compassion on them. His digestion remained good and his sleep restful.

# Chapter Twenty-Three

## May, 1888
## Manhattan

For three nights in a row, Tesla's laboratory assistant Nelle Whitaker was still at work when the midnight hour chimed. An old grandfather clock stood in a far corner of the lab, and in spite of her fatigue she found its musical tones reassuring.

For Nelle, the clock's hourly chimes were the only things about the place that were familiar to her; otherwise, Mr. Tesla's electrical laboratory was unlike anything she had ever seen.

The first and most striking example was its sources of light. The night outside was pitch black with no moon out at that moment, but the laboratory was filled with brilliant white light, so strong that it illuminated every detail. It was nothing like anything Nell had ever seen, as bright inside of there as if the building had no walls, no roof, and it was not the hour of midnight but high noon.

The ceiling over the entire length of the room was strung with arc lamps mounted at precise intervals. They were a second generation, designed using lessons from the Rahway project. Unlike that city's massive generators, the whirling machines that powered this lighting system were tiny. These Tesla motors were built to run on the "impossible to control" alternating current, and they were more efficient, by a factor of thousands of percent.

The lab's bright light always made her eyes more tired after the first twelve hours or so. No matter, she was resolute in her determination that if Mr. Tesla intended to outwork every single one of his employees, so be it, but she would *positively* be the last one to give out. It was partly a matter of professional pride for her, but just partly; the truth was that the gloom in her empty apartment was relentless. She had nothing else to do but face the drudgery of a mounting stack of boring personal errands. And in recent months the thought of spending time with a possible sweetheart seldom even crossed her mind. She saw what mattered and she was where she needed to be.

Nelle was acutely aware that since she had reached the age of twenty-seven without once hearing a marriage proposal, her romantic prospects had dwindled to the point that to even speculate now was an indulgence she could not afford. The aftermath of such flights of girlish conjecture always consisted of a blue mood and the sudden sensation that she was carrying around a lot of extra fat. This happened despite the fact that she was no more than what people would call "pleasingly plump" except for sometimes, she reminded herself, during the Christmas holiday when she tended to add ten or twenty pounds, which she mostly lost again over the summer.

Nights like tonight were the fruit of Nelle's willingness to sacrifice for Mr. Tesla, if sacrifice is what it truly was—she didn't really know anymore. She knew that the life of a spinster was "supposed" to be dry and brittle and boring; Nelle figured that it might indeed be that way if she were in the same spot as most women her age. But on nights like this night, it was freeing to have no social agenda or obligation, with no one waiting for her at home. Most freeing of all, there was no petulant husband to have to appease for the sin of staying late at work.

Nelle's job made her feel deeply and quietly proud, partly because she loved this magical field of electro-magnetism, and partly because of Mr. Nikola Tesla himself. He was not yet thirty-two years old and wore his thick black hair swept straight back from the eyes. The effect magnified the intensity of his gaze.

She looked up from her arduous task of winding layers and layers of fine copper wire around a solid iron bar three feet in length and two inches in diameter. The bar sat braced against her wooden work table, held in place by a rubber-coated iron vise. Every single turn of wire had been laid perfectly against the turn next to it, in order to ensure a precise level of electrical energy over the entire copper mass.

She could still hear Mr. Tesla's enthusiastic voice when he first explained to her the importance of perfection in this new task. "It is as if we are painting layers of metal over the magnetic core, building up coat after coat with such precision that we can weigh out the entire mass of copper wire down to fractions of a milligram and predict exactly how it will shape the magnetic field!" While that sounded terribly important, it was the passionate gleam in Mr. Tesla's eyes that was magnetic to Nelle Whitaker. It shined in her memory.

During the six months since Nelle was hired, the magical force of magnetism seemed to become something he generated along with his fantastic devices. The force was so powerful it held her at the lab, day after day, during the unending work sessions that always followed Mr. Tesla's bursts of creative invention.

The strange magnetic force increased its power over Nelle every time Mr. Tesla came out of his isolated work room to interact with others—he always spoke to Nelle as a colleague, not an underling, always addressed her as "Miss," never by her first name. "Meese," he pronounced it. It sounded so exotic, a recurring reminder of his European background.

To Nelle, Mr. Tesla often appeared brusque with the other workers in a distracted sort of way, but his manner with her seemed special. Her only disappointment about it was that the warm moments were few and brief, but Mr. Tesla was so unfailingly polite that the bubble of formality around him made it unthinkable to attempt a personal conversation.

On this night, she passed the midnight hour with all but three of the dozen lab assistants having already gone home. She was proud of that; the inventor's magnetism again bound her to the place. It even seemed to hold her upright and on her feet while she waited for Mr. Tesla to notice that there was not another soul in his employ who understood and supported him with more commitment than she displayed, every single day.

Nelle blinked her eyes hard several times to push the floating dots out of her vision, then carefully began to turn the next wind of copper wire. By now, all of the other technicians—the one other female and the eight men with families—had been gone for almost an hour. The two remaining men were bachelors, free to give a solid effort at overtime. It didn't matter to Nelle; not only was her willpower fixed in place, but for the past several minutes, every time she glanced up, the increasing slump in each man's posture indicated that both of them were close to calling it quits.

Soon, at any moment now, she would be alone in this place with Mr. Nikola Tesla himself. And if the mysterious gentleman inventor was ready to burn the entire night away on whatever this fabulous thing was that they had been building for the last twelve hours, then so be it.

She blinked back the floating spots once again and stretched her neck from side to side to ease the cramping muscles, then set back to work at making another perfect turn with the thin copper wire. She concentrated on picturing the process in her mind's eye, just the way he described it: painting with copper wires in slow layers, building up a near-solid specific mass of copper around the iron core. She had captured it in her imagination that very afternoon, just for a second or two, during those first moments when Mr. Tesla appeared at her workbench and asked her to take on this special task. He was bashful in requesting her help with a thing of such concentrated drudgery, but he also explained how important it was that the copper circuit be constructed as near to a "perfect wind" as humanly possible.

The strength of the forces which this copper mass would be able to withstand depended upon the copper's overall conductivity. Nelle fell in love with the word the first time she heard him speak it: "conductivity." It referred to the ability to transmit a carefully calculated level of power, below which it *must not falter.*

If the electrical current passing through the copper wiring encountered pockets of resistance in the form of tiny gaps in imperfect wiring, then each of those tiny gaps would act as a condenser of the energy. The current would then have to build up a bit in each location in order to gather enough power to spark itself across the gap and move on. Each release of the condensed energy disrupts flow and reduces power. The gaps in the winding that Mr. Tesla described to her would force the energy to constantly build up, then jump, build up, then jump—across gaps that would only exist if she had failed and left them there.

She had no intention of letting that happen. If she failed here in Mr. Tesla's employ, where would she go next? Nelle felt keenly aware of herself as no more than a spinster with a good job, and even that much was a position she had only enjoyed perhaps "one finger less than a fistful of times," as Nelle liked to imagine herself announcing to a packed church.

The stickler in the situation was that she had no idea what the range of Mr. Tesla's great mental powers might be. He was well known to see things, detailed things, in plain midair. He admitted that. He was said to be able to see those things with such fine details that he built them without ever leaving his chair, built them entirely in his mind before he did a lick of work. She had even heard him explain as much to the rare visitors who asked the question; they seldom listened to the answer as carefully as she did.

Nelle figured the challenging world of invention would not be a bad way to spend her life, too, if she could just get a handle on how he did it. Not that she would ever admit to a soul that she would even *consider* attempting such an arrogant thing as setting herself next to a man with serious brains and a fancy education that he got over in Europe.

Still she dared to think about it anyway, just as she had dared to do so many other things. Nelle's secret motto was "You never can tell 'til you try," a battle cry of optimism for the contemporary American unmarried woman. She owned a dozen embroidered pillows with that very line of wisdom painstakingly stitched across their faces, one by one, over her many years of free time. As far as application of that wisdom in life, she was frequently amazed at how often she was able to bluster her way into situations where she surely had no business—like this very job.

She only applied in one of her rare bursts of overconfidence, not realizing the job involved working in a place with just one other female worker and ten males, not counting the boss. Nelle did not believe that the rest of the men shared Mr. Tesla's appreciation for a working woman's value, and she frankly did not think that her female co-worker shared it either, as she hoped to one day point out to the pathetic creature in no vague terms.

Be that as it may, Nelle could not doubt that she never would have gotten the job at all except that Mr. Tesla insisted on doing all the hiring interviews himself. Even though two of the young male technicians laughed derisively at her before the interview, snickering in a vaguely sexual manner while she passed on her way to Mr. Tesla's private office, Nelle found that the inventor himself invited her in, offered her a chair, closed the door to give them privacy and then began to quietly ask polite questions. He listened to her answers without interrupting her. Not one time. While he listened, he looked at her so hard that Nelle's thighs felt warm and she was glad that he allowed her to sit down for the interview because the woozy feeling was starting already and it always made her knees weak. She tried to deepen her breathing and freshen up her inner air without being conspicuous about it.

Nelle already knew about Mr. Tesla's big success over in Rahway, New Jersey; she had even seen it herself. Daylight outdoors—at night! She wondered what kind of man thinks up something like that? Could he read her mind? She felt sure that he must have some such ability that average fellows apparently lacked, something that allowed him to see whatever was about her, because he had not only hired her, but introduced her to everyone in the lab himself. He showed her such respect that it commanded the same from the other men.

In the coming days, Mr. Tesla trusted her with one vital task after another. Her diligence was such that she did not stop to eat unless Mr. Tesla also did, except that he seemed to go without eating for days at a time. She had to resort to keeping cookies and sandwiches in the pockets of her lab coat. At least she did not gain any weight and woke up every morning happy to go to work, even when she had only had a few hours to sleep. Such was her hunger for a chance to not merely be in his employ, but to make sacrifices for Mr. Tesla's wonderful work and to keep right on sacrificing until he noticed her, really noticed her. She dared to hope, and even to secretly suspect inside of her heart of hearts, that life had only held her captive in her ridiculous prison of spinsterhood in order to save her for something better.

That life was beginning now. A life which truly mattered in some way, and a life with a man companion who also mattered in some fine way. And so Nelle found it to be so perfect that Mr. Tesla himself brought this most difficult task of precision winding to her above all the others. Why, with his mysterious mental gifts he obviously perceived that Nelle would do anything, anything at all for the chance to toil with him in this unreal place. She perfectly comprehended that this latest task of precision-winding was only "drudgery" if one looked no deeper than the face of it. She continued winding for five more complete turns, each perfect, until finally, finally, *both* of the bachelors called out to Mr. Tesla and pleaded the need for rest.

Mr. Tesla was drawing at his drafting table with such energy that he appeared surprised, once he looked up, to see that the two men were even there. He laughed sheepishly and assured them both that they could go, and that they should come in late the next morning, as well.

Nelle was resolved not to put up with any of that nonsense about going home. She remained bent over her winding task with such steely concentration that she offered Mr. Tesla no opportunity to catch her eye and dismiss her with some easy remark, perhaps to merely call across the lab, "Oh by the way, Miss Whitaker, I did not realize the hour was so late, and please you must go home and also come in late tomorrow."

But not now, when things were finally getting good. Tonight was her first time to be alone and in private with Mr. Tesla himself. She marveled. Where else in the world could such a thing happen? What ruse could she employ in any other land that would present her with such an opportunity? It was quite extraordinary for any woman to spend time alone with such a man.

Best of all, because the occasion was not social, she did not have to carry any burden of "polite conversation," since it was conversation, after all, where Nelle's disasters always took place. Having to talk.

For all these reasons and in spite of her fatigue, Nelle's contentment filled her.

Nikola finished the last in the series of cutaway battery drawings and was glad to be done with that uninteresting chore. He stood up and stretched his arms high over his head, pulling his lower back muscles as taut as he could. When he lowered his arms and glanced across the lab, his gaze took in laboratory assistant Nelle Whitaker. She appeared thoroughly engrossed in her winding. For a moment Nikola was distracted by the depth of her concentration, but eventually a sense of appropriate reaction came over him. He smiled and called out to her while he approached her workbench.

"Miss Whitaker, please forgive me. I am afraid I was quite unaware of, well, everything else. Certainly you appear to be doing a splendid job, first rate, but I made a terrible mistake if I gave you the impression that it had to be completed before you go home." He paused for her response, but she seemed to not have anything to say. She merely flashed him a shy smile and nodded.

He stood looking at her, sure that she would want to say *something*, or at least acknowledge his remark and rise to go home. Instead she turned back to the wiring and began to carefully lay another turn.

Nikola watched in consternation. Surely he had made some communication gaffe but he could not guess what it might have been. Why was she still here? Everyone else was gone. He had assured her that it was all right to go home, but she politely ignored him and returned to her task.

"Miss Whitaker, I must compliment your tireless work ethic. You certainly stand out among all the other employees—"

She flicked her face toward him and flashed an expression of gratified delight so intense that he realized he had stumbled onto words she truly wanted to hear. But still she was not moving. Why was she not going home?

"Ah, at any rate, I would be a complete villain to allow you to work another minute more."

Nelle Whitaker let out a tiny sigh which barely indicated her level of resignation before she began her familiar struggle to speak past her stutter, "Mister teh-teh-teh TES-la, I'm hap— hap— I'm glad to be— be— be—" she stopped, took a deep breath, and appeared to be regrouping for another try.

"Yes thank you very much. And you have certainly been giving a fine effort here, but please—I am ashamed to have allowed you to stay this long already. If I had not been so caught up— well." He shrugged and gave her an amiable smile. "Please, you must not come in until after the lunch hour tomorrow." He started to walk away, turned back, "Is it agreed then?" he asked in a mock-stern voice.

Nelle smiled, nodded her head and instead of speaking, just mouthed the words, *yes thank you.* He gave her a quick little bow, then returned to his drafting table and sat back down.

After Nikola dropped back into his former state of concentration, he lost all awareness of Nelle Whitaker while he began jotting down notes for his speech of May 16 before the American Institute of Electrical Engineers. It was to be his first scientific speech in America and his first ever before such a large congregation of the day's leading scientific minds. He planned a physical demonstration of his complete alternating current power system. It seemed best to keep the text of the speech "short and sweet" as Americans liked to say. He could start with—

"Nikola!"

Karina's voice whispered in his left ear. A hot blast of fear shot through him. He was careful not to move or react.

"Why do you shut me out?" she insisted.

For that first moment, he remained frozen.

"Without new bursts of inspiration," she went on, "you will do nothing more than scavenge your own discoveries!"

Just when Nelle was nearly out the door, she caught sight

of Mr. Tesla. It was at the instant his body snapped backward as if something startled him. The inventor stared wildly around the room until his gaze fixed on a point in empty space at just about eye level.

"No!" Mr. Tesla whisper/shouted and threw both hands over his ears. He turned his back on the empty space and kept his ears covered, holding his eyes tightly closed while he tensed his entire body.

Nelle's heart jumped at the spectacle. At first she feared that somebody had sneaked in and surprised Mr. Tesla, frightened him, perhaps. But an intruder would not explain Mr. Tesla's behavior in the next instant—he burst into a harsh, guttural whisper. As far as Nelle could tell, it was directed to nobody at all, since Nelle and Mr. Tesla were the only ones in the laboratory, and he was obviously not aware that she was still there.

For Nelle, the fascination of watching a genius talk to himself was not as strong as her sense of shame at intruding. A sinking sensation washed through her, equal parts nausea and embarrassment over blundering into someone's intensely private situation. Some instinct told her to turn and run from the room, but more fundamental instincts—the parts going all the way back to humanity's days in the trees—assured her that any quick motion would draw his eyes to her.

Nelle tried to move smoothly toward the door, hoping to melt from the room before anymore strangeness took place and before he could accidentally discover her. She had no idea where she would even begin any efforts to assuage him after such an intimate confrontation as that. She kept her movements as slow as syrup.

She had not taken another three steps before Nikola screamed out in anguish. He sank to his knees, still holding his hands over his ears.

"Because I *don't know what you are!*"

Nelle froze and held her breath, but this time only for a moment. Instinct again controlled her and now feet and legs moved with smooth urgency, back-pedaling first toward the nearest wall and then around the perimeter toward the exit.

She realized that if she made any sound at all Mr. Tesla was likely to open his eyes. So far he had continued to keep them tightly closed, and Nelle was especially glad for that once he began screaming.

"Because disaster follows you! Yes, it *does*! And then you desert me!"

Nelle stopped merely sneaking along the wall and now headed at a fast walk directly toward the exit.

"Nooo!" Mr. Tesla bellowed into the empty room, swinging at the air as if shooing away birds. His eyes were open now, but he was not seeing the same room Nelle was in. She ran the last few steps to the door, pulled it open, stepped outside and only turned to glance back in at the last instant to make sure Mr. Tesla was not following her.

She did not have to worry. Mr. Tesla was still on his knees in the middle of the laboratory floor. He had finally stopped trying to swat away the invisible birds or whatever they were and was now stretching his arms straight out like a child straining to reach for something wonderful. All sense of torment was gone from his face. His relaxed body swayed slightly while he stood on his knees and reached into the emptiness.

Nelle felt certain that what she saw on his face was the happily stunned expression of one from whom all fear and shame has been removed. She was more frightened of Mr. Tesla's childlike delight over a roomful of nothing than of his emotional outburst.

She made it a point to step out through the door without closing it, just in case a sound should draw his attention to her and bring his madness down upon her. Perhaps he would ravage her in some way——the madman/genius now struck Nelle Whitaker as being capable of anything one could imagine, perhaps also a great deal one could not.

She hurried out of the building, down the deserted sidewalk, and at last into the comfort of the moonless night. Her pace was quick along the darkened, quieted streets. She was cheered by the thought of sleeping late in the morning. Nelle had worked so much overtime in the past six months there was enough money to allow her to wait a week or two before going back out to look for a job—perhaps someplace in an entirely different part of town.

And this time, Nelle thought, she really must go for something with normal hours. A dependable job that would leave her enough spare time to try a modest social outing now and again, to develop respectable social contacts and perhaps make a few friends. To begin steering her life with utmost determination in the opposite direction of such God-awful aloneness as she had just witnessed inside of that place, that frightening and disturbing place. That haunted laboratory.

# Chapter Twenty-Four

## May 16, 1888
### The American Institute of Electrical Engineers
### New York

The American Institute of Electrical Engineers (A.I.E.E) ended their formal reception and dinner for Mr. Nikola Tesla so members and esteemed guests could retire to the main lecture hall for the evening's main event. Everything else up to that moment was preamble. Gourmet dining and vintage wine were merely standard accoutrements; the gauntlet had been dropped before the evening's guest of honor when the A.I.E.E. sent their courier to Tesla with the summons to come and address them about his work. Now the moment of truth approached. It remained for him to justify their purpose in the occasion. Within a crowd of such extraordinary illumination, careers were made or broken every time a voice was raised in public, lives were made or broken whenever one dared to formally announce a discovery, and history itself was written on those blue-moon occasions when one of their kind dared to step forward with an entirely new melding of science and technology. The evening was tight with anticipation because Mr. Nikola Tesla claimed to have done just that, with a wealth of discoveries capable of revolutionizing the field of engineering itself.

Nikola had accepted the evening's honor knowing full well the potential repercussions to his scientific credibility could go on for the rest of his life. Nevertheless, while he waited just offstage for the crowd to finish taking their seats, he had the feeling that the formality of his new and impeccably tailored suit was perfect for the revolution he intended to launch. He did, after all, have more than mere personal conviction to sustain him; it had been five months since the U.S. Government certified his forty related patents on alternating current—and it was the U.S. Patent Office that insisted on officially proclaiming his work an entirely new branch of the field.

Within minutes, the audience began to settle down. The gas footlights were turned up to full, throwing a deep yellow light on the underside of the announcer's face while he stepped onstage and strode out to the podium, raising his hands for silence.

Nikola stood ready offstage while the speaker introduced him to the packed hall of expectant faces. "Those of you who keep a sharp eye on scientific discoveries have already heard about our special guest this evening. And although Nikola Tesla may be unknown to the world today, please listen to him explain the ground-breaking wave of patents which the government recently approved in his name, and you will realize why Mr. Tesla's anonymity is about to change."

He looked over to Nikola's spot in the wings and gestured welcome to him. "Mr. Nikola Tesla ..."

Nikola walked to the podium amid polite applause while the speaker modestly retired from the stage and took his spot centered under the long A.I.E.E. banner. His head was clear, his body felt strong, and the moment was exhilarating. He knew that if only they could be persuaded to set aside what they had been taught and consider the implications of what he was about to demonstrate, he could not fail to amaze the audience.

He remembered the note cards in his pocket and took them out, but after he glanced at them he put them away again. Instead he gazed out into the room, trying to take in every face in the auditorium, to lock eyes with every pair. He took a deep breath; the air felt good, a bit dusty, academic. Perfect for the occasion.

On cue, two graduate students pushed a wheeled table from the opposite side of the stage. It was set with a matched pair of two-phase induction motors that Nikola hand-built especially for the event, to provide a practical demonstration proving his lecture tonight on alternating current was to be entirely fact-based, not a thing of dreams.

With practiced subtlety, Nikola scrunched over and briefly clenched all his muscles to clear his vision. He looked back up and took a deep breath, then began.

"A whirling magnetic field marks today's frontier in electrical power, but that frontier exists on only *one* note, along an endless scale of energy frequencies. By modulating energy as we would music, we can create—*in our lifetimes*—stunning developments in mass transit and mass communication. These small motors you see here will demonstrate why the power of alternating current is important to the future of humanity.

"Still, they are only the first step. Because we will be able—again, in our lifetimes—to create a standing wave of energy surrounding the entire planet, which will provide *free* electrical power to anyone, anywhere on earth! I am not talking about transmitting information. I am talking about transmitting energy itself, anywhere on the planet."

He looked out on an audience so absolutely unmoving that for a moment they appeared to be carved from wax. He had not performed the demonstration yet, but everyone knew it was coming and nobody seriously expected it to fail because of his patent approvals. What Nikola saw was more than the expectation of seeing a demonstration of proven machinery. If some among them regarded him with that familiar look of hurt and envy he knew so well, the details of their faces were too far away to see. The audience as a living body listened with that particular mixture of awe and disbelief felt by elite members of any prestigious trade when they are presented with a groundbreaking truth about their field. He was about to demonstrate to them that this one had been right there in front of their expert eyes, all along. As for the familiar looks, they would come.

Nikola arrived at his laboratory the next morning before the sun was clear of the horizon. He cherished the early hours when no one was in the lab almost as much as he cherished the late hours when no one was in the lab. His level of excitement after last night's event was so high that a single hour of sleep was enough to restore his strength and set him eager for another day.

He stood atop the lab's tallest A-frame ladder positioned next to a giant, half-constructed transformer while he carefully checked the coil wiring. He was aware that the procedure had already been done twice by his staff, but for him the many subtle powers of the number three included the power of a third check in preventing mistakes.

He heard the front door open and close, but it was not unusual for assistants to come in early, so he did not look away from his work. Moments later a stocky, dark-haired man with a thick walrus mustache entered the room. The man was attired in a suit appropriate for royalty and clutched a fat cigar in his teeth. He glanced around until he caught sight of Nikola up on the ladder. He eyed him with a predatory grin for just a moment, then announced his presence by calling out in a deep voice that boomed around the lab.

"*Free electrical power to anyone, anywhere!*" He let out a dramatic sigh. "Magnificent! Who wouldn't love the idea?"

Puzzled, Nikola regarded him without moving down off the ladder. He replied with ritual politeness, "Ah. Thank you."

"I mean, talk about your public relations!" the man bellowed. "And really, as for whether or not it has to be absolutely *free*, well, perhaps it could be suggested that one could also offer 'Low Cost And Affordable' as a worthy alternative?"

"Sir. This is a private lab." He climbed down to emphasize his point.

But the uninvited visitor was already closing in. The man offered an outstretched hand in the customary American greeting.

"Mr. Tesla, my name is George Westinghouse, and your speech last night was brilliant!" Westinghouse reached him and stopped, holding out his hand. The flash of nausea that swirled through Nikola made him regret his studies in bacteriology. When he combined his knowledge of the emerging field of germ studies with his observation that few people ever washed their hands...

There was a single empty moment before Nikola could

make any response at all to this surprise greeting. If he had more time, a few minutes even—but at that point the best he could do was to step to the floor, ignore the man's hand, and instead offer a sincere bow from the waist.

Westinghouse didn't appear to notice anything unusual. He dropped his extended hand and forged ahead. "Hell, I wanted to congratulate you right there on the spot, but the crowd around you was enormous. Any rate, here I am. Your discoveries? Truly brilliant, sir. *Brilliant!*"

"Thank you, Mr. Westinghouse. I know you by reputation of course."

"You should! Hell yes, man; I'm the strongest supporter of the Tesla alternating current that there is! I want to see the whole country running on it!" He glanced around as if making certain that no spies lurked in the shadows, then went on.

"*And* I have a financier who wants *you* to design giant alternating current dynamos that will eventually harness electrical power off of the great Niagara Falls!"

"Niagara Falls?"

"Mm. Heh-heh. Know the place?"

"Yes! Yes I do indeed! I have often thought—"

"They want me to acquire *your* power system for that task, Mr. Tesla. Lock, stock and barrel."

Nikola had to sit. He flopped onto the floor and took a few deep breaths. "Sir, the power of that much water will no doubt run into many millions of volts."

"Then you're in luck! They only want your guarantee that you can put 100,000 volts on a single wire and carry it from Niagara to Buffalo, New York. Permits will take time. You've got a few years to work with, here."

Nikola fought to steady his breath and to keep his vision from sliding into a chaos of overlapped imaginings. Slowly, he replied, "Mr. Westinghouse, please tell your financiers that if they chose to underwrite the equipment to tap 400,000 volts, then we could deliver power to the entire eastern seaboard."

Westinghouse beamed at that. "First Buffalo. Later the entire eastern seaboard, if you don't mind. These people are big on proof. Results. Things that actually work. If you're interested, of course."

"*If?* When can we begin?"

Westinghouse gave out a hearty laugh and clapped his hands together. "How does tomorrow sound? I don't like nitpicking!" He leaned closer to Nikola and asked in confidential tones, "You're not a nitpicker, are you?"

"Ah, actually, I suppose I am a—"

"Because I am prepared to offer you one million dollars for all forty of your existing patents on alternating current power."

Nikola was entirely unaccustomed to thinking of money in such terms. He ran his mind through a series of recollections about the stuff. For this country of America in the late nineteenth century, the finest luxury hotel room cost a few dollars a night. A fine home of equal luxury in the city could be had for ten to twenty thousand dollars. A large sized laboratory could be built on choice land purchased for a thousand dollars an acre, stocked with everything necessary to work with electrical energy, then staffed with well-paid technicians and run for a year, maybe even two years before it would need to turn a single penny of profit.

He had to take a pause. Nikola was in such shock that he could not find his tongue. Westinghouse quickly decided to fill the silence. "*Plus* royalties! Royalties of one dollar for every single horsepower of electricity generated by your creations. Royalties are where a man makes his—"

"One million? One million dollars?"

George Westinghouse grinned and winked like a co-conspirator. "Fifty thousand cash to start. And I mean first thing, tomorrow! I hope you love this country as much as I do!"

"Oh yes, I— I am going to become a citizen one day! My life here would be impossible anywhere else!"

Westinghouse smiled in satisfaction. "There you have it. Me, I'm born and raised here in America and I couldn't say it better than that!" He thrust out his hand. "*This* is how I like to do business! No nitpicking!" He looked down at his hand, then back up at Nikola. "So my man will be by tomorrow with the papers and your check."

"Tomorrow?"

Westinghouse's hand was still out. "Yep. Fifty thousand down. If you accept."

Nikola blinked hard several times but his vision refused to clear. "Are there actually people in America who would *turn down* a million dollars—plus royalties—for an invention?"

Westinghouse was still holding out his hand. He boomed out the big laugh again. "Only the stupid ones, sir."

Nikola smiled in amazement, and then slowly—although without actually looking—he reached out and clasped George Westinghouse's hand with his own.

A few minutes after the surprise encounter Nikola found himself sitting alone on the floor of the silent lab, slumped against the wall in a warm sunbeam. The feeling was that of a beautiful dream. Everything was different now. In one tick of the clock, everything was different. Why, this was an absolute guarantee of a laboratory of his own where he was free to work on anything at all, with plenty of equipment and qualified help. It occurred to him then, that as of this day he was separated from the first part of his life by a breach he would never have to cross again.

"Nikola!" Karina's voice came from somewhere close by.

He snapped alert and looked around. A moment later she stepped out from the shadows, her expression full of concern for him. "Why do you keep turning from me?"

"Shut up! Shut up!" He covered his eyes and took a long, deep breath. When he spoke again his voice was small and tired.

"I am a preacher's son. And he seems to haunt me. I am not proud of that, but I cannot deny it. As sure as I feel about you when we are together, I still hear his voice repeating that every time I listened to you, disaster followed."

Karina moved to him and lightly touched his face. "You have made powerful enemies, but you have already changed the world more than you know."

The pull of attraction from Karina was nothing he could resist for any length of time. As much as he feared her, his strongest abilities to discipline himself and control his emotions faded against her power over him. She wielded that power simply by being in his presence, whether she was inside his consciousness or outside in the hard world.

Sharp metallic sounds came from the large main lab door. It was being unlocked and slid back; the noise pulled his concerns from Karina. Mingled voices of arriving workers mixed with approaching footsteps of heavy work boots. Nikola only had time for a brief and panicky glance around before he realized that he was cornered.

He hunched over slightly and clenched all of his muscles in a huge effort to concentrate, to drive out Karina and her visions before anyone walked in, and only managed to finish half a blink before three of his younger male employees entered. The first one stopped at the sight of Nikola, who was now standing in the middle of the room with a confused and guilty expression. The other two quickly bumped into the first one with annoyed grunts—until all three looked up and saw the inventor.

Nikola looked like a drunk trying to fake sobriety. Plastered with sweat, clothing askew, he turned to face them, moving as if heavy weights were pressing down on his head while he looked up and attempted a smile. "Good morning," he croaked.

The three men's self-conscious pause lasted only a second, then they each muttered a quick good morning and stepped off to their respective work areas. They moved with the timeless manner of experienced employees who know better than to ask.

Thomas Edison did not look out of the window of his Manhattan laboratory one single time after someone told him about the truckloads of equipment and construction materials that were arriving down at Tesla's place. Edison knew his people would be watching him to see how he took the news, the same way farmhands watch the farmer to determine how they will react in a storm.

But all Edison's employees were going to see was a man hard at work doing research. He stood slightly bent over his desk, holding a book out to catch some extra light from the desk lamp. As for his expression, he felt perfectly confident that people could study him out of the corners of their eyes all day long and learn nothing; his face could be stone, for all it revealed.

Edison was already well aware that dozens of men and even a few women had lined up to apply for jobs at Tesla's new lab in the last two days. Whatever was going on, they were seeing a lot of newly hired people down there.

"Whoop-dee-doo," he muttered under his breath, just the way his mother used to do when she was making fun of someone who was getting too high and mighty. Whoop-dee-doo for Nikola Tesla and whatever nonsense occupied him.

None of it was a surprise to Edison, who considered his ability to size up a man one of his greatest strengths. He knew Tesla was trouble from the very first day. Edison generally found that men who are too well-spoken and too polite turned out to be an aggravation once they worked their way into things. It never took long; their soft voices and soothing attitudes more or less put you to sleep, then they robbed you.

Work at Tesla's lab had been going at a constant pace ever since that idiot George Westinghouse handed Tesla a million dollars *plus* a fat royalty agreement. The obvious danger in putting power into the hands of such a man as this Tesla fellow quickly manifested itself when he lost no time in undertaking some sort of massive project that obviously required tons of new equipment and a rash of job applicants.

Why all the secrecy? He knew Tesla wasn't making some sort of explosive weapon. The young immigrant was, however, building a dangerous electrical power system that should never be allowed to exist in a world of fallible human beings who can suffer instant death if they touch the wrong wire. This was exactly what they will inevitably do, Edison repeatedly assured anyone who would listen. The harmless buzz of a direct current shock was nothing compared to the controlled lightning of alternating current. It blackened flesh to the bone and stopped a heartbeat in an instant. No, Tesla was engaged in exactly such a pursuit and everyone in the trade was aware of it, and still the operation was shrouded in secrecy, as if he labored in the black-magic den of some old necromancer, not merely an industrial laboratory built to experiment with electrical energy. There would be precious little experimentation required beyond the state of the art today if direct current was universal in America, instead of the copper-wired thunderbolts that were being employed by this upstart foreigner.

Perhaps, the famed man reflected, it was time to bring one of the boys over from the New Jersey compound—some fellow Tesla is sure to have never met—and have that man apply for a job at Tesla's lab. Now more than ever it was going to be vital for Edison to know his enemy in the war of electrical currents. Maybe he could offer the man a fat bonus for success—a verbal offer, that is.

He realized that he might have to let his man stay on the payroll while the guy also collected a check from Tesla, just to ensure loyalty in the meantime. Let him cash in on his two-paycheck windfall by funneling every tiny fact and nuance of Tesla's work right back to Edison. Tesla was certainly doing more than merely developing elements of Philadelphia's new power grid that the idiot Westinghouse had contracted out to him.

No, something else was going on down the street. It was something much more than the mere manufacture of an urban lighting system. Not that an alternating current system wasn't bad enough in itself, but Edison knew that the real danger lay in whatever line of experimentation Tesla was now underwriting with his newfound wealth.

*If there is anything more dangerous than a crazy man who thinks he's a genius,* Edison quoted to himself, *it's a crazy man who thinks he's a genius and gets his hands on serious money.*

# Chapter Twenty-Five

## Three Years Later
## Philadelphia

Three years went by in the hard world while Nikola lived essentially among his *visions* while his laboratory manufactured working models of his designs. In this manner he gave the hard world its due while he sat back in his tiny rocking chair and kept the lights on inside.

He felt strongly that this time of his life was no less than a full-blown blessing of opportunity, despite the occasional bout of loneliness and the desire for some deeper level of contact than he could find in a billiards tavern. Otherwise his life was exactly as his mother had told him it would be, during that endless carriage ride home from the cemetery after they buried Dane. He may have failed to accomplish great things through the company of Mr. Thomas Edison, but he had prepared himself so well and kept his drive so focused that greatness had come to him by walking right out of the hard world and straight into his laboratory—in the form of George Westinghouse.

His father's ghost no longer held power over him with its accusatory and fearful attacks. The iron spike of fear no longer stabbed his chest when his father's dying curses sprang to mind. As the fear grew weaker, so did his father's ghost. Quieter and gentler moments began to make themselves felt, memories of a man who wanted to be a good father. For the first time in many years, Nikola felt the truth of that.

There seemed to be nothing he could say to persuade his mother to consider moving to America, even though it would guarantee her the best medical care while the cruel frailties of age advanced upon her. But Djouka Tesla derived her *power* from the ground she had walked all of her life; a new land was not a place where she chose to end her days.

At least Nikola's peace of mind on her behalf was boosted by his new ability to send her meaningful amounts of money that ensured that she was as comfortable and secure in her life as he could help her to be. Her pride in him, most of all her approval of his accomplishments, made him feel more solid inside; his feet struck the ground with a less tentative heel and he no longer feared that his personal appearance at social situations required him to be in a tuxedo. Although he kept the same immaculate bathing habits he learned as a boy, he was aware of feeling cleaner in general now, or at least less suspicious that there might be some personal detail he neglected. Over time, it turned out to be a minor revelation of relief for him that despite relaxing his diligence, he continued to arrive everywhere he needed to go in acceptable condition and with matching socks on his feet.

The question if he had been a few degrees too self-critical in the past was a speculation he had no time to pursue. Any part of his awareness not involved in the pursuit, manufacture, and patenting of alternating current devices was occupied in walking through professional association lunches, dinners, publicity gatherings, and in making the rounds of New York City's social elite. They had lately grown frenzied for the company of men who understood this powerful new force, and who, perhaps, had ideas about where a smart investor's money ought to go.

Suddenly, despite being a force reviled by some as a menace to humanity, the so-called "lightning bolt" of alternating current appeared to those in the know as an invisible force that was advancing on civilization with the same inevitability as the thunder trailing a lightning flash. Conjurers of high finance found themselves confronted by the opportunity presented by those many, many thousands and someday perhaps many millions of electrically driven machines, each one waiting to be manufactured by them with operating parts built by Westinghouse Company under Tesla's patents and placed into systems which the conjurers of high finance would devise and sell to, bluntly said, anybody anywhere who needed to accomplish anything.

As the conjurers predicted, within months of buying the Tesla alternating current patents, George Westinghouse's manufacturing wing began flooding all sorts of new electrical products into the marketplace. And because financial mavens do not sustain their lofty heights by sleeping through opportunity, many worldly eyes perceived the same message: *the rotary effect of the whirling magnetic field has proved itself to be perfect for powering any kind of machine. Any machine at all.*

Nearly a year after buying Nikola Tesla's alternating current patents, George Westinghouse sat alone at a table set for two, waiting for Tesla to arrive in the fine restaurant Westinghouse had carefully selected. He had set their meeting in this place hoping the opulent surroundings might somehow dull the blow he had to deliver to his partner and friend.

Now that he found himself actually sitting there, his choice of location seemed ridiculous. What he had been thinking? That a man he was going to rob of a fortune would be mollified if he fed him well first? It hit his conscious mind like a breaking ocean wave; even though Tesla had not even arrived yet, Westinghouse's attempt to tread lightly with the man was already an awkward failure. His wool suit was suddenly too thick for this warm room. It felt fine all afternoon, but now it was a hair-shirt of damp confinement.

He glanced around. The dining room was sparsely filled, so why did it feel so stuffy? He spotted some fellow smoking a pipe by the large fireplace, filling the room with the scent of cherry flavored tobacco. Westinghouse wanted to shout, *What would make a man smoke that fancy garbage?* Did such a man think the aroma recommended him?

Suddenly his lungs felt too small for his body. His chest was that of a big bear of a man and it needed plenty of air; his puny lungs short-changed him with every breath. Thick straps began to tighten around his heart. He could feel the straps, real as dirt, encircling the beating organ and closing in tighter, tighter.

By that point his grim task was already giving him a massive dose of indigestion. His state of turmoil was so intense that he had no idea what he actually felt—or was even supposed to feel. Shame?

Why allow shame? Why should he be ashamed of pouring the company's resources into development of all his alternating current patents? Companies have to grow or they wither, do they not? If his bankers had a mind to call in some of his overextended credit, what was that besides bad luck? The sale of his company was being forced on him, along with the need to think about all his workers and their families.

Of course he could refuse. He could tough it out and try to stare down his creditors long enough to raise sufficient capital. He could defy those who would control him into selling off this company. All he had to do was to be willing to gamble his credibility in the profession and the ongoing needs of his workers and their families. That way, he could heed his moral imperative and pay Tesla's royalties—at the risk of losing everything.

Except that, of course, in the case of a bankruptcy being forced on Westinghouse, the payments to Tesla would stop anyway.

"What a nasty business," Westinghouse muttered into his second slab of buttered bread while he drained his wine glass. "Nasty, rotten business," he added, blotting his mouth with a napkin. "All of it."

Westinghouse knew in his heart that the blessings in his life required his gratitude, but the thought gave him no comfort today. He was especially mindful that the greatest gift he had been granted was not, as many speculated, in having been guided to the inventing of air brakes for trains at the age of twenty. It was not even in successfully winning the U.S. patent on the system that brought him validation from the Universe itself—it was in being allowed to survive the major train wreck that gave him the idea for inventing better brakes for trains in the first place.

And so because he consciously lived on a moral path, Westinghouse recognized that the only morally pure action open to him on this night was to pay the man his royalties and trust in God to bridge the shortfall of capital that would follow. Except that religious faith only requires you to risk your own life for the Lord; it doesn't require you to risk an overall group of men, women, and children who have no say in the outcome, which is what the board members finally made him see after hours of wrangling.

It was, plain and simple, a lesser-of-two-evils situation. He took into account their own bias and still the truth of that remained. Because if God should possibly slip up on maintaining income flow while the Tesla payment obligations were being honored, then along with everyone else who went down with the ship, Westinghouse himself would land on the bottom in ruin, at the age of forty-three. This in an age when a rightly done gentleman retired at fifty.

*You steel yourself by remembering your duty.* The words ran through his mind several times. Everyone kept their job and paycheck as long as Westinghouse allowed this deal. How was he supposed to match up his loyalty to Tesla against that? Still it hurt. It hurt no matter how he explained it to himself, and the hurt got worse for every minute that he waited for Tesla to show. His frustration felt like a mouthful of nails.

The Golden Rule had stood him well as a guidepost all of his forty-three years, kept him away from temptation throughout his long marriage to Marguerite, kept him honest in his business dealings. It had nothing to tell him now.

Westinghouse felt someone's presence close by. When he looked up, Nikola Tesla stood right there next to his chair, wearing a patient smile. He actually looked as if he had been politely waiting for Westinghouse to finish his thoughts. *The man has no idea how to stand up for himself,* he thought angrily while he smiled and gestured for Tesla to have a seat.

He genuinely liked Tesla, despite the fact that most of the man's lab workers resented him for his trademark marathon work sessions. The office joke seemed to be that they should forget about building more efficient motors and instead find out how to manufacture whatever it is that drives Nikola Tesla.

He liked the man in spite of his many eccentricities, but George Westinghouse was no politician and he couldn't bear to beat around the bush over this thing. And so as soon as greetings were exchanged, he cleared his throat a couple of times and launched directly into the news, full of overt apology and the unspoken hope that Tesla would not take him to court in a lawsuit that Westinghouse knew that he could easily lose.

He found it impossible to guess what Tesla was thinking while he regretfully explained about his overexcited business expansion costs and how they may have brought alternating current to the market, well, maybe a little *too* quickly, because now the specter of bankruptcy loomed if the company's cash flow was diverted to pay Tesla's royalties.

Tesla's gaze drilled into him from a face that looked almost empty. He silently already asked himself what he would do in Tesla's position, but the feeling was so unpleasant that he ignored the question altogether and focused his energy on winding up the message.

"So that's the gist of it, Mr. Tesla. And let me tell you, as a man of my word, it cuts me to the quick to have to say it. I know that the royalties I promised you have mounted up, but..." Westinghouse hit a dead end. He could not get the words out.

And the last thing he expected was for Tesla to jump in and save him—

"Mr. Westinghouse," Tesla's smile was broad and warm, "your generous offer made my current work possible. I would not dream of adding to your troubles when every day of my life is now so full of promise."

Westinghouse watched as Tesla pulled a paper from his pocket and unfolded it. Westinghouse immediately recognized the royalty agreement. A cold surge of fear ran through him. It was as if Tesla somehow knew why Westinghouse had asked him here tonight, and came prepared to quote the agreement's language verbatim. He felt a strong need to urinate. Had he severely underestimated this man?

"Here is our royalty agreement, sir," Tesla began.

A moment later Westinghouse's heart nearly stopped in

shock when Tesla tore the agreement in half, put the halves together and tore them in half again.

"What's this?" Westinghouse gasped in astonishment. "What are you doing?"

Tesla tore the pieces in half one more time, then dropped the bits on the table. He spoke quietly, "Men of vision should stand together. Dishonorable behavior is beneath us. Don't you agree?"

For George Westinghouse, the noble sentiment was not the incredible part of the encounter; it was the self-evident fact that Tesla clearly believed every word of it. Quietly, without showmanship of any sort, he spoke with so much conviction his sincerity could not be doubted. He looked Westinghouse straight in the eye, smiled, and patiently waited.

Westinghouse stood up, but carefully; his legs were shaking and felt weak. His eyes filled with tears while he reached out and clasped Nikola's hand. "I won't forget this."

Nikola remained seated and simply lifted his glass to Westinghouse and smiled. "I already have."

Westinghouse sat back down and spoke in quiet and determined tones, "Well sir, then you just say the word and you can stay on here full time with my company and I'll pay you twenty-four thousand a year. That's what my top executives make. You can do your own work in your off hours and live like a king!"

Nikola waved him off. "I appreciate your generosity, but our work here together in Philadelphia is essentially finished and, thanks to you, I can afford to go back to New York." A quick laugh broke out of him. "Now that you have made it possible for my discoveries to spread across the country and soon across the world—think of it!—I am able now to run another lab on a full-time basis for my own experimental work." The same excited laugh got away from him again. He shook his head, swallowed. "There is so much to do." He turned away for a moment and seemed to squeeze every muscle in his body for a couple of seconds before he relaxed and looked back up with a pleasant face.

Neither man was one for small talk. Shortly afterward, when they parted company out on the street, Westinghouse again extended his hand. Tesla regarded him warmly but this time only returned a little bow from the waist. Then he turned and stepped into the street to hail a hansom cab.

Minutes later Westinghouse bounced along in the back of his chauffeured carriage while his indigestion attacked him like a stomach full of burning oil. What just happened?

He came to that meeting prepared to deal with a range of possible responses once Tesla heard the grim news. So much money on the table, many millions perhaps, that it seemed smart to try the element of surprise, hope to get him signed up before he could walk away. And yet there was Mr. Tesla appearing not surprised by this at all, arriving with the royalty agreement already in his pocket.

And at the moment when it seemed that nothing could be any more strange, it turned out Tesla didn't bring the agreement along to use as a legal reference; no, he brought it to tear it up in front of him. He brought it as gesture of thanks and friendship such as Westinghouse had never seen before. So much money, and yet Tesla appeared completely unconcerned simply because he had enough capital to work with, thanks to Westinghouse's purchase of his patents. He showed no doubts about his ability to generate whatever future funding he might need. Apparently, the idea of earning additional money simply to accumulate personal wealth meant nothing to the man.

Westinghouse was boggled. Nothing in his experience guided him in interpreting what had just happened. A reaction of such calm at the loss of such wealth? How could anyone do that?

By this point in the carriage ride Westinghouse was nearly doubled over in pain; he no longer tried to tell himself that it was indigestion. He recognized it for what it was: a combination of the damned shame and the disappointment with his own actions, gnawing away inside him.

He didn't want to feel such irrational rage toward Nikola Tesla. It was just there. He loathed his own sudden desire to destroy Tesla, now the only other person on the planet who knew how badly George Westinghouse was outclassed by a far less wealthy man, a man from another country, a man *ten years his junior.*

He also reviled his burning anger. Although he had no real desire to hold a long knife to Tesla's throat and shove in the tip with the palm of his hand, he would certainly understand if another man did.

He knew the anger reduced him and shriveled his spirit. It was just there. All he could do was hide it and try to think... try to think... but he needed time. He was so full of shame over his anger at Tesla and so diminished by the younger man's equanimity of spirit that he no longer knew how he truly felt about anything.

# Chapter Twenty-Six

### The Fifth Street Lab
### New York

Nikola rode the train from Philadelphia back to New York City, still glowing from the opportunity to make his magnificent gesture of faith and friendship to Westinghouse. After all, the man had done so much for Nikola, bringing his alternating current to the public, allowing him to make that first big step in Nikola's journey to either live up to his gift or outsmart his curse. Why not show him genuine gratitude?

He thought if his current state was typical of what philanthropists feel, then he certainly understood their way of life. The joy of giving; what a thing! His sparkling condition grew deeper when he considered that this was only the beginning of such opportunities to be a benefactor of deserving people. He was barely thirty-three and already a millionaire, a newly-recognized inventor of the first order.

He began to hunger for Karina's presence even more than after she had first appeared to him. While he watched the flickering panorama out the windows, he could feel the hollow place inside of himself that would be perfectly filled if only she were real and there to share the fine feeling with him.

The glowing sensation stayed strong inside of him during the train ride because a definite point of peace had entered his life. He carried the evidence: a letter from his mother received the day before he left Philadelphia. It was full of her love for him, just as her letters always were before the hard world gave him the power to make her old age more healthy and comfortable. But she also told him of her happiness with the extra comforts and the sense of peace he provided to her.

Written confirmation of the good that his work had done for her was a powerful weapon against his father's legacy of torment. The waves of delight and gratitude coursing through him were so powerful that he had to squeeze his muscles especially hard just to carry out normal conversation in the course of traveling.

Once he returned to his South Fifth Street lab in Manhattan, he revived the level of work output back up to what the place had sustained before he left for Philadelphia. There was nothing to interrupt his full immersion in the creative process. Life took on a golden haze so intensely sweet that the only darkness was in his hunger to call out to Karina and try to draw her to him.

It never occurred to him to attempt duplicating the state with anyone he met through his requisite social occasions. Instead he routinely sent the automaton in his place, with just enough awareness to cope with distractions while he curled up in his little mental rocking chair and sat behind his own eyes, observing moments of friendship and loyalty and tenderness passing between others.

Sometimes they were strangers on the street, a mother cooing to a child with such love that she was unaware of anyone else around, or perhaps two lovers strolling arm in arm and quietly laughing at some intensely private joke. He knew that such moments were the things that illuminated most people's lives, but except for his times with Karina, the older he became the less he could find any tolerance for unnecessary human contact.

The fact that his inspirations passed so easily between his imagination and the hard world clearly set him apart from the vast majority of the human race, especially since imaginary objects seemed to appear in front of him. Surely it confirmed that his mission was genuine. Why else had these extraordinary powers come to him? He was after all merely the dunce brother who had been allowed to live after his more promising brother Dane died, and was therefore obligated to bring greatness to the world in the way Dane surely would have done. The mission was so much a part of him that it no longer occurred to him to question it.

But the work was sweet nonetheless. His ability to pay for constructing huge experimental generators gave him the opportunity to experiment with a wide range of frequencies, each one with its own distinct trait. This burgeoning field of discovery captivated him so completely that for days at a time he forgot to be lonely, forgot to sleep, barely ate anything, and lost himself in the beauty of exploring the full spectrum of electromagnetic energy.

Life was so smooth he could barely remember his fears about whether or not the late Reverend Tesla had correctly identified a demon or if Karina's beguiling presence and inspirations were no more than a blend of temptation and trickery. With every passing day, he began to feel less resistance to the idea of trying to bring her back.

The only thing that spared him the urge was to immerse himself in spontaneous number puzzles. He employed them everywhere, distracting himself with challenges such as counting his footsteps and trying to arrive at any destination using a number of steps divisible by three.

At a restaurant table, he could calculate the volume of every bite of food or each sip of water, also limiting himself to amounts of milligrams and milliliters as expressed in numbers divisible by three, but the game could become annoying and get out of hand if he was not sufficiently distracted by other things.

It never occurred to him that there might be a problem with any of this until he found himself compelled to calculate in advance the number of words needed for any verbal response and then speaking in exactly that amount of words and of course making sure that it was always a number divisible by three.

Anytime the game failed to challenge him enough to soak up his extra energy, his old symptoms quickly became apparent. The energy simply bled through his awareness and clogged his visual sense in the hard world. After that, any smooth iridescent surface like that of a pearl seemed to explode with so many moving patterns that it made his eyeballs itch to look at it. The patterns themselves reached out and rubbed the surface of his eyes. Light falling on someone's hair would accent subtle patterns which then lifted up off the hair and got in the way of whatever he was trying to focus on.

Worst of all, unused energy often sprang up on him in the form of out-of-control knowledge. His nearly photographic memory was packed with the latest scientific writings about bacteria, disease, and infection. Coupled with the casual attitude toward personal cleanliness displayed by much of society, he found that he knew far too much about the interpersonal exchange of disease-bearing filth. He was compelled to bring his own napkin to restaurants to wipe down their utensils before touching them, and then went through a stack of restaurant napkins to get through the meal. Eventually his revulsion at the custom of shaking hands kept him from doing it under any circumstances.

Still, in spite of his curiosity and sense of longing, he refused to allow himself to give in the urge to attempt to summon Karina; everything had gone so smoothly for him since he rejected her. As much as he hated his father's interpretation of her presence in his life, he could not overcome the fear of what sort of events he might draw down upon himself by daring to reach out to her yet again.

He curled up for a long rocking session behind his eyeballs and let the automaton take care of everything out in the hard world. His inner mental laboratory was the only place where his attention could be so completely absorbed that he had no time to ache for Karina or feel envious of the tenderness he witnessed passing between so many others around him.

Nevertheless, the knowledge of how deeply his eccentricities were likely to strike anyone who witnessed them convinced him that it was Karina for him, or no one. Public credibility was also essential to his life plan if his inventions were to be embraced by society and allowed to make the contributions they were designed to do. He became convinced that to reveal his eccentricities was to risk being dismissed as a madman.

Which was why it made such good sense to lie low, as the Americans liked to say. His sexuality was so completely sublimated into his work that he retained the ability to admire beauty for its exquisiteness without feeling the need to embrace it. His pain at entertaining an unending series of shallow work and social relationships disappeared into the rocking chair with him while the automaton executed a generally acceptable performance at dealing with people from a formal European style of expression.

On rare occasions when his entire self was needed and he dropped fully into consciousness, it felt like waking from a night's sleep into the middle of a work day. He hit full awareness so hard that he was sometimes vaguely surprised that spray didn't come blasting out of the blow hole in the top of his skull before he remembered that he didn't have one of those in the hard world.

Later in the year, he was able to set aside enough of his energy to memorize the extensive study materials for the U.S. Government's examination to become an American citizen. The process was mostly a matter of quiet patience, but the actual swearing-in ceremony was so moving to him, he entirely seeped back into the hard world to embrace the experience.

He stayed too long. At a large downtown party given in his honor, he had almost completed deflecting an effete young man's persistent attentions by waxing enthusiastic over the similarities between the shape of a bare tree in winter and the forking fan of a lightning discharge. Thus he fell straight into the trap his old professor so vehemently warned him about, allowing far too much of his imagination to flow into ordinary conversation.

"The real difference is time, yes? In both cases, energy is flowing along the arms of the lightning bolt and also along the branches of the tree, regardless of the fact that it operates on vastly different time frames."

And did the young man therefore agree that tree sap was likely to carry the same punch as a lightning bolt, if you have the time to wait around for it to accumulate? And therefore, wasn't the opportunity to harness the energy of a single tree—using that energy to drive a single household, say—simply a matter of manipulating the flow of energy through time? And if that is the case, is not "the manipulation of the flow of energy through time" also an accurate description of the function of an *ordinary electrical condenser…?*

The pretty young man fled, rolling his eyes in boredom. Nikola felt fifty kilos lighter. It was a good time to begin deepening his breathing, allowing his awareness to rise up like a wisp of steam all the way back up to the tiny rocking chair.

But a small, firm hand grasped him just above the elbow and clamped onto his arm like a five-fingered lobster claw. He turned to see the sweetly smiling hostess, Flora, whose gracious demeanor did not match the clutch she had on him.

"Well," she smiled up into his eyes and murmured in conspiratorial tones, "I was afraid I would have to wait all night for everyone else to give you a minute's peace." With her free hand she playfully ran her finger down his cravat and then delicately spun them both toward the wall, giving their backs to the open room and buying a few more seconds of privacy within the crowded place. "I am going to simply come out and say it, Mr. Tesla; my heart jumped, really jumped inside my breast, when I saw that Enrique was not able to, shall we say, elicit interest from you. I know what that would mean. And *I* would have been devastated!" she concluded with a dramatic laugh.

In another few moments, Nikola's automaton would have simply given her its best social smile and babbled with her until an opportunity arose to walk away without causing offense. Her surprise attack interrupted such a vulnerable moment that it was as if all of his nerve endings were suddenly exposed to open air. His physical senses slammed into a state of perception far more open and active than he needed for the situation. The sensory information overwhelmed him. It felt like he was being smothered by a thick wool blanket many times his own weight.

Flora's face was half a meter away, but he could feel her breath on his skin. He could smell the scent of it as clearly as if the eggy flavor of her mouth was pressed onto his tongue. His heightened senses focused on her as well, to the exclusion of most everything else. The smells crowded for attention in his nose, his mouth, his brain. He felt like he could smell her with his skin, with his fingertips. She gave off a symphony of aromas too strong to ignore. Her body was recently bathed and powdered, but a nervous odor was already wafting up from her armpits. Her hair appeared clean and he was thankful that she wore it tied back flat so that it was far less likely to throw off patterns. She had done something to see to it that both sides of her neck smelled like vanilla cookies. Overall, there was a general fecundity to her that convinced him she was so fertile she would become pregnant immediately if the opportunity arose.

She clung to him with a grip that was making his lower arm throb. What did she expect of him, here, in this roomful of people? Nothing about her was clear to him except the curiously disturbing aroma of desperation. She was an heiress, already rich beyond dreaming. What could she want from a man who lived most of his life inside of his mind?

When another guest called out to her he seized the moment and drifted away, eyeing the crowd while he moved. The faces of the other guests looked back at him with a uniquely American expression of unabashed fascination. Their expressions of approval were a new sort of admiration to him, one that seemed to be attracted by a moneyed reputation and fine-tuned by the price of his impeccable suits.

He realized this reaction from the public, even from his peers, was supposed to be tremendously reinforcing, but could not dodge the impression that each pair of eyes was a set of hollow tubes that would suck him down in pieces if they got close enough to attach. He felt ashamed of seeing things that way and was grateful that no one else could hear his suspicious thoughts.

The sensation of not belonging and of being a stranger in unfamiliar surroundings reactivated his hunger for Karina, for the peak rush of energy that always arrived through her. Whenever he imagined the warmth of her presence, he felt a trace of it tease him, the polar opposite of that chilled mental state caused by endless cool reflection. The warmth penetrated him; he could imagine her streaking through his body like deep red light, seeking out the smallest of cold spots and the tiniest of frozen places, penetrating them, warming them back to softness, and restoring them to circulation. He got no more of her than that. A sip to nourish him, to sustain him with a reminder.

In the next moment a sensation of foolishness washed through him like sewer water when he woke up to what was happening. He found just enough self-control to pull away. In another instant and he would have lost his resolve and pitched forward into the desire to will her back.

He clawed his way back to the hard world by constricting his whole body and squinting back the *visions* while he tried to force his attention back onto the party and the physical surroundings.

When he noticed that an imaginary line connecting three of the gas wall lamps formed an equilateral triangle with him at the center point, he held his focus on reality by gazing around for other visual patterns of three. The search itself kept his attention focused on the hard world.

In the end, he escaped his darker suspicions by continuing to move through his rapt audience while he headed for the door. He turned the rest of his escape from the crowd over to his automaton while he allowed most of himself to evaporate back up to the tiny rocking chair behind the picture window eyes.

# Chapter Twenty-Seven

## Months Later
### The Serbian Province of Lika

The telegram warning him of his mother's failing condition pulled him back to earth so hard that slowness itself suddenly became his new enemy. The trip back to Europe nearly drove him mad with anxiety. Throughout the long sea journey he was barely able to avoid being destroyed by his sense of helplessness.

He could afford to travel in fine style, but the comforts of money had scant power to smooth the jagged edges on his dread while the journey dragged. His automaton was left little to do except pace the deck of the ship, regardless of the weather. He retreated upstairs, where he could take comfort in the only genuine luxury of his life. There, while the giant steam engines thundered away in the belly of the ship, his attention began to float away...

*A ship at sea is guided by a magnetic compass, whenever stars are not visible. A magnetic compass is powered by the magnetic field surrounding the planet itself, so that the fact that the ship remains true to its course proves the value of a compass, which in turn proves the existence of earth's magnetic field. A magnetic field must always have positive and negative poles, which implies conductivity of energy within that field. That proves that something inside the planet functions as the core of the battery while the other end is invisibly held in place, high up in the ionosphere, by the planetary field. Therefore the earth itself, along with its atmosphere, may be considered as a single electrical instrument...*

He began to guess at the base numbers for calculating what kind of mass it would require to hold such a powerful field in place. *Existence of a planetary metallic core is strongly implied,* with iron being the best candidate for the core material, given what the crust's substances suggest about the elements deep underneath the surface. It would most likely be liquid iron, because of the heat and pressure at planetary depths...

And since he saw no reason to assume that a gigantic magnetic field would behave differently from the tiny ones generated in the lab, then it would follow that there had to be one or more frequencies that could be generated as harmonic fractions of the basic vibrations of the planetary frequency itself—just as with the basic vibrations of music.

*Working in reverse then, couldn't a signal be generated by an artificial device which would employ harmonic resonation to subtly activate the entire planetary field? These additional vibrations would stand out from the background palate of the planetary field that they could be detected at any other point on the globe, providing universal electrical power without wires simply by inserting a properly tuned antenna into the ground...* And so his reverie went. He stayed out of the hard world until he arrived back at his mother's home.

His emotions held up well enough until he stepped inside the old family house and smelled the faint traces of a home life he thought he had forgotten. Usually his sense of smell was the one he was least aware of; now it opened an unprotected pathway to the part of him who was still a boy who loved his mother. When the hired nurse led him into Djouka's bedroom, his heart sank. He realized that he was about to play out a scene just as he had with his father, sitting by the bedside of one who will not leave it again.

Djouka Tesla had lost nearly all power of speech by this point, but her gaze was fierce and clear when she grasped his hand. Without a word, she somehow radiated messages of love and gratitude and approval to him. He vaguely noticed that some man was crying out in wracking sobs but he could hardly pay attention because Djouka's eyes were locked onto his, caressing his spirit in the private and tender way that no one but a mother can do for her child. He could feel her spirit embracing him, tenderly saying goodbye almost as if she were tucking a warm blanket up around his chin for the very last time. She was leaving the world in a state of peace and allowing no doubt whatever in her son's mind about her love for him.

"You have arrived, Nikola," she whispered. "My pride." She was not able to speak again.

At the funeral service, he remained present throughout the rituals, the burial, and alone at the completed grave site after the others were gone. He tried to pray for her but the sentiments rang hollow. So he gave up and instead just stood silently trying to guess what fates might have befallen him if Djouka Tesla had not been there to keep the jackals away from the strange boy he once was, giving him safe room to grow until he was strong enough to face them alone.

By the time he finished his grave site vigil, evening was falling. He glanced down and noticed that a mist of cool moisture had begun wafting up from the ground. The hint was all he needed and the time was right. He dissolved most of himself into mist, rising through his fatigued automaton and all the way up to his favorite little seat.

After he returned to America, the automaton took on most of the drudgery of running the successful lab, patenting and manufacturing dozens of new devices with commercial appeal. So much money came in that the need for an adequate accounting system was not immediately apparent. To him, cash seemed to flow in on the morning tide. There was always enough credit to cover any shortfalls that came up. Current bills were reliably paid with the next wave of cash.

He accepted frequent requests for speeches at society's top parties for the elite, where he described worlds few people comprehended, made predictions no one believed, and then nearly caused heart attacks with practical demonstrations involving leaping arcs of electrical discharge. He remotely activated lights and gas-filled tubes that lit up in his hand without being wired to any sort of power. The deeply religious observers and the secretly superstitious were often seen fleeing in distress before he finished, not because they were stupid or immune to inspiration, but because it all seemed so out of place at this time and on this planet. Many of them felt as if his inventions must surely be in this world by mistake, intended for some darker place.

Sometimes while Nikola stood at his demonstration table and watched upset audience members bolt for the door, he felt that he loved those people most of all. In another situation, the fleeing ones might come across as brilliant—after all, the first rats to desert the ship have the best chance to survive if it goes down. And so he thought while he watched them flee, *how can you not love them?* In another version of reality, they would be leaving just ahead of certain disaster, perhaps saving their lives.

When Nikola was too busy in his invisible mental workshop to attend a scheduled promotional appearance or an investor's demonstration, the automaton handled speeches well enough that his public presentations became status events. Fame and fortune mounted.

The early 1890s moved ahead so smoothly that he was able to leave just about everything up to the automaton while he rocked in the tiny chair, chewing on the question of the energy of visible sunlight and the energy of an electrical generator and the energy of a growing tree being essentially *the same thing*, with related practical applications. Despite his hours at the lab, he spent most of his time toiling in the one place where he could never invite someone else to watch him work.

New York Society got most of its news from the daily papers and the rest of it from the yeasty fizz of party gossip. As in any era, only a tiny slice of society paid attention to the scientific journals of the day.

But the people with the all money and power did. Thus everybody who mattered among the hard world's movers and shakers heard about it when Nikola Tesla's Manhattan laboratory was awarded a stunning contract from the Westinghouse Electric

Company. He was to design and build an entire alternating current lighting system for the Columbian Exposition at the 1893 Chicago World's Fair. This was a guaranteed bully pulpit for promoting alternating current and getting the public used to the best methods for handling its dangers. The prestigious breakthrough also brought massive new economic forces into the "War of the Currents," as the papers called the struggle between Edison and Tesla.

Nikola gave no thought to Thomas Edison's dismay while interest mounted in the Serbian inventor throughout the public sector—whether or not they comprehended anything he said. The brilliant Serbian preacher's son lacked the passion of his father's faith, but the lessons were not lost on him during the many years of watching Reverend Tesla keep the congregation's rapt attention while gently rattling their pockets.

What Nikola offered in his public demonstrations was better than magic and more personal than a stage show, because he had things of far greater value than fancy scientific words and brilliant displays of logic. He had toys. He had wonderful toys. These toys went far beyond tricks of prestidigitation. They flashed and crackled and zapped the air with showers of sparks that seemed to spew from nowhere. They radiated the same kind of power that could drive entire cities.

The amount of laboratory space consumed by prototypes of innovation was nearly equaled by space consumed with useless show devices. They were built specifically to dazzle visiting congregations and help them understand they were staring into a glimpse of the future.

The practical magic of the demonstrations staggered witnesses: a room made bright by a hundred different light sources while no fireplace, no candles, and no lanterns burned anywhere. For the first time in their lives, speechless visitors were confronted with glowing tubes of colored light. Some of the tubes were twisted into fantastic geometric shapes. The lights shone with such intensity that it hurt to look at them. This astounded people who had never had to turn their eyes away from the brightness of anything but the sun.

Nikola found that his need for sleep was down to a mere two hours a night with no ill effect. He sometimes worked for two days straight with no rest at all.

Now, with his parents gone and his sisters married off and absorbed into their own new families, Nikola's own limited lifespan confronted him with the question of how to invest his remaining years. His challenge was to keep moving toward the visions Karina always brought without being swallowed into the irrelevance of permanent reverie, whose potential grip on him was as real as the hard world.

The Columbian Exposition of the Chicago World's Fair emerged as a gigantic, glittering testimony to the power of the Tesla-Westinghouse electrical systems. Nikola felt the public adoration shine onto him like infrared rays. Their heat passed through his skin and muscles and warmed the very marrow of his bones. Since he could not alter the number of hours in a day, the demands of his increased work schedule forced him to keep on deploying his automaton to handle public appearance duties while he visualized his laboratory, mentally entered it, and spent his time busily content.

His working trance was long and deep. The Exposition glittered all around him while he walked the grounds engrossed in a thought experiment that was soaking up much of his head time. The challenge was to visualize a clear and provable way of testing nature to determine if gravity is generated by *mass itself,* or whether *gravity might instead be formed by pre-existing pockets of electro-magnetic attraction, into which planetary or stellar mass eventually accumulates?* In that case, a star or a planet would not generate gravity on their own; they would simply be there because that is where the attractive force holds them. If that were the case, then the physical matter itself could disappear and the gravitational force would remain.

Either way, he reasoned, since gravity is a fundamental force, there must also be a correct frequency capable of resonating with the gravity waves and canceling them out.

That would create levitation.

And if so, with further adjustment, could such artificial frequencies be increased to overcompensate for gravity's force? This would create thrust. The thrust could then be channeled in any direction and allow rapid travel to any point on the planet, or anywhere in the reaches of outer space.

It was late in the evening on his last night in Chicago when he took a final solitary stroll around the Exposition grounds. His mental wrestling match with the nature of gravitation consumed him so completely that the dazzling lighted spectacle had little effect; it had already existed in his mind for years.

He was still wrapped in his reverie when he passed by Thomas Edison and a gaggle of newspaper reporters while he toured the grounds.

One of them spotted Nikola and called out to him—was this alternating current thing of his going to be an affront to Mr. Thomas Edison's worldwide reputation? The hardened reporters grinned at the effrontery of the question.

Nikola didn't hear them and never saw Edison's face turn red while he passed by without acknowledging any of them. The solitary inventor kept walking, unaware.

Such was the power of Nikola Tesla's aura in that place and on that night, nobody chased after him. None of the reporters called out to him a second time. They just let him continue on.

And so he remained ignorant of the pall that fell over the reporters when they coughed, shuffled their feet, or cleared their throats. Then they turned to Edison to see how the Wizard of Menlo Park was taking this snub from the man of the hour.

They got nothing for their trouble. Not even the pointless insult of a public snubbing was enough to cause Thomas Alva Edison to forget the importance of a man's need to maintain dignity. Edison was nothing if not someone who could bide his time. When you grow up having to sit without fidgeting at every single meal while daddy or mamma offers prayers that can easily go on until the food gets cold as proof of spiritual sincerity, you learn the power of patience.

* * *

It took nearly a year for Edison's carefully restrained outrage to find the appropriate outlet. When the moment arrived, he would have sworn it actually made him feel ten years younger and twenty pounds lighter. Filled with its power, he stormed, or rather walked briskly, into J.P. Morgan's office and threw down, or rather set down, a copy of the July 22, 1894 edition of *The World*. He then bellowed to Morgan, or rather spoke energetically, while Morgan appeared consumed with the task of eating a large bowl of thick soup.

Morgan crunched bits of baguette between his fingers to sprinkle over the surface of the soup. His actions strongly implied there was a great deal more to the business of eating soup than most people understood.

After another few moments of being ignored, Edison cleared his throat and pointed to the magazine. "That is the Sunday edition! Read that part, the part I circled, there. It's just the one paragraph." He waited for a moment and got no reaction, so he bent over the magazine and read the paragraph aloud himself.

"*'Even before the great generators which are now being built at Niagara Falls have been completed, Dr. Tesla has assured this reporter that anyone in good health may expect to live long enough to see the entire country powered by alternating current.'* The entire country!" Edison added, then paused and stepped back for dramatic effect. He wanted a good look when Morgan replied, so he focused on watching the man's lips just to make sure he got everything.

Morgan glanced up at him and nodded in a way that told Edison nothing, then returned to his soup-eating project and crushed another hunk of baguette with his fists. He sprinkled it over his soup in careful circular motions. Edison watched the ritual, suspecting that it was some sort of a Continental thing, and decided to ignore it and keep the topic on the matter at hand.

"Do you see now?" Edison implored. "Do you see *now* what happens when you let a godless lunatic who talks to rain clouds actually gain some measure of influence in the world?"

Morgan glanced up again. "What happens? Hm, what

happens…" He stroked his chin and pretended to ponder, "Let's see: he figures out a way to get power off of Niagara falls, without doing anything to destroy the beauty of the place. A million light bulbs go on, many sold by you, profiting you. Right?"

"People are not—" Edison shouted. He stopped himself, cleared his throat and continued in respectful tone. "People are not qualified to handle this power. Not the general public. You watch, Mr. Morgan, you mark my words when I tell you people will *die* from this alternating current! It's too strong! People will accidentally make contact with those wires in more ways than we can imagine, and every one of those ways will be deadly!"

Morgan spoke with his mouth full, without looking up. "Can't direct current kill people?"

Edison paused, took a breath… "No. Sir. Not at the levels my devices use. You touch it and you get a little buzz that couldn't kill anybody!"

Morgan took a little breath of impatience. Fatigue was setting in. When he spoke it was in a murmur, almost as if he was fresh out of energy to converse. "Using your nice safe sort of power, we have to put up a generating station every mile or so, yes? So that it would require three thousand of them to reach from coast to coast on a *single wire?*"

Edison's heart sank. The butler would be escorting him out momentarily, at Morgan's command. There was no choice left but to play his trump card. It risked blowing the volatile man's temper so completely that Edison's relationship with him could go through the ceiling, but now the move was unavoidable.

"The last part of the article, Mr. Morgan, I did not circle it, but— but— perhaps you should read it!"

Morgan did not move.

Edison continued. "Perhaps you should read it most of all for your *own* interests!" He pointed to the section, waited, got no response. So he continued it himself, "Tesla is already preparing the public for the idea of doing away with transmission line systems as his next phase. No power lines. You hear me? No power lines! 'Unnecessary,'" he calls them.

Edison leaned closer and lowered his voice. "He is referring to hundreds of miles of copper lines that *you* have already invested in, lines that *you* are going to control when electricity reaches the whole country. But now Tesla says the world should not be made ugly by stringing electrical wires all over the place. Power should be wireless. And why not? What should *he* care if he introduces the world to the future?"

Edison knew that if his last ditch effort was to work at all, he had to be bold enough to press the blade home. "*He* won't be the one left stuck with how many millions of dollars' worth of copper wire and the labor to string it, miles and miles and miles of it, all over the country."

Edison turned away and spoke his last sentence without looking at Morgan, then twisted the shaft a second time. "He won't be the one history laughs at."

Edison wanted to jump and scream, dance and shout. *Look! Look at the man's face!* Oh, that one did it, all right. *Shrug that one off, my friend! Laugh about losing your fortune!"*

And because Thomas Alva Edison was nothing if not a practical man, he spoke not another word. He also made certain his own expression did not flicker while shock and anger and outrage traded places on J. Pierpont Morgan's well-fed face, reddening that boozy bulb of a nose. Edison had correctly gambled that Morgan would not direct his rage at him; the financier seemed to recognize that Edison was only speaking the truth. The farm-boy inventor had landed a solid punch. He was surprised that it could feel so good to strike an old man—it was a fine feeling. Edison would have had no moral qualms with the idea of boot-kicking the fool down a long flight of stairs.

*So shrug that one off, Mr. Morgan,* he thought to himself. *Yes sir, imagine a country covered with countless miles of copper wire, a scattered fortune in copper wire: "Morgan's Folly."*

*And then have that manservant of yours bring you more soup.*

# Chapter Twenty-Eight

## 1895
### Hotel Restaurant
### Manhattan

"Mr. Tesla?" Nikola looked up from his restaurant table to see a tall man with thick gray hair and a salted walrus moustache.

"Well," the man added, "you look like the drawings they print of you in the papers." He spoke with the voice of a lifelong American. Nikola was still trying to place the regional accent when the man leaned in close and imitated a conspiratorial tone.

"Your letter mentioned that you dine here every night…"

"I beg your pard—" but then Nikola felt the hard world fall back onto him like a thick book landing on a bare floor. He jumped to his feet, beaming. "Oh! Samuel Clemens! You are Samuel Clemens, yes?" He laughed with delight. "Mark Twain!"

"Whenever necessary." Twain touched the empty chair across from Nikola and asked, "May I?" He was already pulling the chair out by the time Nikola replied.

"Yes! Please! Of course, I am honored!" Caught up in enthusiasm, Nikola began counting off book titles on his fingertips: "*Tom Sawyer*— *Huckleberry Finn*— Why, the name alone: 'Huckleberry.' Brilliant! Who would think of such a thing? And *A Connecticut Yankee in King Arthur's Court*, sir, the truth with which you satirize the concept of royalty is—"

"*But!*" Twain interrupted, holding up his hand. He inhaled deeply and then went on, "I have also read about *your* work, sir." Twain took a moment to light a fresh cigar. "And I was intrigued to hear of an esteemed man of science such as yourself who dares to confess that he is also a reader of popular novels."

"Oh! Well, yes," Nikola enthused. He leaned closer and pleasantly confided, "sometimes it's the only thing I can do to avoid thinking."

"...Ah."

Nikola happily went on, "When my mother died last year, the voyage home was so hard. It was the fine stories in your books that kept my spirits up while we were at sea."

Twain slapped his thigh in delight. "There! *That's* more like it! I came here trusting that you would be a fine conversationalist and already you show promise! As for the distraction factor of the books themselves, I can only say that I wish it worked on me. But come, my place isn't far from here." He glanced around with mock disapproval. "I'll wager my Cognac is better than theirs."

Twain stood and gestured toward the door with his cigar, smiling. "And of course I am eager for more admiration. Feel free to wax eloquent regarding the fine stories in my books, that sort of thing, whatever you like."

Twain politely ignored it when Nikola stood up wearing an undignified smile of delight. Instead the famed writer took Nikola's arm and walked him toward the door. "Use your imagination with the compliments. An inventive fellow like yourself? You'll do fine."

On the front steps of Twain's Manhattan townhouse, he and Nikola each sat on comfortable padded rocking chairs. Nikola was especially interested in the way the chair fit him, and Twain stared intently into the sky. Each one held a glass and both men had long since lost track of time. A nearly-drained decanter of cognac sat on a small table between them.

At Nikola's South Fifth Street laboratory, the front door splintered with a loud crash. Two dark-clothed men in heavy boots ran inside the darkened building.

\* \* \*

"All right, then," Nikola said to Twain, "what about the moment you first became aware of your destiny as a writer?"

"Oh. Well! Without hesitation, it was at the end of my very first day as a riverboat pilot." Twain took a sip and sighed at the memory. "Just as I stepped ashore, this extraordinary young beauty came strolling by, with her aged auntie."

"Auntie?"

"Auntie, mother. Point is, I knew they saw me, in my Captain's hat, and I wanted nothing more in this world than to meet this stunning creature. At that moment I could feel, for the first time, that I had the power of words and images that would reassure the older lady while beguiling the younger."

Nikola laughed out loud, enthralled.

Twain continued, "Of course, by experience I also knew that I would become hopelessly tongue-tied in the close presence of such beauty, and so I just watched her pass, with her auntie."

"It was her auntie, then. Not her mother."

"She even glanced back. I was too shy to smile! Can you imagine? What a waste. At that moment, that very instant, I realized that I would come to no good in this life. Lie, steal," he took another sip, "write novels. A shameless activity, to be sure. I just love the idea of being a freelance writer. My lance is free, bound by no flag, servant to no royalty."

"I understand! Yes. Mine too."

Unseen hands poured kerosene all over the floors of the darkened lab, the walls, the equipment. A flaming match fell into one of the puddles and a greasy blast of orange and red boiled upward. It rolled across the ceiling and throughout the room.

Nikola was feeling loosened by the wine. "Mr. Twain, surely you realize that your work has an element of magic to it. I truly believe that."

Twain raised his glass in salute. "Thank you. My magic is powerless to return my daughter from the dead, but thank you. I may despise my isolation but I do love well-phrased flattery. Your isolation, however, appears to be something you've chosen."

All three floors of the South Fifth Street laboratory—Nikola's creative home for six highly productive years—were fully engulfed in flame within a matter of minutes. The searing heat soon began to eat deep into the supporting timbers, which began to give way, one by one.

Nikola nodded. "Most of my isolation is necessary to my work. But there is someone. It's fair to say she sets me on fire with inspiration. The difficulty is that when I accept her creative gifts, it seems to attract disasters. They then destroy the very work she made possible. Some sort of a curse. A man doubts his sanity when that happens… And so for a long time now, I only work. Perhaps if I am to live up to my destiny, I must do without female companionship, the responsibilities of marriage, children. Do you agree?"

Twain threw back his head and laughed a full belly laugh for the first time that evening. It took him awhile to recover his voice. Even then all he said was, "Well now, Mr. Tesla. Perhaps you're not as smart as people say."

Nikola asked what he meant by that, but the author didn't seem to want to discuss it any further. He urged Nikola to relax and have another cognac while announcing his intention to do the same.

The entire laboratory building was fully engulfed and ablaze against the black sky by the time the fire company set to work. All they could do was save the neighboring buildings while the roof and the floors of the lab collapsed into each other and the iron and copper machinery inside the laboratory melted down to piles of slag.

\*   \*   \*

Nikola realized that if he was ever going to dare the Big Question that he craved to ask this renowned author, a man he so greatly admired, this would be the time. "Mr. Clemens, when I first read your work, I thought perhaps you also—" he stopped, took a deep breath. "Mr. Clemens, could there be such a thing as a muse? I mean, have you got, ah…"

Twain appeared to need a moment to grasp the idea. "Have I got a muse?"

"Yes!! Yes. Or anything one might, one might call…"

"A muse."

"Well. Yes."

Twain let out a long sigh, rubbing his eyes. "Mr. Tesla, everyone—or I should say, everyone in that tiny slice of today's civilization who can and does read—where was I? Yes. Everyone is aware that you have successfully designed magical machinery that will soon harness the energy of Niagara Falls. Astounding feat! There is even cause to believe that you will provide the world with free electrical power. And yet, your major point of *concern* is a question like this? Are you not essentially trying to determine how many angels can dance on the brim of your grandmother's hat?"

"No, I am referring to an unseen, conscious entity! One whose sole purpose in this world is to inspire." He dropped his voice and whispered intently, "Sir, I need to know. I *must* know!"

Twain leveled a penetrating gaze at Nikola. He held it there while he sipped his drink. He sipped again. Finally he turned toward the stars and stroked his moustache a few times before he replied, "I can only take it that your intention is to goad me, sir," he took a puff on his cigar, "until I am forced to reach over and slap the backside of your head."

Nikola stared at him for a moment, absorbing the reply, then lifted his glass and quietly sipped his drink.

Shortly after sunrise the next morning, Fritz Lowenstein stood with a group of lab assistants at the site of the South Fifth Street lab building. All of them wore gray faces and expressions of shock while vapors from the smoldering remains wafted all around them. Lowenstein was beside himself, speechless with horror. He turned to a recently hired young assistant, a young cub in his early twenties named George Scherff. Scherff somehow managed to look even more badly shaken than Lowenstein. And in Lowenstein's stunned state he spoke to Scherff as if they were intimate friends.

"God in Heaven!" Lowenstein's voice broke. He swallowed and started again. "All of the Company assets were in that lab! And Mr. Tesla plowed every cent of his own fortune back into it as well!"

Scherff took a stab at the positive side of things. "Yes, but everyone is safe. And with the fire insurance, well, surely Mr. Lowenstein, everything can be rebuilt! Can it not?"

Lowenstein averted his eyes. It took Scherff a moment to make the connection, then the question tore itself out of him, "The business *does* have fire insur…" He stopped when Lowenstein dropped his head so far that his chin touched his chest.

Scherff ventured again, "At least you remembered to insure the equipment? Right? Or the tools? At least the *tools*?"

Lowenstein's anguished reply seemed more like part of an appeal to God than an answer to Scherff. "Mr. Tesla trusted me to handle business matters ever since we met!" He spun to Scherff and fiercely whispered, "And I have been honest! To the *last cent*!" Then Lowenstein's face fell, his eyes went dull, and he turned away, shaking his head. A moment later he ventured a final glance at Scherff.

"But I've always been absent-minded about things. Certain things. Always just little things, though. Damned details. Little things."

"*Little* things?" Scherff repeated.

At that point Lowenstein covered his mouth with one hand and walked away without looking back. He kept walking, even while he took a deep breath and barely spoke aloud, "It's a curse in my life, that's what it is. A goddamned curse."

George Scherff turned toward the ruined building and

studied it in the emerging daylight. Nothing was left but a pile of blackened rubble and the wisps of smoke. His vision was blurry; there had been no time to grab his glasses when Lowenstein pounded on his door that morning before sunrise and yanked him outside, shouting about disaster at the laboratory. Now Scherff had to squint his eyes to make out a vague form before him in the rubble.

The lanky form was familiar. He moved toward it and soon found himself walking toward his employer, who seemed to be alone there in the smoking ruins. Scherff didn't mean to intrude, merely to get close enough that his eyes could focus on the details of the wreckage. It felt as if there was some duty to see this, an obligation to look closely and see for himself what had happened here.

Scherff had worked with the Tesla lab long enough to be aware that this devastation was a loss to the world's future, more so than the public would ever suspect. When his eyes finally focused, he was within a couple of yards of Mr. Tesla, who was down on his knees sifting ashes next to the charred remains of a piece of apparatus. Scherff stopped in his tracks. The agony inside the inventor was carved into his face. Scherff's heart was torn by the sight of it.

The thought that he was looking at the remains of an accidental fire never occurred to George Scherff. Neither did it cross his mind to believe that the perpetrator(s) would ever be found. But now this cruel twist of fate about nonexistent insurance coverage, why, it was almost as if somebody had connections good enough that they could find out in advance if someone else was insured against fire.

Nikola rose to his feet and shuffled forward a few steps, wandering in shock. The torment of the moment extended beyond the loss of the lab and all of its contents. The rusty blade of it was twisted by the knowledge that for him to have sacrificed years of her presence had been a foolish waste. He had feared allowing her into his consciousness, thinking disaster would follow, but disaster found him anyway. The sacrifice was for nothing.

*It was a cowardly waste, worst of all,* he thought. By closing himself off to her in some bid for his own safety, he gave away time they might have had together.

The burned smell of the ruined laboratory was sharp enough to cut at his nostrils. The effect was like a strong waft of smelling salts. Things once murky became transparent; if disaster was to stalk him whether or not Karina was manifesting in his life, then he wanted the experience of her back again.

In one changed moment, he accepted her without reservation and without needing to understand her. How much, after all, did he truly understand about his own abilities? And yet he had based his whole life on them.

Was such an unlikely thing as bringing her back into his life even possible anymore? If it could be done, he swore never to entertain any notion that demonic forces could be behind her. Never again.

He wondered how he could have feared such a thing. In spite of his father's raging curses, why had he not seen then what was so clear to him now?

Another wisp of acrid smoke caught in the back of his throat and set off a racking cough that doubled him over. He became dizzy, and out of the dizziness rose a realization so powerful that it struck him with an explosion of vertigo. He saw with clarity that if his life should end at that instant, and if consciousness truly survived the death of the body, then when he looked back on his existence, his greatest memories would revolve around Karina. It did not matter that he was unable to define her. He was unable to define himself.

*But I shut her out. I closed my heart to her.* With that thought, fear struck him again with the suspicion that he had made a terrible mistake, one he might never repair. After this awful day the single ray of light shining on the ruins of his life was that the destruction of his work had also annihilated his reasons to close her off. The destruction was stark proof that avoiding her never advanced his mission, bolstered his work, or even saved him from calamity. After today, there was nothing to be done about the pointless sacrifice but to end it.

He stumbled a few steps in a small circle, muttering under his breath while he tried to give words to his feelings. The words made no sense and he did not care; he only needed to feel her energy in his life. The words would not come to him but the feelings poured out of his heart. He apologized for failing to understand her and he begged her to return.

A young woman's shadow passed across the ground next to him; he glanced up from the wreckage and saw her outline silhouetted by the rising sun. He nearly blurted out her name, but she shifted in the light and he saw that she was not Karina. The young woman who was not Karina scowled at the crazy man among the hot ashes.

His strength faded again, and he sank to one knee. He was still in that position when another shadow fell over him. This time it was George Scherff, who had seen enough, glasses or not. When he kneeled next to Nikola his breath was ragged.

"Mr. Tesla?" he spoke softly. "It's me, George Scherff."

Nikola offered a vacant smile and resumed sifting through the ashes, as if in a trance. "George Scherff. I know. Good man. Enthusiastic. George, there must be something we can salvage here."

"Mr. Tesla—"

"Out of all the tools, the equipment. There must be something."

"Sir. Mr. Lowenstein can't bring himself to face you. He knows that this terrible thing has left you completely stranded, sir. Foolish as he was, I'm sure he made an honest mistake."

Nikola's voice was barely audible, "I don't doubt that."

"It's odd that sometimes the worst things that happen don't come from our enemies, but from our friends."

Nikola burst into an unhappy laugh and squelched it as quickly as he could. "Oh, yes. And I hope you can forgive me, Mr. Scherff."

"Why? Whatever for?"

"You have only been with us for a few weeks, and it's already over. Everything was taken and there's nothing to rebuild with. I am forced to send you out to look for work."

"Sir, I've followed your developments for years. I don't want to go anywhere else."

"Mr. Scherff, we are in the middle of a pile of ashes."

"Yes, sir. And I want to stay with you anyway. I know what you're trying to achieve. I want to be a part of it. I have to. That's all."

Nikola smiled in spite of himself, charmed by Scherff's youthful enthusiasm. "Thank you kindly, young man. But unless you fancy eating ashes for supper, you will have to do something to earn a living."

"I already am, sir! When Fritz hired me, I kept my old night job at the factory." He grinned sheepishly, "in case you didn't approve of my work."

"You've been working all night while you work here every day?"

"Just these last six weeks. I didn't know if I could go on such little sleep, but being with you has been so exciting. I'm hardly ever tired."

"Even so, your work has been exemplary."

Scherff beamed at that. "You see? To hear you say that!"

"...Well. Small enough consolation now."

"I don't ask for consolation, sir. I want to offer it."

Nikola was not sure he heard that right. "You what?"

Scherff jumped in excitedly, "If you'll only allow me to stay on with you, help you rebuild. I'll work for no salary. That's the thing—I still have my night job!"

Nikola's hearing still seemed to be playing tricks on him. "Work for no salary?"

"I mean it, sir! I'm sure we can find a way to continue. I'll knock on every door of every financier in New York. I only ask that you promise you'll let me stay on with you if we can get started again. *When* we get started again."

Nikola's eyes filled with tears. "Mr. Scherff, you are an outstanding young man. I will make you that promise, but I want one in return."

"Name it."

"If this schedule begins to take its toll, give me your

promise that you will abandon me before you risk losing the job that feeds you."

Scherff beamed. "There's an easy promise to make, because I won't have to quit! I know we'll find help from somewhere!"

Nikola could only gaze at him, speechless. Scherff grasped his arms and helped him to his feet.

"Come along now, sir. This is no place for you to be."

Nikola started to object.

"No, Mr. Tesla," Scherff protested, "You go home and rest. I'll stay here and sift through to see if there's anything we can salvage."

Nikola stared at him, stunned. His lips formed a tiny smile. "That we can salvage."

"Yes, sir." Scherff gently led Nikola out of the smoldering ashes while he signaled one of the men to hail a taxi for the boss.

The following day the *New York Times* trumpeted that "The wizard and rival of Thomas A. Edison was completely burned out."

*The New York Sun* labeled the destruction a "misfortune to the whole world" and added, "It is not in any degree an exaggeration to say that the men living at this time who are more important than this young gentleman can be counted on the fingers of one hand, perhaps on the thumb of one hand."

Nevertheless, the origin of the fire was never placed under criminal investigation.

# Chapter Twenty-Nine

## The Hotel Gerlach
## New York

George Scherff was determined to avoid disturbing Mr. Tesla until he could bring him news worthy of lifting a broken man's spirits. He knew how rough things were at the Hotel Gerlach, over near Madison Square Garden; Mr. Tesla was incommunicado and would not even respond to visitors by speaking through the door.

But George also knew he was the ideal candidate for this challenge. His internal voltage was high and provided hope that he would find someone to pull Mr. Tesla out of this jam. It overrode any hesitation he might have otherwise suffered about such a mission.

He had to wonder how much money it would require to restart the operation. Certainly not much from some rich fellow's perspective. George had worked with Mr. Tesla long enough to know that the only challenge to this new mission lay in getting somebody, the right somebody, to just *watch* the man demonstrate his work. Then if they were smart enough to put together two plus two, they could see here is someone who has to be given working space and plenty of raw materials: sheet metal, copper wire, an array of tools. It was only right. This inventor was actually bringing forth an entirely new branch of scientific exploration and all of its opportunities.

When Scherff asked himself who would have knowledge of where to go for funding, he realized that Fritz Lowenstein would have plenty of information on who had the money and the inclination toward this new field. First thing the next morning, if Lowenstein was still too badly shaken to offer any personal help, Scherff determined to somehow persuade him to hand over that information, a few names if nothing else. That would be enough for him to approach them himself.

Nikola lay in the shadows of his darkened hotel room and kept himself as numb as possible by focusing his attention the intricate patterns of the room's Victorian wallpaper. He reached out with his eyesight as if he were touching a fingertip to the wall and slowly, steadily, traced the pattern's curves and twists. He never allowed his vision to focus on an area wider than a few centimeters. The rigors of his careful tracing project numbed most of the scalding pain that the disaster burned into him. The process helped prevent the remnants of his life from crushing him.

His eyes tracked the curling lines on the walls and slowly rode the interlocking patterns from one corner of the room all the way around and back to the other side. Each circuit took him approximately ninety minutes and nine seconds—handily divisible by three and more reassuring for it. He did three circuits in a row each time without interruption, then took a few moments to move around the room or to relieve himself down the hall. That much physical activity drained him, so he lay back and started the tracing process all over again.

It was late on the second day before sleep found him. By the time his eyelids at last began to droop, small gaps between the window curtains showed that the second day's light was nearly gone.

He felt no awareness of falling asleep or of feeling his eyelids close, so he failed to notice that he had switched from the view of wallpaper patterns to the view in his mind's eye. The transition was so smooth it never occurred to him to wonder why or how he found himself gazing far out into a night sky.

His vantage point seemed to be above the misty cloud cover beneath a crystal-clear dome of stars. He began tracing the patterns of recognizable constellations. He didn't get far;

a tiny movement in the corner of his eye made him shift focus slightly below his eye line. In the next moment, she was there. And just as it had always been with her, his sense of need to demand answers about her origin and resolve the question of his sanity completely left him.

"Where are we?" he felt himself whisper.

"Nowhere," she smiled. "This is a dream."

There was an explosion of light and sound that overcame his senses for a moment. When he got them back, Karina was in his arms with her own arms tightly wrapped around him. The feel of her grip was real.

She laughed and the sound of her laughter ran through him. When she lightly stroked her fingers across his face, he immediately reappeared back in his hotel room and found himself flat on his back in bed. There was still almost no light coming into the room from outside and no lamps lighted within, but now he saw the brightly colored wallpaper as clearly as if one of his arc lamps illuminated the area. The scrolling patterns separated and defined patches of color in their hollow spaces.

And with the first sight of the bright colors, her message arrived in one fell swoop: *colors are distinct from one another because the colored surface only reflects back those wavelengths of light that would be associated with each color. Just as different wavelengths express different tones of sound, so do differing wavelengths express what is called color.*

With that he realized he could allow each color to represent a musical tone, translating each color's light waves into their comparable component in sound waves. Combined shadings of color could become complete chord structures and make music.

In that single instant, the knowledge became real to him— all he had to do was run his eyes along the same wallpaper patterns, and this time the colors translated themselves into sounds, tones, chords, full melodies. He moved his gaze from one piece of the wall to the next, and the walls sang to him. He flicked his gaze around the room, searching out other color patterns—all of them sang. Some sounded their melodies in tune while others screeched a torture of noise. Some were brief little bird calls; others played out subtle chords and complex interwoven melodies.

His spirits gradually began to lift, and after a few more days was finally enough to lift his spirits and lure him out of the darkened room in search of new patterns. Store windows would be full of them, he realized. The park too. Even the sky, it turned out, was a symphony of shaded clouds amid the blue of the atmosphere.

The hunt for color him out of isolation. He set the automaton to the task of taking care of rudimentary chores and listening to the unbearable speeches of condolence that well-meaning others hastened to offer as soon as he emerged from his self-imposed isolation. The automaton offered terse answers to the same few questions over and over, cringing every time it was necessary to admit that the lab had not been insured. He knew from their eyes that most people figured such carelessness deserved harsh consequences.

Since the automaton barely felt pain, he allowed it to take most of the blows for him while he played sky music with his eyes. He kept a reasonable illusion of social function in place while his true self swam in the sea of images. He never mistook them for the hard world, but they were just as clear and present to him, all the same.

The automaton was sitting alone on a wintry park bench tossing seeds to pigeons when Nikola found himself yanked back into the hard world so abruptly he was left reeling. It happened at the moment his eyes focused on George Scherff, who had apparently come looking for him. Scherff radiated excitement and delight.

"Sir! We have it! You have it! Congratulations! The support is out there! There are people who understand! They know your work must not be allowed to falter!"

Scherff explained that he had indeed found a benefactor, a Mr. Stanley Adams, who would put up an immediate forty thousand dollars, plus provide work space. He was willing to do it on very favorable terms just for the privilege of being in partnership with Nikola Tesla. The money was available at that very moment, waiting in Mr. Stanley Adams' New York office.

The only proviso was that Tesla should employ his benefactor's grown son at the new laboratory. "Naturally," Scherff explained, "I accepted on your behalf, because as long as he shows up, there's always something he can do. And if he doesn't show up, problem solved!" He laughed in spite of himself.

Nikola was so moved by Scherff's loyal accomplishment that the two men spent the rest of the evening over a long celebration dinner. Throughout the evening, he stayed inside of the present moment and there was no pain. The company was as warm as those friendships Nikola sometimes watched between other men. For those few hours, he got a glimpse into what kind of relationship he might have had with his brother Dane. Even though George Scherff was a good ten years younger, the protective attitude he displayed toward Nikola made him feel safeguarded in a way he had not in many years.

The routine of setting up the laboratory was enough to fill the coming weeks. Most of it was automaton-level work, so Nikola had no real need to attend. His excess energy manifested an abundance of fresh compulsions if he left it alone. His senses themselves were thus affected, strangely heightened. The noise of a crowd was deafening. The smell of a warm room full of people nearly took him off of his feet. He occupied his compulsive energies with challenges such as counting every step he took throughout the day and adding up the sub-totals of steps used to walk to and from any given destination. He forced himself to work it out, so the last step he took from the floor into bed at night created a final total that was evenly divisible by three. He had no conscious reason for it, merely a strong sense of taboo over failing to do it.

After the new lab got up and running, Stanley Adams' son proved himself so incompetent that he was a genuine detriment. Nikola had to return to physical reality to finesse his way through the tricky challenge of firing the boss's son without having to close down the lab altogether. As it turned out, either the father understood his son's shortcomings more than he cared to admit or else he had begun to understand that the Tesla partnership was too valuable to jeopardize. The lab stayed open.

With that crisis averted, Nikola disappeared back into the timeless place to work on the continuing mystery of whether or not gravity could be vibratory in origin. *Even if a solid granite mountain range was measured as having more gravity than the surrounding land because of its greater density, perhaps that density itself merely reflects a harmonic overtone of the same vibratory energy which creates the gravity pocket that attracted the planetary matter into a revolving ball, so the harmonic points within the earth's gravity field would be where the denser matter would congeal.*

He mentally searched for any proven science that prevented the concept from being possible. One problem especially consumed him: how to design a means to seek the proper vibrations to create or negate gravity? Just as he once discovered through experimentation that a sound wave can be "cancelled out" by an identical sound wave travelling out of phase with the original, it stood to reason that if the vibration of gravity could be experimentally determined, then the same cancelling-out procedure of beaming the wave back at itself in opposite wave phases should stop the pull of gravity in that location. His imagination staggered under the implications for the fields of heavy construction and transportation.

It was in that private place where he ceased to have any meaningful grasp of the flow of time. The through-line of his work and its challenges were the only markers of his life. If not for the loneliness, it would have been as close to heaven as he could imagine.

Even more of Nikola had to stay present in the following year, when the great Tesla/Westinghouse generating plant at Niagara Falls successfully started up and created international acclaim. It required a major portion of his energy each day to cope with the promotional speeches and the society party appearances and the unending social challenges, because they often blended with technical conversation that required his full attention. When slow moments between occasions allowed his senses to overflow with excess energy, his compulsion to count things and divide them by three returned in full force.

His heightened sense of smell also began to trouble him. He repeatedly found himself feeling physically revolted during encounters with men and women who seemed to know little about personal hygiene and to care even less. His fertile imagination plagued him with thoughts of the many kinds of microscopic colonies that lived in the unwashed head hair of such people. When they brushed their hair against him in a crowd it nearly caused him to vomit. Now that people on the streets were regularly recognizing him in the wake of the Niagara publicity, he found it necessary to wear cotton gloves everywhere he went because so many people insisted on grabbing his hand and pumping it up and down.

He realized that such things bothered him more than they had in the past, but there was no accounting for the feelings when they arose. Physical concerns were dwarfed by his increased awareness of his own loneliness. It flooded him whenever too much of his awareness was present in the hard world. The sound of public laughter made it worse. More than anything else, the sound of crowds of people getting together and talking and laughing made him realize his choices had sealed him off from such things. With practice, he had developed a smooth and charming demeanor for use at social occasions which served its practical purpose but brought no real pleasure.

Karina sometimes came to him while he slept, or at least he had perfectly convincing dreams that she did. In them he celebrated all the reasons why he had no cause to envy anyone over anything. In them there was no need to seek comfort elsewhere.

He could feel her leading him farther down her mysterious trail when he was compelled to spend several months of 1898 attending to a dazzling exhibition to be held at Madison Square Garden. The compulsions she visited upon him held him in their grip, but through them he managed to stun a capacity crowd with his newly patented remote-controlled boat. It shocked them to see an iron boat barely two meters long maneuvering itself in intricate patterns across the surface of a giant water tank. When he concluded the demonstration by removing the top of the boat so that people could see for themselves there was no dwarf pilot inside, those who didn't suspect witchcraft were openly amazed. The concept of radio communication was itself a brand-new idea for most of the public, and the invisible control of a mechanical object was a futuristic phenomenon that boggled everyone who witnessed it.

She led him further still. Later the same year, when his patent was approved on a guidance system for use inside of a remote-controlled rocket, he was flushed with gratitude for the turnaround in his fortunes and so confident of having hit his professional stride that an expansive mood spread through him.

That mood and its attendant generous spirit motivated him to write to the U.S. War Department with the news of his new invention. He asked for an appointment to come in and meet with someone who could listen to his plan to build an arsenal of automated weapons that would be capable of operating in battle without human presence, saving many lives. He insisted that automated machinery could do heavy and dangerous work while human controllers stood back. He openly suggested that the specter of possessing such powers, once demonstrated for all the world, might in itself serve to keep enemies at bay.

If his fascination with the field of remote-controlled machines had not absorbed so much of his mental energy, he might have followed up on the letter to the War Department. But he remained in an ecstasy of creative inspiration while Karina led him further into his visions.

And so, having sent that letter, he simply let go of it. The tiny amount of mental energy that it took to write it went back into his general mission. He never bothered to mention to anyone at work that he had written to the government about robot workers and automated war machines, so there was no one else to follow up on it for him after he became distracted by his next project.

This effectively removed all opportunity for anyone to inject a common sense point of view into the situation and ask Mr. Tesla whether he was absolutely certain that the response to such a letter would represent a nation's gratitude.

## Chapter Thirty

### 1889
### New York

J. Pierpont Morgan's office was still as much the Lair Of The Alpha Male as ever, but on this particular day he found himself sitting upright with his hands folded neatly atop his desk and an attentive expression fixed to his face. Morgan even squinted a little while he listened, just to make it clear that he was paying careful attention to the man from Washington.

"So this was the fifth attempt we made," the man continued, "and I just happened to be the one who got lucky and managed to get hired. George Scherff told me that he was doing the interviewing that day because Tesla was occupied with something he couldn't interrupt. We understand that he usually does all of the hiring himself."

Morgan nodded, just to make it abundantly clear that he had listened and understood. "Yes, well I'm sure he has to. There must be plenty of inventor types who would love to infiltrate the laboratory of a *bona fide* electrical wizard."

"If that's what he is," the G-man countered.

"Oh well naturally. If. Cigar?"

"Do you mind not lighting up while I'm here?"

"Not at all! Filthy habit, truth be told."

"Tesla," the G-man prompted the topic.

"I'm listening."

"He needs to prove himself to the country that adopted him. To the people who run things. After all, this place made him rich and famous."

"He's not rich anymore. Lost it all in a lab fire."

"Is that America's fault?"

"Well no."

"Of course not. So. The question is, *why* would he contact the federal government with such fantastic claims and then drop the matter entirely?"

"And as I've said, I don't know."

"Was it a veiled threat?"

"I don't know."

"Did he just want our *top people* to think that if they don't help him achieve these things, he is just as likely to go somewhere else?"

"I couldn't say."

"Seek support from some monarch who would be happy to turn around and use them to attack American interests?"

"Our way of life."

"Precisely! Now Washington is curious; a man with the brain capable of doing half the things this Tesla can do... *what kind of politics* does this man have?"

"He's never said a political word to me, you understand."

"Never?"

"Oh no. Not one time."

"Do you find that odd? I mean, isn't it normal for people to make political remarks—you know, just passing remarks about politics? Maybe a particular politician?"

"Mm, now that you mention it, I'd have to agree. Most people *I* know do that."

"Of course they do. It's normal. American. Washington knows that."

"Really? The whole city?"

"Mr. Morgan, are you employing an ironic tone?"

"I'm sorry. It was just the way you said 'Washington.'"

"Because a tone like that indicates to me that you may not appreciate how deeply it will affect your little personal empire here if Washington gets tired of turning a blind eye to your attempts to build an industrial monopoly."

"I *told* you—there are no monopolies! It's a free country. People can go into any business they want."

"Unless it's something *you* want."

"All right let's remain calm here. I was having a little humor about the way you said 'Washington' which I can see is not what you care for, yourself. So that's it. No joking."

"Thank you."

"So you were saying?"

"I was saying that Washington is interested in infiltrating him because we need to answer these questions. He took a sharp breath and got down to the core of things. We cannot help but wonder if you are a loyal enough citizen to offer to bankroll his so-called worldwide power research."

"Bankroll? With whose money?"

"As an investment."

"Mm. How much of my money, then?"

"Well. I'm not a businessman, but enough for him to do the work. I'll be there to see that the experiments are continuing; somebody else will keep in touch with you."

"What? Who's going to keep in touch with me? I've only spoken to you."

"So that's it for tonight. You have ten days to get the financial connections put together."

"All right... all right. But I should stay out of it myself, correct?"

"It's late. Good night, Mr. Morgan. I'll show myself out."

"Just a moment! Now then, in return for my cooperation — which I am happy to provide, but nevertheless we are at a delicate stage right now. May I safely assume that Washington is willing to guarantee that it will not involve itself with my business concerns?"

The man from Washington smiled the gratified smile of a petty bureaucrat who has just humbled an industrial giant.

"Yep. The whole town."

"Now see here just one minute!"

"We'll be in touch! Toodle-ooo!" the man from Washington openly sneered while he walked out and shut the door.

Morgan sat staring at the closed office door with outrage flashing in his eyes. He did not move or speak a word. For several silent moments, all he could do was breathe.

\* \* \*

Nearly a week passed before the poisoned arrow found its mark. Nikola was halfway through a relaxed dinner in the dining room of the Waldorf Astoria hotel, seated at his customary isolated table for two. For some reason, he had pulled the chair across from him slightly out from the table and appeared to be concentrating on his plate while he idly played with his food.

From time to time, he glanced up at the empty spot across the table. Each time he looked back down, the corners of his lips twitched with a barely concealed smile.

"Mr. Tesla, I believe?"

Nikola looked up to see an expensively tailored man who appeared to be about Nikola's age. "Yes?"

The gentleman extended his hand. "John Jacob Astor, at your service."

Nikola quickly stood and did a slight bow instead of grasping Astor's hand. "How do you do, Mr. Astor. I know of you, of course."

Astor withdrew his hand and smiled. "Well, only because I was lucky enough to be born into my father's fortune. But sir, I see you are alone and wonder if you might allow me a few minutes of your time?" Astor grabbed the empty chair across from Nikola and plopped himself down in it without waiting for an answer.

"I have a most interesting business proposition, Mr. Tesla. Please, sit! Are you all right?"

Nikola clenched his muscles and squinted, then stood up straight and smiled. "I'm fine, thank you." He took his seat.

Astor's eyes gleamed with excitement while he began to speak in confidential, urgent tones. "I am not here representing the Astor family's interests, sir. I have a private source of funding—confidential source, you understand—and I would like to use it to sponsor your experiments with the worldwide power system, just as you've described it for the press."

Nikola laughed. "I see you do business in the same fashion as George Westinghouse."

"Excuse me?"

"Bluntness. Very American. I like it. Saves time."

"Well. Thank you." He leaned close and again adopted the confidential tone. "The plain truth is that I'm thrilled to be able to make you an offer like this; I've been following your articles for years now, and this grasp that you have—of the very fundamental nature of energy, as I understand it—well, it's just extremely interesting to anybody at all who cares to ask himself what the future is going to look like in this country. And by that I mean the near future, Mr. Tesla. Say another decade or so."

"I suppose the frank answer to that is that electrical science will transform every level of motive power, both commercial and industrial. It will affect every single member of our society."

"Without a doubt! I could not agree more!" He dropped his voice to a secretive murmur. "Mr. Tesla, I will advance you thirty thousand dollars to begin this research now! My bank can honor a draft tomorrow morning."

"Sir, if you have read my articles, then you know that I have determined that to do such experimentation, the work must be done in Colorado, on the eastern face of the Rocky Mountains."

"Well yes, I read that, but I thought you might not have to actually—"

"It's a combination of the high altitude the very high ore content within that mountain range. There is an ideal situation for encouraging an electrical charge to pass from the earth to the sky."

Astor slapped his palm down on the table and beamed. "Colorado it is, then! You will have what you need to do this work. Just allow me to represent your financial partners, and you will retain half ownership of every dollar of profits!"

An excited flush filled Nikola's face while he considered the possibilities. "Mr. Astor, you have overwhelmed me with this, this wonderful..." Nikola reeled, suddenly dizzy.

"No need to rush, sir. Take your time."

"But I do! I do need to rush. Time is one thing in which I will always be poor. The strangest thing here is simply that someone I know told me to expect something like this, but I would not believe... this person."

Astor grinned and winked. "Well whoever she is, she's got herself a crystal ball, Mr. Tesla! Because I tell you, I only got approval for the funding this afternoon. I'm so excited that I couldn't even wait for tomorrow's business day to begin!" He shrugged. "As you can see."

Nikola's eyes flicked up to a point above and behind Astor's right shoulder. The same curious tug twitched at the corners of his mouth. He nodded to himself.

"Mr. Astor, the sum of money you mentioned is certainly enough so that I could take my crew to Colorado, build the laboratory and begin the process. But within a few months we would need more to complete the work."

"Of course!" Astor beamed, smelling success. "Of course! The results you achieve with the first round of funding will determine how much the second round will be!" He extended his hand, ready to shake on the deal. "Fair enough?"

Nikola stared at the extended hand for a moment. Finally he smiled in gratitude and reached out to return Astor's handshake. He remained sitting while they finished their goodbyes so that he could wipe his hand under the table with a fresh napkin and drop it to the floor while Astor walked away.

# Chapter Thirty-One

## 1899
### The New Tesla Lab
### Colorado Springs

It was late evening when a rolling pack of thunder heads boiled over the eastern slope of the Rocky Mountains and collapsed into furious storm activity while they approached the town of Colorado Springs. The strip of mountains overlooking the town, capped by Pike's Peak at more than fourteen thousand feet, left the thin mountain air to swirl over the ore-laden peaks until it became so highly charged that brilliant lightning streamers fizzed through the sky.

Rain was not falling yet, but the ozone produced by electrical discharges gave the night air its familiar pre-rain smell. The patch of sky farthest from the mountains was still clear enough to allow a few stars to shine in the silent pause before the storm took over.

The break in the sky hovered over Nikola's new laboratory on the southeastern outskirts of town. The approaching discharges revealed dreamlike glimpses of a strangely shaped two-story wooden building in the middle of a field at the intersection of two dirt roads. A tall fence surrounded the property, with each fencepost bearing the same sign, "Keep Away—Great Danger!"

The new structure's freshly cut timbers still oozed pine sap, helping to seal the new joints against the coming rainfall well enough to effectively keep out every forbidden drop of water. The roof above the second story was topped by a level platform that looked like a large raft balanced on the peak of the slanted roof. The platform was as long and wide as the building itself, and braced with strong timbers. A one hundred and forty-foot mast extended up from the ground, through the platform and into the sky, tipped by a hollow copper ball several feet in diameter.

Nikola was with his crew gathered on the second floor to celebrate their first night in the newly completed laboratory. The tone of the meeting was strange from the outset. George Scherff and half a dozen local hired helpers joined three others from the New York lab, standing on the far side of the room and maintaining a respectful if somewhat embarrassed silence. Nikola lay on a sofa next to an open window and stared out into the approaching storm, conversing with the lightning displays as if they were treasured pets.

"Come on now, my friends! We need the best you can throw at us, tonight! We want to know how much power this place can push into the air!" As if to answer him, an unusually large lightning bolt fired off in the distance and sent Nikola into a gale of delighted laughter. The new men winced at this behavior but took their cue from the experienced ones, who had seen it all before and made no other reaction.

"There! You are getting close. More! Show us!"

At that point another gigantic bolt fired off above the mountain range and fanned its way to the ground nearly three miles away. This one was far bigger than anything the men had seen there.

"Yes!" Nikola shouted. "That's the one!" He pulled out his pocket watch, quickly checked it and turned to the other men. "Duck! We have about thirteen seconds!"

He hopped off the sofa and hurried over to a spot behind a massive, half-assembled generator. "Five seconds!" he happily called to the men, who still had not moved. George needed no further encouragement. He hustled over to Nikola, then turned to glare at the other men.

They finally broke and stampeded behind the dynamo, arriving just as Nikola bellowed, "Now!"

A rumbling blast rolled across the plain delivering a shock wave with such force that it rattled the glass in the windows and shook the building. When the rumbling subsided and Nikola leaped to his feet, he was the only one to rise.

He laughed in triumph and shouted to the others, "There, you see? Our *first night* in the completed laboratory and we have already witnessed the truth that the ore in these mountains resonates with the storm clouds and produces lightning which can be many times its normal strength!"

The workers remained squatting behind the dynamo for another moment, spooked and ready to bolt. But George stood and patted a couple of them on the shoulder, pulling them to their feet while Nikola prattled on, "And gentlemen, tomorrow night—tomorrow night the lightning will be created here!"

Sunset arrived the following evening in a clear sky. Nikola stood outside with a direct view up to the tower mast and its copper ball. It seemed to glow against the reddening sky.

"George! He called out. "Is everyone in place?"

"All set inside, sir!" George hollered back from his position on the ground floor. He stood just inside the door at a large iron switch wired to a huge copper coil, and the coil was made of thick wire wrapped around a circular wooden fence fifty feet in diameter and ten feet high. In the center of the coil stood the bottom end of the tall mast, anchored deep into the ground.

Half a dozen of the other men worked at various checkpoints around the large coil, while several others stood by to observe a series of smaller coils inside the lab. These coils were not wired to anything. But Nikola had calculated that the size ratios of the smaller coils should allow them to "attune" to the output of the giant coil, so they would receive energy from it and throw it off in the form of electrical discharges. The exercise itself tested the men's loyalty, since it was apparent to anyone with a working knowledge of science that free-standing electrical coils could never receive a "charge" from any source, unless they were connected by wires.

Some of the workers stayed at their posts out of a blind belief in Nikola's ability, even if he was experimenting with equipment that everyone else expected to fail. The more critical among them were already convinced that the experiment was an expensive exercise in madness. A few only did their jobs out of curiosity, wondering just how spectacular tonight's disaster was going to be.

Under those watchful eyes, Nikola called to George Scherff, who was inside the building standing by the control switch, "Open power to the coil!"

George slammed the big switch forward, releasing the flow of electricity from the town's municipal generators. The city had granted full cooperation to the strange experiments that were being conducted in their town by this world renowned inventor. The municipal utility had even closed off power to other customers so that Nikola's lab would have all the current that it needed during the few minutes that the experiment was expected to take.

Now a deep and powerful hum began to rise from the giant coil. It resonated with every object, living or inanimate, throughout the building. It grew louder and more powerful until the four-by-eight beams of the foundation itself began to vibrate in response.

Nikola stood holding his breath and watching the big copper ball at the top of the mast, waiting for any sign of electrical discharge. Seconds passed. There was nothing but noise and powerful electrical vibration until finally, it began…

A halo of sparks formed on the surface of the copper ball, discharging excess electricity into the open air. The halo steadily expanded in size until the sparks were long enough to give the ball a coating of fiery hair.

"Yes! George, yes! It's working! Keep the power on!"

Nikola could barely hear George's "Yes sir!" over the snapping of the sparks, which were still continuing to grow. Suddenly they were an English foot in length … then five feet… ten feet… and soon sparks twenty feet long began leaping from the surface of the hollow copper ball atop the hundred and forty foot wooden mast.

"There it is, George! The energy we are pumping into the ground is reverberating back!"

But no one could hear him. By that point the sounds of the giant discharges exploded like cannon fire.

Back inside, the frightened workers found sparks several inches long jumping from their fingertips to the nearby coils. George tried to close the big switch, but the shock of the touch was too strong and he recoiled away.

Nikola leaped and twirled beneath the tall mast like a child on Christmas morning. Now the din of the discharges was deafening, and an artificial lightning bolt over a hundred feet long snapped out of the copper ball and crackled in the sky. It hung in the air, lasting several long seconds.

"It works!" Nikola screamed. "The planet is bouncing the energy back to us! It works! It wooorks!"

Meanwhile George frantically bellowed, "Sir, the coil is overloading! I can't shut it down!"

The smaller coils that were sitting around the shop and not yet connected to anything at all began to resonate with the charge of the master coil, so that they now also spewed showers of sparks by pulling power from the air. The men staggered from their posts in terror.

Nikola gave no sign that he heard Scherff's warning while he stared in fascination at the aerial display. Now lightning bolts of more than a hundred feet were snapping into the sky one after another, arriving so fast that they overlapped while they fanned the air.

He threw his arms high and bellowed with glee. "You see? Do you *see*? There's no limit to the power! This force can carry humanity's labor! It will take us to the staaarrrs!"

The tower shorted out with a huge bang and two brief fizzles. A second later, it fizzled a third time, billowing smoke from the superheated copper.

Then everything fell silent…

After a moment, George Scherff staggered to the door. Little wisps of smoke rose from his frazzled suit.

"George!" Nikola yelled. "What have you done? I never gave the signal to shut down!"

"It wasn't me, Mr. Tesla. I wasn't able to shut it down! It's the supply. The city power has been shut off. Nothing's coming in at all."

At that moment the other men appeared at the door behind George, wide-eyed and silent. George glanced at them and then back to Nikola. "Also, another inch of rubber under our boots would be good, I should think."

The largest of the men leaned in toward George and whispered, "A good inch, Mr. Scherff."

George turned and repeated out loud to Nikola, "A good inch."

Fifteen minutes later the door to the Colorado Springs Municipal Power Company flew open and Nikola rushed inside.

"Who cut power to my lab?" he demanded. "Our experiment was not finished! Why would you…" He stopped cold and took in the scene.

A small crowd of disgusted municipal workers turned to glare at him, faces black with soot. Huge wrenches dangled from their hands.

Both of the two giant municipal generators were dead silent, nothing more now than blackened hunks of smoldering metal. Nikola's mind raced.

"Ahhh. But! You see? If my tower pulled so much power that it overloaded two large commercial dynamos, then that proves that the coil was resonating with the earth itself! Fed by it! Where else would it get the power? Fed by the planet's own charge!"

He ran over to one of the dynamos for a closer look. "See? If these dynamos had not melted down, the power could have built up to an infinite degree. Starting from only a very small current! Tiny!"

He paused, noting their expressions. "Why, the possibilities…" he weakly finished.

The grimy workers only stared back at him.

"And! Gentlemen! Of course it goes without saying that I will bring my entire team over and we will repair these, uh, these—" He gestured to the generators. "Both of them. Immediately! Like new! *Better* than new!"

The disgusted workers still did not respond. Nikola stepped to the closest dynamo and patted it. His hand came up filthy.

"Not that these were not fine already, I am sure." But then a detail on the generator's main circuit caught his eye. "On the other hand, gentlemen, this entire method of handling the pressure behind the load is—" The men's expressions stopped him from going any farther.

"I'll get my men. I'll get them right now. We'll work all night."

He turned and hurried out.

Two weeks later, with the city generators back in working order but with power no longer coming to the lab free of charge, George Scherff arrived at work early one morning and was pleasantly surprised to see that one of his men was already waiting for him to unlock the place. George was so impressed by the fellow's initiative that he invited him to share his coffee and set a pot to boil on a lab bench over a handmade electric heating element.

George observed that it was the newest man, the one he had hired for Mr. Tesla back in New York shortly before leaving for Colorado. He had already noticed with admiration that the fellow consistently showed interest and initiative greater than the others, second only to his own. It was a natural opportunity to get to know the man a bit better. Minutes later they sat sipping the brew and casually talking.

"Anyway, Mr. Scherff," the fellow remarked, using the formal means of address that the boss encouraged everyone to maintain at work, "I wonder if you couldn't get Mr. Tesla to write down more of his ideas for us. I mean, if we had complete schematics to work from, then on a day like today when we arrive before he does, we could already be at work when he gets in."

Scherff smiled. "I appreciate your enthusiasm, but Mr. Tesla seldom writes down any more than one worker needs in order to make one part. He takes almost no notes at all and has a photographic memory for detail, so I think he feels that putting a lot of things on paper is an unnecessary drain on his time."

"Mm. I see. Why do you suppose he doesn't publish more?"

"He does, usually after the patents on any given device are granted, but personally I think he can't be published much more than he already is because at the outermost reaches of his imagination, where he is most comfortable, the scientific community either does not believe or will not accept his thinking."

"Mm," the man nodded, sipping his coffee. He seemed to get another idea. "Don't you suppose that he has reason to fear that if he doesn't publish, someone like Edison will get wind of his discoveries and publish them himself? Claim credit for them?"

Scherff frowned. "How could anyone do that?"

"Who knows? I just mean that Edison almost succeeded in stopping Mr. Tesla from getting his alternating current power to the public. Maybe a man like that will want to find a way to jump the gun on him the next time."

"Don't worry," Scherff reassured him. "Mr. Tesla is so far ahead of Thomas Edison and every other experimenter working today that without him, the things he is working on might not be discovered at all for many years to come. Perhaps many generations."

"That's for sure. Like that "free power to the world" scheme? I mean, without Nikola Tesla to figure it out, it might not happen at all."

"Exactly," Scherff replied.

The curious man nodded with a grim smile and resumed sipping on his coffee. He didn't ask any more questions that morning.

Late that summer, Nikola Tesla and George Scherff stood one evening on a windy plain twenty-six miles east of Colorado Springs. They had just finished setting up a bank of exactly two hundred light bulbs of fifty watts each, all mounted on a large wooden table. The bulbs were wired together, but there were no wires leading from the table to any source of power other than a metal ground stake and a small tuning box.

Scherff was terribly agitated and looked around as if he expected to be confronted by armed men. He held a lamp just high enough for Nikola to work at inspecting the connections, but watched with increasing anxiety until he glanced at his watch and shouted over the gusting wind. "Sir, if we burn out the city's generators again, I seriously doubt that we'll get away with just fixing them this time."

"Ha! They should thank us!"

The wind ate his words. "What?"

"I said they should thank us! They'll get an extra five years out of those dynamos with the thicker coiling we installed!"

"But sir, I'm not at all sure that they really grasp what you did for them. If we overload them again—"

"No, no, no—tonight we are only drawing enough power to light these bulbs." He glanced into the sky. "This is perfect! I love windy nights!"

"Well then, now that we're alone out here and there's no way anyone could eavesdrop on us, perhaps you could share a little more of the detail with me, I could feel more assured."

Nikola grinned. "Assured? George! There's no danger to us! The concept is simplicity itself!" He drew George close to him and put one arm around George's shoulder while he pointed to the bank of light bulbs with the other. "The receiver your team constructed is right there under the lights and wired to all of the bulbs. This time, when the tower crew activates the main coil—even at a relatively low charge—the receiver will vibrate in resonance the same way that a crystal glass vibrates in resonation to a high note of music! You see?"

"But sir, just tell me—please—is there really no power source inside the rig? I mean, you didn't have one of the other teams building, I don't know, small hidden batteries or something?"

Nikola laughed, delighted. "No! No! You see? Unnecessary! All of the power we use tonight will come from the lab, 26 miles away from here! It will work because I learned the correct frequencies from lightning storms. Sky music! Enough power for all the world!"

"I hope so, sir," George replied, trying hard to hide his misgivings. "I do hope so." He checked his watch by the lantern light once more. "And if the tower crew is on their mark, your 'concert' will begin in five... four... three... two... one...

Nothing happened. Scherff looked to Nikola, then back to the still-dark bulbs.

Nothing happened some more.

Nikola frowned and checked his own watch.

Still more nothing.

And then... all 200 bulbs flickered. Scherff gasped. They flickered a second time, then began a weak but steady glow. He cried out in amazement and dropped the lantern to the ground while the bulbs glowed brighter, brighter, until finally both men stood in a patch of intense light from all two hundred of the fifty-watt bulbs. Scherff's face went rapt with wonder. He stepped to the bank of lights, coming very close, studying them, then turned to Nikola and shouted, "Mr. Tesla! In the name of God! It really..."

Nikola stood staring at the glowing bulbs with a calm smile, while Scherff reached out his fingers to touch the brilliant lights. "Power," he muttered. He went on, louder, "Power without wires! We are transmitting power to light bulbs without any wires! You are making history tonight, Mr. Tesla!"

Nikola inhaled deeply and clasped both of Scherff's arms. "No. We both are, Mr. Scherff. We both are." He checked his watch again. "That should do it."

A moment later, the power faded as scheduled and the lights went dark. This time George Scherff was the one to place his arm over Nikola's shoulder. "Congratulations! It's unbelievable, sir! But it's true all the same!"

At that point Nikola was so overcome he felt weak on his feet. Scherff reached out to steady him. "Come away now, sir. I know you haven't slept in days. I'll bring a crew back to gather up all of this tomorrow."

"What if someone finds it first?" Nikola asked, suddenly troubled.

"Finds *what*, sir?" Scherff laughed. "There's nothing here

but a rack of light bulbs, mounted on coils, with a ground wire and an antenna! What would that tell them?" He gently led Nikola toward their waiting carriage. "Come away now. Get some rest. Then you can go back to New York and announce your success to our backers. Now they'll have to give us all the funding we need!"

Nikola was so lost in his reverie that he made no reply; he simply allowed George Scherff to lead him off while he muttered, "Think of what this is going to mean to the world! We have to get back to New York City right away."

Scherff laughed again. "None too soon, either! The people around here have no idea what you're up to. You make lightning and talk to storms. To them, it looks like magic."

Nikola climbed into the carriage and replied under his breath. "Magic. I wonder if she agrees?"

# Chapter Thirty-Two

## Two Days Later
### Aboard a Passenger Train

It was late at night while the thundering locomotive hauled the eastbound train toward New York City. Every passenger on board had been lulled into sleep by the rocking motion of the cars, leaving no one besides Nikola awake at the late hour except the engineer, the brakeman, and two conductors. This night was a thing of special reverie. The joy of this journey filled him so completely that he felt as if he would never need to eat or sleep again.

His newly proven reality of the transmission of electrical power without the use of wires was the first and most vital step in his quest to deliver free energy to the world. All that remained was to build perhaps half a dozen transmitting stations large enough to boost the electrical waves until they encircled around the planet, providing electrical power to anyone with a receiver which would be little more than the antenna and a ground wire. The poorest peasants would soon have the ability to pump their wells and irrigate their fields. People of slightly greater means would be able to power all manner of machines for no more cost than the machines themselves. With universal access to free electric power, crops could be grown almost anywhere and poverty itself could be made to vanish.

For the first time in his life, Nikola had a definite sense of deliverance from his fear of proving his father's dire predictions for him to be right. He had recently learned the perfect American word to describe this new feeling: gramercy. He acquired the word when he was made an honorary member of the highly prestigious Player's Club. The Club was located next to a tiny urban haven known as Gramercy Park, and the salient moment came for him when he arrived at the appointed hour.

He noticed the adjacent little park and saw the sign naming it, and found himself so captivated by the word that he immediately confounded his hosts by showing no interest in the occasion itself until he located someone who could explain the origin of the word "gramercy" to him. It was no easy task. None of his American hosts could define it or particularly cared to try. It was only when an English butler happened to overhear Nikola's request that an answer was obtained.

While Nikola listened, he made a mental diagram of the word, beginning with its original root in French: "Le Grande Merci," a phrase describing an overwhelming experience of gratitude. In English, the "Grande Merci" of French had evolved into Grand Mercy, adding a color of compassion to the feeling of thanks. In American English, the term was contracted down to a single word and became the current "Gramercy." The answer delighted him the first time he heard it.

And now on this night it was a perfect description of his mental state. Gramercy filled him. He overflowed with it.

"It is so perfect," he whispered to Karina when her image appeared.

"This night?" she asked.

"Well, yes," he replied. "But that's not what I mean."

"Do you mean something like this?" Karina asked. She reached out and stroked her fingertips along his forehead.

Nikola felt the impact of her energy hit him so hard it collapsed his body and left him inert while a mixture of images and feelings poured into him. With it the very essence of *gramercy* sprang to life for him.

He felt her making him aware that the emptiness of space was an illusion. Instead he suddenly saw space as packed at every point with an invisible and un-seeable force that transmits energy vibrations in the same way that the surface of a pond hosts the ripples made by raindrops. He saw that the force was as unknown to the world's living as the pond's water is to its fish.

Gramercy expanded his *vision* until his awareness left his body and expanded in all directions. He understood that all physical matter was nothing more than varying combinations of vibration, appearing solid only because the physical body cannot pass through them because of its conflicting vibrations. He saw this vast conglomeration of vibration weave itself through the vastness of so-called "empty" space. He saw plainly that the human mind may experience some of these vibrations as physical matter, but in his state of gramercy he saw they can all be defined as the living tissue of the mind of God.

# Chapter Thirty-Three

## Grand Central Station
## New York City

"Mr. Tesla!" cried John Astor, grabbing Nikola's hand and pumping it up and down. Nikola's smile was so broad that Astor didn't notice his attempts to pull his hand away. The bustling chaos of the debarking passengers filled Manhattan's train station with a din that made it almost impossible to hear, but Astor took Nikola's arm and led him off, happily jabbering away despite the noise. George Scherff hurried along beside the two men, laboring to keep up. He carried a heavy valise under each arm, having insisted on handling Nikola's as well as his own.

"Let your crew go on back to their homes or else back to your laboratory, Mr. Tesla!" cried Mr. Astor. "I was so delighted to receive your cable about the success of your Colorado experiments that I immediately told our benefactor! He has asked to see you right away!"

Scherff called out over the noise of the train station, "I prefer to stay with Mr. Tesla, if you don't mind, sir."

"Quite right, Mr. Scherff!" Nikola hollered back, adding to John Astor, "George Scherff has been an indispensable part of this operation, Mr. Astor."

"Fine, fine!" Astor fairly sang it. He was giddy with excitement, anticipating the welcoming response into which he was about to usher them.

The three men and the two heavy valises all piled into a taxi carriage amid an urban hustle that barely lessened after they left the train station. Moments later they were on their way downtown.

Nikola was so drained by his sleepless journey that he failed to ask about the identity of their financier. The name hardly seemed to matter, only the fact that the benefactor could not fail but to be delighted over the results he had sponsored.

The mutual state of joy and the flush of success was so strong with all three men that Nikola and Scherff barely blinked when the carriage pulled to a stop in front of the office building of J. Pierpont Morgan. "So this is the secret you have kept from us?" Nikola exclaimed with delight.

"Only because Mr. Morgan insisted on anonymity," Astor assured him. "However, after hearing of your splendid success, he is no longer concerned about remaining a silent partner."

"Wonderful!" Nikola cried. "It is only right that he step forward and take credit for his part in a ground-breaking discovery!"

The three men headed up to the top floor office. By now they were in such good spirits that Nikola and Scherff both forgot their travel fatigue.

Half an hour later, when they came back out and happily flagged another taxi carriage, the heavy pedestrian traffic on both sides of the street prevented them from seeing another of the men who had worked in Nikola's Colorado lab. This other Tesla lab worker crossed the street and hurried inside Morgan's office building as soon as the high-spirited men rode away.

The man didn't bother to knock when he walked into Morgan's office, but when he closed the door behind himself, Morgan showed no surprise at seeing him.

"How did it go with our man Tesla?" the visitor asked.

Morgan stared back at him with a blank expression that he had spent years perfecting into an unreadable mask. Not a trace of hatred or rage showed on his face at the indignity of being manipulated by some underpaid government bureaucrat.

"It's all taken care of, my good man. I praised his genius, assured him of more funding, and allowed as to how I'm going to be sleepless while I wait for his next round of stunning results."

The man laughed. "Oh-oh! That sounded awfully friendly, Mr. Morgan! You sure he won't find your attitude out of character?"

"Is that some sort of joke?"

"Pretend it isn't."

"All right... No. He was not suspicious, I am quite sure. The process of flattering an inventor is no different than that of flattering a stage actress. They're so busy hearing what they want to hear that nothing else gets through."

"So what's the deal, then?"

"Like you asked—I congratulated him and agreed to bankroll what he calls "phase two," for one hundred and fifty thousand dollars."

"But in return you keep control, right?"

It was Morgan's turn to sneer. "Do you have any *idea* how long I have been successfully doing business?"

"On your inherited money."

"Yes, damn it! Yes! I will hold sole control over his wireless technology for as long as I continue to fund its development. All right? Now if you don't mind—"

"I do mind, Mr. Morgan. I have a job to do for this country, just like you do. Now what is this 'phase two' of his?"

"He wants to use the money to buy a little piece of seacoast land that he has his eye on near the New York shoreline. He calls it Wardenclyffe. Or maybe that's what the locals call it. Anyway, it's close enough to his Niagara generators to tap into their power and drive his new system."

"That 'system' will be the one broadcasting all of that, ah, free power?"

"So he says."

"Any chance he's just deluding himself?"

"Why ask me? Hell, you just spent months working with him out there in Colorado. He says he can do it; what do you say?"

"I think just the fact that he's *trying* to do it is enough to make him a very dangerous person. I also observed that he managed to pull off everything he attempted to do while we were out there. I mean all of it."

"There you have it. Are we finished now?"

"Almost, Mr. Morgan. So it's understood that you will give him the money and keep him under control until we notify you otherwise. Then you will cut off the funding while we see to it that the press discredits him."

"You know, a lot of people consider him to be some kind of people's hero. Have your bosses thought about what they're going to do if the public gets wind of this?"

"How would that happen? We're the only ones who know, and *I'm* sure not going to tell him. Are *you* going to tell him?"

"Don't be absurd," Morgan growled, lighting another cigar even though he had one burning in the ashtray.

The man laughed again, clearly enjoying his work. "Good enough, then." He turned to go. "Better be on my way now. I have to report to the lab bright and early. You know, start helping him spend your money."

Morgan made no reply to that. His face spoke volumes about the rage felt by a man with no experience at taking orders.

The visitor opened the door and stepped out. "I'll be in touch," he called over his shoulder.

"Imagine my relief," Morgan muttered under his breath. A moment after the man disappeared, Morgan's butler opened the door and pushed a wheeled cart into the room, loaded with the usual one-man feast.

All Morgan had to do was glare at him. The butler turned the cart around and pushed it back out the door.


The following July, Nikola published a magazine article entitled "The Problem of Increasing Human Energy." It was not a treatise on healthy living, rather a series of predictions based upon his own experiments and visualizations regarding the potentially sweeping changes for the better that he planned to bring to the world with his fundamental new source of energy.

When the magazine hit the newsstands early one summer morning, copies were snapped up by various interested parties who knew better than to dismiss predictions made by a man with Nikola Tesla's history.

At his Manhattan lab, it was one of those rare mornings when Nikola stayed home to rest after another three-day work marathon. This one was spent designing the facilities for the

Wardenclyffe installation on the land that he had just purchased with Morgan's funds. George Scherff stood in the center of the lab reading aloud from the article while the other workers gathered around him and listened.

"The Worldwide Power System plant can be in operation in nine months. It will produce up to ten million horse power, and among the possibilities it can create will be—"

Thomas Edison also read the article in his own lab to several of his men, speaking with a grim face and a flat voice, "—interconnection of all telegraph exchanges in the world, interconnection of all phone exchanges all over the world, establishment of instant worldwide communication for private and government use, each one completely individualized to be non-interferable—"

J.P. Morgan read to himself from a comfortable seat in his private dining car, but the shock of the words rang through him as if he shouted them, "—interconnection of all the stock tickers on the planet, a world system of musical distribution, universally tuned clocks that are inexpensive and completely accurate—"

The G-man who work undercover for Nikola Tesla paced back and forth in an unmarked government office, reading aloud to the people who actually owned his loyalty. "—facsimile transmission of typed or handwritten documents, a universal marine service allowing all ships to be guided without a compass, anywhere in the world, and instant reproduction anywhere on the planet of photographs and all kinds of drawings or official records."

The man paused and cast a loaded look at his superiors.

J. Pierpont Morgan dropped the article on the table in front of him and stroked his chin with worry.

Thomas Edison wadded up the article and threw it at the wall.

George Scherff finished reading the article to the other workers and turned to look at them with his face full of worry. "What will the world say—what will it *do* to a man such as this?"

Either no one heard the question or nobody wanted to venture a guess.

# Chapter Thirty-Four

*Two Years Later*
*New York*

After two years' worth of work, the site that Morgan's money allowed Nikola to buy was now home to a newly completed brick building specially constructed to house the new Wardenclyffe World Power System. In size and shape, the structure resembled a large single-story home. All similarity ended there.

Behind the building, towering over a hundred feet into the air, was a wooden framework that looked something like a giant windmill. At the top, instead of wind turbine blades, the tower was capped by a half-dome steel cage another twenty-five feet in height. Both the cage and the "windmill" structure were designed to be clad in a stainless steel shell that would complete the broadcasting antenna for the Wardenclyffe World Power System, serving up a colossal standing wave of electricity that would invisibly surround the entire planet in vibration between the surface of the earth and the stratosphere. It would thus provide the basic power for the world's power users to tap into with the accompanying antenna devices. Since the devices were made to resonate with the standing energy rather than pulling power out of it, they would not detract by tapping in. Any number of users could draw power at the same time without diminishing the basic charge.

The inside of the building was still empty at that point. It lacked the specially designed generators and transformers that Nikola had ordered from George Westinghouse.

But strangely, Westinghouse's company was demanding payment before they would agree to ship them. J.P. Morgan's seed money of $150,000 was already spent on the land, the building, and the tower structure. Nothing more could be done until another round of financing was in place.

A week later, early in the morning, Nikola and Scherff stood in the Manhattan office of J.P. Morgan, waiting for him to acknowledge them. Morgan, however, stood with his back to the men. He simply stared out the window and down toward the street. His back was still to them when he pulled a piece of newsprint from his pocket and unfolded it.

Then his voice boomed out, "Imagine my surprise, Mr. Tesla, when I opened the New York Times yesterday and saw this article wired from Wardenclyffe: *Eccentric genius Nikola Tesla,*" he looked up and added, "who spent his time in Colorado and at Wardenclyffe on *my* funding, *is reported to lie next to open windows during thunder storms and converse with the lightning bolts!*"

Morgan gestured to his butler for a fresh cigar, then paused long enough to properly light it before he continued. "In the name of Holy Christ, man, what goes on in your *mind*?"

Nikola looked at Scherff in consternation, but Scherff could only shake his head, mystified. "Mr. Morgan," Nikola began, "I gave no interviews in Colorado *or* at Wardenclyffe."

"Yes. It seems you were also careless enough to allow a *spy* into your ranks at experiments that I paid for and that I ordered you to keep secret!"

"I *did* keep it secret… What spy?"

Morgan only sneered and glanced over at George Scherff. Scherff gasped in shock and immediately protested, "I never! I never, Mr. Tesla! Not a word! I would never say a word about—"

That was as far as he got. Morgan gestured to his butler, who immediately took Scherff under the arm and firmly escorted him from the room.

"What are you—?" Scherff shouted in alarm. "Let go of me! Mr. Tesla, you know that I'm no spy! I would never do that to you!"

But by that point the butler had Scherff through the

door. He pulled it closed after them. Nikola stood stunned and speechless.

Morgan stepped whisper-close and leaned toward him. "You have embarrassed me, Mr. Tesla."

"I— Sir— I have done *nothing* but what I promised to do, and proven that electrical power can be sent using very little energy and no wires and that it can be used by anyone, anywhere!"

"So you say."

"You have just removed my witness from the room, sir! He can testify that I succeeded in transmitting power wirelessly, at a distance of 26 miles! Not just messages, Mr. Morgan, not merely information, but wireless electrical power. All that is left for me to do is to use the Wardenclyffe system to find the precise frequencies needed to transmit small amounts of power, which the earth itself will magnify to huge levels at almost no cost!"

"And who authorized you to tamper with the public's energy cost?"

"*Tamper?* Sir, this power can provide universal access to unlimited energy anywhere in the world!"

"Exactly." Morgan calmly took another puff of his excellent cigar. "People don't need to be that free. What are they going to do with themselves?"

"Improve their lot, of course!"

"At whose expense? Let me tell you, I am deeply concerned about your attempts to throw our American economy out of balance!"

"Sir, the entire world's economy is badly out of balance already! I have brought you a *gift* for you to pass on to people everywhere!"

"And you have done so with no thought for the effect on existing governments! Industries!"

"Governments and industries adapt! It is the *people* who need this!"

"Mr. Tesla, the long and the short of it is, as your sponsor— and as the controller of fifty-one percent of your patent rights on this technology—I intend to hold those patents in my company vault, and continue to finance conventional power sources."

"Sir. Please, sir. Why are you doing this? We are talking about supplying electrical power to every person on earth, for practically no cost!"

"No, *you* are," Morgan quietly replied. "Which is why I am withdrawing all further funding at this point."

"No! No, Mr. Morgan, I—"

"Why don't you do some more work like your hydro-electric plant at Niagara Falls? That's the kind of thing we can put a meter on. That's good business." He smiled and blew another puff. "Unlike the very bad business of you letting Westinghouse talk you out of your royalties on your patents."

"...That was done in secret."

"...Apparently not."

"I told *no one* about that!"

"Your royalty was one dollar per horsepower. Since there is currently about twelve million horsepower being produced in this country on technology that you invented, why, that's twelve million dollars of your own money that you gave away."

Morgan looked at Nikola with revulsion and added, "And that, no doubt, would have been more than enough for you to fund this 'worldwide power scheme' yourself. As for me, I do not feel disposed to make any further advances."

Nikola staggered backward as if he had taken a blow to the gut.

"However," Morgan added with a generous smile, "I'm sure that you can continue patenting little inventions on your own. Right? Make enough money to keep a small lab open?" He blew a large puff of smoke followed by a perfect smoke ring.

Nikola turned and stumbled out of the room.

# Chapter Thirty-Five

## Immediately Following
## Manhattan

The moment Nikola emerged from Morgan's office building, George Scherff came running up, full of quaking denials that he had ever betrayed his benefactor. Nikola allowed Scherff to take his arm and walk away with him. He looked at Scherff with such open trust that Scherff burst into tears in his gratitude to see that Nikola did not believe Morgan's story against him.

The two men walked a long distance through the city, moving slowly and barely talking at all, while they each reeled under the day's events. Around noon, they reached the park behind the New York City Public Library and moved toward an empty bench, with George still supporting Nikola's arm as if he were a man many years older. Ground-pecking pigeons formed a living puddle that parted around their feet. As soon as they sat down, the flock washed back in all around them, hoping for bits of food.

Nikola patted George's hand, then wordlessly gestured to indicate that he should leave him there. George's reluctance to go was clear while he rose and walked away, honoring Nikola's request to be left alone to wrestle with his agony and his unanswered questions. However he could not disguise the worry on his face.

Nikola remained alone on the bench, gazing around at the rustling trees like a man waiting for someone to arrive from an unknown direction. Mid-afternoon arrived and Nikola still sat on the bench.

Sunset came and went and the park lamps switched on for

the night. They were modified versions of the same arc lamps he invented for the town of Rahway years before. Passers-by moved through the pools of light with no idea that they were so close to the man responsible for them. Nikola still sat quietly alone on the bench, still waiting.

Darkness fell and Nikola remained in the same spot, but by that time his shoulders were slumped and his head was down.

When dawn began to break he was still on the bench, just waking up after sleeping there for hours. He climbed off of the bench and rose to his feet, stiff from the comfortless night.

When he walked around to the front of the library and emerged on the street, he passed a newsboy hawking the fresh morning paper. He bought a copy. There was no need to open it; he saw the article right at the bottom of page one: "STOCK MARKET GIANT J.P. MORGAN WITHDRAWS ALL FUNDING FROM INVENTOR NIKOLA TESLA." The lead paragraph made Morgan's reasoning clear in a single stark phrase. "...the man's renowned genius has decayed."

The entire business world would hear of this. He dropped the paper into a street corner wastebasket, feeling so full of heartbreak and shame that he let the automaton handle the job of taking the long walk back to his hotel. The rest of him drifted up into the tiny rocking chair and concentrated on the task of reaching out to Karina.

It did no good to passively wait for her, so he now reached out with all of his energy, sending a silent call so clear and strong that he knew she had to hear him if she was there. No matter what she was or wherever she resided during the long stretches between her visits, she had to sense this plea. She had to come to him, now. She had to.

Time passed... Time passed... Time passed...

He had long since given up fearing that his father's morbid interpretation of her presence could be true, and it did nothing to stop the cold blade of dread from pushing into his chest. Whether she was a demon from Hell or not, the awful message was too clear to ignore. She had deserted him.

In the same fashion that the foolhardy world had judged

him unworthy of support, she had abandoned him, abandoned his struggle to carry out his life mission, abandoned humanity's dire need to be lifted out of squalor by the fruits of his most meaningful discovery. The cruelty of men with the Robber Baron mentality was hard enough to bear, and the frustration of trying to bring his *vision* into the hard world was costly enough to his spirit. But the heaviest blow came with the realization that Karina had filled him with sweeping solutions to the world's poverty and then left him to carry the answers in neglected silence.

*Do not do this!* the plea went out from him like the soundless beam from a lighthouse. *Whatever your purpose in my life, do not leave me like this. If you will not help me, at least give me some understanding of why this had to happen.*

The automaton got Nikola safely back home, but every face he passed was that of a stranger; Karina remained unseen.

With every step he took, the anger and bitterness coursing through his blood were converted to sheer outrage. There was nothing he could do but allow the mortifying truth to flow through him; she was, in some terrible way, a part of the nightmare. His muse, his Karina, might not be the Satanic demon his father had labeled her, but she might just as well be. No matter how anyone defined her, she had served as a cruel beacon urging him down this primrose path to failure. She had left him to the open ridicule of the world whose collective burden he had made his own. As a result, he did not merely fail to achieve his goal, he even misfired in using his spectacular abilities to secure his own lot in life.

The bright morning air was clean and clear, but he had no sense of the new day. He felt suffocated by the smell of death. By the time he reached the door to his rooms, his shaking hand could barely fit the key to the lock.

The man who appeared to work for Nikola but who was actually with the federal government heard the key hit the lock. He spun away from the pile of papers he had just finished pulling out of Nikola's tall safe, but it was too late to get them back in place. It had taken him most of the night to pick the safe's lock, constantly checking over his shoulder for any sign that Nikola might come home. Once morning arrived he had decided that the inventor must be on another marathon work session, so he slowed to make a more thorough search. It was a calculated risk that he was not prepared to lose; before he could secure a hiding place, the door opened and Nikola stepped inside.

The intruder was in Nikola's direct line of sight. Both men froze in place. Several seconds passed.

The man was well trained in physical combat and carried a small revolver under his coat, so he decided to wait to see what Nikola's reaction would be before he took action. He felt prepared for anything that might happen—except for what came next.

Nikola made no objection to seeing him there. He did nothing to question the man's invasion of his privacy and did not mention having his safe opened or his papers rifled. He merely turned away, calmly removed his coat, stepped to a nearby closet, and placed it on a coat hanger.

The intruder remained silent and still, waiting for the outcry that had to come. Instead, Nikola moved over to the bed, sat on the edge of the mattress and removed his shoes and socks. When he spoke at last, his voice was quiet. His tone was calm. He did not bother to look at the government man. "So. Are you here for yourself or are you here for someone else?"

"…I'm not supposed to say."

"You just did." Still not bothering to look over at the man, Nikola busied himself in removing his tie and loosening his shirt.

The man gave a dry little laugh. Nothing in his training prepared him for this sort of reaction. He decided to keep quiet and wait for Nikola to speak again.

"I hope you did not damage the lock in opening my safe."

"Uh, no. It's still good."

"Imagine my relief. Well, it was clearly wrong of me to think of myself as your employer. Have you stolen anything?"

"I'm not here to steal anything, just— just to look."

"Ah. To look." Nikola lay down on the bed with his shirt and trousers still on and pulled the bedspread over himself. "If you have done enough looking, do be kind enough to leave now. I need to sleep." He fluffed the pillow a couple of times, then rested his head on it and closed his eyes.

The government man shook his head in disbelief. Of all the odd behavior he had witnessed from this Tesla fellow since going undercover in his laboratory, this apparent lack of concern was the strangest yet. He shook his head once again and started for the exit. When he reached the door, the inventor made one last remark, this time without bothering to open his eyes.

"Please tell whoever sent you that the only papers here are patent drawings for devices that are already a matter of public record. Everything else stays in my head until it's time to construct a working model." With that, he turned onto his opposite side and faced the wall.

A tiny smile of disbelief crossed the man's face, but without attempting any further comment he opened the door and stepped out of the room. Before he could close the door behind himself he heard the inventor quietly add, "Please be so kind as to have any of your belongings out of my laboratory before I return."

The man dropped his head with a small sigh and closed the hotel room door, which automatically clicked into the locked position behind him.

# Chapter Thirty-Six

## Seven Years Later
## New York City

They were able to keep a modest lab open at 165 North Broadway for the next seven years, even as the Wardenclyffe tower stood unfinished, primarily because of George Scherff's relentless scrounging on Nikola's behalf. Nikola's life continued on a level of success that most inventors would have envied; he developed a turbine engine so tiny and efficient that it was dubbed "A Powerhouse In Hat" and perfected refinements in the control systems for his existing turbines, generators, and transformers.

The alternating current technology he sold to George Westinghouse spread through the country and around the world—all without payment to him. Westinghouse remained enthusiastic in his public support for the fruits of Nikola Tesla's mind, but even after reviving his personal fortune, he never attempted to restore any portion of the many millions of dollars in royalties that Nikola forgave him.

For any other inventor, Nikola's continued work would have signified a triumph over adversity. For him, it was nothing more than small change. He still enjoyed a certain amount of fame, although with every passing year his name was recognized by fewer members of the public. Lately it was known more exclusively by those rare tradesmen and scientists capable of grasping the importance of his work.

His steadfast refusal to make public comments against Westinghouse or any of his former supporters meant that the public remained unaware of his borderline poverty while he recycled every cent he earned into laboratory expenses. When visitors to his lab noted the humble surroundings that he and his tiny crew worked in, rumors flew that he was stashing his loot and saving up for some momentous new creation—perhaps for the good of humanity, perhaps some darker purpose.

And all the while, those rare newspaper and magazine interviews that he granted were filled with descriptions of futuristic inventions few people could imagine and accept.

A persistent rumor remained on the street: the old genius was secretly building giant secret weapons. He had threatened to sell them to another government if the United States refused to pay for them.

No basis for the rumors was ever discovered. It was never determined where the rumors originated or who kept them afloat.

In reaction, Nikola grew more isolated than ever, sending his impeccably dressed automaton out to high society functions whenever he was granted the chance to speak. An opportunity to raise funds could never be ignored. But up there in the tiny rocking chair behind the picture window eyes, the bitterness of Karina's desertion secretly festered. It was necessary to block all thoughts of her if he hoped to get anything done.

He continued to greet the uncounted women who fawned upon him and the men who attempted to cultivate his friendship with universally polite rejection. Attempts to distract him from his work were as useless as worldly temptations proffered to a devout monk.

Author Mark Twain was a rare exception. During the last years of Samuel Clemens' life, he and Nikola cultivated a friendship that included late night philosophical discussions and private laboratory demonstrations of whatever new device Nikola was working on at the time. Clemens was especially fond of Nikola's healing apparatus, which bathed Clemens in a magnetic field so powerful that it warmed him inside and produced feelings of euphoria that only peaked when the vibrations went on long enough to produce galloping diarrhea. Clemens even forgave Nikola this indignity. For his part, Nikola never got over his sense of appreciation for the approval and interest of a man whose writings taught Nikola so much about his adopted country. Clemens repeatedly assured him that if not for his own constant financial difficulties, he would have been delighted to finance the World Power System himself.

# Chapter Thirty-Seven

## 1912
### New York City

The year 1912 found Nikola's tuxedoed automaton sitting at a table of dignitaries during a formal dinner at the French Embassy in Manhattan. Even though he was elegantly attired, his lined face now told the story of years of effort and frustration.

He did not recognize most of the luminaries seated around him, but the chair at his right was occupied by a smiling Samuel Clemens. The fact that the great author had died two years earlier did nothing to deter Nikola's experience of the man he admired beyond any other.

Because Nikola sat quietly throughout most of the evening, the rare comments that he made to Clemens were overlooked by the other guests, usually with no more than a roll of the eyes or a poorly smothered grin. Meanwhile he was experiencing the things around them all as a drone in the background. It was not until the talk at his table turned to the upcoming Nobel Prize award that the conversation grew lively; the Nobel Committee had just announced that the prize was going to be awarded to both Thomas Edison *and* Nikola Tesla for that year.

One dignified older man whose name Nikola did not catch leaned across the table and looked at him with astonishment. "And sir, you will actually *refuse* the Nobel Prize?" The man rapped his knuckles sharply down on the tabletop. "*No* one does such a thing, sir. No one!"

Nikola came back to awareness and smiled. "It would seem that I do. Not because of what Edison and his peers kept from me for so many years, but because of what their sabotages have kept from humanity itself. I will not endorse undeserved adulation."

"You say that your adversaries are keeping some important something-or-other from humanity?"

"That is a fact. And needless suffering continues all over the country and around the world because of it."

No one offered any further argument, but the other guests regarded him with doubting eyes. People who would have gladly stabbed one another's backs with daggers of gossip just a moment earlier now experienced group closeness in their unity of attitude toward him.

The next morning, Thomas Edison paced the floor of his Menlo Park offices in a raging fury, holding a copy of the day's *New York Times*. Yes-Man #1, Hawkins or Harper, stood by with a telegram in his hand and waited for the right moment to reveal its contents because the Boss had not stopped fuming for the better portion of an hour.

"This article can't be right! This absolutely cannot be true! Cannot! Be! True! What are they trying to make us believe, that Tesla and I are selected to share the Nobel Prize—the Nobel Prize, mind you—and the damned fool *refuses to accept*?"

"Um, yes sir, but, well—"

"Speak up!"

"Yes sir!" he shouted. "However I'm afraid that's not all. Besides the newspaper, we just received this."

Edison was still powered by raging momentum. "When I was a boy they told me I was too stupid to have a future! But I came this far on a grade school education! Damn it all, that Nobel is mine!"

"Yes sir, no doubt about it. Except that... well..."

"Speak up, damn it!"

"Sir! This wire just came." He held up the telegram.

"What? Hawkins, right? Hand me that, Mr. Hawkins."

Yes-Man #1 handed over the telegram with a shaking hand. Edison scanned it, eyes widening, then gasped. "God Almighty! The Nobel Committee has retracted the entire award because of the madman's refusal! They're giving it to some Englishman named Henry Bragg, and his son!"

"Excellent choice," Hawkins muttered, knowing that Edison would not hear him. The Boss stepped to a window and gazed into the distant night sky. He focused on the indifferent stars and whispered to Hawkins as if Hawkins cared, "Whatever goes on in that lunatic's mind?"

Late autumn found Nikola and George Scherff slowly walking a Central Park pathway at sunset. Nikola scattered bird seed from a paper bag to the massive flock of pigeons that surrounded and followed them. Among the countless gray pigeons was a single snow-white dove. Nikola found her to be so beautiful that he made sure to toss extra seed her way. She responded to the special treatment by fluttering up and lighting on his shoulder. This delighted him so much that he placed a little pile of seed there for her.

"I checked both afternoon papers," George ventured. "They are confirming the initial reports that out of the few survivors of *S.S. Titanic*, John Astor was not among them."

Nikola stopped in his tracks and seemed to grope for words. "And we think we have troubles. That was a man who deserved to live if anyone does. Family man, philanthropist…" He sighed. "The fellow was truly attempting to do right by the world."

George gave him a look of admiration. "He was not the only one, Mr. Tesla."

Nikola smiled ruefully. "No, but perhaps the only one left who believed in my work enough to help us with financing."

George spoke with a frustrated sigh. "I still don't understand what is the matter with the investment community. They treat us like lepers, despite the fact that in the twelve years since Colorado, your lab—even as small as it is—obtained dozens of new patents!"

"Gadgets," Nikola replied with a dismissive wave. He turned to George. "But your loyalty has been extraordinary. I am certain you will receive other offers of work. At higher wages, no doubt."

George duplicated Nikola's dismissive wave. "I don't want to work with others. I want to work with the Wizard." He smiled at Nikola's puzzled expression. "I know that some call Edison that, but I know who the real Wizard is!"

Nikola fondly placed his hand on Scherff's shoulder and smiled at him. "I hope you will always consider me a friend, George. The simple truth is that you will do better elsewhere."

"Surely your remarks last night were only born out of frustration! Eventually we will find some way to retire the lab's debts. But Mr. Tesla, if you close down the lab, if you stop working—"

"Stop working?" Nikola interrupted. "Oh no. Not stop working, oh no. I will maintain a small lab for a while yet. But without building any models. I won't even file patent drawings. You see? That is my only hope of protecting any new science from wealthy thieves. At least until everything is ready."

He stopped and spoke with a stronger note of hope than George had heard from him in many months. "Perhaps we can get together once a week or so and work on general matters. We may yet live to see free power go out to all the world."

George was suddenly too choked up to talk. All he could do was embrace Nikola, who gently patted his shoulder in return. The two men walked on. For a long time neither one spoke.

# Chapter Thirty-Eight

## Winter, 1915
### The Bowery, New York

By the winter of 1915, Nikola's outstanding bill at the hotel Waldorf Astoria peaked at nineteen thousand dollars. To settle the score, he had no choice but to deed the Wardenclyffe property to the owners of the hotel. They knocked down the incomplete tower in hopes of making the land easier to sell. Even though Nikola had settled his bill, the hotel refused to extend him anymore credit. He had to leave the suite of rooms he had occupied during all of the years since returning from Colorado.

He resorted to a single room in a seedy hotel on the Lower East Side. There were few belongings for him to move. He carried them over on a dead gray day that gripped the neighborhood in a dingy blanket of snow and dirty ice.

Looking up and down the street, he saw nothing but the last stop for staggering winos, raving outcasts, and one nearly forgotten man whose inventions were, at that moment, powering a large portion of the hard world.

Early on his first evening in the new location, he sat in the tiny room surrounded by his unpacked bags and the room's few sparse furnishings. Despite the cold, he had the window wide open and was dressed in nothing more than a worn robe. His concentration was occupied by the process of sketching birds in flight on a large tablet.

There was a knock at the door, but before he could respond, a heavily worn hotel maid with deep lines carved into her face entered carrying a small paper bag. He glanced up at her and smiled, then returned to his sketch. She set the bag down on his chair.

"All right, Mr. Tesla, here is the bird seed you wanted."
Then she added, crafty as hell, "I'm afraid there's no change…"

"Fine, that's fine. But please just set it over by the window."

"Well all right. But if you're going to stay up here without
coming out, maybe you should let me go get some food for
you. You should feed yourself before you feed wild birds." She
started to close the window.

"No, no. Leave it open, please."

"What, you want to freeze?"

He looked up from his sketch and smiled. "What is life
without risk?"

The maid regarded him with exasperation, whether at his
refusal to protect against the cold or his refusal to allow her to
cheat him out of some more pocket change. She sighed and left
the room.

He put his sketch aside, stepped over to the window and
sprinkled some seed on the sill, then sat back down and picked
up the tablet again. Within moments he was so engrossed in the
drawing that he didn't look up again until the rustling of a bird's
wings caught his attention. His eyes widened when he saw that a
white dove had flown in and landed on the sill.

"Ha! A customer! And not an ordinary pigeon, but a
beautiful white dove…"

He squinted at the bird for a few seconds, then took a
deep breath of surprise and stepped closer to it. After another
moment, a delighted smile spread across his face. "Why, I
do believe it is the same one! From the park! Now this is a
noteworthy event! Welcome, my little friend, I am delighted to
have you as a guest."

The dove seemed to ignore his presence altogether in favor
of pecking away at the seeds. Amused, Nikola decided to address
the dove as any other visitor. He turned the sketch pad to reveal
another page filled with tiny handwriting.

"I am so honored by your appearance here, that I shall read
you something of my latest writing, taken from a speech of
mine. The money from this magazine article will keep us in bird

seed for many weeks! Ha!" He began to read aloud.

*"The problem of increasing human energy can also be addressed by increasing humanity's food supply."*

He paused and added, "You see, little bird, if only I could discover the right frequencies, my multi-phase oscillating coils could be placed next to all farm fields. They break up air molecules, release pure nitrogen. And the crops! The crops love nitrogen the same way you love that seed! Oh yes! And so the crops are *vastly* increased without anyone doing anymore work!"

At that moment, the amusement fell from his face. He stared at the bird, then moved closer to it, staring harder…

"What?" he breathed. "What did you say?"

The dove tilted its head toward him until Nikola saw a blinding flash of light explode from its eyes. The light engulfed him. He cried out in wonder. After one brief moment, the light faded back down, but now the dove was gone, and a golden fountain of energy appeared in the middle of the room, spewing silver showers into the air. All around the energy shower, translucent plants appeared. They seemed to be growing furiously right before his eyes, winding their way up into the air.

Nikola gasped in shock and in recognition. "Those are the frequencies to split the nitrogen from the air? Yes? They must be!" A moment later Nikola's knees grew so weak that he fell to the floor.

Karina stood in front of him, as real and as lovely as if they had never been apart. "You!" he whispered. "Why have you come in such a form?"

She smiled and spoke in the faintest whisper. "Your anger kept me from reaching you."

"Stop it! It is *you* who have avoided me! I have called to you endlessly! Looked for you everywhere! Is this some new cruelty that you—"

She stopped him cold with a stroke of his cheek. He immediately saw the energy shower grow huge—the "plants" filled the air around him. He fell to his knees and reached out to her with trembling hands.

# Chapter Thirty-Nine

## Years Later
## Manhattan

Old Thomas Edison sat on a rocking chair alone on his front porch. He clutched a large copper ear-horn with one arm while he lifted a tall glass of iced tea with the other. It was just at that moment when one of the new generation of Yes-Men came hurrying up the steps, fellow name of Tilton or Milton. The young man waved a magazine.

"Mr. Edison!" he cried in excitement, appearing delighted to bring good news. "This is the new Tesla interview! He says—"

"What's that?" Edison picked up the big copper horn and held it to his ear.

The fresh-faced Yes-Man leaned forward and hollered directly into the ear horn. "Nikola Tesla, sir! It's as if he *wants* to destroy any reputation he has left! Listen to this: *The struggle toward sex equality will end with females superior to males. Once free of the bonds of domesticity, they will not willingly take it up again. Society will form centers for the care of children, much like that of the bee.*'"

"The what?"

"The *bee*, sir! If the man wasn't finished before, he surely is now! The boys at the lab are saying—"

Edison raised his hand to silence the young man. He lowered the ear-horn, a most effective signal. "I appreciate your enthusiasm, young man. But I am done battling with that fellow. My family is secure, my place in history is secure. Whatever response Nikola Tesla deserves from the world—as far as I'm concerned, he can have it."

He raised his glass of tea to the disappointed sycophant

and took a long sip, staring at some faraway point his visitor could not see.

By time that the winter of 1933 rolled around, old age had a firm grip on Nikola and his fortunes had plunged. He found himself reduced to shuffling down the sidewalk in a worn out suit. This time he carried his belongings in two dilapidated suitcases, having been evicted for nonpayment from his room at the Hotel Pennsylvania.

In that grim moment, he did not see the corpulent hotel manager at first. The man came hurrying up behind him, hardly able to catch up to the much older man. Finally he called out, "Monsieur Tesla! Wait! Wait!"

Nikola turned around just as the manager reached him, panting hard.

"Sir!" The Manager began with an obsequious smile. "Just after you left, an envelope arrived from the estate of the late John Jacob Astor! They have been trying to locate you— although I must say that after all these years it does not seem that they were trying very hard—but his will ordered the estate to look after you if you needed help. The bequest, it will be enough to completely pay your back bill, plus a year in advance! I'll get your bags!"

The manager dutifully picked up Nikola's suitcases. Nikola stared in confusion and happy disbelief, then began following the manager back toward the hotel. The man prattled on, "You also have a five *hundred* dollar credit in the dining room, Monsieur! I did not realize you had such influential friends! Why did you not contact them yourself? They only just discovered that you are in need of assistance."

Nikola managed a stunned reply. "I... do not know what to say." He decided to try making light of it. "Tell me, by any chance did the trustees mention paying for a new laboratory?"

The manager sniffed, clearly offended. "Certainly *not*, Monsieur! As you are well aware, we have one at the end of the hall on every floor!"

Nikola said nothing and kept walking, so the manager added, "We are so sorry about having to be strict regarding outstanding bills. Monsieur, but they keep raising our power bill and we must pass on those costs. Well. No matter. All taken care of now! However, refresh my memory if you would. What was it that Monsieur used to do?"

Nikola soon moved on to occupy a small double room in the Hotel New Yorker, farther away from the downtown area. He was living there when he appeared at the offices of *Collier's Magazine* in 1937 for a rare personal interview with writer John J. O'Neill. O'Neill was well aware of Nikola's accomplishments and his impact on all of modern society, having spoken informally with the inventor off and on for a number of years. He also knew enough of Nikola's personal situation to be appalled by the man's poverty.

O'Neill planned the article as an unabashed piece of praise for a man he knew to be deserving of a far higher place in the world than an anonymous hotel room and a laboratory in his imagination. The writer's agenda for the interview was simply to ask the aging genius to tell what he had been doing to employ his mental powers in recent years. O'Neill figured that if he could just get Tesla to open up about his life, there would be nothing more to do than let him expound while he took notes.

Within the first half hour after they started, writer's cramp was setting in and O'Neill struggled to keep track of the inventor's flying thoughts.

"—so you see: a magnetic field intersects between the physical world and the unseen realm by causing iron to move, just as *consciousness* intersects between the spirit and the body, allowing *us* to move! I've spoken extensively about this."

"Mr. Tesla!" O'Neill blurted out. He took a breath. "We are not a scientific journal, you know. Really, how can the public be expected to understand a concept like that? How are they even going to understand this Universal Power System you propose?"

"They don't have to. They can still enjoy the benefits of it, and it will work anyway."

"Of course they have to understand it, Mr. Tesla! They are my reading public."

"How many of them drive an automobile without understanding how it works?" He paused for an answer, but O'Neill looked like he was done for the moment, so he went on. "Thus, properly controlled magnetic fields can deliver *conscious thought* to any point in the physical realm! Not messages, I am stressing to you, but *thought*!

At that point O'Neill held up his hand to stop him. He rubbed his eyes for a moment before he spoke. "Mr. Tesla…" He sighed, then went on. "I take it that you are talking about mind-reading?"

"Why yes! Of course!"

"Uh-huh. With people connected up to machines?"

Nikola laughed at that. "Connected up." He stared into space for a second, picturing it, then laughed a second time. A moment later he gazed all around the room and whatever he saw made him laugh louder, completely thrilled.

He stopped himself and threw a guilty glance at O'Neill, then squinted in concentration for a second or two and cleared his throat before he went on. "More like using the telephone, really. The rest of the time, of course one's thoughts would remain private."

"And you have no qualms about the impact of such a thing? Or doubts that you can actually build it?"

Nikola smiled at that. "Sir, I have never failed to build a working model of every invention I had the funding to construct." He leaned in closer. "Never."

"But such an invention, in the hands of the wrong people…"

"Yes! The wrong people! Precisely! Which is why I cannot use government funding! But with a silent partner," He finished in a whisper, "We would only be within a few months of manufacturing every single component."

"Mr. Tesla, please! Sir. Please." He dropped his pen with a sigh and rubbed his eyes again. "I can't print any of this."

"But why?"

"Because it sounds… I know your work has lighted our entire country. I know much of the benefit was stolen from you. But sir, I have to wonder if years of public ridicule haven't scarred you more than you realize."

This time it was O'Neill who leaned in close to speak. "Tell me, surely you must have *some* source of joy in your life?"

"But of course! My muse!" Nikola laughed. "She last appeared to me in the form of a white dove." Beaming, Nikola spoke for the next half hour, revealing the details of his strange relationship with Karina.

When he was finally done, he ended by saying, "And so you see, Mr. O'Neill, she has always been my best secret."

O'Neill sat without comment for a moment, then slowly shook his head. "And a secret she shall remain, Mr. Tesla." He closed the cover of the notebook. "In fact, out of respect for you, sir, I will print nothing of what you have told me today."

"But Mr. O'Neill, the world has such great need of—"

"*Please*, Mr. Tesla!" O'Neill extended his hand in farewell, signaling an end to the occasion. "That's all, then."

Nikola just looked at him, seeming not to comprehend. O'Neill extended his hand farther. "Good day."

Nikola finally rose, shaken. He bowed slightly to acknowledge the handshake, then turned to leave.

Minutes later Nikola was walking the streets and still replaying the scene, wondering how he might have edited his remarks while still being able to communicate what he was trying to say. The riddle held his concentration so well that he absent-mindedly stepped into the path of a barreling New York City taxicab.

The blow felt like he was struck with a giant hammer. He landed on his back in the middle of the cobblestone street. He was still struggling to sit up after the driver pulled to a stop and hurried over. "Hey! Hey, Grandpa! You alive? You all right or what?"

Nikola managed a sitting position, which measurably cheered the driver.

"Yeah, there you go! There you go. So you in any pain, or anything like that there?"

Nikola's voice was nearly a whisper; the driver had to strain to hear him over the background noise. "How will I get to the park to feed the birds?"

"To do *what*? Hey look, is there anything I can do for you here?"

"Please," Nikola murmured to him. "Take a bag of seed to the park."

"The park. What is this with the park?"

"If you see a white dove there…"

"Oh! A white *dove*, In the park!" He grinned and called out to the world in general, "He wants me to go feed the birds!"

Nikola allowed the driver to pull him to his feet. He rose carefully until he managed to stand. "Thank you. You're right, I should do it myself. Never mind. I can still do it." With that, Nikola shuffled away.

The driver yelled out to the few remaining bystanders who hadn't already lost interest, "It's all right, no problem! He's gonna go feed the birds himself."


When Nikola's health remained frail after the taxi accident, a small cadre of supporters persuaded the new Yugoslav government regime to award him a modest lifetime pension to their most accomplished native son. His homeland granted the relief despite the fact that Nikola had long since taken on American citizenship, because no individual or group in his adopted country considered it necessary to provide him with any help at all. His unbelievable proclamations had eroded all support from the worldwide scientific community, American government agencies, or even the private industries that ran on his inventions.

The small monthly stipend assured his essential survival costs: the price of his pair of rooms at the Hotel New Yorker and for the crackers and warm milk upon which he had come to subsist. Luxuries were his writing and sketching supplies and a daily bagful of bird seed. On days when he was too weak to walk to the park, he lay piles of it on his window sill and spoke to the birds as if they were friends when they came to feed. A few became so familiar he gave them names.

From time to time, special occasions arose when he was invited to be an honored guest at scientific awards dinners, eastern European state dinners, and the odd private dinner party hosted by social luminaries who still sought to acquire some additional reflected light from his remaining reputation. It was usually Nikola's automaton that attended, while most of him sat in the tiny rocking chair behind the picture window eyes.

The twilight lasted for six years.

# Chapter Forty

## January 7, 1943
### New York City

By the time the new year began, the United States had entered its second long year of the great global conflict that was already being called World War II. This effectively forced the renaming of the war that was formerly called "the war to end all wars" to the far more ominous "World War I."

Within that climate, Nikola Tesla wrote to the U.S. Army and Navy and offered to provide the plans for energy beams that could destroy ships at sea and drop airplanes from the sky. For reasons never explained, his offer was rejected. However his work became a topic of keen interest within certain government agencies whose purview included national security and defense. No small amount of paranoia went to work in questioning the true motives of anyone who could do the things Nikola Tesla claimed to be capable of doing. Where did such a man's loyalties lie?

Darkness was falling amid freezing temperatures on the night of January 7 while George Scherff's son, George Jr., made his way along the streets from the subway stop to the Hotel New Yorker. Razor sharp wind made an unpleasant ordeal of every moment outdoors, but he was responding to a written summons. The old inventor himself had sent the note, and so there was a duty to attend even though the message was addressed to his father.

The old inventor did not realize his longtime assistant was battling with health concerns. The only reason George Jr. was present when the note arrived was that he was on an emergency furlough to help his father arrange his things. Still the elder Scherff sent his son to answer Nikola's call.

George Jr. hurried through the freezing gusts hating the way his childish feelings of intimidation were flooding back to him. He especially disliked having to spend his short time on stateside furlough with a visit to the man who had given him so much grief during his teenage years.

George Jr. had always loved the mystery of his father's workplace and shared his father's admiration for Tesla's genius, but he had no talent for the science being done there. "Curious George," Tesla had teased him, chiding the boy's fascination with every piece of equipment in the laboratory and his clumsiness in handling them. Whenever he came to visit his father and poke around the lab, his only contribution to the work was to bump into things and risk destroying delicate apparatus or getting himself electrocuted.

"Curious George" had sounded like a pet name at first. Eventually he came to take it for the scold that it was. He was glad that none of his mates on the ship ever heard it; he would have carried the damned title for life. Now, against the evening's cruel wind, all he really wanted to do was turn around and head back to his father's place and finish with the grim business of his emergency shore leave.

But he was carrying a personal note from the great Nikola Tesla. He had read it by the light of the system that Tesla invented, and his ailing father wanted him to go. That was enough to carry him all the way to the Hotel New Yorker.

He arrived at old Nikola's small double room, numbered 3327 and 3328 at the L-shaped end of the hallway, and heard a feeble "come in" in response to his knock. He tried the knob and found the door already unlocked. Inside, the old wizard sat next to a large window, which was wide open in spite of the bitter cold. Tesla appeared far more feeble than George remembered him; he had shrunken into himself.

Nikola stared in surprise for a moment, then his eyes registered understanding and he smiled. "Curious George," he said. But the old man's tone was one of fond respect. George noticed this time the nickname had no sting.

"Good evening, sir. It's good to see you again. My father sent me with his regrets that he's too ill to attend to you. He hopes to come in a few days. They only granted me emergency shore leave to get him taken care of at the hospital and handle some of his affairs. But he wanted me to see you.

"Your father is a fine man. I am sorry to learn he is ailing."

"Thank you. He didn't want you to have to wait."

"I would never intrude upon you this way if it were not a matter of supreme importance."

"Never a doubt about that, sir." George nodded and waited for Nikola to continue. The old discoverer sat holding an unmarked leather portfolio, but although his grasp was tight, his attention was focused on the open window. Finally, he rose with a disappointed sigh and shuffled over to sit on the bed. Only then did he turn his full attention to his visitor.

Nikola cleared his throat and extended the thick leather portfolio toward George Jr. with both hands. It appeared difficult for him to lift its weight.

George Jr. took it while Nikola explained, "Mr. Scherff, this file holds detailed notes for the Universal Power System. I understand that my critics consider free electrical energy to be impossible, but this is only because so many of them think I am talking about sending electricity through the ground itself. Shooting sparks through dirt! Or just blasting the power through the air like lighting. Ha!"

His face formed a sly grin. "But the actual method is to create a standing wave of invisible energy between the planet and the stratosphere: a hollow ball of energy surrounding the entire planet, with its poles on either side of the Earth and with the Earth itself as the center core! That's why the energy can be tapped anywhere, by anybody!"

When George glanced inside the big leather folder he saw that it was stuffed with pages and pages of schematic illustrations, each one covered with liner notes. George felt his jaw drop. "Sir, I've heard my father talk about this, but I thought it was just a pipe dream."

"It is nothing of the kind," Nikola replied. "It is only a problem of politics. This current war we are in with these Nazi forces reminds us what human beings can become. So the question is, *what to do* with this power? I have done everything I could to keep my discoveries from falling into malevolent hands." He shook his head. "Recently I gave different portions of my plans for a directed energy beam weapon to the American government along with Canada, Britain, and Russia. I told them since mankind is not conscious enough for any one government to have such power, they will only be able to develop it by working together—"

Nikola smiled, "—of course they all have very good spies. But I don't know what else I can do. And that is why I can only entrust this to you. It must remain hidden until the world understands the importance of universal free energy so clearly that humanity itself will not allow the power to fall under the control of any government or industry. Mr. Scherff, I am glad for your youthful energy and that your father sent you."

A racking cough shook his body and left him gasping for several seconds before he could continue. "I am instructing you to keep this file from prying eyes until you can find a way to make sure that the world learns of it and it is not buried. When the time is right."

George could only stare. This sudden turn of events left him stunned. He had been given a single day's leave from his duties to visit his ailing father. Now when it was long after nightfall and time for his return, he was confronted with this.

Still, George Jr. knew the world well enough to understand that the forces feared by the old discoverer could be found everywhere. He looked straight at the old man and solemnly patted the thick folder. "You can trust me, Mr. Tesla," he said with a grim smile. Then he kneeled next to the bed to take Nikola's frail hand and whisper, "Let them try to find it."

Old Nikola sighed with relief. "Good." He patted the younger man's hand. "Good indeed. I know I can count on you. My 'Curious George,' such a nuisance when you were young, now you are my salvation in this, entrusted to keep this safe for the world. As for the other papers in the room, they can go to whoever they will."

The sounds of a cooing dove caused both men to turn toward the open window to see a single white bird standing on the open sill. Nikola cried out with joy. George Jr. had no idea what was happening.

"Is that you, then?" Nikola breathed toward the bird. "Are you back?"

"Is that who, sir?"

Nikola ignored him and stared at the bird. "What? I didn't get that. *What?* Say it again!"

A moment later, his expression shifted to one of sheer amazement. Nikola pulled a shuddering breath deep into his chest and stared off at some faraway place. A blissful smile crossed his face.

"George, she's still so…" And then the old man's face flashed with amazement. He fell back flat back onto the bed and his spirit sank straight out of his exhausted body. One moment he was there in the room with young George, the next he was gone.

George glanced at the window sill; the dove was gone too. There had been no time to do anything but look on in helpless shock. He struggled to control his disbelief. Moments earlier, the great Nikola Tesla was speaking directly to him about his most powerful secret. But George Jr. had already seen enough death in the war to know Nikola was already gone.

He felt the heft of the fat folder under his arm and instinctively clutched it tighter. At last he exhaled a deep sigh. His breath came out as a cloud of steam in the freezing draft. He set aside the file long enough to gently arrange Nikola's body in a supine position on the bed, then folded the hands over the chest and closed the unseeing eyes. George Jr. picked up the file again and tucked it under his coat before turning to give the room a long, sweeping gaze. Then he stepped out and closed the door. He went to inform the hotel staff about their deceased guest.

The night manager responded to young George's news by dutifully calling the office of the New York City Coroner. The manager had no way of knowing his hotel line was tapped. At the mention of a deceased resident in the dual suites 3327 and 3328, the information was intercepted and relayed through a host of government offices.

In less than half an hour a large black government car pulled up outside the hotel. Four federal agents hurried inside the building and up to the inventor's room. They left the body in place while they rushed to box up all of the inventor's papers. They made several trips to carry them away. The team moved through the process with such a practiced level of skill that most of the confiscated materials were already loaded up before the coroner's team arrived to claim the body.

Meanwhile in the darkness half a block away, George Jr. stood shivering inside the shadowy brick cave of a recessed doorway. He clutched the secret file beneath his coat and remained in spite of the deepening cold, standing watch until the body was eventually carried out to the coroner's wagon.

The loaded wagon pulled away from the curb and proceeded down the street running only on its emergency lights, not bothering with a siren. The red strobes played across his features until the vehicle rounded the corner.

The feeling of isolation that fell over him then was as heavy as the file under his coat. He wondered how he could ever manage to protect such a treasure? How could anyone?

A thing of unlimited value.

George Jr. was fully aware that considering the damage free electrical power would do to existing political and financial structures, surely there were those who would kill him a hundred times over to prevent it from reaching the general population.

It occurred to him that the game for him had begun the moment he accepted the file. Now his role in the contest was sealed. He had to hide it somehow, and then he had to get back to the ship without attracting attention, then he had to keep it safe until there was a way to get it out to the world without being repressed. There would be no trial run.

As if in answer to the thought, a man's voice called from across the street. "Hey buddy! Come over here a minute, will you?"

He whirled around too hard for an innocent man and saw one of the government agents standing next to a large black automobile. The man appeared to have been waiting around as if he had nothing else to do. George Jr. wondered if he had attracted the agent's attention when he emerged from the shadows or whether the man had been watching him for some time.

The agent held up a badge and waved him over, "Yeah, over here. So what's going on there, pal? I seen you watching the hotel. So why don't we have a look at what's under your coat there. That all right?" The guy grinned at him through a sly face.

Young George's heart sank. The agent had already seen too much, and his attitude pegged him as a lover of petty authority, a candidate for a lifetime on Shore Patrol.

George Jr. smiled over at the agent and started in his direction like a man who fully intended to comply. Nice and relaxed, he took three or four steps toward the waiting officer, using his posture and his attitude to broadcast the message: *yes officer, of course, officer, not a problem, officer.*

He silently counted: one for the money... two for the show... three for whatever that one is... then wheeled and broke into a dead run, instinctively aiming for the corner alley. The first "halt!" rang out behind him before he reached it.

Young George was in good condition and felt confident enough that he could outrun most pursuers, but he clearly sensed he would to need all his speed for this; the agent's interest was more than casual.

He plunged into a shadowed service lane behind a large factory building and risked a quick glance back. There was no one in sight at the moment, so it was vital to get as far away as possible before anyone spotted him again. He pumped his legs until he could barely keep his feet under him.

Somewhere a few blocks behind him, the first siren started up. Quickly a second, a third, a fourth... maybe six? It was hard to tell, with the echoes, the overlapping sounds. Fear and confusion mixed. *Six cars?* With two cops to a car, that meant at least a dozen police had been mustered into the hunt for him, all within less than a minute. What could make the authorities respond this way? Everything was happening too quickly to comprehend.

But the police response had already convinced him the old discoverer told the truth about the file. And somebody else appeared to have their own ideas about it.

The sirens sounded like a pack of circling dogs. The wailing grew incrementally louder until, as if abruptly responding to a single cue from somewhere, every one of the sirens fell silent. The telltale noises of the patrolling cars disappeared back into the camouflage of background city traffic.

George guessed there was no reason for him to react by changing direction. He had to assume they remained in motion and that one of them could appear anywhere. What he most needed to do was stay aware of his surroundings and keep moving—perhaps he could still escape through a random hole in the dragnet.

He had only traveled a few blocks when he emerged from the alley at the intersection of a wide boulevard. Moving too fast, he trotted out from the cover of the shadows and was immediately caught off guard. The artificial daylight on that street was so bright it brought him to a cold stop.

New lights had been installed all along the boulevard: arc lamps perfected by Tesla were mounted in street lights powered by Tesla's alternating current, which came from Tesla's Niagara Falls generators.

George Jr. began to move again while panicky realizations struck him like blows to the head. On top of the extra challenge posed by the bright new street light system, his pursuers would also be using Tesla's invention of radio to organize their patrol cars. He had been trusted with Tesla's secret file but was now up against the fruits of Tesla's genius while they aided the authorities' pursuit.

He inhaled and forced himself to adopt an inconspicuous walking pace, camouflaging himself among people going about ordinary things. He remained hidden among them until he reached a small intersection with another darkened alley and turned in. Back in the shadows, he gradually increased his speed with every step. Soon he was moving as fast as the limited visibility allowed, barely keeping his balance while he dodged obstacles looming in the darkness. He could hear the screeching tires of the patrol cars closing in. The sounds flushed every drop of his adrenaline into his bloodstream. Fear cramped his stomach, but the weight and the heft of the file bolstered his determination. He clutched the secret papers to his chest and plunged deeper into the pointy darkness of the hard world.

*The End*

# Afterword

This book is a work of speculative fiction that imagines what it may have been like for Nikola Tesla to live his singular life, and which invites the reader to peer out through his eyes.

For all those who would now like to pursue more factual information about the life and work this of leading light among the world's greatest inventors, there are several publications available in nonfiction form.

A number of excellent nonfiction sources can be combined to get a feel for the full breadth of his life. The seminal reference will always be John J. O'Neill's *Prodigal Genius*, the only biography by an author who actually knew Tesla and interviewed him (remember the *Colliers' Magazine* senior editor).

Margaret Cheney's *Nikola Tesla: Man Out Of Time* is also essential reading for anyone interested in the biographical treatment of Tesla's life. The PBS documentary, *"Tesla, Master of Lighting"* is available in video form, as well as the excellent companion book of the same title. All offer important facts and insights.

This story's use of his 1888 lecture before the A.I.E.E. is a brief and fictionalized version of his highly technical remarks, but for those looking for the engineering details, many of his most cogent writings are found in *The Inventions, Researches, and Writings of Nikola Tesla*, compiled by Thomas Cummerford Mann for Barnes & Noble Books. Most of his lectures can be found online.

I believe the portrayal of Tesla in this book to be honest and fair, even as I acknowledge there will be those who would do it other ways. The historical characters surrounding him are also drawn with regard to their known traits. These documented personalities and their known accomplishments allow for reasonable speculation as to their behavior.

The historical record is riddled with mysteries regarding Tesla. Why was he compelled to carry out his mission with such single-minded purpose that he declared himself a monk to science? What was his relationship to the white dove who was so important to him in his later years?

For so long, it has been effortless to ridicule his eccentric behavior and his claims of solving the design for his worldwide Universal Power System. But it must be pointed out that unless such critics have read about him under natural light or battery power, then they must have done so under lights powered by energy generated and delivered on a system he alone conceived in all its detail, and this in a horse-and-buggy era of gas lamps and oil lanterns.

— A.F.
Seattle, 2013